I0600199

RUIN'S END
BAR·LOUNGE

VOLUME ONE

A WING TO BREAK

CALLA TATE

A Wing To Break: Ruin's End Volume One
Copyright © 2026 by Calla Tate

All rights reserved.

No part of this publication may be reproduced, distributed, or transmitted in any form or by any means, including photocopying, recording, or other electronic or mechanical methods, without the prior written permission of the publisher, except as permitted by U.S. copyright law. For permission requests, contact callatatebooks@gmail.com

The story, all names, characters, and incidents portrayed in this production are fictitious. No identification with actual persons (living or deceased), places, buildings, and products is intended or should be inferred.

Book Cover Design by Calla Tate
Editing by Laura Pu-Syska www.lapsstudio.com
Published by Sinbound Print in the United States of America

First edition 2026

ISBN: 979-8-9998540-0-1

Hardback ISBN: 979-8-9998540-1-8

For anyone who's ever swallowed their pain, bit their tongue, and told themselves to carry on.

This is what happens when you don't. When the ache demands to be named, and you stop asking for permission to feel it.

For anyone who's ever swallowed their pain, bit their tongue, and told themselves to carry on.

This is what happens when you don't. When the ache demands to be named, and you stop asking for permission to feel it.

Trigger Warning

This book contains mature content that may not be suitable for all readers. It includes open-door sexually explicit scenes, themes of stalking and online harassment, the use of firearms, and elements of vigilante justice.

While this story is infused with humor and emotional depth, please take care in choosing whether and when to engage with it. Your well-being always comes first.

PROLOGUE

Sable

A little red notification bubble pops up like a tiny digital middle finger.

Great. Another interruption. Because raising a ten-year-old, managing two businesses, and shacking up with someone who's common-law eligible but still not husband material isn't a handful already.

Social notification. Not even a text. Just the algorithm, mocking me from the void.

My furniture restoration business is finally launching. Thorne Revival. I've graduated from garage hoarding and online-only sales into a bona fide workshop with a legitimate store front. Everything is moving in the right direction... even if it's slow.

I refresh the page, wired for response and starving for that tiny spike of validation.

Two thousand followers.

It's not viral, but my marketing brain soothes the anxiety rising in my throat by reminding me it's respectable for a niche business.

I fire off a joke to my best friend, Demi.

> **[Sable]:** Omg. 2K followers. Clearly, I'm crushing it. Where's my six-figure home decor deal??

Demi responds instantly.

> **[Demi]:** HELLO BIG SHOT!!! Ride that algorithm, you filthy capitalist queen!

My comeback dies at my fingertips as a new follower notification flashes across the screen.

A dog account.

Huh.

Normally, I wouldn't give it a second thought, but something makes me pause. The profile pic shows two scruffy terriers, the kind my Aunt Mel always posts about on her Facebook account in nauseating frequency. For a second, I think maybe she's finally figured out Instagram and migrated over to the more "trendy" platform.

Nope. Random person.

Still, the account name seems weirdly familiar. I click on it, check the following list, and that's when the first needle-prick of unease hits.

The account is linked to another in the About Me section. I tap on the human profile picture linked to these dogs, blowing it up to a size these aging eyes can actually handle.

And there she is.

Blonde. Fit. Slightly more muscular than I usually find attractive on a woman, but hey, I can appreciate a solid bicep. She has that effortless athletic hotness that suggests she wakes up at dawn to lift weights for fun in a matching sports bra and coochy-suffocating spandex.

I can relate. That used to be my whole personality (*RIP*)... five hobbies ago. Hell, it's how Andrew and I met. But running two businesses, I've turned from a water-hauling wellness warrior to a caffeine-fueled machine. I eye and swipe my sweating, extra-large iced coffee and take a long, satisfying sip.

My gaze lingers on the girl's photos. Studying, not savoring. Comparing, not craving. Attraction, for me, has never been about gender. However, I've found the male organ plays a crucial role in the experience—for me at least. There was that whole exploratory phase in college, of course. Tequila shots and impromptu make-out sessions with friends during parties. Less about self-discovery and more about the room spinning and someone daring me to kiss Jessica—again. Still, I can't pretend this woman is not objectively hot.

And, apparently... she's obsessed with my page.

Interesting...

My fingers hover over my screen as I put the pieces together in real-time.

- She lifts weights at the gym that my long-term boyfriend Andrew's a member of. (*Weird, but fine?*)

- She follows my business page. (*Potential client?*)

- She has a second, more private account... and that account is also watching my stories. (*Um??*)

- There's a third account—also hers—lurking on every single post.

Three accounts? This isn't normal interest. There are no *I love vintage furniture* vibes I'm picking up from any of her posts. Just ass shots of her squatting more than I weigh and selfies taken at all the wrong angles for her square jawline.

This is dedicated surveillance. Single white female shit.

Then I see it. Another gym selfie, but this time she's placing a kiss on aforementioned long-term boyfriend's smug fucking cheek.

And suddenly... the habitually late... always-distracted... non-committal father to my child feels way more suspicious.

The picture confirms the link.

A creeping, sick thought blooms—

That son of a bitch is cheating on me.

And I'm being stalked... by a fucking dog account.

I should be heartbroken. Devastated. Enraged. But all I feel is this hot pulse of irritation curling low in my gut. Like my body's too tired for heartbreak and too smart for denial.

I've just opened my own brick-and-mortar—something real, something mine—and now this is what I get?

Of course it is. So perfectly, pathetically *him*.

It explains everything. The distance. The weird excuses. The sudden need for privacy while I've been bleeding myself dry trying to build something that actually matters.

The weasel's been acting sketchy for months.

I should've known. And maybe that's what pisses me off the most.

Objectively, I'm intelligent. I put myself through college. I run two businesses—*successfully*. I've carried the bulk of our household expenses for years, which... depending on your definition of "mutual contribution," could make a strong case *against* my intelligence.

I digress.

Meanwhile, Andrew's latest excuse for his faltering funding efforts is still that elusive *deal*. The one that's been "almost final" for nine months. He talks about it like it's a weather system he can't quite predict. Unfortunate, inevitable, totally out of his control.

But he *does* graciously offer to "pitch in more," as if paying his own damn bills is some kind of charitable act.

On top of being the lead accountant of this dysfunctional union, I've packed every school lunch, folded every piece of clothing in our house, and mastered the delicate art of hiding vegetables in meals without raising suspicion. I know how to unclog a drain, file taxes, and schedule back-to-back meetings without breaking stride. I sign every permission slip, check every math assignment, double-check the reading logs, and somehow remember to send in the damn Kleenex box during cold season.

I have done everything right.

And still, after over a decade of shared bills, shared bed sheets, and a shared Google calendar, the man I lived with decided the grass looked greener in someone else's delusional little field. A woman so self-assured she didn't even think to ask upfront about his current relationship status before launching a full-blown surveillance mission on *me*, like I'm the threat in this equation.

The woman buying the groceries. Signing the field trip forms. Managing a life while he chases whatever spark he thinks is missing.

To be fair, he's a solid father. We've managed to parent Bash with minimal drama—which, in this situation, is borderline miraculous. But outside of co-parenting logistics, things between us have been circling the drain for a while. Quietly. Consistently.

And now the universe slapped a bow on that slow collapse in the form of a blonde, stalker-y gym rat with too many Instagram accounts and the emotional maturity of a protein bar.

I exhale, rolling my eyes and looking toward the ceiling for the last shred of patience I can muster.

My fingers tighten around my phone. I should stop. Close the app. Walk away. Maybe throw the digital terrorist against the wall.

... Yeah, that doesn't happen.

Instead, I tap the woman's profile again. And with shaking hands, I dive into the rabbit hole headfirst.

CHAPTER ONE

Sable

The mallet slams down, and something cracks open with a sick pop. A sharp snap. A deep groan.

I tighten my grip, breathing hard, my arms aching from the effort. "Sable! What the fuck?!"

Demi's voice barely registers over the pounding. Over Florence and the Machine blaring. Over my ragged breathing.

Another blow. Another crack.

My pulse is steady. My focus is sharp. I must finish this.

A low whimper—or is that the wind?—echoes through the shop.

Then... silence.

I step back, panting, wiping the sweat from my forehead. *Jesus, Mary, and Joseph, that took a lot out of me.*

Demi stands frozen in the doorway, face ashen and eyes darting to the floor with the urgency of someone expecting to find something horrific.

"What the actual fuck are you doing?"

I look down at the wreckage before me. My tools. The pieces of what used to be something whole.

Then I blink.

"Oh. You mean the dresser?" I kick one of the shattered wooden legs aside, reaching for the next tool I need. "I'm restoring it. I have to remove this part to fix it properly."

Demi doesn't move. "It sounded like you were beating someone to death."

I turn the orbital sander on and smooth out the spot I just ripped some trim from. The whirring buzz screams through the shop. I shrug and smile. "If only."

I point the tool and pulse it at her with mock madness.

Demi exhales so hard she nearly deflates. "You're so fucking dramatic!"

"Says the one who nearly stroked out in my doorway!" I holler, turning the sander off.

She barks a laugh. "Yeah, well, for a solid thirty seconds, I thought, *cool,* this is how I become an accomplice, boss."

I snort. "Oh, please. If I intended to commit murder, do you really think I'd do it here? My shop is my sanctuary, Demi."

"You cannot say things like that while holding power tools!" she says, jabbing a finger at my sander. "I think that makes it premeditated."

I grin, setting the sander down and wiping dust off my jeans. The six months since my humiliating breakup—*read: very necessary and ridiculously overdue breakup*—have been therapeutic in a lot of ways. After selling my marketing agency, I've thrown myself into Thorne Revival and mostly ignored the fact my stalker still hasn't moved the fuck on even though I willingly relinquished the pathetic asshole.

The Blonde.

Why do they always have to be blonde? I practically sprinted to my hair girl, demanding she strip every trace of bleach that ever touched my strands, desperate for my natural warm brown to be the only thing staring back in the mirror.

My ex's little side piece turned obsessive creeper.

She stalks my every move. Lurks on my social media even after I blocked all the original accounts. Watches my stories from new burner profiles, a pathetic little phantom who's tragically bad at staying hidden. You would think, with all her watching, she'd know my background in marketing means I have an eye for monitoring all my metrics.

And yet my best friend thinks *I'm* the crazy one.

Demi narrows her eyes. "You're thinking about her again, aren't you?"

I grab another one of my tools, ready to go to town on this piece. "*Maybe.*"

She smirks. "Is that for the dresser or the homicide you are definitely *not* planning?"

I flip the small pry bar in my hand. "Why choose?"

"That's my girl." Demi cackles.

My fiery little redheaded friend crosses over to the stool stationed in the back of the shop where I'm working. She perches on it, owning the space outright, legs stretched, casually surveying the mess around us.

The shop is a contradiction—half gritty, half refined. Not so different from me. The showroom is a picture of effort and illusion. The lighting is warm, drawing attention to the furniture I've restored and vintage pieces I've hunted down, every smaller accent arranged just so to compliment my designs. I've sanded, painted, and curated my way into making it feel delicate, more boutique than a refurbished auto shop.

But back here? Back here is where the *magic* happens.

And by magic, I mean the thick toxic cocktail of dust, paint fumes, and whatever else I've been breathing in. It coats my tongue every time I talk too much. The garage itself still bears the marks of its past life no matter how much I clean. Floor patches stay dark from grease stains, old bolts and washers consistently appear in the corners, and the faint scent of motor oil crinkles my nose whenever the air shifts just right.

My workbench is a chaos of tools, paint cans, brushes hardened with forgotten strokes, and a collection of rags stained with every shade of the past six months. Half-finished projects lean against the walls, waiting for inspiration or the right buyer. A long wooden table is stripped down to bare wood, its old lacquer curling at the edges like dead skin. A dresser stands beside it, missing half its drawers, as if it lost its fight with life and is waiting for me to resurrect it.

The overhead lights buzz, casting a sterile glow over the mess. And I love it. I haven't even lived through all the seasons here yet, but I already know:

- Summer will turn this place into a kiln

- Winter will be a battle between the heat and A/C

- Spring will pretend to save me money on my electric bill before it slaps us with another cold snap

I wouldn't trade it.

And Bash? He's exactly where he always is when Andrew doesn't have him or he's not at school. In the tiny office tucked near the front. I glance over to see the top of his curls as he shifts in the old leather chair that came with the shop. The flickering glow from his tablet screen bounces off the glass partition. The soft melody thrumming from whichever game he's playing is barely audible over my noise and the distant downtown traffic outside. This is as much his haven as it is mine. Surrounded by the humming of tools and entertained by me wrestling beauty into discarded things.

A smile glides across my lips. He's my mini me. He sees the potential in the broken just like his mama.

Demi follows my gaze, smirking. "Kid still obsessed with those weird building videos?"

"*Tutorials*," I correct, rolling my eyes like Bash would. "He could probably rebuild this entire shop in pixel form."

"Little genius. He'll run this whole place before long."

I snort and set the pry bar against the dresser, running my fingers over the splintered edge. "He'd be a better boss than me."

Demi grins. "Debatable."

Drumming her fingers against her knee, Dem's rings catch in the fluorescent light. Everything about her is bold: her tousled red hair, her dark stained lips, the way she commands space without ever asking permission. She's the kind of woman who floats through life untouched by the weight of expectations—a trait I both admire and resent in equal measure.

11

I made a pretty penny from my agency after the split with Andrew. It allowed me to keep my hundred-year-old charming home in the heart of Stillwater Bend, Texas, and kick the jerk out.

Stillwater is a town split in two, not by a river, but by the kind of people who settle here. The rough side isn't rough so much as rugged. It's filled with artists, makers, musicians, and the occasional recluse who keeps to themselves until Friday night when the local bar comes alive. The yuppie side, though, is all polished sidewalks, franchise cafés, and rows of new-builds that lack soul. I settled in the part where the houses have history and the streets feel like they've seen things.

It fits.

So far, this new, quiet chapter has done its best work by revealing exactly who's been in my corner all along. Most friends came from the teams I led. They were people who stayed while I turned nothing into something. And when I sold the agency, those friendships faded, not out of spite, just out of circumstance. It turns out, "We should get together soon!" is the adult equivalent of "Have a great summer!" scrawled in a yearbook.

But not Demi Kincaid. Demi held fast. And in her quiet loyalty, I realized she belonged in my life for all the right reasons.

She was the perfect mix of swagger and sass. During her interview ten years ago, I warned, *"This client will bitch if the logo isn't daring enough."* Demi leaned back, twirled her pen, shot up an eyebrow, and deadpanned, *"Sweetheart, I'll produce a logo so panty-meltingly hot, he'll blow his morning joe all over the place and lose his damn mind—in a good way, of course."* I snort-laughed in the interview, and sealed our contract on the spot.

12

At the time, she swore she "did temporary things" and "couldn't commit." But she listened. She got it. Got me. Stayed for ten years. And when she finally left to start her own whirlwind mix of consulting, design work, and whatever shiny new obsession grabbed her attention each month, I realized we kicked ass even harder when we weren't boss and co-worker.

Demi watches me work for a few beats before stretching her arms overhead with a satisfied sigh. "You know what we should do tonight?"

I don't look up, but I can already hear the trouble in her voice. "Define 'should.'"

"Go out."

I grunt, prying another warped nail from the dresser. "Yeah, let me just pencil that in between my sleepy tea and crashing on the couch at nine."

These days, Demi storms through like a hurricane in unlaced Doc Martens, leaving glittering mischief in her wake and fresh momentum in my bones.

Demi is free in a way I still can't fully grasp. She does what she wants, does *who* she wants, and never seems to second-guess herself. No partner, no kids—though she wraps mine in all her love. Nothing anchors her except her own instincts. And still, she's happy. Genuinely so.

I, however, lie awake with the ceiling sneering at me, torn between worshipping her reckless freedom and wanting to call her at 2 a.m. to scream into the phone, "Spill your secrets, you glorious witch!" until she finally tells me how the hell she makes it look so damn easy. I am a constant analyzer of where I've gone wrong.

"No, I'm serious." She leans forward, elbows on her knees. "Your thirty-ninth birthday is in just over a week, and I refuse to let your last few days of thirty-eight slip by in domestic monotony." She tilts her head at me. "And you, my dear, have not been out past 7 p.m. in—"

"God knows how long," I finish for her, sighing.

"Exactly." She lets satisfaction curl her lips. "So, we're going out. Tonight. Andrew's coming to pick up Bash soon, right?"

I glance toward the office where Bash is still glued to his tablet. "Yeah, any minute now."

"Perfect. No excuses." She claps her hands together. "We'll get a drink, listen to some music, maybe even flirt with strangers if you're feeling frisky."

"You think I remember how to do that?" I raise an eyebrow. "That's funny. I haven't touched a drink in so long, I'll probably be shit-faced after one and picked up any man that can hold three seconds of eye contact."

Demi waves a dismissive hand. "Please. Drinking and flirting are like riding a bike. You never forget, you just are a little wobbly at first. Plus, you'll be a cheap date."

I tell myself I long for the simple life. Lower expenses, nothing flashy. Just enough space to breathe, to work, to *be*. To step outside and hear cicadas chitter in the heat, to know the stories behind the creaky wood floors and the chipped porcelain sink in my kitchen. No grand expectations. No risk of failure. Just a quiet, comfortable life where no one asks what the hell I'm doing with it. Or if I'm ever going to get married. That, in itself, is a palm to the face.

Is that longing or retreat? Am I stepping into something new, or slipping away from the person I used to be? The ambition that once burned like a wildfire has softened into embers banked beneath the surface. It might be growth, or I just stopped trying. Maybe I found peace or simply found a place to disappear. Disappearing sounds suspiciously easy these days.

This is what it is—not dust drifting across afternoon light filtering through my old windows, not the quiet thrum of a smaller life—but me, learning to rest. Soft, steady... enough.

No more chasing.

No more proving.

No more trying to fix what never wanted to be fixed.

I shake my head, but the idea of being out, of being something other than just Mom or business owner for a few hours, feels oddly appealing.

Demi smirks, reading my hesitation as a win. "Come on, Sable Hawthorne. Let's be reckless. Or, you know, as reckless as two women approaching forty can be on a Friday night. Bash will be gone for the weekend; in mostly safe hands with Andrew—"

"Andrew would never let anything happen to him," I correct.

She waves a dismissive hand over my incessant need to still defend him.

I look down at all the dust covering my work clothes, as if I'm actually considering this idea. "I absolutely cannot go out like this."

With an exaggerated slap to her forehead, she lets out a sigh as if I'm hopeless. "It's 4:30 in the afternoon. You've got all the time in the world to wrap things up here, grab a shower, throw some mascara on those lashes, and slap some lotion on those long ass legs—because you are wearing something short to show them off."

I roll my eyes, but before I can argue, my phone vibrates on the workbench. I glance at the notification that glares on the screen, bracing myself.

It's her.

Again.

Another fake account—this one named *JustWondering2025*—commenting on the latest photo I posted of a sun-bleached, knotty-oak farmhouse cabinet with hand-brushed copper hardware.

> **[JustWondering2025]:** *Looks great! I hope your client loves it as much as Andrew loved what we did together last night.*

I grind my teeth. Molars ready to crack

Demi notices immediately. "What? What happened?"

I tilt the screen toward her. She skims the message, then groans. "Oh, for f—" She stops herself, throwing her hands in the air. "This bitch needs a hobby. Crochet a thong, skydive into traffic, I don't care. She's out here stalking your posts like a dumpster rat on meth."

I don't respond. I just stare at the message, letting the familiar irritation flare up. It's been months, and she still won't let me go. I've deleted and blocked every account she'd made, but she just keeps coming back, the digital equivalent of a particularly aggressive fungus.

Demi nudges me. "Okay, no, we're definitely going out now."

I blink up at her. "What—"

She gestures dramatically at my phone. "You need a break from this nonsense. From her, from Andrew-adjacent drama, from your shop hermit tendencies. I refuse to let a grown woman's weird obsession keep you locked up with your pry bars and dust."

I exhale through my nose, still simmering, but she's right. Maybe getting out, getting away, will help. I slap my phone down on the workbench.

"Fine," I mutter. "We're going out."

Demi pumps a fist in victory. "Yes! There is a bar not too far from here I've been dying to check out."

The front door chimes, and we both turn as Andrew steps inside.

Andrew, a car sales manager, could charm an entire PTA into forgiving his lateness. Dark hair, neatly trimmed beard, broad shoulders that used to make me weak in the knees—before I realized they were holding up a man who specialized in manipulation. There isn't much he can't talk his way in and out of. Except when I found out about the blonde.

"Hey, Sable," he says, giving me a nod and completely ignoring Demi, before scanning the shop. "Where's Bash?"

"In the office," I reply. "Where he always is."

The corner of his mouth lifts, mistaking my irritation for a joke.

"Cool, I'll grab him," he says, heading toward the office.

Beside me, Demi crosses her arms and mutters, "You sure you don't need to check with Crazy-Ashley first?"

I choke on a laugh.

Andrew either doesn't hear her or is pretending not to.

A second later, Bash barrels out of the office, backpack slung over one shoulder, his tablet clutched in his hands.

"Mom!" he says, skidding to a stop in front of me. "Dad says we're getting pancakes in the morning. Can I have extra whipped cream?"

I crouch down, brushing his curls back. "You can have all the whipped cream you want, bud."

His face lights up. "Even more than last time?"

"I don't know, that was a lot of whipped cream," I tease, tapping his nose.

Bash giggles. "It wasn't that much."

Andrew checks his watch. "We should get going, bro."

I kiss Bash's forehead. "Have fun, okay? Be good for Dad."

"I'm always good," he says, then hugs me so tight it almost hurts.

I close my eyes, holding on just a little longer.

After I pry myself away, Bash pulls his oversized headphones from his bag, over his ears, and plugs them into his tablet. The faint sound of some over-the-top YouTuber filters through, ensuring he's safely distracted from any impending adult nonsense. *Smart kid.*

And right on cue...

"Hey, Andy," Demi says sweetly. "Do me a favor and try not to introduce him to a new stepmom this weekend. I know you live to keep the girlfriend rotation on shuffle, but maybe let the kid have some consistency, yeah?"

Andrew exhales through his nose, visibly irritated. "Nice to see you too, Demi."

She gasps dramatically. "Oh, I bet it is nice—when's the last time someone was genuinely happy to see you? That reminds me, how is your latest mid-life crisis? Still stalking Sable's socials, or has she finally figured out how to type your name in a search bar and regret her entire life?"

Andrew clenches his jaw, a muscle twitching near his temple. He doesn't take the bait. Instead, he just shakes his head and turns toward the door.

Bash, blissfully unaware under his noise-canceling cocoon, waves as he heads out.

Once they're gone, I turn to Demi, who looks downright smug.

"You feel better?" I ask.

"Infinitely," she says. "Now, let's get you out of these dusty-ass clothes and into something that screams 'yes, I am thriving, and no, I won't be answering any bullshit comments.'"

I grab my bag with the determination of a woman on a mission. If Andrew's tragic taste in women is the most exciting thing happening in my life, I officially need stronger cocktails and worse decisions.

CHAPTER TWO

Hex

The nightmare about owning a bar like Ruin's End isn't the drunks. It's not even the entitled pricks who think money buys respect. No, it's the ones who sidle up asking for "favors."

Not the kind I'm known to do: helping a woman get her kid out of a bad situation, finding someone a place to sleep for the night, making sure someone walks away from a fight they didn't start. I'm talking about the other kind. The kind that doesn't get paid in cash. The kind that leaves your conscience soaked in blood and crawling in filth.

They smile like asking me to clean up their mess is the same as handing over a tip for good whiskey. That's the nightmare.

I lean against the counter, arms crossed over my chest, as I stare down the man sitting in front of me. For a guy wrapped in an expensive suit, wearing a watch that costs more than my truck, he's twitchy. I didn't need to look at him for an extra beat to be convinced his bank account compensates for his missing spine. He probably calls the cops on teenagers for skateboarding near his Tesla but still tells people he's "laid-back."

Every strand of hair is drenched in industrial-strength gel. Everything about him feels poised to implode at the slightest gust of wind.

I'd bet good money he practiced this whole conversation in the mirror before walking up to me.

And yet, despite all that preparation, he still looks ready to piss himself.

"Spit it out," I say, bored already.

He clears his throat, straightens his tie—a nervous tic, since the damn thing's already straight as a ruler. "I wanted to... discuss an opportunity with you."

There it is. The phrase that always means one of two things: a pyramid scheme or some rich guy trying to buy something that isn't for sale.

I raise a brow. "An opportunity?"

He nods. "Yes. I think we could work something out that benefits the both of us."

I let the silence stretch. He shifts in his chair, his cologne flooding the bar with the unmistakable stench of an expensive department store. Finally, I tap the bar in apathy and razor-edged disinterest.

"Buddy, the only thing I want from you is for you to stop sweating on my barstool."

His tongue flicks across his lips, gaze darting, searching for eaves-droppers. I don't rush him. I've found that silence is an incredible motivator. People tend to spill faster when they're left alone with their own bullshit.

Satisfied with whatever peace this bar gave him, he forcefully push-es air through his nostrils, folding his hands atop my counter like a half-wit prayer. "I need something handled."

Of course you do. No one comes to me from the other side of Stillwater Bend just for the cheap whiskey he's got in his hand.

I purse my lips as I repeat the word. "Handled."

It could've meant a hundred different things, but I already know where this is going. He wants a problem removed. Cleaned up. Erased.

"I heard you could help, Hex," he adds when I don't take the bait.

"Hector," I correct sharply. We are not friends.

Goddamn it. I didn't even get both feet down on the ground before the bullshit-of-the-day showed up. I should've known when the ride in didn't suck for a change. We've hit the sweet spot where spring finally warmed things up enough to unclench my teeth against the cold. That narrow window of time in Texas when my balls aren't stuck to my thigh on a long-term contract. Would've been nice to enjoy the post-ride high for more than five damn minutes.

Inside, the bar is quiet, holding its breath before another wild Friday night. Edison bulb light fixtures set throughout the bar cast their brilliance over polished wood, and pair with the sharp tang of lemon cleaner lingering in the air.

We're still closed, but Will's already behind the counter, wiping down bottles as if the health inspector's due any second. I know he's listening. We've known each other since elementary school, and he's one of two people I trust implicitly—with the bar, with my business, with everything.

I roll my shoulders, my leather jacket creaking with my shifted weight. My eyes flick over the mess of a man in front of me once more. Whoever he is, I know his type. He's too soft for the fight he's about to step into and needs someone to do the dirty work.

With a heavy sigh, I push off the counter, reaching for the bottle of Pappy Van Winkle's 23-Year. It's the kind of bourbon that comes with a price tag high enough to make grown men weep.

The cork pops, releasing an oaky aroma rising seductively into the air. This isn't just bourbon. This is patience in a bottle. The kind of thing you sip slow and let linger. And it sure as hell isn't for this asshole.

Pouring myself a glass, I watch the liquid settle, thick and syrupy, before drawing in a sip.

"Do you know how I bought this bar?" I ask, swirling the amber liquid in my glass.

His uncertain eyes dart up to mine. "I—no."

"I fought for it." I take another sip, savoring the burn. I lift my free hand from the bar. He flinches. "Literally. Underground fights. No refs, no rules. Just fists and the grit you carry in your bones. Paid good money if you could survive it."

I set my glass down, watching him. What fucked-up hole has he crawled into that has him convinced I'd be the one to haul him out? A flash of suspicion tightens my gut.

Most of the ghosts from my past aren't trudging some moral straight line. They're slinking through back-alley barters beneath flickering neon, trading favors in smoke-stained rooms and leaving trails of blood money in their wake. Those aren't the shadows I answer to these days, but this bastard radiates that same rotten void. Every flit of his nervous eyes and twitchy fingers tells me he's itching to haul me back into the abyss.

"Ned Stauder suggested you might be interested," the man says, hands shaking as he brings his drink to his lips. His eyes dart to the door, as if expecting Ned to step through it at any second.

The name hits my chest hard, a boot on thin ice.

My jaw tightens.

Stauder.

Old Ned has his fingers in just about every dark pocket of Stillwater Bend. Illegal gambling, rigged fights, backdoor deals. A weathered bastard, tough as boot leather, with a web of connections so tangled it could black out our whole little corner of Texas. I left that life behind, along with every debt and obligation. I swore to myself I'd never owe another favor to men who operate the way Ned does.

Yet he keeps at it, indirectly pulling strings, sending me garbage to clean up.

I stare down at the bourbon in my hand, remembering the copper taste of blood in my mouth, the feel of swollen knuckles and cracked ribs. "Ned should've told you better," I say finally. My voice is low, edged with a quiet threat that leaves no room for negotiation. "I don't owe favors. Not to Ned, not to anyone. When I bought this place, I bought it outright. No loans. No debts. Just blood money turned into business. Done."

His hands clench tighter around his drink. "He said you'd understand."

"Oh, I understand just fine," I say, offering a smile made of broken glass. "And you need to understand that when I take care of a problem, it doesn't come back. Ever."

The implication lands. His throat works around another nervous swallow. "That's what I need. I need her to disappear. She could fuck everything up."

I take another sip, considering him. Considering this.

Once, I didn't hesitate. Once, it felt easy. Violence served as more than a tool; it was survival. I built Ruin's End as my clean slate. Controlled. Less dirty.

And yet, the past always has a way of knocking, doesn't it?

I set my glass down, the sound loud in the quiet of the bar. "Here's the thing," I murmur, leveling him with a look. "If I do this, it doesn't come cheap. And you don't get to pick how it ends."

He nods quickly, too quickly, and slides a piece of paper across the bar. "Understood."

I study him for a long moment, I don't touch what no doubt has the name, before exhaling through my nose. "I'll think about it."

His shoulders ease, the tension melting with the quiet desperation of someone who thinks they've bought themselves mercy.

He moves to go, but I lift a hand. "One more thing."

He freezes.

I lean in, just enough for my voice to drop to something lethal. "If you lie to me about any of this, if you waste my time"—I smile, a lazy, wolfish grin—"you become the problem."

He pales and nods again, this time more carefully. Then he's gone, leaving behind only the faint scent of too much cologne and desperation.

I stare at the warped reflection of myself in the glass.

Ruin's End was supposed to be my way out.

But I've never been good at walking away from a fight.

CHAPTER THREE

Sable

I'm nervous. Nervous as hell. I haven't been out in... forever. I've got that first-day-of-school energy buzzing under my skin. But I need to hold it together, pass for a confident adult and not a mom escaping for one kid-free evening.

Demi's made sure I look fabulous—by her standards, any-way—though it feels a tad more *look-at-me* than I'm used to. But Demi's insistent voice rings between my ears: *"You've got it, flaunt it!"*

Maybe she's right. Or maybe this is a little much for a thir-ty-nine-year-old mother of a ten-year-old. But then again, who the hell knows anymore?

I tug at the hem of the little black dress, then rub my hands over my arms, wishing I had something to cover the top half of my exposed body. The last thing I need is to attract all the wrong people.

Demi's humming beside me, far too excited about the night yet to unfold. We round the corner, and that's when I see him.

The guy leaning in the Ruin's End doorway is a fucking marvel.

He's so tall, his head nearly grazes the frame, broad enough to block out the neon sign behind him. His biceps bulge against his leather jacket's sleeves, clinging to him like a second skin. His hair is that effortless kind of dark and tousled, the kind that says *I woke up this gorgeous* and didn't need to try.

And that jaw—holy hell, that jaw could slice diamonds. Chiseled, exact, a perfect right angle begging to be traced with a tongue.

My gaze lingers—too long—until my pulse drags me back to earth.

He's got to be in his twenties. Maybe thirty, if the universe feels like granting me a bit of mercy. Still too young. *Way* too young. The fact that I even noticed makes my stomach twist.

What is wrong with me?

Because I'm old. Done. Well done. I might as well just settle into my golden years, buy a single-story house in Florida, and maybe take up knitting. I'll be found dead on my lanai. Dead from old age—not loneliness. Or more likely, skin cancer from the sun I'd worship. That's the future I'm looking at.

Not a future with some mysterious, brooding, and *very fuckable* younger man in a leather jacket.

Demi bounds up the steps as if she owns the place. I trail behind her, wobbling through the mental math of the age gap while questioning whether these heels are a young woman's game or a terrible idea, period.

When I finally reach the top, Demi is waiting for me near the entrance, cake box still clutched in her arms. A younger guy—who I definitely don't have the hots for—steps aside to let us in. He doesn't even ask for our IDs, which is honestly a little disappointing. I wouldn't mind the ego boost.

As we approach the doors together, just as I'm mentally preparing to slip inside behind Demi, a low, velvet rumble wraps around me.

"Hold up," the tall one purrs, stepping slightly forward to block both our paths, each syllable rolling off his tongue. "Both of you."

I freeze, my chest tightening as I tilt my head up to that devastating jawline. His dark eyes stare down at me, sharp, and ready to interrogate. *Oh, great.*

Demi and I both step back, giving him space.

"IDs," he says, his eyes scanning my face with an intensity that makes my skin prickle.

Demi hands hers over first with a flirty smile. He glances at it briefly—she's clearly young enough that it's just a formality—then turns his full attention to me.

Damn it, I hoped to sneak by and pretend I'm still in my twenties. Now he'll for sure know the truth of my age. I dig my wallet out, irritated and slightly flustered. He takes my ID and studies it, holding onto it far longer than necessary.

Only a few seconds pass, but the way he stares at the card has me convinced he's committing it to memory. I shift on my feet, suddenly hyper-aware of my own existence, and attempt to make a joke. "No one ever asks a fake ID maker to age them up to *almost forty*."

I immediately regret it. A fart would have been less awkward.

Nothing. Not even a smile.

Okay, cool. At least he's not trying to flirt or anything. It's not as if I'd actually go for someone younger, even if the way that leather jacket fits him is hard to ignore.

Get it together, Sable.

He hands my ID back, his thumb brushing mine in a casual caress. His voice drops to a low, husky whisper: "You're good." That hard-as-nails bouncer façade doesn't crack, but for some reason those smoldering embers in his eyes promise he's not done with me.

Before I can overthink it, another guy steps out of the bar—so impossibly crisp, he looks like he just marched off a GQ cover. His clipped-short caramel hair is slicked back in perfect glossed waves. His shirt is pristine, tucked in just right, and there is an unmistakable air about him that makes me wonder if he irons his jeans. I'm guessing he's a bartender, and in fact, I spot a fresh, neatly folded white towel peeking from his back pocket, ready to be pulled out and swapped for a new one at the slightest hint of a spill.

He sees Demi holding the cake I told her not to bring, and I can already tell this isn't going to go well. His eyes narrow, his lips twist into a tight line, and the atmosphere shifts. Disdain colors his features as he stares at me like a man who's found grime where everything should gleam.

"Absolutely no fucking cakes inside," he says, his tone blunt. "This is a bar, not a Goddamn Chuck E. Cheese."

I glance at Demi, her arms tighten possessively around that triple-layer red velvet cake like it's an arsenal-grade weapon.

"*Okay,* Mr. Aggressive." She's already making her sexy, pouty face—eyebrow arched, lips sucked in just so—like she's plotting a face-icing ambush. "You sure about that? I mean, I'll save you a piece if you play nice." She pops the lid up, runs a finger along the side of the icing, and brings it to her lips, sucking it into her mouth.

"No cakes. Period." No hesitation, no smile. All business.

Demi shrugs and leans in, grinning, clearly determined to push Pretty Boy's buttons. She inches into his personal space. He begins to lean back. "What if I feed it to you? I promise it's not poison."

The new guy doesn't bite, but I watch as the first hint of a smile pulls on the tall and intimidating one's rather perfect lips.

"I don't care how good it is. I don't care if Duff-fucking-Goldman baked it. No cakes."

And that's when Demi decides she's had enough and... *tips. The. Damn. Cake. Over.*

It splatters onto the sidewalk. Red velvet and frosting explode in a mess of crumbs and goo. I freeze, staring in disbelief.

"What the hell, Demi?" I can't help but hiss, but the absurdity of the situation makes me laugh despite myself. It's my cake, and I *didn't* want her to bring it, but now I'm disappointed. In her actions and that I won't get to taste the glorious creation.

I don't miss the youngest of the three guys chuckling into his hand.

But what really gets me is the bartender's reaction. His face gives nothing away. He doesn't speak—just stands there, shoulders squared, eyes fixed on the ruined cake like it personally assaulted him. It's the subtle twitch of his fingers, and the way his jaw tightens that make me think he's already working out how to handle the mess. Not emotionally—literally sweeping, scrubbing, erasing.

I'm staring at the disaster, unable to tear my own eyes away, when I hear that low growl from behind me. "You're gonna need to get a handle on her."

I twist around to find him leaning so close, it sends a pulse of heat through me. His dark eyes flick over the mess, then back at me. I can't help but take every inch of him in—*and there are a lot of inches.* The leather jacket looks even better up close, stretched tight across his broad shoulders, and I notice for the first time the dark tattoo peeking from under his sleeve and running down over his knuckles. It's something intricate but hard to make out. The intensity in his stare pins me in place.

"Clean it up," he says, voice deep and controlled.

Is he demanding I clean up the cake from the sidewalk?

Panic starts to rise in my throat. I'm not even certain I can bend to pee in this dress, let alone clean icing off of concrete.

Demi smirks but seems to back off, thrown by his no-nonsense tone. The air feels charged, electric, and my emotions tear. I'm aching to cry, half desperate for the comfort of sweatpants and half tempted to see where this tension leads by biting back.

I stay rooted in place though, stuck in the wreckage of my ruined cake, while the bartender's sharp gaze tracks from the frosting-covered sidewalk to the behemoth in front of me, clearly recognizing who's on cleanup duty. "Okay, Hex."

The man in the pressed jeans walks down the steps. Without a word, he raises his palm out to Demi who hands over the container. He bends down and uses the container's cover to scrape the cake's contents back into the box. I can't help but admire the precision of the way he handles it. Demi observes him, her expression unfazed by the carnage being removed from the sidewalk. But I find there's something so...*fascinating* about the way he keeps it all together. When he's done, he grabs the towel from his back pocket and wipes his hands clean.

My eyes land back on *Hex*. He's not the kind of man who messes around.

Big guy's name is Hex. He is in charge.

And right now, he's watching me. Watching us. Heat flares in my chest, undeniable and intense. What gets me is that behind that implacable look, I catch glimpses of something darker, more complicated—like he's feeling this tension too but keeping it locked down. The last thing I expect is for it to stir something inside me.

"We aren't getting in now, are we?" I ask, with a nervous laugh.

Hex doesn't smile, doesn't even flinch. "I'm letting you in, but if she keeps this up, you're both out. Got it?"

Demi shrugs. She hooks my arm and leans in. With a wicked grin and loud enough for all three men to hear says: "Cake got bounced, but that's no biggie. Let's find a warm mouth to gorge on our red-velvety sweet spots instead."

I shake my head, already dreading the chaos that will become this night. "I'll be lucky if I make it through tonight without her setting fire to something."

Hex raises an eyebrow. "Watch your back, birthday girl."

CHAPTER FOUR

Alex

I 'm standing outside, leaning against the brick wall of Ruin's End, talking shop with JT—my kid brother and our bouncer. He's just as solid as I am, but where my presence keeps people in check, JT's easy going demeanor makes them forget what he's capable of. Stupid mistake. I taught him how to fight, and at the drop of a hat, he could put someone on the ground before they even realized they fucked up.

We're going over the night, and I'm hoping things stay quieter than last Friday. I'm not in the mood for another repeat of that mess.

"I don't expect any trouble tonight," I tell him. "If anything pops off, just give me a shout. I don't want you dealing with shit alone."

JT smirks, rolling a toothpick between his teeth. "Man, you act like I don't live for a little entertainment." He scans the street, unbothered, cool as ever. "But yeah, I got you. It's been slow so far. We're probably in the clear."

I exhale through my nose. "Good. Keep it that way."

JT chuckles. "Sure thing. I'll tell the drunks to schedule their dumbassery for another night." He leans back, stretching his arms over his head, the picture of someone without a care in the world. But I know better.

He's a coiled spring, waiting to be triggered and snap.

He won't hesitate.

I'm just about to push off the wall when I see them coming around the corner. Short and spicy, the redhead bounces for the door, energy bright and unapologetic, moving as though the space already belongs to her. She's holding a cake—*of course*. Will will be pissed. But it's not her I'm focused on.

It's her friend.

Tall. So damn tall. She walks with a kind of grace that stops you dead in your tracks. At least five-foot-ten if I'm guessing right, but the heels make her six foot easy. She knows how to carry herself. The black dress she's wearing is... well, it's the kind of dress that makes you think of dropping to your knees in surrender. It's the perfect balance between sexy and strong, hugging her in all the right places, making it damn near impossible for me not to look.

JT tilts his head slightly, amused. "You seein' what I'm seein', big bro?" he mutters just low enough for me to catch.

I don't answer. I don't have to. We have the same taste in women.

Her legs stretch endlessly, sculpted and strong, the kind of presence that turns movement into authority. She has that focused look. Her long, dark brown hair falls in waves, the streetlight picking up those sun-kissed highlights at the edges. And her big brown eyes pull you in, making you forget whatever the hell you were thinking. She's poised but wary, too controlled for someone just looking to have a good time. Or maybe it's just that she doesn't seem to belong here. And yet somehow, she fits anyway.

As they approach the door, JT barely moves. He's leaning against the windows that line the front of Ruin's End, arms crossed. He's about to let them in—no hesitation—until the tall one walks past.

I see it, the flicker in his expression. His eyes narrow just slightly, tracking her a beat longer than usual. Not in the way most guys would, but in a way I've come to recognize is a characteristic of both of ours. He is clocking something, filing it away in that sharp-ass mind of his.

I reach into the moment, and without missing a beat, I stop them.

JT lets out a slow whistle under his breath, rocking back on his heels. That easygoing, nothing-phases-me demeanor still firmly in place.

"Hold up," I say, my voice low, barely a murmur against the street noise. "Both of you."

They both stop, and I could see the surprise flint across the tall one's face. Something shifts in her eyes—just a brief spark of shock, unprepared for the interruption.

"IDs," I add.

The redhead steps forward first, pulling out her wallet with that same bright energy she's had since she bounced up the steps. She hands over her ID with a flirty smile, clearly thinking she can charm her way through this.

I barely glance at it—she's obviously old enough. I hand it back without comment and turn my full attention to her friend.

That's when I catch the hesitation in her face, the coolness under the surface. She was not expecting to be carded, but there's a bit of excitement too that it's happening.

She pulls out her wallet and hands it over without a word.

Sable Hawthorne.

Turning thirty-nine in nine days.

The fact that she's almost forty and looks this fucking good catches me off guard.

I'm thirty-one. She's got eight years on me, but I don't give a damn.

What matters is how she moves. She's not chasing anything. Confident. Not desperate like most women who come through here. She's already found her spot in the world, and from the looks of it, she's not afraid to own that.

Local address. Stillwater Bend. I recognize it instantly. Old houses, the kind with character and history. Wraparound porches you can imagine sitting on with a drink, watching the world pass by. She's got roots here.

I hold onto her license longer than necessary, watching her fidget. She makes some nervous joke about fake IDs and aging up to forty, and I can't help but feel that pull again.

"You're good," I mutter, my voice rougher than I want it to be. She takes the ID back, her fingers brushing mine in the briefest of touches, and my pulse stutters.

I can't help but watch her, her confidence carrying her forward as she steps past me. There's something in the way she holds herself that makes me think she's the kind of woman who knows exactly what she wants, but might be a little afraid of the power.

Her vertically challenged friend, however, is still lit up, clearly looking for any button she can find to push. Will steps outside right on cue.

I know exactly what he is about to focus on.

Will's a neat freak. *No, scratch that.* Will's an obsessive, compulsive neat freak. Used to organize his damn toys by color, shape, and size when we were kids. Everything had its place. We were roommates briefly, and I swear he spent more time folding his clothes than I spent cleaning the entire damn house.

But that's what makes him so damn good at his job. This place is spotless under his watch. Will's the guy I call when things in life spin out and get messy. He doesn't crack under pressure. He thrives on it.

He's going to hate that cake. He's going to treat it as a personal affront, and I'll be damned if he doesn't end up cleaning up the aftermath.

"Will's not gonna like that," I murmur and glance at JT. "I'd have let it slide."

JT chuckles. "Yeah, well, you've gone soft with the patrons. I'm not testing Will's blood pressure by making him scrape cake off the booths. Man's already one frosting disaster away from an early retirement."

I'm focused on the way Sable tracks the tension, reading the situation. Smart. Most people miss the undercurrents, but she's clocking everything—Will's stance, her friend's smirk, the way this is about to go sideways.

Can't wait to watch that.

Then Red dumps the whole damn cake on the sidewalk. A mess in front of my bar.

Sable stands frozen, but I can tell it's not about the cake anymore. It's about what's coming next.

Perfect.

I elbow JT in the gut for chuckling and step into her space, closing the distance between us. I don't say a word at first, just letting the weight of the moment settle in. "Clean it up," I say, my voice low but firm.

Her eyes flick up to mine. Her body tightens, a subtle adjustment that tells me she's assessing me.

I watch her. The flicker of surprise I expected is absent. A little rattled by my command, but she's holding steady.

I can tell she's repeating my three little words over in her brain, deciding whether I'm serious. And I am. I seriously want to see if she'll give up a little grace and relax the death grip she has over control.

Will's probably salivating at the thought of dropping to the concrete to clean up the mess the right way, but that's not what I'm after. It's Sable I'm focused on.

I don't expect her to clean up the mess. Hell, I'm not even sure she could in that dress. *But God, what I wouldn't give to see her on her knees for me, the snug black fabric riding up her tight ass.* The thought has blood rushing to my cock. It stiffens against the seam of my jeans.

Is she scrappy, like her little friend? Or will she hold herself back and submit?

Her lips press together, eyes narrowing just so. She's considering it. *That's* what I'm after. The reaction. Does she let me lead, or does she push back?

Her confidence speaks volumes, but I can feel it—something more hidden underneath.

Of course, Will drops down to pick up the mess, the fucking neat freak tendencies kicking in full force. The guy's practically having a mini meltdown at the sight of cake lying there on a dirty ass sidewalk for even a few seconds.

Sable watches him, a quiet little smirk on those pouty lips, clearly enjoying the show. It's a rare thing to see someone keep that kind of control. But then, she turns her attention back to me.

"We aren't getting in now, are we?" she asks, the words slipping from her glossed lips with an adorable charm. I swear, all I hear is her asking if she's been naughty, waiting to learn what her punishment will be. My mind takes off with the thoughts of what I might do to get her to behave.

She's testing me, no doubt.

It's a simple question, but it lands on me as an unspoken challenge. I step closer, my voice low but direct, my tone still laced with that edge, giving her a warning about keeping her friend in line.

I can see her eyes flicker with something... maybe curiosity, maybe more.

"Watch your back, birthday girl."

I don't know why I said it that way. Maybe I meant it as a warning, but part of me wonders if it came out as something else entirely.

Her friend loops her arm through Sable's, leading her inside. Red's laugh trails behind, that wicked invitation about "red-velvety sweet spots" echoing in my mind.

My pulse kicks up. What I wouldn't give to taste every inch of Sable's sweetness myself. I'd beg to lap up every drop of her.

Sable—*damn*—moves away from me, claiming every inch of my bar as she steps into it.

I resist the urge to follow. Giving myself a minute to let things settle down in my pants. She's a distraction, and I'm not used to feeling this way over a woman I just met.

But I'll be watching. I'll be keeping an eye on Sable Hawthorne.

CHAPTER
FIVE

Sable

My typical Friday nights consist of loungewear and the latest unhinged romance novel. But tonight, Demi could talk me into just about anything.

And maybe that is directly influenced by the low-grade buzz still humming under my skin, ignited by Demi's cake-fueled bedlam. The gold tequila burns on the way down, a languid, smoldering heat that spreads through my chest before settling into something akin to comfort—almost. I'm careful not to take another sip too soon.

Warmth lingers in my core from the raw heat that sizzled between me and the gorgeous guy at the threshold.

Hex.

My eyes flick over the crowd, scanning the room for his leather jacket, and that unreadable expression. I'm being ridiculous. Barely ten minutes in and my cheeks are warm, my body restless from a full-blown schoolgirl crush. I blame the way he looked at me. He didn't just see me. He examined me, piece by piece, the way someone studies a puzzle they fully intend to solve.

I exhale sharply, shaking it off as Demi slides into the booth, settling beside me, her phone already out. "Alright, birthday girl," she chides, angling the screen toward me, "let's get this thirst trap on record."

I give her that flat lip, dead eye stare she's so used to, but lean in anyway. The booth's tucked into the back of the bar, lit just enough to be flattering, and the perfect spot for people-watching or disappearing. Demi knows exactly what she's doing as she angles her phone. If I have to be in this photo, I might as well make it count. I throw on my best sultry smirk.

"Perfect," Demi murmurs, tapping her screen before lifting her glass in triumph. "Posted. Tagged. We are officially on the map."

I huff a laugh, glancing around. There is a perfect blend of history mixed with modern updates here. It's housed in one of the old Main Street buildings, the kind that's been standing for at least a century, but the interior is anything but dated. Dark wood, deep leather booths, a bar top that gleams under the soft glow of trendy Edison bulb light fixtures. Masculine finishes, sleek but warm. It feels... clean. Which, in a bar, is saying something.

Demi chatters beside me, something about the comments already rolling in, but my attention drifts again. My fingers curl around the edge of my glass as I search for Hex again without fully admitting that's what I'm doing.

GQ man is indeed one of the bartenders. He simultaneously pours drinks and wipes down any droplet of condensation he comes across.

The ice clinks as I swirl the tequila, eyes fixed on the golden liquid, searching for answers that aren't there. I don't drink often. I hate the slow unraveling, the way my mind stops filtering thoughts before they tumble out. And more than anything, I hate the morning after. The bone-deep exhaustion, the headache that lingers too long. A greasy breakfast and a couple of Advil pills used to cure a hangover. Now, it's a full 24- to 48-hour recovery period, and I just don't have the time for that.

I glance up and catch a flash of black leather.

It's him.

Hex.

At the far end of the bar, he shrugs off his leather jacket, revealing a fitted black T-shirt that hugs broad shoulders and arms strong enough to lift the damn place off its foundation.

He's standing with a few older guys, faces weathered like they've spent more years outside than in. He didn't seem to be the kind who wastes words. His lips move in such a way I know he's commanding the conversation.

I watch the way they look at him. Not with the casual friendliness you give to a bartender, not with the wary respect you show a bouncer who might toss you out. No, it is something else. They listen—attentive and deferential—giving subtle nods, following every word he says.

An aura of quiet confidence wraps around Hex. As if he has nothing to prove and everything under control. No laughter, not the least bit jovial, yet his posture feels easy. A man who's rarely questioned and often obeyed.

What the hell are you, Hex?

My eyes drag over his arms, thick and corded with strength. The tattoo I saw peeking from his sleeve now visible, running up the length of his arm and leading to God knows what other muscle he has packed into that shirt.

He's just there, fully present in every moment, and somehow that's even more intimidating than his size.

God, his size.

He could throw a man through the window without breaking a sweat. He could probably take a hit and not even flinch—by a fucking car.

The way his fingers drum lightly against the bar top betrays restrained excitement. He doesn't look around. No other ticks or quirks give away whatever emotion simmers beneath his stoic mask. There's a patience in him that makes me wonder what it would take to break it.

He vanishes into the back office, the men he spoke with following close behind.

I shift in my seat, the upholstery sticking against my bare thighs as I slowly exhale, like that'll steady the heat building low in my stomach. I shouldn't be looking at him like this—like I want to unwrap him and taste the trouble underneath. Shouldn't be letting thoughts like that take root.

I take another sip of my drink, feeling the warmth spread through me, and remind myself why alcohol is never a good idea.

Andrew.

I used to convince myself that I could fix things when I drank. That if I just found the right words, the right actions, I could give him another chance, make him and I work.

I know better now.

I didn't feel sad when we ended. There were no gut-wrenching sobs, no desperate urge to win him back. What I felt was emptier than that—like standing in front of a house I'd spent years trying to renovate, only to realize the foundation was rotted the whole time.

What hurt was the failure. The quiet, exhausting truth that no matter how much I bent, tried, forgave, or held it all together with both hands and a smile, it was never enough. And it's also the part I still struggle with—the loss of the illusion that if I just tried hard enough, I could make broken things whole.

Now, my focus is on raising Bash. Trying my best to keep things civil with Andrew. And if I end up alone for the rest of my life? I could learn to be okay with that.

I lift my glass for another sip, the low hum of the bar blurring into my thoughts right up until a sudden commotion cuts through it all, snapping me back to the present.

Two older men are squared up near the pool table, close enough in appearance to be brothers: late fifties, thick beards, biker vests, and years of hard living carved into their faces. Their argument almost looks like playful roughhousing. But then a shove turns into a near swing, and the whole energy shifts.

I set my drink down, straightening.

Demi glances over, barely interested and still lost in her phone. "Let me guess, someone lost a bet?"

"Looks like it," I murmur, but my eyes aren't on them anymore.

They're on him.

Hex steps out of the office, his presence instantly shifting the air in the room. Conversations dip. A few heads turn. He doesn't acknowledge any of it. Just moves with purpose, rolling his shoulders as he crosses the floor. There's no rush. No urgency. Just the kind of authority that says this problem is already handled.

He reaches them just as the bearded man on the left cocks his arm back, ready to throw the first real punch.

Hex doesn't snatch him up. Doesn't shove between them.

Instead, he steps in close, a hand clamping down on the guy's shoulder with a firm grip. He leans in, murmuring something too low for me to hear, but the effect is immediate. The guy exhales sharply through his nose, unclenching his fists. The other man relaxes, too, his body loosening under whatever spell Hex just worked on them.

The walk to the exit starts, one hand on each of their shoulders, steering them out with a gentleness that shocks me. There's no aggression. No posturing. Just a quiet command that the men don't even think to question.

The door swings shut behind them, and I realize I've been staring.

Who the hell is this guy?

"Damn," Demi mutters, leaning on the table, phone now fully abandoned. "That was kind of hot."

I shake my head to bring my focus back to my friend, trying to ignore the way my pulse is suddenly hammering against my throat. Hot. Yes. But also... interesting.

I turn back toward my drink, trying to shake the feeling when—

A flicker of blonde at the bar.

A slow, icy dread trickles down my spine, my skin prickling with awareness.

I know that hair.

My fingers tighten around my glass as cool sweat coats my bare limbs.

This isn't random.

This isn't coincidence.

The gym rat stalker decided to step up her game. No longer watching from a distance—she's here.

Demi suddenly stiffens. Her head jerks to the left, and before I can even brace for it, she blurts out—loud enough for the entire back of the bar to hear: "Oh. My. God. Is that Ashley?!"

I flinch. My stomach twists. I try to ignore it, but Ashley's gaze drips across the bar, dark and crawling, a nightmare dragged out from beneath my bed.

Of course, Demi remembers her name and every detail of how she looks.

I swear, Demi has been stalking her back just as hard, but this... this is new. We've never crossed paths in person. Not like this.

Demi's gaze swings back to me, eyes wide with equal parts disbelief and unhinged amusement. "Oh, this little toxic cockroach just won't die." She dips her head out and back toward the bar, voice lowering to a dramatic whisper. "Do you think she saw my story? She totally saw my story. What kind of unhinged commitment"—she motions wildly, gesturing between me and the blonde at the bar—"does it take to go from commenting on all your posts from burner accounts to showing up in person?"

I stare at my drink, willing it to make me disappear. "Demi—"

"No. No, this is next-level dedication, babe." She studies Ashley, head shaking slightly, as if surprised and impressed all at once. Then, in a complete one-eighty, she slams her hand on the table. "Nope. Nope. I've had enough. I'm going over there."

She's halfway standing when I reach out and catch her wrist. "Absolutely not."

The brief commotion has the put-together bartender snapping his distaste in Demi's direction.

"Sable." She gives me an incredulous look. "We cannot just sit here and let Stalker Barbie think this is okay. This is your side of town. You should be able to enjoy your life, your bar"—as if I've been here before today—"your birthday, without some psycho lurking in the shadows." She waves her hand dramatically, nearly knocking over my drink.

I take a deep breath, lowering my voice. "Demi. Please. Let's just go." I push my glass away. "I just want to leave."

Demi stares at me, mouth gaping, as though I've offended every value she holds dear. "Are you kidding me right now?" Her voice pitches up in pure outrage. "She wins again?!"

Her finger jabs toward Ashley, who remains at the bar, unbothered and out of place in the most infuriating way. "You're gonna let her dictate where you can and can't go? Babe. Babe. Do I need to shake you?"

I rub my temples. "Demi—"

"No, you listen to me. You are Sable *Fucking* Hawthorne. You are hot. You are successful. You are capable of murder if required—"

"That's... not the pep talk I need right now."

"—and this? This is your damn town. Your turf." She leans in, eyes blazing. "You do not run. You do not hide. Let her haunt the corners of this world, playing the deranged ex-side piece ghoul while you live. Let her watch. But you are not leaving this damn bar on your birthday because some desperate gym rat doesn't understand boundaries."

My grip tightens on her wrist, keeping her from charging into whatever she's got brewing inside that wild brain of hers.

I want to leave.

But... she's right.

Demi sees it too, the way my hesitation is giving Ashley exactly what she wants.

I unclench my jaw. "Fine."

Demi bares her teeth. "That's my girl."

I push past Demi and out of the booth, my pulse hammering against my throat. Confrontation has never been my thing. *I do not want to do this.* I don't get into fights. I don't cause scenes.

Thinking through my approach, I know I should keep it civil. Don't escalate. She's clearly a tick short of sane, *kill-me-and-wear-my-skin* levels of crazy, and I have no intention of poking the feral animal.

I straighten, about to make my move, but Ashley's already moving.

She's crossing the floor, heels clicking against the wood in a steady death march. Her foundation is caked on thick enough to crack, and she's wearing a cheap, too-tight, too-short strapless number that belongs under a flickering motel sign. Her overprocessed blonde hair lies flat against her head in a way that makes me think it hasn't been washed in days.

But it's the traps that do it for me. Those things are too big. I have no idea how she's keeping that fabric up. Probably with a combination of industrial-strength double-sided tape and sheer spite.

I set my jaw as she reaches the table, stopping close enough to violate every concept of personal space.

She smirks, gaze flicking over me, then Demi, then back to me again. "Wow," she drawls, crossing her arms under her overinflated chest. "Didn't think I'd see you out tonight. Let me guess, early birthday celebration? Andrew didn't tell me."

There it is. The bait. Andrew's name drops, a lit match in gasoline.

I don't flinch. Ashley wants me to believe they're still screwing like rabbits.

"Probably because it's not relevant to him." I offer her a tight smile. "Or you."

Her smirk twitches. "Oh, come on," she coos, tilting her head. "You don't have to pretend. I know you still think about us."

I arch a brow. "I assure you, I do not."

She laughs—an ugly, breathy sound that makes my skin crawl. "Sure. That's why you're looking so bothered right now."

My fingers curl into my palms. I can feel my pulse in my ears, my body wired tight with restraint. I inhale sharply, count to five. I will not engage.

I open my mouth to deliver something appropriately mature and dismissive—but before I can get a word out, Demi steps up onto the seat of the booth and launches herself off the table.

Full WWE-style aerial assault.

One second, she's nestled safely behind me, gripping her glass. The next, she's flying, clearing the table with terrifying ease and landing on Ashley, arms locking tight in a full takedown.

Chaos erupts.

Demi forcefully tugs Ashley's swinging arms out of the way. "YOU WANT TO TALK SHIT?"

Ashley shrieks, stumbling back as Demi grabs two fistfuls of her hair. "LET'S TALK SHIT, BARBIE!"

Glasses clatter. Chairs scrape. People whip around to watch.

Ashley flails, trying to shake Demi off, but Demi is in it. She's got the strength of someone who has been waiting for this moment, and I'm so stunned, I can't even move.

Then, in a blur of movement, the bartender swoops in. He rips Demi off with an ease that suggests he's done this before. Demi thrashes in his grip, still trying to claw her way back toward Ashley, a rabid squirrel hell-bent on reclaiming her stolen nut.

Hex's voice cuts through the commotion, sharp and commanding. "GET HER OUT OF HERE!"

I whip around to see him grab Ashley. It's not rough, but with enough authority that she stops screeching and stiffens. His grip is firm as he steers her to the front door while the bartender hauls Demi toward the back.

I stand there, chest rising and falling, feeling the eyes of the entire bar on me.

The space where Ashley stood buzzes with tension.

Demi, mid-removal, shouts over the bartender's shoulder, "I RE-GRET NOTHING!"

The back door slams shut.

My skin crawls. My breath shaky. And as I glance at the front entrance, my gut tells me this isn't over. Not even close.

I exit out the back after my friend.

CHAPTER
SIX

Sable

The alley behind the bar reeks of fried food, stale beer, and a lifetime of bad decisions. Dim streetlights buzz overhead, illuminating the collection of cigarette butts, shattered glass, and a dumpster that is convincing me it's hiding something illegal. Or dead.

And right in the middle of all that glory, Demi's clinging to the bartender with the tenacity of a rabid koala. Her legs cinch tight around his waist, arms windmilling, and cursing loud enough to paint the air with so much color it could be sold as abstract art.

"You motherfucker! You cockless, soulless, fun-sucking—"

"Jesus Christ, would you stop?" The bartender—built as if he personally lifts kegs for fun—plants his feet and peels off the stubborn leech in human form.

Demi lands on her feet with the grace of a drunk cat, her hair disheveled and breathing hard, but still glaring up at him with undiminished fire. "Do you have no shame throwing out a woman defending her friend's honor, or are you just an asshole?"

He straightens his jeans and twisted shirt and steps back. "You throw a punch at a barely-legal blonde, and suddenly I'm the asshole?"

"She deserved it. And barely-legal? Do men even look at girl's faces anymore, or is it just straight to the tits?"

"She definitely deserved it," I chime in. My heels click against the cracked pavement as I stop just short of the two of them. "My friend simply enforced some basic street justice."

He crosses his arms, unimpressed. "Justice doesn't usually involve pulling out extensions."

Demi rakes her fingers through that fiery red hair, not a hint of guilt in sight. "They were fucking clip-ins. Bitch can't even afford to get them professionally installed."

The bartender exhales through his nose and presses his fingers to his temple. "Yeah, well, it's a shame you wasted your takedown on someone who didn't deserve that kind of energy. You're banned. Forever."

Demi snorts. "Oh, *forever*? What is this, the fucking Roman Empire?"

He cocks an eyebrow. "No, but I am the fucking justice system in this establishment, and you"—he pokes her in the forehead, pushing her back a step—"are a goddamn liability."

Demi lets out a gasp so offended you'd think he just smacked her grandma. I pinch my lips together and clear my throat to keep myself from laughing.

Then he turns to me, his expression softening as if my obvious mortification still lingers on my face. "You, on the other hand, can come back whenever. But you might wanna consider picking less homicidal friends."

I fold my arms. "Not a chance."

His eyes flick between us, and something akin to amusement tugs at the corner of his mouth. "Figures." He sticks out his hand. "I'm Will, by the way. Y'all got names, or should I just refer to you as Menace to Society and her loyal partner in crime?"

I shake his hand. "Sable." I jerk a thumb at my gremlin of a best friend. "And *Menace* is Demi."

"Charmed," Demi deadpans with a too-honeyed smile as if still plotting her way back in.

Will smirks, then sobers a bit. "Y'all good to drive?"

"We walked," I say. "I live a few streets over." I jerk my head toward Demi. "And nobody's fucking with me while I walk my pitbull home."

Will laughs under his breath and shoots Demi a look. "Yeah, I can see that."

Demi flips him off.

Will shakes his head, already heading back inside. "Good luck with that one," he calls over his shoulder.

I grin, but Demi's not done.

"We don't need luck," she shouts as a final stand. "WE HAVE ALCOHOL AND POOR JUDGEMENT."

And with that, we start walking, Demi still fuming, me still laughing, and Main Street buzzing behind us as if at almost forty years old we weren't just unceremoniously dumped into the alley like last night's trash.

Back at my house, the familiar scent of vanilla candles and old wood welcomes me like a hug. The quiet hum of the refrigerator and the soft tick of the hallway clock feel like a lullaby after the holy mess at the bar.

Demi is already strutting around in a pair of my sweatpants that puddle around her ankles, pure '90s skater jeans energy. She's always treated my space as her own, and there's something about that comfort I love. She feels permanent, unbothered, unbreakable. In one hand, she's sucking down an applesauce pouch with the dedication of a post-soccer game kid, and with the other, she's rifling through my pantry with the determination of a treasure hunter. No sense of order. No shame.

"You seriously don't have any good snacks?" she calls over her shoulder, her voice muffled by the bag of stale pita chips she's digging out from the back.

I glance over from my spot in the living room, where I've been watching the tornado whip through. "Define 'good.'"

She waves the applesauce pouch in the air. "Not fucking these."

I shrug. "Bash likes them."

Her glare lands hard, all righteous indignation and silent accusation. "You have failed him." Then she heads back to the living room with the assortment she's got tucked under her arm and dramatically flops back onto the couch, legs crossed, crumbs everywhere.

I take a slow breath and look around the house, letting my gaze wander over the space that used to be ours—Andrew's and mine—but always mine by law.

The hardwood floorboards betray only the ghost of his passage. Every wall wears the furniture I restored myself—the battered oak chair whose leather I stitched patch by patch, the walnut dresser I refused to sell even when I could've doubled the price. On the far wall, my degree hangs in a matte-black frame—a silent middle finger to everyone who ever said I couldn't. I did all of this on my own.

Andrew never left a mark because he never wanted to. For ten years, he held up a neon sign flashing *I don't belong here*, and I just kept pretending I didn't see it.

Tonight feels different, though. For the first time in years, someone tried to make me run from my own life, and I didn't. Well, Demi didn't let me. The memory of Ashley's smug face flashes through my mind—the way she invaded my space, dropped Andrew's name like a weapon, waited for me to crumble. But I held my ground. Even when every instinct screamed at me to flee, I stayed.

I shake the thought away, watching Demi transform my organized living room into her personal chaos zone. It's oddly comforting—her ability to bounce back from throwing punches to rifling through my snacks like nothing happened. Some things never change.

She pops open my laptop, now buried in a nest of pillows and throw blankets she's yanked from their perfectly folded spots, completely unbothered by the disaster she's made of my couch.

"Alright, so what's the plan for Stalker Barbie?" she asks, fingers already flying across the keyboard.

I groan. "Demi, please tell me you're not—"

"I'm just doing some light research."

I lean over and instantly regret it. The screen is filled with a website that looks dangerous. Dark backgrounds, red text, and a loading bar that gives off a distinctly illegal vibe.

"Demi, what the fuck is this?"

She smirks and wiggles her fingers ominously. "The dark web."

"The what?!" I slam the laptop shut so fast she nearly loses a finger.

My heart hammers against my ribs. After everything tonight—Ashley showing up, the confrontation, getting kicked out—my safe space feels more precious than ever. The last thing I need is Demi inviting actual danger into my home.

She glares. "You're overreacting."

"What are you going to do? Hire a fucking hitman?"

She scoffs as if I'm the one being absurd. "They're not *hitmen*, they're professional handlers. You don't even have to know what happens to the problem... they just *handle* it. I'm outsourcing." She shrugs, as if this is the most obvious, ethical solution in the world.

I rub my temples. "You need to stop drinking."

"You need to start." She gasps, noticing we have no drinks. "And I will not be silenced."

Before I can argue, she's already on her feet, wandering back to the pantry. "I swear I saw a bottle of wine in here."

I sigh and turn my attention back to my laptop, this time with safe intentions.

I type in the name of the bar, Ruin's End, half-wondering if Hex is somewhere laughing about what a disaster Demi and I are.

The website is sleek, moody—dark colors, grunge-style fonts, and obscure, shadowy images meant to fit some mysterious aesthetic. I scroll until I hit the About Us page.

Hector Alvarez.

The name sits there in bold lettering under an artsy, backlit photo that's more shadow than person. *Figures.* Even his picture has a mysterious attitude.

I stare at the screen, remembering the way he moved through the pandemonium of tonight—quiet authority, no drama, just solving what needed solving.

Right beneath the picture is a contact form, inviting guests to reach out for inquiries. My cursor hovers over it for a long moment. What would I even say? Thanks for handling my stalker ex-side piece? Sorry my friend turned your bar into a WWE SmackDown?

Before I can spiral too far into my curiosity, Demi comes barreling back in, waving a bottle of something deeply questionable.

I squint at the label. "Where the hell did you find that?"

She lights up. "Your mom left it. Some random cocktail ingredient she swore she'd master eventually. That woman is sixty-five and thriving. I don't ever want to hear you call yourself old again."

Demi pours us shots into the only thing she can find—Bash's old sippy cups. Then she lifts them, solemn and expectant, as though honoring something bigger than both of us.

"Tractors or puppies?" she asks.

I stare at her. "What?"

She gives the cups a shake, apparently convinced that'll make things clearer. "Which one do you want? Tractors or puppies?"

I sigh and grab the one with puppies on it, thinking about how only several hours ago my biggest concern was whether my feet would survive the night. Now I'm drinking questionable liquor from my son's sippy cups while my best friend plots revenge via the dark web.

"To disorderly conduct," Demi declares, raising her tractor cup.

"To survival," I counter.

Because, apparently, this is my life now.

CHAPTER SEVEN

Alex

"**H**eading out?" Will finishes wiping down the counter for what has to be the third time before tossing his bar towel into the bin.

The stools are flipped, the floors are swept—*twice*—and the last drunk stragglers have stumbled their way home or into someone else's bed.

"Yeah," I say, rubbing a hand over my face. "I'm going to crash upstairs tonight."

Will nods, as if he expected that. He's already got his keys in hand, ready to lock up. "Wild one."

"That's one way to put it."

Four fights. Not our worst night, but entertaining enough. Standard shit—drunken chest-puffing, too much testosterone. Nothing we couldn't handle.

Except the blonde. The curb crawler who threatened Sable. *Something's off about that one.* The moment I grabbed her elbow, she didn't struggle. She simply complied, as if she'd anticipated the escort, maybe even craved it.

Just as I was about to shove her out, she unleashed a tirade I never saw coming. She rattled off every sordid detail she knew about Sable. And Sable's ex.

I didn't engage, but she told me anyway, eyes too damn focused for someone who'd just been tackled by a woman half her size.

"She ruins men, you know," she murmured, dragging her tongue over her split lip, feeding on the taste as though it powered her. "Takes them, wraps them up in all that fire and when she's done? When she's sucked and fucked them dry—" A crooked smile spread over her face that said the thought angered her in a way that pleased. "She leaves them fucking useless. Empty. No good to anyone else."

The crazy ass bitch then tilted her head, looking me over, assessing. "Andrew used to fuck me," she went on, her tone disturbingly casual, as though listing off her morning routine. "Used to be insatiable for my attention. Until she left him." She pointed a finger back at the bar.

The words dripped from her lips, each one coated in contempt.

"He told me once—after a few drinks, when he thought I wouldn't remember—that I can't compare to her." Her gaze dropped to my mouth, then returned to my eyes, gauging how much she could say without giving too much of her crazy away.

My jaw locks, my pulse ticks faster. This crosses every fucking line. *I don't want to hear this shit about Sable.* But every detail she spills tells me more about what I'm dealing with. This isn't just jealousy.

"And you know what the worst part is?" Her lipstick-smudged mouth opened as she stepped in closer, dropping her voice as though we were old friends sharing a dirty secret. "She doesn't even mean to do it. She doesn't even know the power she has. And they keep chasing her, but they never get her back."

I said nothing. Just let her words sink in, cataloging every twisted detail of her ramblings.

She wasn't talking about Sable like a woman scorned.

She talked about her like someone who wanted to be her.

Someone who'd been competing from the start.

Someone dangerously close to losing the game inside her head.

And something told me, she'd never let it end that way.

Climbing the stairs to the loft, her words circle back. *I should let it go.* Chalk it up to drunken rambling. But it sticks. Burrows deep.

I push open the heavy door, exhaling at the quiet. It's nothing fancy up here—open loft, old bones but solid. I put in the work myself. Ripped out dated flooring, exposed the original brick, added modern finishes where they mattered. A king-sized bed sits against one wall, leather couch across from it. The kitchen is small but functional with slate gray counters.

I stay here when the nights run long, but it's not home. That's out in the Hill Country. Secluded. Quiet. Mine.

I'm too damn tired to make the ride back. The loft will do.

I strip off my shirt, tossing it over a chair, and sink onto the couch, rolling my shoulders. My body's exhausted, but my mind is still running, still caught on the image of Sable standing by that booth, watching me as I escorted the blonde out.

She looked... surprised. Maybe even a little impressed.

Or maybe I'm imagining that because I can't stop thinking about her.

I reach for my phone, not even fully aware of what I'm doing. I've pulled up her social media like some goddamn teenager. *Sable Hawthorne.*

The thirst trap photo she's tagged in from earlier is already racking up likes and comments. She looks good. A cocky smirk at the camera, confidence radiating from her with ease. My eyes beg to drink in what lies beyond where the photo cuts off—the long lines of her legs, the curve of her hips, the bare skin she exposed with conviction. *Christ.* The woman's a fucking distraction.

I let out a slow breath, rubbing my neck.

This is not what I should be doing.

I'm about to put my phone down when a chat bubble pops up, the one connected to the bar's website.

I frown. Most people use the Contact Us form for lost shit: purses, jackets, IDs. Last month someone left a prosthetic leg. Don't know if they ever came back for it.

But this message... this one is different.

The text appears in real-time, like someone's voice-to-text is struggling to keep up:

> **[Guest]:** How woud you handle a stalker?

A pause. Then another line.

> **[Guest]:** I don't think I should ask it like that Sable.

Another.

[Guest]: You have to be more discreeet.

Then the final one.

[Guest]: We need a bitch gone. Yes?

I sit up straighter. Exhaustion gone.

What the fuck?

I stare at the words, my pulse kicking up a notch. The sloppy spelling, the phrasing—the whole thing has the energy of drunk texting.

Sable.

Or more likely her spitfire friend Demi.

I glance back at her social profile, at the picture Demi posted. Yeah, that's the one who launched herself across the table, a damn banshee in full flight.

Could this be them? Were they talking about the blonde? The one I took out front?

Or someone else?

And how the hell would they know to contact me?

I don't have an answer. But one thing is clear.

Tonight might be over, but whatever this is?

It's just getting started.

CHAPTER EIGHT

Sable

The bottle of Chartreuse *thunks* onto the coffee table, half-empty of its sickly yellowish-green contents and entirely regrettable. It's bitter, medicinal; every sip clings to my tongue with the smoky sting of an apothecary cabinet gone up in flames. Truly, the highlight of the night will be examining my own ultraviolet vomit.

"I just need to know," I say, blinking at the label, "who the hell takes shots of this?"

Demi, standing on my couch mid–Taylor Swift performance, grabs the bottle and raises it to eye level. "It's alcohol," she says, as if that justifies everything. "And we had nothing else."

That part is true. My house offered one grim option: an ancient bottle of this liquid regret. Either my mother has no taste buds, an iron gut, or a secret recipe that transforms this herbal punishment into something drinkable.

Every time she visits, she shows up with a sack full of bottles and arms overflowing with rare liqueurs, obscure aperitifs, and spirits—each more offensive than the last; no sane person would willingly keep them in their home. But her visits don't end with just alcoholic presents. No—in fact, she turns my place into a makeshift bar for her experiments and constantly nudges me out of my comfort zone.

Although she knows I barely drink, she treats me like her personal blank canvas. Demi on the other hand, delights in whatever mom mixes for her. They both cackle into the early hours while I sit back and listen half-amused, half-resigned. But right now? My mother is not here.

Which means there is no one to make this swamp water remotely drinkable.

And yet, here we are.

Worse? We'd been chasing it with Bash's favorite drinks; the ones he insisted I buy because some YouTuber swears it's the elixir of the Gods.

"You know," Demi muses, taking another sip of *razz me up,* swishing it around her mouth before gulping it down, "for something created by a douche-canoe, these are surprisingly good."

I let out a slow breath. This night has gotten far more out of hand than I ever intended. But we're home. We're safe. Bash is safe with Andrew.

So why do I still feel like I'm doing something wrong?

I shake the thought away and turn back to my laptop, where Demi has been gleefully navigating what she claims is some kind of "dark web" help site.

"This isn't the dark web," I point out, narrowing my eyes at the very basic, very legal looking interface.

Demi waves me off. "It feels like the dark web. That's what matters."

I rub at my eyes, my alcohol-fueled patience wearing thin. "And what exactly are we doing?"

"Getting help," she says dramatically. "You have a stalker, she's crossed the line, and we need a plan."

I'm about to argue when an open chat window on the screen catches my eye.

"Demi," I screech, lunging for the keyboard, "was the voice-to-text on?!"

She blinks down at me, confused. "What?"

I scroll back through the chat history, my stomach dropping with every word.

> **[Guest]:** how woud you handle a stalker?

> **[Guest]:** I don't think I should ask it like that Sable.

> **[Guest]:** You have to be more discreeet.

> **[Guest]:** We need a bitch gone. Yes?

I whip around to face her. "My name is in this, Demi!"

Demi flops back onto the couch, entirely unconcerned. "There are a lot of Sables in the world."

I squeeze my eyes shut, inhaling through my nose. "That is not the point—"

A message pops up.

My heart stops.

I yelp.

Demi's eyes go wide. "Oh my God, I might have peed."

> **[Representative]:** Who exactly do you need gone?

Demi and I look at one another. *What do we do? Do we just tell him her name?*

I slap my hand over my mouth. Demi clutches my arm again as if she is a horror movie heroine about to be dragged into the abyss. We stare at the message, eyes wide, hearts racing.

Demi inhales. "Okay, but is he hot?" She wags her sparkly painted nail at the keyboard. "Ask that."

I whip my head toward her. "That is not the question we need to be asking right now!"

"Sure it is." She sits up straighter, fanning herself. "Because if we're hiring a hitman, I'd prefer one who looks capable of railing me through a wall *and* hiding the body without breaking a sweat. Get something out of it before we go to fucking jail for life."

"This was your idea," I groan, dragging my hands down my face. And as if I were talking to my child, I say, "You need to pee. Go."

She wobbles to her feet, pointing at the screen. "Don't respond without me."

"Yeah, yeah."

She disappears down the hall.

I stare at the laptop, heart still hammering. *How* should *I respond?*

Another message pops up.

> **[Representative]:** I have to know who it is to do the job.

I blink.

And type before I can overthink it.

> **[Guest]:** Are you saying you actually consider requests through the internet? Because that's concerning.

A pause. Typing bubble...

> **[Representative]:** Only concerning if you're not any good at your job.

I shift my legs beneath me, suddenly very aware of the way my skin feels too warm, how I'm still slightly humming from the last shot of the poison Demi poured for us.

My fingers hover over the keyboard.

> **[Guest]:** So, what's the going rate? Asking for a friend.

The response is almost immediate.

> **[Representative]:** Depends. You offering cash or something more... personal?

A slow pulse beats at the base of my throat.

> **[Guest]:** Okay. So. Flirty murder guy. Not what I expected.

"Demi?" I call out.

A small almost-indistinguishable grunt comes from down the hall.

I push up from the floor, and my head swims. I swing my arms out to help my balance and shuffle to my bedroom like a dazed penguin. The light is on. Sprawled out on one side of my bed with one slipper still dangling from her toes is Demi.

She is done.

I sigh, grabbing a throw blanket and tossing it over her. "Guess you're not coming back to the party."

She makes a noise of agreement but doesn't move.

I make my way back to the living room, intending to clean up, but after two minutes of picking up wrappers and shifting things around, I realize the room is swaying. *I'm swaying.*

Not to risk a head injury, I sink back onto the couch. The laptop screen still glowing.

A new message waits.

> **[Representative]:** You're not answering the question. That means one of two things… you're thinking about what I said or you're trying to figure out if this is a trap.

I smirk, shaking my head. Bad move. I inhale deeply, ordering my brain to stop spinning in my head. The last thing I need is for this person thinking I cannot write properly.

> **[Guest]:** Or I got distracted. My friend is officially dead to the world.

> **[Representative]:** Convenient. I got a clean-up guy for that.

> **[Representative]:** You're all mine, Sable.

A slow heat curls in my stomach. He knows who he is talking to.

> **[Guest]:** My name is NOT Sable, and you have an interesting way of comforting someone in distress.

I try to throw him off—assuming this is a him. As if that would help, he's probably got hacking devices that have already run my IP address, and he knows exactly where I live.

> **[Representative]:** Who said I was trying to comfort you? And this is definitely Sable. The typing is significantly better.

I shift, my fingers tightening around the edge of the couch cushion.

> **[Guest]:** Do I get to know your name?

> **[Representative]:** Do you want to know my name?

> **[Guest]:** You think you know mine.

> **[Representative]:** H-

> **[Guest]:** Is that a haha or you go by H?

> **[Representative]:** I'd let you call me anything you want.

I should shut the laptop. Should stop engaging.

Instead, I type:

> **[Guest]:** Cute. So what exactly are your qualifications? For handling problems.

A pause. This is all going to be used as evidence against me in a court of law. I start to shut the screen when I see the words...

> **[Representative]:** Let's just say I have a very hands-on approach.

And, yeah. I feel that one.

CHAPTER NINE

Sable

H ammering...

    ... with a sledgehammer...

... in my fucking head.

Each relentless throb vibrating between my temples makes me want to curl up and die.

And...

God, the taste.

My mouth is a graveyard of bad choices. It's dry, sour, and coated in something acrid that refuses to let go. Every breath reminds me I did something regrettable. I swallow, trying to ease the burn in my throat, but it doesn't help.

I groan, slowly pushing myself up from the couch, regretting every inch of movement as the world tilts. Why would I do this to myself? There is no recovering from a hangover at thirty-nine. Only death.

Any attempts to gather my thoughts, the words scatter. It feels like piecing together a jigsaw puzzle that's missing half the pieces. All I can focus on is the uncomfortable sensation of my pulse pounding in my head.

What happened last night? And how much water can I consume without drowning?

I try to retrace my steps, but everything is a blur. I vaguely remember messaging someone... *no*, who did I message? Did I send anything to Andrew?

My stomach tightens. *Please, God, don't let me have texted him.*

I fumble for my phone, my fingers sluggish, uncooperative. I manage to unlock the screen, and a wave of relief washes over me when I see only old messages about Bash. Thank fucking God.

But then I catch sight of my laptop, sitting innocently on the coffee table. The pull is subtle but insistent, demanding I open it and confront whatever mistake is waiting inside.

I push myself up, nausea rising, but I don't stop. I drag my legs over the edge of the couch. One foot thuds to the floor. Then the other. I haul the top half of me forward and reach. My fingers are slow, trembling as I open the laptop and type my password. The screen blinks to life. A barrage of additional screens open, but a dark broody website catches my eye—

Ruin's End.

My stomach drops.

What the hell?

I lean in. My contacts are dried to my eyeballs. That's it, because I can't be seeing things right. My heart pounds in my chest, eyes scanning line after line. I can't shake the feeling that whatever's on the screen is a mess I can't undo.

Demi appears in the hallway, her energy bouncing off the walls, bubblier than I can handle right now. She stops when she sees me.

"Why do you look like you're about to cry?" she asks, brows knit with concern.

I let out a shaky breath and show her the laptop screen, pointing to the open conversation. "This."

Her brows furrow even more as she leans in to read. Fingertips fly through her sleep mussed red hair. She doesn't say anything for a beat, then looks up at me, lips curling into a smile.

"Oh, come on," she says, almost laughing. "Look at this as a win. A funny story. It's the freaking bar website. *'Ruin's End.'*" She tosses up air quotes, dripping with sarcasm, already prepared to wage eternal war against the place.

"Yeah, let's hope," I mutter, rubbing my forehead. "Nothing went too far, and I didn't hire a hitman. Thank God. The guy said his name was H." I stare at the screen again, my heart still thumping against my ribs. "It could be Hex—Hector, couldn't it? What if he reports me to the police?"

Demi shrugs, clearly more amused than concerned. "He could."

I open another tab on the website, this time clicking on the About Us section.

"That doesn't concern you?" I question my friend.

"One drunken night? Nah. Nothing to worry about. A mistake. I think you actually have to exchange money for it to be a crime. You didn't

CashApp him, did you?" She's making her way to the kitchen I pray to make coffee.

I read about the bar's founding, a couple of years ago, scrolling down to Hector Alvarez's bio.

I pull my blanket around my shoulders and crane my neck to read it again. Sober.

The bio makes him sound... wholesome, oddly enough. The kind of guy you'd expect to be running some upscale lounge, not taking hitman requests. His profile mentions his background in business, and that he's dedicated to making Ruin's End a place where people come for more than just drinks. It even says he's "known for his personality" and "for going the extra mile for his patrons."

I shut the laptop with a sigh, shoulders caving in.

"I'm going to go in and talk to him. Make sure he knows I sent this"—I wave in circles at my laptop—"without thinking. Drunk. Stupid. A mistake, just like you called it."

"It's fine, Sable," Demi says after a long pause. "Seriously. The guy probably laughed it off."

"No," I say firmly, shaking my head. "I need to go there and make sure he doesn't think I tried to hire a hitman. I don't care what he thinks of me. I just need to make it clear. I own a business in this town and so does he. We will cross paths, and I don't need him thinking Thorne Revival is run by a paranoid woman looking to commit murder."

Demi rolls her eyes dramatically. "Babe, WE are banned FOR LIFE. Remember?"

I wince. "*You* are banned."

"You're not going to get in there. But I'd be happy to wait for you outside." She grins wickedly.

I shoot her a look. "So helpful, Demi. I'm a big girl who can go by herself."

"You know what I mean," she says with a shrug. She's shouting from the kitchen now, banging cabinet doors looking for k-cups that are right next to the coffee machine. "You've got time. The bar opens at six on Saturdays if I remember correctly. You can catch 'H' before the crowd comes in. And Bash is with Andrew until Sunday night, right?"

I stare at her, my mind already working through the conversation I am going to have with him. If I get there early enough, it might not be too bad. I can apologize, explain the mix-up, and get the hell out.

I make my way down Main Street, realizing just how close Ruin's End is to my shop. Only two streets over. My jeans are comfortable, not too tight. My T-shirt is simple, but maybe a bit low cut. But again not tight, so really it's not a big deal. This is my go-to mom ensemble. Sweet, harmless, and just convincing enough to fit the identity motherhood carved out for me.

Still a little jumpy, but significantly more hydrated, I'm inching back toward basic human functionality after last night's mess. I'll just apologize to this guy, clear the air, and get the hell out and back to my normal, safe existence where I don't drink alcohol and try to hire hitmen or "handlers."

The bar looks mostly closed, which makes sense, since it's two hours before opening. But surely someone has to be here, right? People have to get a bar ready. How long does that take, I wonder?

I see a light on through the glass of the front window, so I step closer and knock on the door. I wait a beat, but there's no answer.

Frowning, I peer through the window again. I can see movement in the back. They likely can't hear. Maybe they're getting ready. Without thinking, I decide to walk around the building to the alley. I'll try the other door.

The alley sits quiet in the midday light, framed by the faded brick of the century-old establishment. I nearly turn on my heel, but then catch sight of a familiar door, the same one they escorted us out of last night. I knock again—this time harder—my knuckles rattling the warped wood as a pulse of impatience thrums through my fingertips.

The door creaks open.

A shirtless Hex.

Black sweats slung low on his hips, his hair damp and slightly curling at the ends. The scent of soap still clinging to the air around him. He looks surprised to see me, smoldering brown eyes widening as the afternoon light glints off their depth. Then his brow knits into that inscrutable crease.

I'm caught off guard by the sight of him looking... too good.

I realize I'm leaning into his space, and I immediately straighten.

"Can I help you?" he asks, voice rough, still carrying that commanding tone, but there's something new in it, something that makes me freeze for a moment longer than I should.

I swallow, words suddenly lodged in my throat. It takes a second to gather myself, but I push through the moment.

"I—uh—I just wanted to check in. About last night. You know, just to clear the air."

He doesn't move. Just watches me, his gaze more intense than it should be for a simple encounter.

"I didn't think you'd be... here," I say, trying to pull myself together. But it's hard when he's standing there, looking like *that*. His warmth unexpectedly makes my senses go awry.

Hex leans a shoulder against the doorframe, arms crossed, studying me. A flicker of amusement crosses his eyes. "Then who were you looking for?"

I hesitate. My throat suddenly feels dry.

"H?"

I say it as if the letter's a stranger to my mouth, a foreign sound I'm clumsily trying out for the first time.

His mouth twitches, but he doesn't smile. "That's me. Hex."

I blink. Stare. Process.

I need him to acknowledge the conversation. The messages—along with the wildly unfortunate implication that I drunkenly tried to hire a hitman—linger like a storm cloud over me.

I try to have the conversation with my eyes, willing him to give me something.

But he doesn't.

He just stands there. Bare chested. Looking so fucking hot.

I shift my weight from foot to foot, cross my arms, uncross them, feel my palms get weirdly clammy. This is me—showcasing the subtle grace of someone trying not to piss themselves.

Finally, he nods toward the apartment. "You wanna come in?"

"Yes."

I freeze. *I said yes?*

Something shutters in his gaze before he steps back, giving me space to enter. I swallow hard and follow him up the stairs, nerves buzzing.

His apartment surprises me. It's not the open, loft-style that catches me off guard from this man who runs a bar. It's the intention across the space: clean lines, dark woods, a balance of modern and masculine touches. There's no clutter.

Out of place, yet wholly *home,* my eyes snag on a piece of furniture, a buffet cabinet tucked along one wall. Solid walnut, unmistakably 1930s. The lines are curved, the craftsmanship stunning. My breath catches as I move toward it without thinking.

I run my fingers along the edge, feeling the smoothness of the original finish, the age in the wood. "This is incredible," I murmur. "You don't see pieces like this often, especially not in this good of shape."

Hex watches me, arms still crossed. "It belonged to my grandfather. My mom left it to me."

I glance up. I don't miss how he says *left.*

His eyes dart across the piece, jaw tightening as a quick shadow of conflict crosses his face before he masks it. "She wanted to get rid of it, but she knew I liked it and would take care of it."

I can't help the chuckle I release, shaking my head. "You like old things."

He lifts a brow. "That funny to you?"

I press my lips together, a teasing glint in my eye. "No. Not at all."

That earns me a slow, considering look. One I feel in my stomach.

I clear my throat, running my fingers along the edge of the wood again. "I own Thorne Revival, the furniture restoration shop two streets over. If you ever want this piece completely restored, I'd be happy to help. It wouldn't take much. Just some sanding, stain, and varnish."

His gaze lingers.

"I know of that place," he admits. "Haven't been inside, but I've seen it in passing. I'm usually here in the evenings, so I only catch it when everything's closed."

I nod, a quiet understanding settles between us.

Or maybe something else.

Something I'm definitely not ready to name.

Hex moves toward the kitchen area, and my eyes instinctively follow.

It's stupidly nice. The kitchen resembles a scene from a luxury design magazine, with its matte black cabinets, dark stone countertops, and an expansive island that—much like him—commands attention. There's a row of industrial pendant lights hanging above it, their warm glow making the deep tones of the space feel rich instead of cold.

I shift my weight, trying not to think about how much I like it.

He plants his hands on the island, leaning in slightly, and my focus snaps to the way his muscles flex. It holds me in place, demanding every ounce of my attention.

His forearms tighten, veins prominent beneath dark skin; the black and gray tattoo moves with him, the design shifting as his muscles contract.

I drink in its intricacy. An angel that starts at his fingertips and winds its way up his arm, across his hard bicep, over bite-worthy capped shoulders, and up the side of his neck. Every feather, every shadow of its wings, is shaded to perfection, the kind of artistry that takes multiple sessions. I find myself drifting closer to the island, drawn by the warm light casting shadows across his skin.

I'm staring. Hard.

His voice cuts through the quiet. "Didn't you say you wanted to clear the air about last night?"

I flinch slightly, my face heating. Reality.

I clear my throat and drop onto one of the barstools. The second I sit, I pull my knee up to my chest and wrap my arms around it, seeking some kind of comfort, but also there is an underlying wave of embarrassment.

Hex lifts a brow, eyes roving over my posture. "You've got long-ass legs to be sitting like that."

I huff out a laugh, still slightly flustered. "I can never sit right." I pause, then mutter, "Or apparently act right, for that matter."

His steady gaze pins me in place. I can't for the life of me tell what he's thinking, and unease coils in my chest.

I exhale, forcing myself to meet his eyes. "I want to apologize. My friend and I were... out of line at your bar last night."

He tilts his head slightly. "You weren't out of line." He leans forward, voice dry. "The little one? Yes."

I let out another breath, part relief, part amusement.

Then I hesitate. My fingers tighten slightly against my shin.

"About the messages," I finally say.

Hex doesn't react right away. He just watches me. Then, after a pause—

"What do you need me to do?"

My brain short-circuits for a second because that is not the response I expected.

"I—" I fumble, shaking my head. "Absolutely nothing."

His brow lifts, a subtle nudge for me to keep going.

"It's nothing more than a reckless, alcohol-fueled screw up," I continue, my words tumbling out too fast. "I don't drink. I mean, I did, obviously, but I usually don't because of"—I wave a hand vaguely—"reasons. It was stupid. I'm a mom for God's sake. I don't"—I gesture wildly toward the counter as if there is a laptop in front of me —"do that."

His mouth twitches, but he doesn't smile. Instead, he tilts his head, studying me with that same quiet intensity that's lingered since I walked in.

Then he leans in just a fraction. "Is it the blonde?"

I freeze. My stomach twists, and my hands pull my knee a fraction closer to my chest.

"The blonde," I echo.

His gaze stays locked on me. "The one I took out the front. Is she the one bothering you?"

My pulse kicks up, my throat dry.

Yes.

And no.

And suddenly, it feels wrong to be having this conversation with someone who's still a stranger in all the ways that matter.

But he's watching me in a way that strips everything bare. The hesitation. The fear. He already knows the answer.

For the first time in a long time, I don't know what to say.

CHAPTER TEN

Alex

A mom.

Why the fuck is that a complete turn-on?

I lean against the island, watching her curl into herself, one leg tucked close, trying hard to not take up space.

But she does.

She takes up space that's impossible for me to ignore.

The way she moved through my apartment, straight to my grandfather's buffet as if it called to something in her. I didn't miss the way she kept herself facing forward without thinking about it. Whoever's been fucking with her has her well-trained. But beyond that, the way her eyes lit up catches my attention. Full of awe you only see when someone stumbles onto something worth treasuring. I didn't expect that. Hell, I didn't expect her.

She's more than I could have imagined.

Sable turned my head last night—any man with working eyeballs could see her beauty. But up close, in my space, she's simultaneously sharp and controlled, yet not. There's something beneath the surface, something I want to pull out piece by piece until I see every last bit of who she is.

She's so fucking different.

And the blonde is bothering her.

She hasn't said it outright—not yet—but I can see the hesitation in her eyes, the way she's testing my reaction before she says too much.

I exhale slowly and tilt my head. "You gonna tell me what's got you looking like you don't know if you should be here or not?"

Sable worries her bottom lip and lets out a noise that is something caught between a laugh and a sigh. "I *don't* know if I should be here."

My jaw ticks, but I keep my voice even. "But you are."

She looks down for a second, fiddling with the hem of her jeans before glancing back up. "I just... I didn't want you to think I meant any of it. Last night. The messages."

My fingers drum against the counter. She's nervous, shifting slightly in her seat, the kind of restless movement that says coming here might be making things worse.

"I didn't," I say simply.

Her shoulders relax a fraction. "Good."

"But that doesn't mean you don't have a problem."

Her fingers grip tight, just for a second, and she swallows.

Bingo.

I don't know the details... yet. But I know one thing with absolute certainty: Sable Hawthorne doesn't deserve a single ounce of bad in her life. Not from what I can see. Not from what I've learned.

When our conversation faded into silence last night—early this morning, really—I did what any rational man with a particular set of skills would do. I looked into her. Lightly. Casually. I didn't have to dig deep to confirm what I already suspected—Sable is a fucking force. Graduated top of her class with a Master's in Marketing and Communication. Built her own marketing agency from the ground up, then sold it for what I assume turned out to be a substantial payout. Now, she runs a décor shop that restores furniture. A passion project stemming from an extensive home renovation she documented on a blog for Thorne Revival.

The information existed in plain sight, readily available to anyone who cared enough to look. And if I needed to go deeper, I could. But nothing about her raised a single red flag.

The blonde, though? That's another story. I need the full dossier on her. Who the hell is she, why does she think she can mess with Sable, and what's the best way to make her vanish if she steps out of line.

"I can help you."

Sable startles. "I don't want to kill her. I mean clearly, she is mentally unstable—"

"I wouldn't kill her." I push off the counter and lean back against the cabinets, letting out a small chuckle. "We just met."

Her chin drops at the implication of what I might mean. That *I could*. The raised leg drops next to stabilize herself on the floor and arched brows pull together. "So... what exactly does helping me look like?"

I prop my hands against the counter behind me, watching her. "We break the stalker."

She lets out a dry laugh, shaking her head. "Break her. Right. Not ominous at all."

I shrug. "You take away the thing she wants—control, fear, your attention—and she's got nothing. She loses."

Sable exhales, rubbing her temples. "Okay, so what? I just... ignore her?"

I tilt my head. "Ignoring her hasn't worked so far, has it?"

Her silence is my answer.

"She needs to believe she's already lost," I say, keeping my voice even. "And the best way to do that is stop looking like a target."

Sable flexes her fingers where they rest on the counter. "And how do I do that?"

I taste the words before I let them out.

"You let her see that you're mine."

Sable freezes.

Her eyes snap to mine, wide and unblinking.

I don't move.

"*Yours*," she echoes, measuring, processing and turning the word over in her head.

I nod once. "We spend time together. Publicly. She needs to see it. Needs to believe that someone bigger, meaner, and far less stable than her has his eye on you."

Shaking her head like that will physically reject the idea, she says, "So, what? You're going to be my... bodyguard?"

I smirk. "Truthfully? I'm thinking boyfriend."

Pink lips part slightly, but no sound comes out.

I watch realization settle in from the way she adjusts herself in her seat, dragging one knee up again, chewing the inside of her lip. Aside from getting her a restraining order and signing this blonde up for a padded cell, this is her best option. Even if it scares her.

"Tell me I'm wrong," I say, voice low.

She doesn't.

She just swallows, lifts her chin. "I read a lot. Fake dating is one of the cringiest tropes."

I smirk, cocking my chin. "Who said it will be fake?"

Her breath catches, just for a second, before she says, "I'm old, Hex." *My name on those lips.* "You're young. I've got a kid, a whole boring life. And you"—she waves her hand as if dismissing the idea—"you've got freedom."

I push off the counter straightening to my full height. "You're not old. You're thirty-nine, and I'm thirty-one." I step closer, keeping my gaze locked on hers. "There's absolutely no problem."

Her mouth parts, but whatever words she's reaching for don't make it out. Instead, she just looks at me, her eyes betraying the uncertainty.

"You were studying my ID." It slips out in a murmur meant more for her than me, a half-formed excuse to believe I couldn't have remembered. "Still... you're young, and I'm..." She trails off, shaking her head. "Not."

I lean my forearms onto the counter in front of her, my voice dropping to something more serious. "You're exactly the right kind of *not.*"

Those lips pop open again and take the shape of an 'o'. I don't think she expected that response. She feels it land—every word, every truth—heavy and immediate. But I'm not done. I've only just begun.

"Tomorrow," I say, leaning in a little. "Let me take you out. We'll talk more about all of this. You'll tell me what's going on, and maybe we'll have a good time."

The chestnut glow of her eyes drifts away from me, searching the room for somewhere to hide. "I'd love to, but I've got to mow the lawn tomorrow. Yard work is usually my Sunday thing."

I let out a soft breath. "Yard work, huh?"

A tight smile shows up on her face. "Yeah. Bash, my son—he's ten—he'll be home tomorrow afternoon from his dad's. He's got him every other weekend, so I like to get things in order before he's back."

I can't help but study her. Mentioning her son lights up her eyes, and something about that pulls me in deeper.

Just as I'm about to say something else, her phone buzzes on the counter where she had pulled it from her back pocket and set it beside her. She flinches, telling me she's been getting messages she doesn't want. Probably for a while. She grabs it quickly. Her face drops as she reads something on the screen, lips pressing together in a way I've quickly learned means she's stressed.

"What is it?" I ask before I can stop myself.

Sable tries to brush it off, but the tension in her face doesn't lie. "Nothing," she mutters, but she doesn't move.

I step around the island and closer into her space. "Show me."

Her hand stills over the phone for a beat, then she slowly turns it my way.

It's a meme someone has posted—from the blonde I assume—of a picture of a bar fight with a caption *"how professional"* and a tag to @ThorneRevival.

I see her gnaw her lip. "Nobody gives a shit about things like that," I say, my voice softer than before, but the words are meant to push her, make her react.

"One-hundred-fifty-two likes, twenty-two comments, and seven shares. Those numbers could devastate a small business."

Her shoulders sag, and she spins on the chair to look out toward the light pouring in through the windows over my bed. Then she pushes herself to her feet, clearly trying to escape the weight of it all.

I move faster than I think. Without even meaning to, I reach out and loosely grab her wrist, trailing my touch down her hand to her fingers.

Her body freezes for the briefest second as her eyes drop to the connection, just long enough for me to notice the subtle change in her.

I pull her gently toward me, my fingers lingering against her skin. "Let me help you, Sable. I don't care who she is. I'm not letting her tear you down."

The words hit her harder than I thought. She swallows and meets my eyes, but there's a deep tiredness in her gaze that makes me pause.

"Sometimes I wish I could just disappear, you know?" she says softly, her voice barely above a whisper. "I don't even know how to fix this. How to make it stop."

My hand grazes her fingertips. I lean in closer, not letting the small touch go. "I'll help you make it stop."

There's hope in her gaze, brief but real. The warmth of her hand retreats, and her face schools itself to composed and cautious.

"I have to go," she murmurs. "I took up too much of your time."

She doesn't give me a chance to respond. She hurries down the stairs, her footsteps echoing within the distance stretching between us.

I stand there, thoughts swirling.

I'm not letting this go. Not with her.

This isn't a job.

Giving her exactly what she deserves is no trouble for me.

This is going to be *fun*.

Or maybe the blonde was right. Maybe Sable Hawthorne does ruin men.

I'm already ruined. There's nothing left to tear down. No clean edges. No innocence to corrupt.

So go ahead.

Take me apart.

Make it mean something.

Fucking ruin me.

CHAPTER ELEVEN

Sable

Zzzzzzzzzzz *pop*.

I wake to the sound of zipping and snapping. It stammers through the room, stopping and starting, relentless in its rhythm, dragging my focus with the frustration of something that won't stay fixed. Brain fuzzy, I roll over in bed and squint at the clock.

7:45 AM.

I groan, rolling onto my back. I don't normally sleep this late—possibly residual effects from the hangover and underestimating the recovery time my aging body needs.

Then a tractor roars to life, the engine's vibrations shudder the old widows of my house, pulling me out of the last threads of fog clouding my mind. I bolt up, heart pounding a little too fast. I'm not sure if I want to strangle the guy with the damn tractor or thank him for getting me out of bed.

Another groan, I pull myself out of the sheets and shuffle to the window. I peer behind my curtains. A whole damn crew is working in my yard, their various tools orchestrating a mechanical symphony nobody wants to hear on a Sunday morning.

One man's down on his knees by my flower beds, picking at weeds with meticulous care. I wince as I see another man running the hedge trimmers over my once-beautiful bushes, now long overdue for a makeover.

What the hell is going on?

I rub my eyes, willing the sleep away. Maybe I'm still dreaming. But no, the guys are real. The hum of the tractor is real. And the way they're working is way too... much.

I grab my glasses off the nightstand, focusing on my reflection in the mirror. *Damn it.* I look like I've been dragged through a bush backward. It's the only reasonable explanation for this level of disarray. Shaking my head, I throw a cardigan over my cotton shorts sleep set, head to the front door, and swing it open.

The morning air is a little too cool against my skin as I pad across the porch to the older man working on my flower beds. He looks up and grins, that easy kind of smile that says I've just made his day by showing up.

"Excuse me," I say, trying to sound polite despite my confusion, "but can you tell me what you're doing?"

He gives me a nod, his hands continuing to pluck weeds from the soil. "Well, ma'am, it's important to weed these flower beds in Texas in the spring, especially with the heat coming in. These weeds'll take over faster than you can blink if you don't stay on top of 'em." He pauses for a moment, looking over to the hedges. "And these overgrown bushes need trimming. I'll get 'em cleaned up real nice, don't worry."

I feel my face flush with a little embarrassment. The weeds, the hedges... I've been putting it off for weeks, maybe longer. I try to get in as much yardwork as I can while Bash is with his dad. I could've sworn I touched those hedges last month, but life has a way of slipping past when you're not looking.

I clear my throat. "Thank you for explaining all that..." I pause, looking for his name on his work shirt.

"Allen."

"But what I'd really like to know, Allen, is... why are you here? I mean—what's going on?" I ask.

His smile widens, and he wipes his hands on his knees. "Well, ma'am, Mr. Alvarez called us yesterday. Said to come by and take care of everything. You don't have to worry about a thing. I owe Mr. Alvarez a favor. Real good guy. Shouldn't take but a few hours to get it all looking right."

Hex.

I don't know whether to be grateful or freaked out about this unexpected turn of events. But it's definitely leaning toward the latter.

My phone buzzes, and I nearly jump out of my skin. I tug it from my cardigan pocket, heart stuttering as I glance at the screen, half expecting the stalker to be back with a new early morning shit storm for me.

But no. It's not her. It's not the blonde psycho.

[unknown number]: Mornin' Legs.

I blink, reading the simple message again. This has to be Hex. My gaze flicks around the yard, nerves sparking with the sense that he's already watching, just out of sight. I pull my cardigan tighter around myself, glue my thighs together, and smooth my hair down instinctively.

I respond, trying to keep my cool.

> **[Sable]:** How did you get my number?

His reply is quick—almost too casual.

> **[unknown number]:** It's on the Thorne Revival website. Not so suspicious.

I can't help but laugh a little, but I'm still a bit wary. He's not exactly the by-the-book type, but there's a strange comfort in how direct he is.

> **[unknown number]:** Get yourself ready. Coffee or tea kind of girl?

I bite my lip and pull it inside my mouth, fingers hovering over the screen.

> **[Sable]:** Definitely Coffee. Are we going to breakfast? What's happening?

> **[unknown number]:** I'm in charge. I'll bring your caffeine fix, but you'll need to get dressed. Long pants, thick jacket if you've got one. I won't let you go hungry.

I freeze.

> **[Sable]:** Like a parka? Ice fishing in Texas?

He doesn't miss a beat.

> **[unknown number]:** I'd love to see you in leather.

My stomach does a triple-fucking-axle, and I can't stop the involuntary shiver that runs through me. *Damn, this man is not subtle.*

> **[unknown number]:** I'll be there in about an hour and a half. Get moving.

My head spins as I read his last message. Leather? What the hell? Is he being serious or just messing with me? I glance out at the yard where the men are working.

My heart is hammering, and I rush inside, nearly tripping over my own feet. I have no idea what I'm supposed to wear, but I'll figure it out.

Twenty minutes later, I jump from a knock at my door. Panic floods my veins. *I'm barely ready!*

I scramble out of my closet and to the door, smoothing my cardigan down and hoping I look somewhat presentable. I haven't even slipped into what I'm painstakingly deciding on wearing.

When I open it, I sigh in relief. The youngest guy from the yard crew holds out a cup.

"Good Morning," he says, glowing with amusement. "From Mr. Alvarez."

I let out a relieved breath and smile. "Thank you," I say graciously, taking the beverage from him. It's warm in my hands, a nice contrast to the cold panic settling in my chest.

I nod to him. "Tell... Mr. Alvarez... thanks. Really."

As he walks away, I stand in the doorway for a moment, staring at the cup in my hands. This is insane. I've never experienced anything like this. I head back inside, clicking the door closed behind me.

The house is quiet, but my thoughts are anything but. I walk into the bathroom, set the coffee on the counter, and brush my hair out of my face. I start to work through my routine, but my mind keeps circling back to the glaring difference between Hex and Andrew already.

Andrew. *God.* It's like he never even tried.

Ten years, and he couldn't remember the smallest things about me. How do you take your coffee? How do you like your eggs? You'd think after a decade, he'd have those things locked down. But no, I had to tell him everything. Otherwise, default *nothing*. Kind words only left his mouth when working to persuade.

What do you want to do today?

That would've been a start, right? But no, I never got that. He never made plans, never surprised me. Not even on my birthday.

I used to wait for something, anything, to show me he gave a damn. A call, a text, a gesture. But they never came. And after a while, I stopped expecting them. Stopped even getting upset when birthdays would come and go with no recognition.

It dawns on me: I've never felt what it's like to have someone remember the little things. That old ache stirs in my chest. The ache that hits when I realize I'd been alone in that relationship, despite living under the same roof. Even after creating a life with him.

I drag myself back to the present, checking myself in the mirror as I move through my morning ritual. I let the water from the sink run over my hands like the thoughts streaming through my head. *What should I put on?*

I glance at my underwear drawer, hesitating as I take a sip of my deliciously warm coffee. *Should I make sure my bra and panties match? Do I even have anything like that? Should I even care? Would that be trying too hard? I'm not trying to impress him. It's just a first date... right? Is this a date?*

But the possibility of getting it wrong, of giving the impression that I'm barely holding it together, sends a rush of heat straight to my chest.

I go for the one matching set I own. Simple. Comfortable. Nothing too flashy. Anything could happen and I'll be damned if I'm accidently wearing period panties today.

I wrinkle my nose at the thought. Then again, maybe I should wear them. I shouldn't get all worked up about what he'll think of my underwear on the first damn date. *That's ridiculous.* He's not going to see under my clothes. I do have a shred of standards left. *Don't I?*

I let out a breath and move on, keeping my underwear choice and working on more pressing matters. I glance at my legs in the mirror and groan. Okay. Fine. I snatch my razor for the hasty job. I don't have the luxury of time to do it right. Mentally, I can already feel the burn. But whatever. If I don't do this, I'm going to panic and regret not trying.

Thank God Demi talked me into a discounted Brazilian wax with her last week. Because nothing says *great idea* more than ripping hair off your vagina at half price. I'd never waxed anything before, and the thought of getting smooth on the cheap sounded... tempting.

I left that hellhole with my right lip swollen to botched-filler proportions and the distinct feeling they'd torn each hair straight from my central nervous system. Still, I'd achieved dolphin-smoothness in all the right places, one bright spot in the freefall of my mental health.

I finish in record time, and one glance in the mirror confirms the job looks rushed. I grimace at the stubble I already see I missed at my ankles, but I shake it off. I'm wearing pants for fuck's sake, but I'm determined to look presentable for him. Hex... whatever this is with him feels different, and I'm starting to panic in a way I'm not used to.

Hex is coming, and whether I'm ready or not, I've got to go figure out what the hell this is all about.

I'm so caught up in my thoughts that I barely notice time slipping by. Thirty more minutes.

If Hex can help me deal with my stalker, in a non-murdery way, then hell, I'd throw myself at him. Not that I wouldn't throw myself at him just for the coffee. Or for the HGTV-level yard makeover. But putting a lid on Stalker Barbie? That would make my life infinitely better.

Twenty-eight minutes. That's all I've got to get my life together and pull myself into a semblance of normalcy. How do I even begin to act like this isn't all a little crazy?

I settle on a pair of tight jeans, my favorite worn-in combat boots, and a casual shirt that clings in all the right places. I reach way back into my closet, fingers grazing over something familiar.

A leather jacket.

It's from my college days, back when I worked promotions for a motorcycle shop and spent my nights line dancing on bar tops without a care in the world. Those gigs were wild, and I liked to pretend my marketing skills got me the job, not my ass in a pair of Daisy Dukes. But that false confidence built something real. It built my agency. My career. Over time, my clients became more corporate, more buttoned-up. And, somewhere along the way, so did I.

I had shoved that side of me—the reckless, fun, alive side—into the back of my closet with this jacket.

And as I slide my arms into it, rolling my shoulders to loosen the stiff leather, I feel an ember of my old self flicker. I flip my hair out from under the collar, then catch my reflection in the mirror.

And I smile.

Because I recognize the woman looking back at me.

CHAPTER TWELVE

Hex

"Plant some Angelonias next to the porch," I say, pointing to the spot along the railing. "Give her some color she can see when she sits out here."

Allen nods. "You got it. We've got the playscape ready to put in the back as well." He shoves his hands in his pockets, rocking back on his heels. "Anything for you, man. And thanks again for helping me out with that... problem."

I smirk. "No problem." I grab a shovel, testing the weight in my hand. "And thanks for letting me borrow these." I nod toward the pile of landscaping tools: shovels, bags of fertilizer, and a few other things that could do more than just tend a garden.

"I'll drop them off at the bar when I'm done." Allen chuckles, but doesn't ask questions. That's why I like him and help him whenever I can.

The sound of my bike must've caught her attention because the door swings open, and there she is.

I take every inch of her in. Scuffed and paint-splattered combat boots, worn down in places but still tough looking. Then those tight-ass jeans, hugging her hips just right, leading up to a leather jacket that scream she *understood the fucking assignment.*

Her hair's curled like she didn't try. But from what little I've discovered about Sable Hawthorne—there's intention in every effortless wave. That rich brown catches the light of the morning sun, making me think of a slow pour of whiskey and darker things I shouldn't want this bad. Her makeup's subtle. No glitter, no tricks. Just her.

She looks real.

And real is dangerous.

She catches me looking, and I don't bother hiding it.

Her eyes flick to Allen, then to the landscaping materials scattered around the yard. She frowns, but it's not anger. It's a quick flush of embarrassment she doesn't seem to know how to hide. The crease between her brows deepens, and her mouth presses into a thin line like she's biting back an apology that won't fix anything.

"This is too much," she says, folding her arms across her chest. Her weight shifts, subtle but uneasy. "I should've never let it get this bad."

I step closer into her space. "You've got nothing to be embarrassed about." I meet her eyes, making sure she hears me. "Your ex should be the one embarrassed."

Her jaw tenses, but she doesn't argue. Not directly, anyway. "I don't need a man to take care of everything for me."

I nod. "No, you don't..."

Her brows lift, eyes full of challenge, like she wants me to test her. I don't flinch.

"But a partner," I continue, voice low, steady, "a *real* partner, doesn't stand by and watch the person they care about drown under a workload too heavy to carry alone. It's not about who's capable. It's about who gives a damn."

Her throat bobs. And something twists in my chest. She's never experienced someone picking up the slack *without* being asked.

And it makes me want to hit something.

Before I can spiral, she peeks around me, arms still crossed, hair falling off her shoulders at the motion. "I can now officially guess we're taking the bike somewhere?"

I smirk. "Got something in mind I think you might like. You ready?"

Those bright eyes rake over me before tipping her head once.

We head toward the bike, and I can't help but feel that familiar sense of satisfaction looking at it. A Harley I built for my hands and no one else's. *Mine.* Blacked-out, customized to hell, tuned to purr under me. The tank's got a custom-painted angel, dark and detailed, wings stretching back toward the seat.

Sable steps closer, tilting her head. "That's beautiful." Her fingers hover above the design, as if she wants to touch but isn't sure she's allowed. She glances at me. "Reminds me of your tattoo."

I nod. "It's in memory of my mother. She passed just after I turned eighteen."

Her face softens. Something deep flickers behind her eyes, but she doesn't push. Just gives me a look like she's trying to say, it's okay to say however much I want.

I reach into the saddlebag and pull out a helmet, handing it to her. "Here."

She takes it but doesn't put it on. Instead, she watches as I throw my leg over the bike, settling in with the ease of something I've done a thousand times.

I glance up, and damn, she looks cute as hell standing there, holding the helmet, torn between courage and second thoughts.

Sable exhales. "It's been a long time since I've been on a bike. My uncle... that had to have been the last time."

"Good. You won't have any bad habits to break." I smirk, but I mean it. If she's going to ride with me, I want her to be safe.

There's the briefest pause when I face forward, barely noticeable, before there's movement behind me. Boots crunch gravel, then one foot plants itself on the peg. She swings a leg over with confidence—unbothered, unaware of the slow burn that sparks under my skin as she settles in close behind me.

Fuck.

Her body presses against me, warm and fitting just right. My cock comes to attention. Her hands hover at my waist before resting there lightly. Then, with measured movements, she wraps herself in, carefully exploring the space between us.

The engine roars to life, and the second it does, she jumps, squeezing me tighter.

I grin. *There it is.*

I reach down, patting the long, toned leg pressed right up against my side.

Those fucking legs.

CHAPTER
THIRTEEN

Sable

This does not feel like my uncle.

My hands rest comfortably around Hex's hard abs, the leather of his jacket warm from mild spring sun shining down on us as we ride. It's the same jacket he wore that night at the bar. Something about it—maybe the way it clings to his broad frame—feels just as dangerous now as it did then.

We've been riding for a bit, pulling into a town not too far from Stillwater Bend, but far enough that I have no clue where we are or what's about to happen. Hex is impossible to predict. That's part of the problem... and maybe part of the appeal. He's in complete control of this situation.

We pull up to a nondescript building, the kind that could be any-thing: warehouse, mechanic shop, underground fight club. A few cars are parked out front, but nothing about this place gives me a hint as to what awaits us inside.

I climb off the bike, handing him the helmet while I fuss with my hair, trying to smooth out the smashed and windblown strands. Meanwhile, he grabs a backpack from the saddlebag, tossing it over his shoulder, as if we're off to tackle something important.

I raise a brow. "Okay, if you're about to lead me into some dark, dangerous place where I have to fight for my life, I'd like to state for the record that my upper body strength is on par with a T-Rex."

Hex smirks, and my stomach tightens just a little. "Noted."

He pulls open the door, and before I can step inside, the sound hits me. A sharp *pop-pop-pop*, then another, louder this time.

I freeze.

Hex just chuckles and nudges me forward. I step in.

Oh. *Oh.*

A gun range.

I glance across the stalls with people lined up, safety glasses and bulky ear protection on, taking aim at targets I can't quite see yet. The acrid scent of gunpowder lingers in the air, sharp but not unpleasant.

"I've never done this before."

I'm not opposed to it. I'm kind of excited about it if I'm being honest. But I have absolutely no idea what I'm doing.

Hex leans in, his voice low and teasing. "I'm very well-equipped to teach you things you've never done before."

There's something in the way he says it—so deliberate, so sugges-tive—that has me clenching my thighs. Great. *Just great.* Now all I can do is hope these barely-there panties are enough to keep the dampness he caused between my legs from soaking through my jeans and giving me away.

Looking for a way to distract myself, I take in the atmosphere. Outside of the gunpowder and oil smells, there is a quiet bond between the people here. People who move with certainty, weapons in hand, as if they're a natural part of who they are. The guy at the counter lifts his chin in acknowledgment, eyes locating Hex before offering a nod of respect. It's subtle, but I catch it, and it sends a ripple of curiosity through me. I've known men who command attention, but this is something different. It's earned, not demanded.

Hex removes his leather jacket, revealing an olive-colored T-shirt stretched across those round shoulders and arms that make my fingers itch with entirely too many inappropriate thoughts of touch. The man is solid, his body a testament to something more resilient than what most of us are made of. His jeans emphasize thick thighs and the casual confidence in the way he moves.

He pulls a set of ear protectors and safety glasses from his bag, handing them over. "You'll still hear me. Won't hear the gunshots."

We both slip the protection on, and when his voice comes through perfectly clear, I blink. "What kind of witchcraft—"

"*Technology.*"

I narrow my eyes at his smirk that is quickly becoming a favorite of mine, but he's already pulling two cases from his bag, setting them on the counter in front of us. He pops the first one open, revealing a sleek, compact handgun. "Sig Sauer P365. Good for beginners, easy trigger pull, solid accuracy." He taps the second case. "Glock 19. Bit bigger, more control once you get the hang of it."

I eye both weapons, then him. "You're assuming I'll get the hang of it."

"You will." There's no doubt in his voice, just quiet certainty that does something traitorous to my stomach.

He checks the chamber on the Sig, ensuring it's empty before handing it to me. "We'll start with the basics."

I take it slowly, both hands steady but not quite sure. The grip is colder than I expected and the weight, heavier than it looks. I shift it in my palm, the metal pressing into my skin, foreign and intimate all at once. My pulse ticks up. Not from fear exactly. From the knowing. From what it means to hold power like this.

"Were you in the military?" I ask.

"No."

I glance up at him, expecting more, but that's all I get. The pieces are easy enough to fit together, though. The way he handles the gun, the way the guy at the counter acknowledged him—Hex has experience. More than casual. More than just a hobby.

After holding the gun for a little bit and getting more comfortable. I hand it back and he gets it prepped.

"First rule of gun safety: always assume it's loaded. Never point it at something you don't intend to destroy. Keep your finger off the trigger until you're ready to shoot."

I nod, absorbing the information. "Got it."

Hex moves in behind me, his hands settling lightly on my hips before adjusting my stance. The heat of his palms burns through my jeans, and I catch the scent of him—leather, something clean and sharp, and underneath it all, something purely male that makes my mouth go dry. Warmth rolls off him, wrapping around me, and suddenly the cold steel in my hands isn't the biggest threat. It's the way my body reacts to his. The way his fingers linger a heartbeat too long. Focusing on the whole life-or-death weapon thing? Yeah... not exactly top of mind.

He reaches forward, guiding my grip, his chest pressing flush against my back. "Tight, but don't strangle it. You're in control, not wrestling it into submission."

The vibration of his voice travels through me, and I have to bite back a gasp. His hands completely engulf mine, callused fingers sliding over my knuckles as he adjusts my hold. Every point of contact between us feels electric.

I exhale a laugh, then inhale sharply when he nudges my arms into position, the movement bringing his chest flush against my back. "Like this?" My voice comes out breathier than intended.

"Good girl." His voice rumbles through his chest, vibrating against my back as much as in my ear protection. "Now keep your eyes on the target."

Easier said than done when the real source of my attention stands behind me, heat radiating from him as though he's a furnace wearing human skin. Still, I manage to center myself, swallowing past the sudden dryness in my throat.

Hex's voice drops lower. "Squeeze the trigger, don't jerk it."

The double meaning isn't lost on me, and heat pools low in my belly. I take a shaky breath, trying to focus on anything other than how perfectly I fit against him. I line up with the target and pull.

The shot cracks through the space, the power behind it vibrates through me. The kick surprises me, making me stumble back a step. Hex is there, steady hands catching my waist, pulling me against the solid wall of his chest.

For a moment, we're frozen like that—his arms around me, my back pressed to his front, our breathing in sync.

I tilt my head back to look at him, and something dark flickers in his eyes. His gaze drops to my mouth for just a second before rising again.

He leans in, voice smooth and amused. "Not bad."

I twist my head to look up at him. "I missed completely, didn't I?"

He bares more teeth than I've yet to see, and damn it, a little dimple makes its first appearance. "Maybe."

I roll my eyes, but he's already repositioning me, settling his hands over mine to correct my grip. His touch is firm, instructive, but there's an undertone to it, a subtle tension coiling in the air between us.

As he helps me line up another shot, I glance at him. "You learned all this just because you wanted to?"

His brows dip. "Needed to."

The weight of that answer catches me. I want to press, but something about his tone makes me hesitate.

I swallow hard, the dryness in my throat scraping like sandpaper. My eyes drift back to the target, that flimsy paper fluttering paces away. I picture it solid, three-dimensional, breathing. A person. Flesh and bone. Someone's son. Someone's friend. Someone who might've hurt me or might not have had the chance yet. The image settles heavy in my chest.

I can almost feel the recoil before I even pull the trigger. The sound. The flash. The way it would rip through something real. Someone real.

My grip tightens, but my stomach twists.

"I don't think I could ever shoot someone," I murmur, the words tasting like doubt and guilt and something just shy of fear.

Hex is quiet for a long beat. Then, his voice is calm and clear as day in my ear protection. "If someone you love is in danger—if it's shoot or they get hurt, maybe even die—the choice gets a lot easier."

A shiver traces down my spine. The way he says it, the certainty, makes me wonder. About his past. About what's shaped him. If he has made that decision himself.

My eyes narrow, tracing the outline of the target until everything else fades—the other people, the sounds, the gnawing doubt. Just me and the target.

Hex doesn't step away. He stays close, his chest at my back, steady and solid. His presence threads through me like a second spine, anchoring the nerves that had scattered through my limbs.

Somehow, I stop shaking. I stop thinking.

I think about Sabastian and what I wouldn't do to assure his complete safety.

I pull the trigger.

And I don't miss.

We empty a few magazines, and I surprise myself by not completely sucking. Hex lingers behind me, his hands staying on my hips, but I don't complain. He's patient, offering just enough praise when I land a shot and smirking in that way that makes me want to try harder when I miss.

Eventually, I graduate to the bigger gun. My aim sharpens. My confidence builds. And when I finally hit dead center, I don't miss the way he looks at me. It's as if he's seeing something he wasn't expecting. Something he likes.

When we wrap up, he turns to me, tilting his head. "Hungry?"

"Yes." I exhale, only just realizing I've been running on the sad remains of an old yogurt I grabbed in a rush this morning. "Starving, actually."

Hex nods and leads me outside. When we get back on the bike, I expect him to head for a diner or some tucked-away breakfast joint.

Instead, we pull up to a place that seems to have sprung from a child's sugar-fueled fever dream with bright colors, a ridiculous sign that reads *Pancake Panic*, and cartoonishly oversized stacks of waffles and bacon decorating the windows.

I blink. "This is the place?"

"Best damn breakfast around," he says, completely serious. "Besides, they've got a pancake challenge, and I wanna see you try and hang."

The inside is no less ridiculous. There are booths shaped like eggs, a neon sign that shouts *Let's Get Stacked*, and a menu built by someone who worships butter and laughs in the face of cholesterol.

We slide into a booth, and just as I'm settling in, a waitress swings by with two mugs, filling them with steaming coffee before either of us even has the chance to ask. Hex nods his thanks, lifting his cup to take a relaxed sip. I take a moment to breathe in the rich, roasted smell mixed with the delicious scent of syrup and fried dough.

It's oddly... homey. Comfortable.

Then I notice Hex watching me over the rim of his mug, as if he's waiting for something.

"What?" I ask, raising a brow.

He nods toward my phone I placed on the table. "Make sure you snap a picture of us and post it. Tag the bar."

I squint at him. "Why?"

That fucking smirk. "Because it's the only social media I have, and I got a feeling our blonde friend might be watching."

"Oh, you are *diabolical.*" I grin, unlocking my phone. "Alright, but we need a picture together first."

I slide off of my bench and ease in beside him, phone in hand, angling for the perfect shot. Hex doesn't miss a beat. He drapes his arm around my shoulders, pulling me in until I'm pressed against the heat of him.

On instinct, I tip my head toward him, and the screen captures us perfectly. Hex with his no-nonsense smug look, a knowing glint in his eyes, the scruff on his jawline sharp against the buttery glow of the restaurant lights. And me, slightly flushed, smiling just enough to show I'm enjoying this, even if I won't admit to myself that this might just work.

He might just work.

I snap another, and Hex tilts his head just enough so his mouth is near my temple, the warmth of his breath teasing my skin like he's about to say something mischievous. It's the kind of photo that *looks* intimate, even if it isn't.

I scooch back over to my side, scrolling through the shots before finally choosing one. "What's the caption?"

He barely hesitates. "Bangin' in the morning, stackin' for lunch."

I nearly choke on my coffee. "Hex!"

"What?" He leans back in the booth, all easy confidence, as he makes pistols with his fingers. "It's the truth."

I bite my lip to hide my smile and type it out, tagging the bar as instructed.

The post goes up, and not even a minute later, my phone buzzes with a notification.

Right on time.

The username makes my stomach twist. @MuffinsMommy.

Of course. The damn terriers.

Then I see the comment.

> **[@MuffinsMommy]:** *Didn't take you long to spread your legs for someone new, huh?*

My fingers tighten around the phone.

Like six months isn't long enough? *Wait.* What am I talking about? I haven't even spread my legs... *yet.*

The comments aren't even subtle anymore. She's dropping all pretense, going straight for the kill. My stomach knots with equal parts irritation and unease. She wants me to react. She wants me to feel watched.

Before I can react, Hex reaches across the table, his large, calloused hand covering mine. His fingers are steady as they ground me. "I got you," he says, low and certain.

Then, with the kind of unbothered confidence I wish I possessed, he pulls out his own phone. A few taps later, another notification pops up.

> **[@RuinsEnd]:** *I'll take care of Sable's legs. You can deal with the fact even Muffin fakes excitement when you come home. And maybe unpack whatever unresolved trauma told you this post needed your opinion.*

My jaw drops.

That's when the floodgates open.

Notifications explode as the patrons of Ruin's End—at least, that's what their usernames tell me—come out swinging, each comment funnier and more ruthless than the last.

[**@IPAinMyVeins**]: *@MuffinsMommy just got served harder than the tequila shots on half-price Wednesdays.*

[**@GinAndChronic**]: *A moment of silence for @Muffins-Mommy's dignity. Thoughts and prayers.*

I slap a hand over my mouth but not before a snort giggle escapes.

[**@TequilaMockingbird**]: *She really thought she could slide in here and not get roasted? Ma'am, you don't mess around with Ruin's End.*

[**@MargaritaVillain**]: *Nothing pairs better with a vicious clapback than a cold beer and @MuffinsMommy's shattered ego.*

[**@NeatOrOnTheRocks**]: *Bartender, get this girl a drink. She's gonna need something stronger than delusion to recover from that one.*

[**@HennyThingIsPossible**]: *Plot twist: @MuffinsMommy is actually just Muffin logging into her account to ask for help. *Bark* Help me. *Bark* My mommy is crazy!*

My shoulders start shaking with suppressed laughter.

[**@OldFashionedRevenge**]: *You come for one of ours, you get the whole bar. Hope you brought back up, @MuffinsMommy.*

[**@DrunkInLoveAndPetty**]: *Oh, we roast AND serve at Ruin's End. Welcome to the party, sweetheart.*

> **[@CraftBeerComebacks]:** *@MuffinsMommy really said, "let me embarrass myself publicly" and we said bet.*

Full-bodied, belly-clenching laughter bursts out of me, drawing looks from people at nearby tables.

My stomach hurts from laughing at the absolute onslaught happening in real-time.

Hex reclines against the booth's cushion, unfazed, sipping his coffee, as though he didn't just end a woman's entire online existence with a single comment. He glances at me, amused. "Problem handled."

I wipe at my eyes, still breathless from laughing. "Remind me to never get on your bad side."

"Oh, Sable. You're already on my favorite side."

In a blink, my face is burning with what I can assume is a bright red blush.

This might be the best first date I've ever been on.

CHAPTER FOURTEEN

Alex

I can't believe she ate that many pancakes. A shit ton. They sat down twelve fluffy round, buttery and steaming pancakes, each as big as a dinner plate. Her eyes lit with fire like she had something to prove and no patience for anyone who dared doubt she'd own it. Each bite looked effortless, and as the stack briskly dwindled, I caught myself watching her, forgetting my own plate.

I'm not sure what's hotter: the way she's putting down pancakes without breaking a sweat, or the fierce, determined look on her face. Most people would be tapping out by pancake four, but not Sable. She powers through pancake eight like a pro.

I try to hide a full smile behind my fork. "You're actually gonna finish all that?"

She pauses mid-bite, her cheeky smile breaking through. "Hell yeah, I am. I'm not backing down from this."

The competitive edge she's got is almost... intoxicating. The way she's tackled anything I've thrown at her today—regardless of what it is or how comfortable she may be—with full commitment. Yeah, that's definitely something that gets my attention.

And she downs every last bite. She's full but relaxed, looking far too satisfied for someone who inhaled their body weight in carbs without flinching. Impressive. Kinda sexy, if I'm being honest.

When the waitress comes to clear the plates, I lean back in the booth, still staring at her in disbelief. "Damn. You really did it."

She flashes a smug little smile, then consciously wipes her syrup-glossed lips with a napkin. "Told you I could. Pancakes are my thing. My son loves them, and I make them on the Saturdays I have him. But there is far more whipped cream involved."

I shake my head, completely impressed.

Her eyes narrow playfully, and she crosses her arms, raising an eyebrow. "Don't judge a girl by her looks, Hex. You'd be surprised what I can do when I set my mind to it."

And damn, there's that fire again.

"Alright, well, after that performance, you've definitely earned something a little more... active." I grin. "I know a place we can go to work it off."

I can't help but beam as I watch her. She's practically bouncing in her boots, eyes wide with curiosity as she takes in everything the outdoor market in Stillwater Bend has to offer. This place is not far from the more commercial part of town, but the kind of hidden gem locals swear by but most mimosa-sipping twats and silk-tie soldiers wouldn't know to look for.

The smell of street food and incense greeted us, wafting through the air. Handcrafted art and quirky trinkets line various wooden tables across the line of bright color tents. It's artsy, it's alive, and it's exactly the kind of place I figured Sable Hawthorne would love.

Her fingers trail over hand-woven scarves, vibrant pottery, and jewelry that looks like it was shaped with love and patience. She moves through the market with that wide-eyed wonder usually reserved for kids in candy stores.

The way she talks to the vendors—polite, engaged, genuinely interested—is a refreshing change from the superficial small talk I'm used to hearing at the bar. There's nothing fake in her voice. Just real curiosity. Honest appreciation.

The sun is high now, the heat in the air a welcome relief from the morning chill. We've shed our leather jackets, and they're both draped over my arm.

I watch with a half-smile, amused by how easily she gets lost in this world of handmade things. It's hard not to notice how different she is. The women I've known—even the ones I've taken upstairs—weren't like this. They wanted something I don't offer.

Call it a commitment-phobia or just knowing myself too well, but it runs deeper than that. I'm not built for the long term. Not with the life I lead. The only constant has been me, and I've learned to prefer keeping my adult life casual. When your business dips into the gray, there's not room for much else.

Keep it simple.

A few drinks, some laughs, but always transactional. No promises. No expectations. Just fun and the quiet understanding that it ends when the night does. That's it. I don't call. They don't either.

It's been a long time since I even tried to get serious. Back in my early twenties, maybe. She had checked all the boxes: good girl, easy to like. But she wasn't my type, not really. We went on a few dates, looked great on paper, but the moment she started talking about the future, I couldn't breathe.

She didn't do anything wrong. I did. It never stood a chance. Not with underground fights, busted knuckles, and injuries I couldn't hide, let alone explain. I couldn't drag her into that. The secrets were too heavy, and letting her in felt harder than pushing her away. So I did.

For a split second, I think about my mother.

Tough as hell. Kind-hearted. Dealt a hand no one deserved. She loved her boys fiercely and did what she could with what life gave her. I don't think the right man ever came along. Not one who saw her for what she was. She moved from one bad decision to the next, and I wasn't exactly easy on her. But I respected her strength more than I ever said out loud.

Losing her too soon... broke something in me. I never got the chance to say what I should have. Never got to make it right. And maybe that's why I've kept things shallow ever since. All surface-level, clean exits, no real weight to carry.

And that's worked for me.

Until now.

Sable is different. Not like the women I've known, not chasing something I can't give. There's this insistent pull I've never felt before. It's not letting go. And I'm starting to wonder if I might actually be okay with more.

I shake off the spiraling thoughts. There's no need to get ahead of myself. I've still got a lot of ground to cover, and a hell of a lot of walls to keep up until I know she'll be ok with my *extra-curricular activities*. But damn, she makes me want to reconsider everything I thought I knew about myself.

Sable's still distracted, talking to a vendor about a leather bracelet. She's so into it that I hesitate to interrupt.

But as I glance at my watch, I'm tight on time. I've got something to take care of, and I need to keep this date moving without raising any alarms. I'll give her a few more minutes to enjoy herself, then slip out, handle what needs handling, and be back before she even realizes I was gone.

No ripples. No questions.

I follow her as she moves to a nearby booth. She picks up a carved wooden spoon rest, studying it with reverence, gently turning it in her hands before deciding to buy it. The vendor—an older man with a face lined by time and long days—offers a soft, approving smile, clearly pleased she's not just another customer looking to haggle.

And damn, I respect that.

"Nice choice," I tell her, sliding my hands into my pockets as I lean against the booth.

She glances up, the sunlight catching her hair, giving it a golden shine. "Thanks, it just felt like it needed to be mine. You know?"

I chuckle softly. "Oh, *I know*." I hold her stare for a beat longer than expected. "There's something about this place that makes you wanna take everything home."

My words aren't lost on her. A casual but knowing smile curves her lips. "Exactly."

I'm enjoying this way more than I expected to.

She catches me staring, her eyes narrowing with that teasing smile I'm starting to crave. "What?"

I shake my head, feeling my lips curl. "Just admiring you. That's all."

"Right," she says, raising an eyebrow. "You're full of compliments, aren't you?"

"When I mean them," I tell her, walking a little closer as we make our way through the crowd. "You make everything seem... interesting."

There's a twitch in her cheek.

"Alright, let's do this." I stop her in the middle of the market.

"Do what?" She asks, wide-eyed, a little nervous at what might come next.

"Pull out your phone and let's make this a good one."

I nudge her toward the nearby food truck, where they're slinging fresh tacos. A massive mural with vibrant colors covers the side of the vehicle. Perfect spot.

"I want to see if I solved your problem."

Pulling her phone from her back pocket, she lifts it, searching for the perfect light. The moment her arm rises, I step in behind her instinctively, close enough for her to feel every inch of me. I press in, letting my body align with hers like we've done this before.

I shift our jackets to my other arm, freeing the closest. My hand finds her waist, fingers tracing the curve just above her jeans. Then lower. I hook my thumb, my knuckle grazing her skin just inside the waistband, slow enough to make her breath hitch.

Lace.

I tug the denim back just enough to see it with my own eyes. Black. And fuck me, it's even smaller than I imagined.

Wordless, her body responds, arching into me with an unspoken invitation that makes my restraint stretch thin.

But I'm not finished.

I lower my head, my breath feathering the curve of her neck. She shudders enough to tell me she feels it. Feels *me*. Her pulse kicks beneath skin so soft it makes my mouth water.

I bring my lips to the hollow below her ear, barely grazing it. Not a kiss—*not yet*—just a promise in the shape of a breath.

The shock crashes over her face in a wave. Her whole body stiffens for a fraction of a second, but then she melts, tilting her head to let me in deeper. Her pulse under my lips is a steady hum, matching my own.

Her phone snaps the shot just as I pull back, the ghost of a kiss still hanging in the charged air between us. She lowers the phone, like she's forgotten what she's holding, and turns her face toward me, eyes wide and dark with something that wasn't there a second ago.

Those soft, parted lips—kiss-ready and stunned—make my thoughts go straight to places I'd die to explore in private. A blush blooms across her cheeks, as if her body's betraying the effect I have on her before she can form words.

And fuck, if that isn't the best thing I've seen all day.

I can't resist a smile now. She stands there with a quiet, dreamlike glow.

Dropping her attention back to the phone in her hand, she begins typing, her fingers moving fast over the screen, and I can tell she's trying to compose herself. A few seconds go by, and she glances up at me with a playful twinkle in her eyes.

"Tacos are surprisingly good," I read over her shoulder. A small laugh escapes her lips as she taps 'Post.'

I gaze at her, feeling the weight of what just happened hanging between us, but it's not awkward.

It's charged. *Alive.*

Her phone buzzes almost immediately. I lean in to kiss her cheek, brushing past her ear.

"Let's see what happens now," I say quietly, my voice low, the tension still thrumming between us.

The comments start rolling in.

[@WhiskeyAndWings]: *I've heard of hot tacos, but this is a whole new level of spice. Get it, Hex?*

[@ShotgunSips]: *I think the tacos just got jealous.*

[@HighballHopper]: *That kiss cost extra like the guac? I'm here for it.*

[@TequilaTaps]: *Tacos, tequila, and a neck kiss? You two are making me question my lunch plans.*

[@MargaritaMaven]: *Who knew taco trucks could serve like this? Damn.*

[@BarstoolBabe]: *I'll take two tacos and a side of that.*

[@RumRunner87]: *I swear, if I hit up this truck and tacos don't come with a kiss like that, I'm demanding a refund.*

[@VodkaVixen]: *I'm reconsidering my whole diet.*

Sable's smile widens with each new comment, her fingers scrolling through them all.

Then it hits her.

"This is the first post she hasn't instantly commented on in over six months," she says, a little amazed, as though that silence is its own kind of win.

I raise an eyebrow. "Glad to be part of the experience."

But as the last comment drops, my phone buzzes.

I glance down.

"Will," I mutter, reading the message. "Uh, sorry. One of the taps went down at the bar. I've gotta take this call real quick. You good on your own for about fifteen—twenty minutes?"

Sable nods, already turning her attention back to the next booth she's eyeing. "Of course. I'm fine. Go ahead and handle it. I'll just be in this general area."

"Cool. I'll be back before you know it."

I pull out my phone as I step toward a quieter corner, tapping the screen to fake a conversation with Will. I look back only to make sure she doesn't notice me ducking away and making a very quick exit out of the market.

CHAPTER FIFTEEN

Hex

Going to the market was the perfect play. Not because I knew Sable would love the artistry, but it put me exactly where I needed to be. A quick walk from the luxury condos. No wheels, no mess. Just a clean break when the time came.

In and out.

The social posts also played double duty, taking care of Sable's problem while accounting for my whereabouts.

My phone vibrates in my pocket.

[JT]: Down. 20 minutes, 25 max.

I type back.

[Hex]: Won't even need it. Got a set of legs I'd rather be spending time between.

[JT]: She could have been mine.

[Hex]: In what world, kid? She's got steaks in the freezer older than you. You still need permission to rent a car.

[JT]: Anything you can do, I can do better.

[Hex]: Sure. Now go color or whatever it is 24-year-olds do, you little shit.

[JT]: Just don't miss, old man.

I huff a bitter laugh, shaking my head as I shove my phone away.

Didn't matter how much I wanted to keep JT out of this life—I never had the choice. Our mother was already a cold body in the ground by the time he was ten and I turned eighteen. Old enough to sign custody papers, too young to understand what I was signing up for.

JT followed me everywhere. He had to. I was his whole world by default, which meant he saw everything. The fights. The blood. The men with dead eyes who smiled while calling it business. Worst of all, he saw Ned Stauder for what he really was—not just a threat, but a parasite in pressed slacks. The kind of man who could make you disappear in pieces and still have the paperwork come back clean.

Ned doesn't have charm or brains. No, what he's got is a sick instinct for sniffing out pain. He finds the cracks in you like he was born to break people. After my mother's death, he offered me money for one fight. Then another. Then ten. Before long, I was bleeding on concrete for cash while he sat in the corner, sipping bourbon like it was the fucking ballet.

He made sure it was always in his rings. His name behind every drop of blood. I fought until my knuckles split and my soul went quiet.

But he didn't stop with me.

He watched JT. Waited. Knew my brother's brain worked like a machine and saw dollar signs. When he finally made his move, it wasn't with fists. It was with wires and cameras. Started him on surveillance gigs, tech runs, hacking jobs no fourteen-year-old should've been anywhere near. Told him it was "just work," like that made it better.

I found JT once, scrubbing footage clean after someone got shot during a backroom brawl. He didn't flinch. Just looked up and said, *"I tried not to watch."*

That night, I made a deal.

Told Ned he could have me—every fight, every broken bone—but JT stayed clean. No more jobs. No more blood.

He laughed in my face, but he took the offer. Said it was a shame, really. JT had promise. Maybe one day, when I finally broke, he'd come collect on the kid again.

That was the leash. Still is. He never really let go, just loosened the rope enough to make me think I had breathing room. That's how men like him operate. They don't kill you. They keep you alive long enough to watch everything you love hang from a hook.

JT got out. Got him in front of the right people: tech contracts, security firms, clients who paid for his mind instead of poisoning it. But Stauder's shadow is long. You see it in the habits we still carry. The way our stomachs tighten when an unknown number calls. The way JT keeps cameras in every corner of his place, footage rolling even when he's home.

Eventually, I found a way to get us both out.

But some nights I still wake up with blood under my nails and the sound of his voice in my ear telling me it's never over.

20:00

Back to business.

The market buzzes behind me as I slip out the side street, keeping my pace easy, unhurried. One block away.

18:45

I slip on black latex gloves, the material snapping against my wrists as I reach the service entrance. It's exactly where JT said it would be—discussing the plan late after the bar closed last night—tucked out of sight, away from the main street. A steel door with no markings, nothing to make anyone look twice. I yank it open and step inside.

The hallway smells of fresh paint and industrial cleaner. No security. No cameras. For now.

17:30

The elevator panel is sleek, keycard only, but JT took care of that too. I tap in the code he sent me, and the 14 button lights up.

I lean against the wall as it climbs, eyes locked on the numbers ticking up.

16:15

The doors slide open to a quiet, pristine hallway. Security cameras are spaced out along the ceiling, but JT assured me they'd be looping yesterday's footage for the next half-hour. All marble floors and recessed lighting. It doesn't smell like people actually live here, just expensive candles and new money.

I move straight to 1407.

The door is unlocked. As predicted.

14:50

I push inside and let the door shut softly behind me.

The place is too clean. Too impersonal. Will would like it. The kind of staged luxury meant to impress guests, but not actually used. Floor-to-ceiling windows stretch across the living room, giving a view of the skyline.

The kitchen is spotless except for a single plate in the sink. *Someone ate a late breakfast.*

Too bad it'll be their last.

13:30

The sound of running water pulls me forward.

Down the hall. Master suite. Door's cracked just enough.

12:45

I slip inside.

The bathroom is all sleek marble, fogged mirrors, and warm steam curling into the air. The shower takes up half the space, glass walls offering no protection. The water runs steady.

They don't know I'm here.

11:55

I reach behind me, pull the Glock from the back of my jean's waistband. The one I conveniently grabbed from my saddlebag before we walked into the market. Adding the suppressor with ease.

10:30

I step closer.

10:25

They don't hear me over the shower, and I leisurely pull open the door.

10:20

Finger on the trigger.

10:19

I raise the gun.

10:17

A breath.

10:15

I squeeze the trigger.

The shot snaps through the silence. The body drops. I step back to avoid the splash.

Twitches once. Goes still. Blood runs from the chest wound and begins to swirl down the drain.

Less than ten minutes and I'm on my way back to those legs.

But as I walk, the high of death doesn't fade.

It never does... not right away.

Not when the man I just killed had it coming. Not when the world's better without him breathing in it. Not when the thought of what he did is still sharp in my chest.

What scares me isn't the act; it's how clean it feels. How *easy*.

I remind myself I don't kill for fun. I kill because someone has to, and men like him don't get warnings. Only endings.

But there's something wrong with how my pulse is still steady. How the weight in my chest isn't guilt—it's *satisfaction*.

That's the part that keeps me up at night. Not the blood. Not the body. But the voice in my head that whispers, *you liked that, didn't you?*

And I did.

God help me, I did

CHAPTER Sixteen

Sable

"That was quick." I smile as Hex strides toward me, still holding his phone to his ear. His expression is mostly flat, but there's something about the way he moves—controlled, with that ever-present confidence—that makes my stomach tighten.

"1407. Thanks, Will." He ends the call and slips his phone into his back pocket.

I notice something in his hand, a small object, and tilt my head. "What's that?"

Hex stops in front of me, holding it out between his fingers. A small, round wooden token, about the size of a poker chip, with an intricate design burned into the surface. I take it, turning it over in my palm. Bet he got it from one of the booths during that call with Will.

It's a pair of stacked pancakes, dripping with syrup, and the word *Champion* charred into the middle.

A burst of laughter escapes me, rich and unrestrained. "Oh my God." I press a hand to my mouth as if he just gave me a diamond ring, shaking my head. "Hex, seriously?"

His grin spreads wickedly slow. "Hey, you earned it." His voice dips, a low rumble that resonates deep within me.

I narrow my eyes at him, lips twitching. "Is this your way of saying you appreciate a woman who can handle a sizable... *stack*?"

The look on Hex's face sharpens, eyes dark with mischief. "Oh, Legs, I have no doubt you can handle whatever I put in front of you."

A blush warms my cheeks as I stick my tongue out at him, holding up my new token in triumph.

Before I can come up with a comeback, he steps in. Closer than before. Close enough that the air between us vanishes in an instant. His hands slide to my hips, rough fingertips pressing into the soft curve as he pulls me flush against him.

My breath hitches in my chest.

There's no second-guessing. Just heat and certainty.

His mouth claims mine with the quiet hunger of a man who's spent all day reining himself in. I open myself to him and he deigns what I'm offering. He tastes of lingering syrup and heat, something rich and heady, something entirely him. His hands tighten at my waist, fingers pressing into my skin, not out of fear I'll pull away, but to anchor me there with him.

I'm not going anywhere.

A small noise escapes the back of my throat, and it only makes him deepen the kiss, taking what he wants. His body is solid against mine, the warmth of his skin seeping through his shirt, his muscles tensing beneath my hands as I grip his shoulders.

One of his hands glides up my back, threading into my hair, tilting my head just how he wants it. A shiver rolls down my spine. It's been a while—*too long*—since someone kissed me like this. Like they meant it.

Like they needed it.

My fingers curl into the fabric of his shirt, trying to ground myself in the middle of this storm he's pulled me into. A storm I'm not sure I ever want to leave.

When he finally pulls back, just enough to catch his breath, his thumb brushes the corner of my mouth, and his voice drops into something rough, something dangerous.

"If you stick that tongue out at me," he murmurs, "I'm gonna claim it."

He steps back, weaving his hand with mine. It's bigger, rougher, and threads through with a possessive kind of ease. Our jackets still hang over his arm, and he carries them the same way he's carried this entire day—with quiet authority, intent, guiding me through every new turn with the kind of certainty I didn't know I craved.

Hex has kept me on my toes from the moment we met just two short nights ago.

At the gun range, he showed a steady patience with me. Teaching, not just showing off. He stressed safety, control, protection. His hands were firm but never intrusive, his voice confident but never condescending.

The pancake challenge tore through his serious exterior, exposing a man who lived for competition, thrived on teasing, and somehow made it all impossible not to love.

He wielded influence without force, turning the loyalty of his bar patrons into a shield. With a single picture, a well-placed tag, and a self-satisfied look, he shut down the person who spent months making my life hell. And he did it without blinking, the kind of reflex that comes from instinct, not decision. As if protecting me lives in his bones, woven into who he is.

Now, here, in the middle of a bustling market, he's shown me yet another side of himself.

He kissed me.

A surprise tucked between his teasing, his stupid little gift, and the heat in his eyes... *Jesus, Mary, and Joseph*. A kiss that had no business being this good. A kiss that stole the breath right from my lungs and has me reeling. A kiss I want more of.

I squeeze his hand, feeling the solid weight of it, the warmth of his palm against mine. I don't have time to overthink any of this, and for once, I don't want to.

I just want to know more. Every little last detail about Hector *"Hex"* Alvarez.

The memory of Hex's kiss still lingers two days later as I sit behind the wheel of my SUV, Demi beside me with her newest dark romance obsession in hand. The glossy cover practically casts judgment over the madness she dragged me into—hauling me out of the shop, pulling me from the piece I'd been working on, all for what she insisted was a *proper* lunch break to hunt down some well-earned smut.

With Bash at school, I couldn't come up with a decent excuse to say no.

"So?" she presses, taking the book from me, already launching into her interrogation. "Recount how it ended? I need details, bitch. Don't you dare skimp on a single thing."

I light up from the inside out as I merge into traffic. "It was perfect. I couldn't have asked for anything better. He was—" a dreamy sigh slips out. "A perfect gentleman when he dropped me off, and the yard? Demi, it looks fucking phenomenal."

She gasps. "Landscaping and romance? Be still my fucking heart."

"I got another toe-curling kiss before he left," I admit, and just saying it makes them twitch again. "He knew Bash and Andrew would arrive soon, so he didn't push for more."

Demi lets out a strangled sound. "So, what I'm hearing is... you still haven't climbed that man like a goddamn tree?"

I burst out laughing. "Not yet."

"Not yet?! Bitch, when will you see him again?"

I sigh, shaking my head. "We haven't made any plans yet, but yeah... I'm dying here. And also"—I glance over at her, suddenly feeling awkward as hell about what I'm about to admit—"I'm, uh... kind of spiraling about something."

Demi's brows shoot up. "Oh no. What? Is he bad at sexting? Weird kisser? Please don't tell me he moans like a haunted house ghost."

I snort. "No! God, no. It's me. I'm the problem."

She narrows her eyes. "The fuck are you talking about?"

I grip the wheel of my SUV, hands securely now at ten and two. "What if I'm bad at... you know. *Stuff.*"

Demi blinks. "*Stuff?*"

"You know, *stuff.*"

"Use your damn big girl words."

I gesture wildly with my hand and mouth and watch as realization dawns on her.

She sits up straighter in the passenger seat. "Wait. Are you talking about handies and blowies?"

I groan, pressing my forehead against the steering wheel for a brief second as we come to a red light before forcing myself to focus back on the road. "Yes! It's been so long since I've been with anyone but Andrew, and let's be real, foreplay with him basically meant he did a little playing, then straight to penetration."

Demi makes a disgusted noise. "Ugh. Classic."

"What if a man like Hex expects me to *initiate*?" I ask, fully spiraling now. "What if I just... reach down his pants and start tugging it like a goddamn thirty-nine-year-old amateur?"

Demi turns in her seat, face full of the kind of judgment that only a best friend can deliver. "Babe. No. You get in there, you find your inner Demi, you spit on that hand and theeeennn you start jerking."

My hands slap the wheel. "Whoa, whoa, whoa! Spit on my hand? I can't do that."

Demi throws her hands in the air. "Why the fuck not?!"

I shake my head, fighting a full-body cringe. "That's something I feel like I need to practice."

There's a beat of silence before Demi bursts into a fit of uncontrollable laughter. "You—wait—you think you need practice? To spit?"

"I do! I don't wanna be out here embarrassing myself! What if I do it wrong? What if I get stage fright and my mouth just dries up? The goddamn Sahara trapped behind my teeth."

Demi gasps for breath between cackles. "Sable, babe, you don't need a fucking training regimen for giving a hand job. Jesus Christ, I love you so much."

I groan again, pressing my foot down on the gas a little harder as if speeding will somehow get me out of this conversation.

Demi wipes tears from her eyes. "Okay, okay, listen. I'll help you."

I side-eye her.

She throws her head back, laughing. "If you're scared of your own damn spit, we've got work to do."

I groan, gripping the wheel tighter. "I am not *scared* of my spit."

"You just said you can't spit in your hand." She lifts a brow, clearly enjoying my suffering. "And babe, if you can't do it alone, how the hell are you gonna do it in the heat of the moment?"

I open my mouth to argue but immediately close it.

Fuck. She's got a point.

She sees my hesitation and knows she's got me too.

"Exactly."

My best friend rolls her shoulders as if she's about to give a hand job seminar.

"Now. It's all about commitment. No half-assed dribbles. No weak, last-minute regrets. You own that spit, you mean that spit—"

"Demi—"

"—because if you hesitate, if you fumble the spit—" She shudders dramatically. "That's how you ruin a moment."

I bark out a laugh despite myself. "Speaking from experience?"

She gives me a look. "Sable. I have *thrived* in the streets."

I shake my head, eyes back on the road. "Demi, I swear to God—"

She ignores me completely. "Alright, watch and learn."

Demi spits into her hand, unfazed by the fact we're barreling down the road in the middle of a casual weekday afternoon. As if that's a totally normal thing to do.

A perfect, glistening glob lands in the center of her palm, like she's demonstrating something off the back of a porn set.

I shriek. "Demi, what the fuck?!"

She holds up her hand proudly. "See? That is how you do it."

"Oh my God, wipe it off!" I swerve slightly, heart pounding as I lean toward the glove compartment and grab the extra napkins from the fast food I pretend I don't eat.

She laughs and rubs her hand down her jeans. "You see the form? The control?"

"I see that you're a fucking menace."

She props her elbow on the center console and smirks. "Alright. Your turn."

I whip my head toward her so fast my neck pops. "Are you out of your damn mind?"

Demi shrugs. "Practice makes perfect."

"I am driving!"

"So? Just do a little one."

I gape at her, scandalized. "I am not spitting in my own hand while operating a moving vehicle."

Demi sighs dramatically, shaking her head. "This is why men keep winning, Sable."

I huff a breath, long and suffering, and glance at Demi. "You're not gonna let this go, are you?"

She just folds her arms and leans back in her seat, smug as hell. "Nope. You wanna rock his world or not?"

I groan, adjusting my grip on the wheel. "Fine."

Demi perks right back up. "Yes! Okay, just remember: not too much, not too little. And for the love of all things holy, do not hock up anything nasty. This *is* allergy season."

I cringe but extend my free hand, palm up.

"This is ridiculous," I mutter, trying to make sense of the foreign limb in front of me, as if it's not attached to my body.

Demi gestures encouragingly. "Just go for it."

I take a breath, hype myself up, and lean in—

—and immediately freeze.

Oh my God. I can't do this.

What if it's too thick? What if it's not thick enough? What if I just start drooling mid-moment, helpless and mortified, a grown-ass woman with the motor control of a teething baby? Oh, fuck. What if it lands weird and I get spit on the floor? Jesus Christ, what if Hex is looking down at me, waiting, expecting something sexy and confident, and I just spit a sad little string onto my fingers?

My heart rate spikes. *Oh my God.*

"Sable." Demi's voice is sharp, reeling me back in. "You're thinking too much. It's spit. Not a science project."

I swallow hard. "I just—I don't want to mess it up."

She snorts. "Babe, you're not deactivating a bomb. Just spit."

Right. Okay. Just spit.

I steel myself, open my mouth—

And at the last second, panic wins. I barely produce a weak little pffft of moisture; an embarrassingly dry attempt that barely even registers.

Demi gasps with the intensity of someone watching their legacy go up in flames. "Oh *hell* no."

I groan, clenching my eyes shut. "I told you I can't do this!"

Demi swats my arm. "Pitiful! I've seen toddlers with more control over their saliva!"

I slap my hand onto the wheel, exasperated. "I don't spit, Demi!"

"Well, babe, that's gonna be a problem. You're going to have to find an alternative."

I groan again, throwing my head back. "Fucking kill me."

Demi sighs dramatically. "Alright, pull into the grocery store up here."

I snap my head toward her. "I am absolutely not buying lube from the grocery store at 12:30 p.m. on a Tuesday."

Demi bursts out laughing. "No, dumbass, we're getting bananas." She pauses, tapping her chin. "Or do you think we need a"—she glances at me, eyes gleaming with mischief—"bigger vegetable?"

I nearly swerve into the next lane.

She hasn't even seen how bad my gag reflex is yet.

CHAPTER SEVENTEEN

Hex

Wednesday nights are slow, but I don't mind. Gives me time to think. And right now, all my thoughts are on *her*.

Elbows braced on the bar, I roll my glass of bourbon between my hands, watching the amber liquid catch the dim light. It's been three days since I kissed her, and I'm already losing my goddamn patience. The date felt perfect—better than I could've imagined it going—but now comes the tricky part.

How the hell do I play this?

I'm not trying to push, but I'm sure as hell not going to wait around, lovesick and passive, hoping she decides to act.

I want to see her. And not just for another dick-hardening kiss, though I wouldn't complain if that's all she wants to give. I want her time. Her attention. I want to learn everything about her. All the little things that don't get put on display for the world.

A familiar blonde enters my periphery, walking past the bar outside. Again.

Ashley Vaughn.

I pretend not to notice, but she's there. And unlike Sable, I already know everything I need to about *her*.

A little digging turned up more than I expected. She rolled into town using a fake last name, but her Georgia record under the real one made for an entertaining read.

Shoplifting, bar fights, credit card fraud. She had filed a restraining order against a man who turned up dead six months later. I don't know if she did it, but I'd bet every dollar in my register she knows who did.

I flex my grip around the glass, keeping my expression neutral.

She came in the next night after Sable and mine's very public-social-media date. A Monday, when the bar is practically empty. As if I wouldn't clock her reemergence.

Ashley's a bloodhound locked onto a scent she refuses to lose. And she's not subtle about it. Not in the way she watched me from across the room. Not in the way she lingered too long when she ordered a drink. And definitely not in the way she keeps sniffing around Sable's life.

It took one loose hand around her arm and a whisper in her ear to make her tremble: *"You're not welcome here. Not tonight. Not ever. And if I catch you so much as breathing too close to Sable again, I won't be polite."*

She hasn't stepped foot inside since.

Apparently, though, that message didn't register past the threshold. She's still hovering by the curb, vermin eyes scanning for a crack she can squeeze through.

If she tries anything again?

Well. I'll handle it in a much different way.

The only thing keeping me from being in a worse mood tonight is the fact that I look out now and see the usual bar regulars. The ones who aren't predatory psychos. Just good people looking for salacious gossip and cheap pours.

And while the constant questions about Sable make me want to bash my head against the counter, I get it. I did what I needed to do. I made a statement.

Now I get to live with the consequences of opening my life up to people who know too much already. Nosy as hell, sure. But most of them are genuinely happy for me.

"*Hex, my man, didn't think I'd live to see the day*," Gus said last night, chuckling over his beer. "*She's a looker, that one.*"

Lisa—bakery downtown Lisa, the one who keeps her pink nails pristine and pretends she's not an espresso martini fiend—had raised her glass with a wink. "*She seems like the kind of woman who won't put up with your grumpy ass.*"

I smiled back without word.

Because these are the same people I've done things for. Things we don't say out loud.

Gus? Sweet old man now, sure. But back when his daughter's ex wouldn't stop showing up at her job, it was me who cornered him in a gas station parking lot and shattered his kneecap with a crowbar. No cops. No charges. Just a whispered promise: You come near her again, I fuck up the other one.

Lisa? She used to be married to a guy who dipped into her business funds and threatened to take everything. One night, he ended up in the ER with a busted orbital and a broken wrist. The story was he got jumped outside a grocery store.

I was the jump.

Even Frank—the younger guy sitting at the end of the bar who has a NASCAR shirt for every day of the week and stocks shelves at the corner store—once caught me in the middle of a Friday night shift, whispering about someone who'd been blackmailing his sister with a video she didn't know they took of her.

I didn't ask questions. I just made sure the video disappeared. And the man who took it left town with a permanent limp and three fractured ribs.

So yeah. These people? They smile when they see me. They clap me on the back, and I let them talk about love like it's something soft and redeeming.

But I know better.

I'm not just the guy behind the bar. I'm the shadow they send their messes to.

And sometimes, I worry they like me more for it.

Even JT smirked when the topic of Sable came up, shaking his head with that familiar look that said I'd gone too far to save.

I could put up with it.

Because, for the first time in a long time, I have something *good* worth talking about.

Will drops onto the stool beside me, drumming his fingers on the bar top. "JT's got some updates."

I glance over at my younger brother, who's perched on the opposite side of the bar closest to the door, scrolling through something on his phone. I have no doubt he's got his eyes peeled in case Ashley enters.

"Anything interesting?"

"Just Bat Shit out there." JT hikes a thumb toward the door and blows out a low whistle.

He shifts his focus back to the screen. "They know he's missing. Only whispers. No names. No connections." Then he glances up. "You're in the clear."

Good. Exactly how we planned it.

"Anyone sniffing around?" I ask.

JT hesitates for half a second, then nods. "Had a couple of Ned's boys swing through earlier. Didn't stay long. Just a beer and a little too much interest in the place, if you ask me. Didn't say much, but they were watching. Not the kind of casual that feels natural."

I exhale through my nose. "Ned himself?"

He shrugs, but I can see the tension in his shoulders. "Not yet. But when his bitch boys show up, it usually means he's not far behind."

I lean back, jaw clenched so tight it clicks. Ned Stauder doesn't lose sleep over loose ends. He cuts them off before they fray. If this guy I killed was part of his portfolio, he's already clawing through every missing dollar, hunting whoever made it vanish like blood in the water.

JT taps his phone once, screen going dark. "I'll keep my ears open."

"Yeah," I mutter. "Do that."

Will taps a clenched fist once against the bar and smirks. "By the way, the shovels and fertilizer? Nice touch. You really went for the full serial killer starter pack."

I grunt. "Felt fitting. And I'm a fucking vigilante, not a serial killer."

He chuckles, shaking his head. "Yeah, well, I scrubbed the shower, took care of the mess. Body's buried. No one's finding him."

"Good." I glance at JT. "Make sure you get the shovels back to Allen."

JT gives me a lazy salute. "Already handled."

I nod, taking a reflective sip of my drink. Job's done. I'll save worrying about Stauder until it firms up. For now, all I want is to focus on more important things.

Like the long-legged woman who's been taking up every square inch of my mind since Friday night.

I pull my phone from my pocket and tap out a message.

> **[Hex]:** Afternoon, Legs.

Doesn't take long before she replies.

> **[Legs]:** Legs?

> **[Hex]:** You expecting me to call you something else? Pancake Champion?

> **[Legs]:** I just didn't realize you were fixating on one specific part of me.

> **[Hex]:** I assure you, I'm fixating on a lot of parts of you.

> **[Legs]:** Oh?

[Hex]: Mhm. But I figured *"Tits"* might be a little forward for a nickname.

[Legs]: Jesus, Hex.

[Hex]: Just saying. But if you prefer something else, I'm open to suggestions.

[Legs]: Legs is fine.

I smirk, leaning back against the bar.

[Hex]: I've been trying to figure out how to see you again. Not easy when we work opposite schedules.

[Legs]: You could just ask. I know you're a professional planner, but I'm pretty good at figuring things out too.

Direct. No bullshit. I like that.

[Hex]: Fair enough. I don't want to impose on your time with your kid. We're still figuring this out, and I respect if you want to take some space before bringing a new man around.

Her reply takes a little longer this time.

[Legs]: I appreciate that. Really. But I'd like to see you too. I can work around my schedule with him. He's in school Monday-Friday.

Exactly what I'd been hoping for.

[**Hex**]: I'll be in town early on Friday. Got a delivery coming in around lunch. Figured since you're just two streets over, maybe you'd like to eat with me. *Not competitively.

[**Legs**]: Sounds good. I'll drop in.

Not what I wanted to hear.

[**Hex**]: I could come get you.

[**Legs**]: I can walk two streets, Hex. I'm happy to come to you.

I grin, fingers poised over my phone before deciding to type my message.

[**Hex**]: Fine, fine. I'd be a lot happier if you'd come *for* me.

The conversation bubble pops up. Disappears. Pops up again.

[**Legs**]: You're shameless.

[**Hex**]: And yet, here you are, agreeing to lunch.

I can practically hear her sigh through the phone.

[**Legs**]: I'll see you Friday.

I pocket my phone, smiling to myself.

Yeah, Friday can't come soon enough.

CHAPTER
EIGHTEEN

Sable

I t's Friday.

The walk to the bar feels longer than it should. My body knows the way, but my mind is somewhere else, hovering between anticipation and anxiety. I can't tell if the pressure in my chest is excitement or something heavier like the beginning of change.

Because it's not just Hex I'm walking toward. It's whatever this *thing* is between us. Still unfolding, too fast to overanalyze but too real to ignore.

The morning passed in a blur at the shop, my hands deep in the layers of an old bookcase with glass doors and carved moldings that deserved more than a rushed job. Paint stuck to my forearms, a few faded streaks still visible no matter how much I scrubbed.

I didn't dress for a date. I dressed for work. Paint-splattered pants. A basic tank under a zip-up hoodie.

Maybe that's the version of me I trust the most—the one covered in dust, focused on something real, with nothing to prove and no interest in standing out.

But that doesn't mean I don't feel it.

That faint prickle at the back of my neck.

The unmistakable sensation of being watched.

I glance over my shoulder. Nothing. The street is quiet at this hour, only the occasional car passing by or the soft hum of conversation drifting from an open shop door.

Maybe it's paranoia.

Maybe it's nothing.

Still, I pick up my pace.

By the time I reach the bar, my fingers hesitate on the door handle. Should I have gone around back? Before I can decide, the lock clicks, and the door swings open.

Hex stands there, filling the doorway like he'd been waiting for me.

"Hey, Legs." His voice holds that familiar warmth, laced with teasing, but his eyes cut through the moment, darting past me. He's looking for something. Someone.

Something about that soothes me more than I expect.

He steps back, guiding me inside.

"Delivery's already handled," he says, nodding toward the empty bar. "No one else will be in for a while."

The scent of food hits me first. Smoky, rich, and warm. My stomach growls. I glance at the bar lined with the containers of brisket sandwiches, pulled pork sliders, baked beans, and potato salad. The protein bar I had this morning, as I rushed Bash into the car so we didn't miss drop off, had long been digested.

I arch a brow at him. "What, no dessert?"

Unfazed, Hex grabs a container and opens it. Steaming fluffy, golden pancakes are stacked inside. *Of course.*

"Since you said you liked whipped cream..." He reaches behind the bar and pulls out a can, shaking it.

I let out a small laugh, in disbelief of this insanely thoughtful man.

He didn't ask what I wanted for lunch. Didn't make me pick a place, send options, or expect me to decide. He just... handled it. And after years of making every single decision and keeping track of every single thing: what we were having for dinner, which brand of paper towels we used, even the last time the damn washing machine drain needed cleaning—it's nice not to think so much.-

Hex places the whipped cream on the counter and shifts his weight against the bar, steady gaze locked on me, carrying the quiet certainty of a man who never doubts his next move.

I shake my head, reaching for a plate. *He's a handler, all right.* Just not the kind I thought he might be after our drunken website chat.

I scoop a portion of baked beans onto my plate, then potato salad, stealing a glance at him. He keeps his eyes on me, that coy twitch of his lips playing on his mouth, as if certain he's living rent-free in my thoughts.

"Something funny, Hector?"

"Not at all."

I shake my head again, reaching for a pulled pork slider. "I've got limited time," I remind him, even as I unzip my hoodie, removing it and taking my seat on the stool nearest me.

Hex makes a plate and sits next to me. "You're the owner. Make your own rules."

I huff out a small laugh. "Irresponsible."

"Yeah?" He leans in slightly, voice dropping. "And you're nothing but responsible, huh?"

"I mean..." I gesture vaguely, picking up my fork. "The fact that I've seen the inside of a bar twice in a week is already two more times than I have in the past decade. I'm a little out of character at the moment."

Hex studies me, arms folding over his chest. "Not a big drinker?"

I shake my head, scooping up a bite of potato salad. "Don't like feeling out of control. I like my faculties intact. And at my age, the hangover isn't worth it."

He smirks, the kind of reaction that says he's reading between the lines. "You just aren't doing it right."

An amusing thought, but something about the way he's looking at me makes my stomach feel tight behind my belly button. He's still, letting the silence stretch, knowing full well I haven't told him everything.

I exhale and set my fork down. "No. It's just..."

Hex picks up his brisket sandwich, taking a slow bite, waiting me out. He doesn't push, but he doesn't let me off the hook either.

"I drank plenty in college. My early twenties too. Had my fun. But then..." My fingers toy with the napkin beside my plate. "Then I became a mom, and it just... didn't feel right anymore."

Hex chews, his focus unwavering.

"I didn't want to be the parent who couldn't wake up in the middle of the night if Bash needed me. Or who wasn't completely present if something went wrong." My jaw tightens slightly. "And my ex... he didn't like it. Made it clear early on that he didn't want me drinking. At first, it started with little comments. Then, after a while, it just became something I didn't do."

Hex doesn't react right away, but I see something shift in his expression. He leisurely chews, each bite buying time while he sorts through whatever it is he's about to say.

"I respect that," he finally says, voice low and certain. "Wanting to be present for your kid. Making sure he always has someone steady to rely on."

A lump forms in my throat. I reach for my water to try and clear it, but Hex notices.

His smirk returns.

"But there's a way to enjoy yourself without all the guilt," he says. "A way to let go a little without losing control."

I arch a brow. "Oh yeah?"

He leans in, voice dipping lower. "Yeah." He taps his fingers against the bar. "It helps if you've got the right partner. Someone you trust, who's got your back even if you were truly gone. Someone who'd take care of you, make sure nothing bad happened. No judgment. Just care."

There he goes again with the *partner* comments.

Something warm spreads through me.

Hex stands, moving behind the bar, and pulls down a dark, unlabeled bottle.

"Bourbon isn't about drinking to get drunk," he says, pouring two fingers into each glass. "It's about appreciation. Being in it. Savoring it."

"Are we talking about partners still or alcohol?" I ask with a coy smile.

His lips twitch. "Both."

He slides one of the glasses toward me, the amber liquid catching the light. Then he moves back around and takes the stool beside me once more.

A shiver stirs in me and works its way down my spine. The goose bumps raise on my bare arms.

Hex swirls his glass, watching the liquid spiral. "Drinking like this... it's about patience. You don't rush it. You don't just take what you can get and move on. You let it breathe, take your time with it. Feel every part of it."

I arch a brow. "And what happens if you just throw it back?"

"You miss everything that makes it worth drinking in the first place." And with a careful tilt, the rim meets his lips, his eyes never leaving mine.

I wrap my fingers around my glass, pulse kicking up between my ears. I lift the bourbon, breathing in caramel and vanilla, followed by something darker. Richer.

Hex watches me with that same patient intensity in his eyes he had at the gun range. There's no hint of nerves. No smile. Just stillness. Quiet observation. Like nothing I do could rattle him.

Meanwhile, I'm barely holding it together.

I take a drawn-out sip. The warmth rolls over my tongue, settling deep in my chest like liquid fire. I can't take my eyes off this man.

"So what's next?" I ask, my voice coming out softer than I intended.

With a knowing quirk of his lips, he continues, "Second lesson: you pair it right." He gestures at the food spread between us. "A good bourbon with the right meal? It changes everything."

I pick up a bite of pork, chewing thoughtfully. He's right. The smoky sweetness blends with the lingering warmth of the bourbon, deepening it.

Hex watches me, his gaze flicking to my mouth, and I swear his brown eyes darken.

"You get it now?" he asks with a smooth candor.

I swallow, chasing it with another small sip, and nod.

"I think I do. But..." I look at him through my lashes. "Tell me again about *feeling every part of it.*"

Before I can set my glass flush to the counter his hand brushes mine, catching my wrist gently, and setting the glass down for me. He keeps hold of me as he turns on the stool to face me. His knees bump against mine beneath the bar.

Leaning in, there's heat in his eyes, but control in every movement. Like he's not rushing this. Like he's about to savor it.

His other hand slides to my waist, fingers skimming just under the edge of my shirt. He doesn't pull me forward. He coaxes, guiding me off the stool with the barest pressure of his fingertips, like I might spook if he asks for too much.

I go willingly.

The heels of my boots hit the floor. Hex stays seated, knees bracketing my hips as I step between them. His chest lifts in a long, measured breath, as if steadying something dangerous inside him. Then his mouth finds mine.

The kiss is unhurried at first, all testing and teasing. The kind of lip-to-lip connection that makes you ache because it's not trying to steal breath, it's offering you a choice: lean in, or walk away.

My hands slide up his chest, exploring the planes, tracing the curves of muscle beneath his shirt, then higher into his hair. I curl my fingers in the dark strands and tug, just enough to pull a groan from deep in his throat.

That's when the kiss shifts.

He strokes my tongue with his, coaxing a response that coils heat deep between my legs. One of his hands fists gently in the fabric at my lower back. The other is already reaching up, brushing the side of my breast with knuckles rough and unrepentant.

Neither of us is pretending we care about lunch anymore.

He shifts forward, forcing our bodies flush. Then, he sweeps the plates across the bar in one swift motion. No care as to where they land. A fork skitters. My breath hitches as he hooks a finger inside my waistband. A question.

"Yes," I manage to whisper.

I want him to.

Because something in me is snapping. Not from fear.

From *freedom*.

All my life I've followed rules. I've been polite, responsible, measured. I've kept things together, even when I was falling apart. And what did it get me?

Pain. Betrayal. A ten-year stretch of pretending fine was enough.

I'm done being fine.

I'm done being careful.

Hex presses a kiss to my jaw, then another to the spot below my ear, and murmurs, "Let me take care of you, Legs."

My body answers before my mind can protest.

I nod. Just once.

And in that single movement, I say everything I've never let myself say out loud:

I don't want to think.

I don't want to lead.

I want to break something inside me that's always stayed too controlled. And damn it, I want him to be the one who does it.

He eases my pants down, slow enough for the fabric to drag across my skin, creating a teasing friction that makes me shift against him and pulls a quicker breath from my lips. My thong, while basic—black cotton—is appropriate for a Friday lunch date. I did not try too hard, thank God.

Hex then lifts me onto the bar as if my five-foot-ten-inch frame is weightless in his muscular arms. The wood is cool beneath me and in stark contrast to the heat building between us. His hands trail back up my thighs, thumbs pressing into the soft flesh, parting my legs just enough to fit his body between them.

I lean down, my palms cradle his jaw, fingers skimming the coarse stubble like I'm memorizing the texture of power held in check. He tastes like want and bourbon, and when our lips meet again, it's gentle only for a second. Then it's hungry. By the time he pulls away, I'm wrecked. Mouth parted, breath ragged, thoughts unraveling like ribbon between his lips.

I hesitate at what comes next, pulse thumping between my legs. His hand splays across my stomach, pressing just so—proof he can feel the tremor I can't hide.

"Lay back," he murmurs, not a suggestion but a command. "I've got you."

And I do, I believe him, so I listen. My spine arches as my elbows reach for purchase on the polished wood behind me.

He watches the whole time, the corner of his mouth twitching like he knows exactly what he's doing to me—because he does know.

"Now slide your panties to the side," he says, voice rough enough to scrape down my spine. "And spread those pretty lips for me."

Oh my God.

Heat shoots through me, every nerve buzzing like I've been struck by lightning. My hands shake—just a little—but I do what he says, dragging the cotton aside and parting myself for him with trembling fingers. The way he watches me do it. The weight of it. The approval in his eyes makes my skin feel too tight for my body.

He lowers his head, eyes drinking in the sight of me spread open for him, a reverent exhale ghosting across my heated flesh. My breath snags in anticipation. Then his mouth finds the sensitive flesh I've bared to him and all thought slips away.

His tongue traces a slow, torturous path over me. A primal groan rumbles against my core. The vibrations shoot straight through me. My fingers scramble desperately across the bar. Need something. Anything. To hold onto. I knock things over. Fuck. I should be thinking about how exposed I am. About how easy it would be for someone to walk in or catch a glimpse through the windows.

But then Hex makes eye contact with me as his tongue dips inside me.

Whatever reasoning I had left dissolves on the spot.

My breath shudders. I squeeze my thighs around him, but his firm hands grip my flesh, holding me open.

He presses a kiss to the inside of my left leg, smirking against my skin. "For the sake of time, and because you're *so* responsible and need to get back to work..." He hooks a finger under the thin strip of cotton I'm still holding open for him. "...you can leave these on this time. But next time I'll have you completely bare."

A sharp inhale is all I manage before he leans in. His tongue caresses me with a hunger that says this is what he's been starving for.

A whimper slips past my lips, head tipping back as sensation rips through me, pleasure curling, building. My hips jerk against him, my body seeking more, needing more.

"Oh, fuck—" The words barely make it past my lips before the velvet sin of his mouth does something wicked, something that bows my spine and sends my hands clawing at the bar again. I need to ground myself. Need to hold onto something. The only thing within reach is him.

I clutch his hair, fingers tightening as he groans against me, igniting every nerve ending. That wicked muscle moves relentlessly, working me open, unraveling me inch by inch.

He does it so well.

So. Damn. Well.

"This... definitely my favorite pairing," he says, lips grazing my inner thigh before he dips back in.

Pleasure builds. Coils tighter. Tighter. Pressure crests higher until I teeter on the edge.

"Hex—" His name falls from my lips, half-moan, half-prayer.

His grip tightens around my quivering legs, fingers digging in hard enough I'll feel it tomorrow. His mouth doesn't stop. Doesn't relent. Tongue dragging maddening circles that have me gasping for air.

Then I feel it. His hand shifts. Fingers slide lower, wet with how ready I am.

The first one slips inside me. I gasp, hips lifting in eager response.

He lets me adjust to him, just a breath. Then the second finger follows, stretching me. My body tenses, then melts around the pressure. He thrusts them in that same ruthless rhythm—his mouth still sucking, stroking, teasing my clit. Building me up, pushing me higher.

And then—

He curls them.

Hits that spot.

The coil snaps. I shatter completely. Head flung back, a cry tears from my throat as the orgasm crashes through me—hot, blinding, breathless. I can't stop the way I buck against his mouth. Can't control the tremors that seize my thighs.

The sound I make is lost to the haze. I barely manage to hold myself up on the bar.

My fingers tangle in his hair. My hips twitch, overstimulated, as he licks me through it—that sinful tongue catching every last aftershock.

I can't breathe. Can't think.

Only feel.

It takes a moment—*several*—before I manage to pry my hands from his hair. My body still buzzes. Still trembles.

He pulls back, sliding his fingers out of me, lips shining, looking too pleased with himself.

Cocky bastard.

I blink down at him, still lightheaded, every limb boneless. But something inside me stirs. Something reckless.

I want to touch him.

No—undo him the way he just undid me.

My hand reaches blindly for the bar, fingers closing around the can of whipped cream. I hop down, legs weak beneath me but determination giving me strength. A wicked smile curves my lips.

Hex watches—eyes dark, heated, devouring—as I close the space between us.

His hands go to his belt, but I swat them away.

"Mine," I murmur, locking eyes as I take over.

He lets me. Lets me unbuckle the leather, pop the button, drag the zipper down slow.

He leans back against the edge of the bar, elbows braced. Then, like he's reading my mind, he grabs the hem of his shirt and lifts, holding the fabric between his teeth.

Muscles ripple. Light and shadow play across his skin as I drag my hand down the straining bulge beneath thin cotton.

I bite my lip, the heat in my belly reigniting.

His chest rises. Falls fast. But those eyes—those tantalizing eyes—track every move like a man seconds from snapping. My fingers skim the carved ridges of his abdomen—then dip, slipping beneath the band of his boxer briefs.

His cock is hot. Heavy. Thick in my palm as I pull him free.

Of course, he's big. I would have expected nothing less from this mountain of a man.

But still—

A flicker of nerves sparks low in my stomach. My inexperience gnaws at the edges of my boldness. I know I won't be able to take much—not with my unreliable gag reflex—but Demi gave me tips. And damn it, I want to make my best friend proud.

Hex watches, breath shallow, chest rising and falling in anticipation as I give the whipped cream a good shake. I press the nozzle. A dollop lands on my tongue. I let it melt into liquid and drip from my mouth onto his waiting cock. I use the cream to slick my hand, gliding up and down his thick shaft, watching the muscles in his thighs tighten.

His jaw clenches. Then I lean in, pressing my lips to his. Soft. Sweet. Sticky. I kiss him, sharing the sweetness of it between us.

When I pull back, I press and trail the nozzle down the length of his cock.

The sound he makes is guttural as I lower myself to my knees and lick up the mess I just made.

His fingers thread into my hair. The grip tugs at my roots.

And I show him just how much I've been learning.

CHAPTER NINETEEN

Sable

I smooth my hands down my tank and, after wiping the potato salad and whipped cream—among other things—off my underwear, I button my pants and try to pull myself together. My heart's still hammering.

Hex looks far too composed for a man who just ruined me six ways from Sunday. He runs a hand through his hair to fix the parts I thoroughly tousled.

The bar is a mess.

My skin's still tingling. My breath won't settle.

And right on cue, the universe shows up in the form of a creaking door and its usual middle finger.

I jerk upright so fast I nearly knock over my drink, panic flooding my system as I take in the disaster around us. Plates shoved aside, silverware scattered, lunch remnants smashed between the unmistakable evidence of what just happened.

A man steps inside, hesitating for half a second as his gaze sweeps the scene. Middle-aged, with weathered skin and the kind of presence that says he's seen more than he ever asked for. Five minutes earlier and he'd have had one more story to add his wild tales.

A gray polo stretches tight over the roundness of his stomach, tucked neatly into khakis that look a little too crisp for the rest of him. His boots are worn, scuffed at the toes—but they are the kind that hit more pavement than dirt. A cowboy hat sits back on his head, casting just enough shadow to soften the sharpness in his eyes. It gives him a vaguely relaxed appearance, one that doesn't quite match the weight he carries in his expression.

His lips twitch—somewhere between amused and politely horrified—as he takes in the mess on the bar. Then he clears his throat.

"Sorry to interrupt."

I could die.

Hex, on the other hand, doesn't flinch. He just leans against the bar, easy and unbothered, like he wasn't just... *God.*

The unexpected man shifts his weight, his belt creaking softly as he adjusts his stance, then flashes a badge clipped to his hip.

"Detective Bryant," he says, introducing himself.

Were we that loud? Oh God, was there a noise complaint?

He exhales, giving the room another once-over. "Brandon Dillinger. Local business owner. Runs a pretty big startup. Lives in those new high-rise condos on the other side of town—the fancy ones they just put in. Ya heard of him?"

What does this have to do with Hex's bar?

Hex stares blankly at the detective, but I'm starting to pick things up, to learn *him*. A subtle shift. A tightening of his jaw. A flicker in his eyes I haven't learned how to name yet.

"Doesn't sound familiar. We don't get a lot of people from that side of town in here," Hex says, voice calm, controlled. "What can I do for you?"

"Well, that's interesting," Bryant replies, rocking back on his heels. "Because we have reason to believe he came through here last Friday afternoon."

Hex shrugs. "Maybe so. I don't remember everyone who comes and goes."

The detective watches Hex carefully before continuing. "He's missing. Last seen Sunday. One of the last charges on his card showed a purchase here."

My pulse kicks up, a tight coil of unease winding through me. What exactly does he think Hex knows?

I glance at Hex, searching for some flicker of a meaningful reaction to this detective's words, but his face stays infuriatingly evasive.

Jesus Christ. What if that whole hitman thing wasn't just a joke? What if I just let him give me the best orgasm of my life, only to find out he's actually dangerous?

I'm going to need a better vetting system. Immediately.

I shift, eyes catching on the discarded whipped cream can on the floor, then across the scattered remains of our reckless indulgence. Could I have been any more vulnerable?

Bryant exhales, his expression even. "We checked his condo. Unit 1407. No sign of him, no indication of where he went. Cameras were conveniently down throughout the day."

1407. I've heard that before. The day in the market, when Will called Hex about a broken tap.

I glance at Hex, but if the number means anything to him, he doesn't show it.

"And now? He's just... gone. Disappeared sometime Sunday. Came back from the gym, and that was it. No sign of him since.

"Here's where it gets more interesting," Bryant keeps going, his voice sharpening slightly. "Dillinger was under investigation for the rape of an underage girl. And he's also rumored to have ties to Ned Stauder."

The detective pauses, letting the name settle into the room like a brick dropped into water.

Hex can no longer hide that not-so-subtle clench of his jaw.

Bryant smiles, but it's humorless. "I figured you might recognize that name. You know, given your history, Hector." He says Hex's real name slow and mockingly. "Or is it still Hex these days? Ned Stauder's known to prefer nicknames too, ain't he?"

What history? What the hell kind of history gets you on a detective's radar when a man disappears? And who exactly is Ned Stauder?

Hex doesn't blink. "I'm familiar."

"Thought so," Bryant says dryly, clearly amused. "Given that Dillinger's business dealings apparently crossed paths with Stauder's illegal ventures—fights, gambling, all the usual—figured I'd check in with someone who might know the players."

Hex's smile spreads, but it's unsettling in its ease. "Can't say I've been keeping tabs on Ned's social calendar—" He pauses, just long enough to make the silence stretch. "But you're welcome to ask him yourself."

Bryant's eyes sharpen, hand pulling out a business card from his pocket. "Funny you say that. We tried, but Stauder's memory gets awful fuzzy around details like this. Since Dillinger stopped here, and you have your own history with that crowd, I thought, it'd be wise to ask about your whereabouts Sunday."

Hex doesn't hesitate. "We were on a date."

Bryant tilts his head, unimpressed.

Hex smirks, knowing he's covered. "About twenty-five comments on social media posts with pictures from that day will confirm it."

I clear my throat, still struggling to keep the heat out of my face, the bourbon and orgasm not helping the effort. "It's true," I add quickly. "He was with me. I can show you my social posts. They have locations and time stamps."

Bryant holds my gaze a second longer than I'm comfortable with, his expression keen and assessing.

Does he think I'm lying? That I'm just some naïve idiot covering for a man I barely know?

Worse—*am I?*

Finally, he nods. "Alright." He taps his fingers against the bar, his card resting just beneath them.

"If you think of anything else—anything about his visit that day, or Stauder's dealings with Dillinger—give me a call."

He doesn't wait for a response. Just turns and walks out, leaving the odd encounter hanging between Hex and me.

I wait until the door clicks shut behind the detective before letting out a breath I didn't realize I'd been holding. The tension unspools in frayed strands, coiling tight again just beneath my skin. I don't need to look at Hex to feel the pressure building, radiating off him. I feel I've just been caught in the middle of a storm brewing beneath that calm exterior.

Maybe I'm standing in the eye right now.

But what the hell happens when I step out and right into its fury?

I grab a napkin—because that feels like the normal thing to do—and start wiping at a spot on the bar that definitely won't make a dent in the mess. My brain is caught somewhere between *what the actual fuck* and *play it cool, Sable.*

Hex doesn't say anything, just patiently watches me, which somehow makes it worse.

I shift a glass. Move a plate. Straighten a bottle that's perfectly aligned with the containers.

Act casual. Keep it together. Don't let him know you're mentally falling through the goddamn floor.

"So," I say, voice a little too high, "that was... uh, interesting."

Hex hums in agreement, offering nothing more.

I nod—because nodding seems like the right move—and adjust another glass two inches to the left.

"And when he asked about your whereabouts Sunday..." I glance at him, forcing my expression into something that probably doesn't look as normal as I want it to. "That wasn't... a weirdly tense moment for you at all?"

Hex leans against the bar, arms crossed. "Not really."

I blink at him. Wait. Then—because I'm not as cool as I want to be—I blurt out:

"That market we were at is right next to those condos the detective talked about..."

"It is."

"Did you kill Brandon Dillinger?"

"Yes."

I drop the glass. It clatters against the bar.

Okay. Okay. Okay. You can process this.

"Oh. Right. Of course. You just..." My brain whites out for a second. I clear my throat, reaching to pick it up, my hands visibly shaking. I turn back to him. "Wait, what?"

"I killed him." He says it with the kind of certainty reserved for obvious truths.

I open my mouth. Close it. Open it again.

"I—okay." I nod too many times, the glass forgotten.

Hex just fucking calmly watches me, and I can't tell a goddamn thing he is thinking with that perfect, expressionless face of his.

That's it. I hate that look!

I spin on my heel, taking two steps before coming right back because where the hell am I going?

Nowhere in my thirty-nine fucking years of existence did *"accidentally give an assassin a blow job"* make an appearance on the bingo card. It's hot...

IN THEORY!

"So," I say, trying to swallow the mild hysteria bubbling up. "You just... casually... commit murder."

Hex exhales through his nose, a subtle sound that means he's either amused or pretending not to be annoyed. "It wasn't casual."

"Oh, wasn't it?" My voice cracks. "Because you sure as hell made it sound that way. Do you like football? Yes. Have you ever been on a plane? Yes. Have you ever murdered someone? YES?!"

He sighs, rolling his neck to perhaps relieve tension. "The underaged girl he raped? I know her. Her dad is a regular here."

I stop fidgeting, my stomach twisting. "*Oh.*"

"Dillinger came in Friday," Hex continues. "Wanted the girl taken care of. Thought she'd fuck things up for his business if she came forward with her story.

"He runs a shell company for Ned Stauder and has to keep up appearances. Got the feeling he'd done this before and gotten away with it. He heard things about me and how I take care of problems."

Hex reaches for Bryant's card and studies it. "What he didn't realize was that I don't clean up the messes of depraved bastards who dig their own graves while preying on the innocent. So, I contacted her dad."

My mouth goes dry. "And?"

"And he showed up that night with his brother—the girl's uncle. They were gonna handle it themselves."

I stare at him. I recall the two men I saw him talking with that night. "But?"

Hex meets my gaze evenly. "I'm more experienced."

My whole body locks up. *Experienced.*

My stomach does a slow, uncomfortable flip. I lick my lips, my voice coming out way too thin. "So you're a hitman."

Hex smirks, shaking his head. "No."

"Oh, forgive me for being confused," I snap. "You just confessed to murder, *and somehow* made *'I'm experienced'* sound like a goddamn Yelp review for plumbing."

"I'm a handler."

I blink. "Excuse me?"

"There's a difference."

I throw my hands up. "So I've been fucking told. But please, do tell."

Hex leans forward, elbows on the bar. "I handle shit for people that need the help."

I gape at him. *Handle shit. For people.*

So... Murder? Vengeance? Finding lost dogs?

I take a deep breath, pressing my fingers to my temples. "Okay," I say, my voice faint. "What you're telling me is... you're the kind of guy people call when they need a problem *solved.*"

Hex nods.

"And sometimes the solution is"—I wave my hands erratically—"taking someone out?"

He doesn't answer right away, just watches me, calm as fucking ever. Finally, he shrugs. "If it needs to go down that way."

I take a measured breath. Credit to half a Wim Hof YouTube video and a panic attack last April.

Right. Cool. No big deal.

Just exchanged oral sex with a man who straight-up unalived someone last weekend. During our fucking date.

I stare at him for another long second before my brain short-circuits completely, and the only thing I can think to say is: "...Well. That's not terrifying at all."

CHAPTER TWENTY

Hex

*O*kay. *She's freaking out.*

Maybe if I stay calm, she'll calm the fuck down too.

I lean into the bar, arms folded, watching her move the glass again—left, right—grasping for order after hearing something that can't be neatly put away.

I didn't sugarcoat it. Didn't try to ease her into it. I just dropped it in her lap, a brutal fucking housewarming gift.

Welcome to the real me, sweetheart.

Decidedly so, maybe she should have known this information before I feasted on her pussy. Too late now.

She exhales sharply, hands braced on the counter, eyes darting anywhere but toward me.

"So," she says, voice a little too high-pitched. "You're a... *handler.*"

She lets the word stretch, like she's trying it on, but worried it just doesn't fit.

I watch her carefully, resisting the urge to speak too soon.

She's not the kind of woman who panics, but not the kind who's been given a reason to stand still, either. Always moving. Always calculating.

And still, I told her.

I told her because something about her tells me I can.

She plays by the book, yes, but she's too sharp around the edges for that to be easy.

I've seen the streak of defiance in her eyes when she's trying to do the right thing and hating every second of it. In the way she chews her bottom lip when she's holding herself back. In the way she squares her shoulders before doing something she knows she shouldn't enjoy.

There's a wildness buried under all those rules. Something real.

And that's why she gets the truth.

I nod. "Yeah."

Sable swallows, and I watch her throat bob. "Excuse my ignorance, I don't see how it's any different than a hitman?"

I let out a gust of breath, keeping my tone even as I get ready to explain.

"Hitmen take contracts. They kill whoever pays the most. I don't do that. I handle problems for people who don't have another option. People who deserve justice."

I feel my jaw tic as I finish, remembering the many faces I've helped and the depraved things I've done to right wrongs.

She drums her fingers against the bar, the kind of jittery rhythm that betrays someone silently debating fight or flight.

"You knew," I say after a beat. "At least, you must have heard something. When you contacted me about the blonde, you knew. *Didn't you?*"

She scoffs, crossing her arms.

"We didn't know what fucking website we were on. Demi called it the *dark web,*" she says while wiggling her fingers in a hectic manner.

I arch a brow.

"The dark web?" I question, having a hard time holding back a snicker.

Her mouth opens, then closes, and I watch as her eyebrows scrunch together almost in embarrassment. "Is that not a thing?"

I shake my head, smirking despite myself.

She's rattled, but she's still Sable. Still quick. Still standing here listening instead of running for the door. That has to mean something.

I step closer. She doesn't move away.

"I'm not gonna lie to you," I say in an effort to build some trust.

She presses a hand to her chest. "*Bless your heart.*"

Sable blinks up at me, searching my face. I don't know what she's looking for. Reassurance? An explanation that makes all of this easier to swallow? Hell, if I knew, I'd give it to her.

After a long beat, she exhales.

"Well, that's refreshing. Finally, a man who can give me a proper fucking orgasm *and* doesn't want to lie to me."

I chuckle, the tension in my chest loosening a fraction.

She rubs her temples, then says, "Okay, so let's pretend I—again, *hypothetically*—accept all of this as my new reality. What does that mean?"

"It means you don't have to be scared of me or anything in this world for that matter," I tell her, voice steady. "I know you've got a kid. I know you'd never want him around someone dangerous."

My fingers ache to touch her, but I hold myself back. Not the time. I shake my head. "I'm not dangerous, Sable. Not to you. Not to anyone who doesn't deserve it. I protect the people I care about. But you do what you need to do. Process. Tell Demi if you need to."

Something shifts in her face. Softer now. She bites her lip and nods.

She's going to tell her little redheaded firecracker of a friend. I can already see it. And maybe that's okay. If this thing between us goes anywhere—hell, if it becomes what I think it might—her best friend's going to know everything anyway. Including the size of my dick.

Might as well let her in on the little murder secret while we're at it.

Sable parts her lips on an exhale, her shoulders lowering just slightly. "I need to go."

I nod. "Yeah. Okay."

She pauses. Her eyes move across my face with the quiet urgency of someone trying to memorize it. Then she grabs her phone, heads for the door, and walks out.

I run a hand through my hair, watching her go.

She knows.

She didn't run.

And if I read her right... she'll come back.

Good.

I drop my hands to my hips, turning back toward the bar.

Before I can even process where to start on this hazardous zone, the back door swings open, and Will walks in.

He stops dead in his tracks, eyes scanning the mess. Discarded plates, half-eaten takeout containers, overturned glasses, and spilled liquid.

Silence.

A slow inhale. A slower exhale.

Then very carefully: "What. The. Actual. Fuck."

I press my lips together. He'll flip if I smile.

Will blinks at the crime scene. At the potato salad. The whipped cream. The napkins scattered like confetti. Then back at me, his gaze sharpening, calculating whether I've lost my entire goddamn mind.

His eyebrow twitches.

Then, in a very calm, very controlled voice I hear my name.

I brace myself.

"Why," he continues, scanning the damage, "is there potato salad everywhere?"

I glance at the sad, overturned potato salad cup on the barstool. "Things got out of hand."

Will's eyes narrow. "No shit."

His glare flicks to the whipped cream. Back to me. Back to the whipped cream.

His nostrils flare. His mouth opens, then he immediately shuts it.

A slow crawl of recognition pulls across his face until only horror remains.

"Oh my God." He steps back, mimicking physical repulsion. "*Oh my God.*"

I stay silent.

He jabs a finger at the bar with the kind of wounded indignation usually reserved for personal betrayal. "Hex. Please. Tell me that is not—"

I hold up a hand. "Will."

"*Tell me* that is not *sexually involved whipped cream.*"

I scrub a hand over the stubble on my jaw. I level him with a look. "Will." I repeat.

He leans closer, voice barely above a whisper, as though bracing for something he doesn't want to hear. "Hex... was the potato salad also *involved?*"

I exhale through my nose. "Not in the way you're thinking."

Will visibly shudders. "That's somehow worse."

I shake my head, walking past him, and leaving him to deal with what he does best.

Behind me, I hear him mutter, "God help me, I'm going to have to disinfect the whole damn bar."

CHAPTER
TWENTY-ONE

Sable

"So he's like Batman."

Demi pops a grape into her mouth with the same ease most people reserve for commenting on the weather, not unpacking a weekend murder confession.

I blink at her. "No. Not Batman. Batman doesn't kill people."

"Are you sure?" She lifts a shoulder, unconcerned. "Okay, The Punisher, then."

I pinch the bridge of my nose. "Demi."

She leans forward, eyes lighting up. "Wait. Hold on. Did he kill someone while you were on your date? Like, mid-pancake challenge? Did he just get up, murder a guy, and come back all, 'Hey babe, wanna head to the next stop on my sexy as hell motorcycle?'"

I stare at her.

She glows with amusement. "That's a yes."

"Not *mid-date*. I mean, technically we were still on the date, but I wasn't *there*... just nearby... *allegedly*."

Demi sighs dramatically and slouches back into the couch. "Lame. Would've been more exciting if you got to watch. A fucking rapist? I'd have asked to do it myself."

I throw a pillow at her. She cackles.

Across the living room, I spot my mom at the bar cart she just bought "me" for my birthday, humming as she experiments with her latest questionable cocktail. Her short, tousled dark hair—laced with unapologetic gray—looks effortlessly stylish. She's tall and athletic that makes people assume she once played competitive tennis or hiked remote trails. But her confidence doesn't come from adventure or sports. It's just who she is.

She waves a hand at us while the other pours vodka into something that looks suspiciously like darkened pureed watermelon.

"Girls, I'm telling you, this is going to be the next big thing. Came up with it last weekend at Gloria's lake house. She threw one of her 'Sangria and Seniors' parties."

Dabbing her finger and tasting her concoction, she smacks her lips. "Oh, that's good."

I side-eye Demi, who perks up instantly. "Oh! Tell me about it?"

"Oh, yes," she stirs, adding a dash more of black licorice? *What else would be black?* "Everyone talked a big tequila game, but by nine, half of them were barefoot in the grass, belting Cher's greatest hits. Anyway, one of the new gals helped me concoct this drink, and let me tell you—they *loved* it."

"Name it, Marilyn," she challenges, pointing at my mom.

Mom lifts the shaker proudly. "The Black Velvet Meltdown."

Demi holds out her hand. Fingers wiggling. "Pour me one."

I groan. "Demi, for the love of God, she just made that up five seconds ago."

"And? You know I live for this."

I shake my head. "I'll pass. The memories of the Chartreuse are still too fresh."

Mom rubs some glittery sugar on the rim of the martini glass and hands it over to Demi.

No matter what life throws my mother's way, she finds a way to turn it into a good time. Tornado warning? Marilyn's making cocktails by candlelight. Car trouble? She's befriending the tow truck driver. The woman has never met a stranger.

Demi takes a sip, considers, then nods approvingly. "Ten out of ten, Marilyn. Would black out again."

Mom beams. "I knew you'd love it."

I shake my head at their nonsense.

Bash is outside, thankfully, playing with a friend from the neighborhood. Last Sunday, I came home to a freshly landscaped yard. Weeded flower beds, a new seating area under the oak tree, and a playscape obstacle course that Bash immediately claimed as the greatest thing to ever happen.

Through the window, I catch a glimpse of him gripping the rope swing, his friend cheering him on.

Good. That means he won't hear me telling his godmother that I let a hitman—excuse me, "*handler*"—give me the best orgasm of my life on top of a bar.

Demi turns back to me, hazel eyes gleaming with mischief. "Alright, back to the more pressing matter. The bar. Tell me everything."

I set my glass down. "It was a moment. A very... intense moment."

She tilts her head. "Intense. Sure. That's one word for it."

"Demi."

She holds up her hands. "I just want details, okay? How many surfaces did you desecrate? You said there was barbeque. Wait—oh my God, were baked beans involved?"

"No, baked beans were not involved."

She snaps her fingers. "Damn. That would've been iconic."

I drop my head into my hands. "I hate you."

"You love me."

I sigh. "I do. Which is why I'm telling you this."

Demi props her chin in her hands, practically vibrating. "You're telling me this because you know you're in too deep, and you need me to tell you that it's totally fine that you're dating a killer."

I point at her. "*Handler*. You said it yourself. He confirmed. There's a difference."

She snorts. "Suuuuure there is."

I groan, grabbing my water. "I can't believe I'm having this conversation while my mother is five feet away mixing potions, and my child is playing in the backyard."

Demi clinks her glass against mine. "Happy birthday, babe. Best one yet."

A knock at the front door cuts through the room. It's a sharp interruption to the easy rhythm of conversation. I glance toward it and my curiosity flares. I'm not expecting anyone.

I get up and open the door to find a delivery guy, too bright-eyed for a Sunday afternoon, holding a massive pink box like it's filled with The Crown Jewels. He sets a small envelope on top and smiles.

"This is for you," he says, his young voice too calm for my current level of intrigue.

Demi appears behind me and squints at the box. "Is that a fucking cake from Lisa's Bakery downtown?"

Taking the package from the guy and shutting the door behind him, I open the flaps, and the breath leaves my lungs.

Red velvet. Frosted to perfection. Thick, creamy layers that could be described as nothing but sinful.

"Oh my God," I whisper, resisting the urge to lick the frosting from the lid.

"I might just cream in my panties."

"You're disgusting," I reply, barely juggling the oversized box.

Demi giggles, takes the cake and hands me the envelope. "Open it. I need to know who sent this."

I tear it open and slide out the card. One glance confirms what I already expected. It's Hex. Short. Sweet. Warm enough to melt steel.

"Happy birthday, Sable. I wanted you to know I'm thinking about you today. If you need space, I get it.

But I owe you a cake, and I wouldn't dare let your birthday slip by without acknowledging such a beautiful woman.

If I'm lucky, one day I'll get to taste that cream cheese frosting with you... and maybe a little more of you too.

Enjoy—H."

Demi clasps a hand over her heart. "Aww, Frank is so sweet. And hot."

I freeze. "Don't call him Frank. He's not the fucking Punisher."

I take back the cake and walk to the kitchen.

Behind me, I hear her murmur something that sounds a lot like, *"he punished that pussy..."* and I nearly drop the box.

Mom spots it and beams. "Ooooooh, who's the cake from?" she teases, her eyes glinting mischievously.

"A maaaann," Demi drags out the word to get a reaction.

I roll my eyes, but my pulse spikes. I can already feel heat creeping up my neck and into my cheeks.

"A man, huh?" Mom's smile widens as she leans in to inspect the cake. "What kind of man sends cake to a woman's house?"

"Oh, you know, just a guy who knows I like red velvet and thinks I'm hot." I try to downplay it, but Demi isn't having any of it.

"Uh-huh, hot, that's all," she says, leaning against the counter, enjoying herself way too much. "What's his little nickname for you? It wouldn't happen to be *Legs* would it?"

"Fuck off, Demi."

My mom and Demi continue, but I'm gone. I stare at the cake, and my thoughts go right back to Hex. His card. His words. His admission.

He kills people.

Can I get past that? Or is it not about moving past, but accepting it?

He's dark. Dangerous. But kind in a way that's rare. He doesn't go after innocents. He protects the people he cares about.

I swallow hard. I'm so damn conflicted.

But the cake? It's drool-worthy.

And so is he.

185

Fuck.

My pocket vibrates and I pull my phone out, half-expecting it to be Hex, but the moment my eyes catch the unfamiliar number, my stomach drops. It's not him. My pulse spikes, and my hands go cold, but I can't look away as I unlock the screen.

The first image lands hard, knocking the air from my lungs.

It's me—on top of the bar at Ruin's End—legs wrapped around Hex—

No. No. No.

My body freezes. Blood thunders in my ears. Another image appears. I'm kneeling. Hands gripping his thighs. His cock in my mouth. The angle leaves nothing to the imagination.

I want to look away. I really do.

But I can't.

I want to run from the trainwreck, but I'm stuck staring at the threat encased in a blue bubble.

My stomach sours.

> **[unknown number]:** Hope ur having a good birthday, slut. If u don't want these going public, u better work on getting me back in good graces with Andrew. If I don't see any effort from u, I'll make sure ur precious business gets a healthy dose of scandal. Let's see how long u last with the reputation ur company deserves.

Ashley.

I know it's her. This whole damn thing. All of it. I didn't want to believe she'd go this far, but here it is. She's blackmailing me with these fucking pictures, demanding I fix whatever damage exists between her and Andrew.

I never knew how serious things got between them. Didn't care.

What I do know, I sure as hell don't want the father of my child dragging that unhinged woman into Bash's life. And now, she wants me to undo whatever crazy she showed, effectively scaring him off from the way her message reads?

I rub my eyes, a headache already pounding at my skull.

My pulse thrums in my ears. No. Absolutely not. This is insane. I can't—*won't*—play along. But Ashley has been fucking with my life for too long, always finding new ways to twist the knife every time I cauterize her last jab. She's become desperate.

Now, she's coming for my entire goddamn life. She is threatening to affect my business. Affect my *son*.

I want to hurl my phone across the room and hear it shatter, but I don't. I won't give her that kind of power over me.

Across the room, my mom and Demi are laughing, completely unaware of the storm tearing through my chest. I'm supposed to be enjoying my birthday. Instead, I'm here, hijacked by the fallout of Ashley's madness.

How the hell am I supposed to fix this?

I inhale deeply, trying to steady myself, but shit is getting too real, too fast.

A plan. I need a plan to take back control, to cut her out of my life for good. But every path I think of ends in a dead fucking end.

My hand trembles as I run it through my hair, the weight of everything closing in.

No more games, Ashley.

I'll handle this on my terms, but right now, I don't know how.
I need Hex.

CHAPTER TWENTY-TWO

Hex

Boots planted on solid stone, I'm out on the back patio of my place in the Hill Country. Sundays the bar's closed, which is the reason I'm here and not under the neon lights. Forty minutes from town, tucked between cedar trees and limestone outcroppings, the house blends into the land instead of bragging about being part of it. The sky stretches far in every direction without obstruction, making me feel like I'm the last person left.

Quiet. Remote. Peaceful.

The house isn't flashy—clean lines, big windows, vaulted ceilings with heavy wood beams—but it's nice. Moderate by rich-people standards. Pricey by mine. It's got enough space to keep my life spread out, enough privacy to take care of business without a neighbor peeking through the blinds.

The sun's sinking low, casting gold over the hills. My bourbon catches the light where it rests in my palm, and for the first time all week, the edge starts to dull.

My phone lights up with her name, and the glass nearly slips from my hand.

Sable.

Calling me.

She's never done that before. Not once.

I figured the birthday cake might earn me a flirty thank-you text, maybe a sexy photo if I got really lucky, but an actual phone call? Unexpected.

I answer before the second ring. "Hey."

There's a pause—just a breath—but I hear it immediately. The tension.

"I didn't know if you'd be busy..." she says, her voice tight with the kind of pause that makes me think she's considering ending the call short. "But I got the cake. And, uh... my little rabid friend hasn't smashed this one yet. So that's progress."

I lean forward, resting my forearms on my knees, the bourbon forgotten in my hand. "I hear something in your voice, darlin'. What's going on?"

Another pause.

Then, faint and unmistakable: "*You tell that toe-faced bitch if she wants to blackmail you, she better learn to spell first!*"

I blink. "Is that Demi?"

"Yeah," she sighs. "She's... fired up."

"Well, I hope Bash isn't within earshot of *that*."

"He's outside," she says quickly. "Backyard. On the playscape you installed. He still can't stop talking about it, by the way. Keeps asking when he gets to meet the guy who made him cooler than every other kid in the neighborhood."

I smirk, even as something clenches tight in my chest. "Smart kid."

But the feeling doesn't let go. I want to go to her. Now. Drop everything and just be there. But she's with her son. And besides the whole *does she even want to be with someone who's killed* dilemma, I can't assume I'm welcome around her kid. It has to be her call. Her terms.

She clears her throat. "I didn't just call to thank you. I... I need to tell you something."

My grip tightens on the glass. "Alright."

"I got a text. From Ashley."

The name alone makes me clench my jaw. "I assumed that is what Demi is shouting about."

"She sent pictures. Of us. From the bar."

My blood boils beneath my skin. "What kind of pictures?"

"The kind that make me want to dig a hole and never come out." Her voice is tight; each word threaded with the effort of not breaking down. "Me on the bar. You between my legs. Then... me on my knees in front of you."

My brain goes straight to the thoughts of those moments, and despite the fury flooding my veins, I can't help the possessive twist low in my gut. Those memories weren't meant to be shared. The way she looked. The way she felt. Her body. Her sounds.

They're mine.

191

But I won't lie, there's a wicked part of me that's selfishly glad the pictures exist.

"Text them to me," I say, voice low. "Now."

She hesitates, then I hear her phone clicking. Mine pings a second later. I swipe the notification and open the thread.

Yup. There it is. Clear as day. My hands on her and my face disappeared within her, her head bowed at my crotch ready to consume me, both of us completely gone for each other.

I want to jerk my cock and put my fist through a fucking wall.

"She said if I don't get her back in Andrew's good graces... she'll make them public. Said she'd trash Thorne Revival. Essentially destroy me."

"Jesus Christ," I mutter. "She's fully off the rails."

"You think?" she snaps, then catches herself. "Sorry. I'm just... I don't even know what to do."

I inhale through my nose, working to keep my voice steady. "You don't have to do anything. I'll take care of it."

"How?"

"My brother's a tech genius," I say. "JT can make sure those photos disappear. She sends them to anyone else? We'll know. She tries to post them anywhere? They won't make it past the first upload."

There's silence on the other end. She's contemplating it.

"I know this is a lot," I say, softer now. "But I got you. You don't have to fix this alone."

Sable still doesn't speak.

"I just want you to enjoy the rest of your birthday," I add. "Eat the cake. Let Demi say some wildly inappropriate shit. Sit in that beautiful yard of yours and let yourself breathe for a damn second."

Nothing.

So I push it a little further, just enough to draw her out. "You reached out," I say. "That's something, right? Means you're still thinking about me?"

Her voice returns, this time lighter. "Maybe I just wanted to make sure the cake wasn't poisoned."

I chuckle, resting the bourbon glass on the side table next to me. "If I wanted to poison someone, Legs, I'd use something they wouldn't see coming."

"That's not exactly comforting."

I shrug to myself. "But it's honest. I know how much you appreciate that."

And she laughs. A real laugh. Short, but real. And fuck if that doesn't settle something wild inside me.

We sit there, only breath passing between us through the phone.

"You're really going to take care of it?" she asks softly.

"You have my word."

She sighs, a quiet, trembling sound that carries the weight of everything she's been holding in since the pictures showed up.

"Okay," she says. "Okay."

And just like that, I know I'll do whatever it takes to fix this. Because she didn't just call me.

She *trusts* me.

I lean against the end of the bar, sipping burnt black coffee and watching Will line up coasters with military precision. Lemon oil and bleach cover every inch of the bar's air, which means he's been here since the ass crack of dawn scrubbing out the sins of last Friday's lunch.

JT's perched on a barstool nearby, hoodie up, headphones slung around his neck, wearing that smug little smirk he gets right before doing something deeply illegal.

"She still alive?" Will asks, not looking up from the rag in his hand.

JT grins without humor. "Unfortunately."

Ashley. No one says her name anymore. Around here, she's just Bat Shit.

"She's made a big fucking mistake," I say flatly. "She's screwing with someone that's mine."

JT taps away on both his laptop and phone, then flips the screen toward me. A tangle of code, routing pings, and server logs flash across it.

"Got her cloud access. Phone's wide open. Emails, texts, app data—everything. She's been using a third-party vault for the pictures, but once I isolate the backup pathway, they're gone. Permanently."

"You're sure?"

He raises a brow. "Hex. If you want me to nuke her digital footprint from orbit, I can make it look like she never existed."

Will snorts. "Or we could just make sure she doesn't." I glance at him. He shrugs. "What? I'm just saying. Fewer loose ends."

JT gives him a lazy side-eye. "We're not doing body disposal on a Monday. That's a weekend problem."

I drag a hand down my jaw. "We're not killing her."

Yet goes unspoken.

JT leans in. "But we are taking everything. Her files. Her backup accounts. Even the hidden burner she's been using to send the texts. I've got a tracer on it. If she tries to upload or send those photos to anyone else—"

"They'll disappear," I finish.

"And?" Will adds. "We send her a warning?"

"No." I shake my head. "She won't even know she lost the power. We let her try to swing first."

JT raises a brow. "And then?"

"Then I swing back."

Silence settles over the room.

Will wiggles the last coaster into perfect alignment and tosses the rag over his shoulder. "You want me to tail her again?"

"Yeah," I say, tipping my coffee toward him. "But take the *beater*. Not the Challenger."

Will groans, dramatic as hell. "Come on, man. I spent two hours under the hood yesterday. She's spotless. Even the damn spark plugs are shining. She's sex on wheels right now."

I shoot him a look over the rim of my coffee mug. "Yeah, and she sounds like a jet engine and turns every head within a ten-mile radius. You really want to tail Bat Shit in a bright red muscle car with blackout tint and racing stripes?"

He throws his hands up. "It's not even that loud."

"It backfires when you downshift."

Will winces. "Okay, yeah. But the beater?"

The beater's a war-torn 2001 Ford F-150, sun-faded paint, rust spots on the bumper, and a mysterious smell that might be mildew or old jerky—we've stopped investigating. The headliner sags low enough to graze your scalp, the driver's side window jams halfway down, and the windshield sports a crack shaped suspiciously like a boot print.

He stares at me in disbelief, as if I just asked him to throw loyalty out the window and light it on fire. "I just vacuumed the Challenger."

"And now you're driving the rolling crime scene. Because that truck doesn't get noticed. It gets ignored. And that's exactly what we want."

He sighs long and loud. "Fine. But I swear to God, if I get tetanus from touching the steering wheel—"

"We'll add it to the list of things you've survived."

He mutters something about hepatitis and lost dignity as he heads toward the back.

I watch him go, and that old familiarity tugs at my chest.

Will grew up with parents who forgot to pick him up from school, and never asked where he went at night. He used to show up at my house just hoping for leftovers. Looking for structure. Looking for rules.

It calmed him. Still does.

Now he makes good money. Keeps his life clean and in perfect order. The car. The shoes. His damn sock drawer. That Challenger is spotless because he's earned the right to own something beautiful. Proof he finally has something good, and he knows how to take care of it.

But when I need him in the mud, he never blinks.

Even if he bitches the entire fucking time, making sure we all know how put out he is.

JT starts packing up his laptop but pauses, looking at me. "You good?"

I sip my terrible coffee and think about Sable's voice in my ear last night. The sound of her laugh. She called me.

Chose me.

"I'm good," I say. "I've got something to protect."

JT's expression is sharp, almost proud. He really thinks he's looking out for me by asking, like we've quietly switched roles. But I've never stopped protecting him.

Not when he was ten and already too smart for his own good.

Not when Mom died and the world got real dark, real fast.

He's a man now. Dangerous in all the right ways. But my instinct doesn't leave. The weight in my chest stays the same.

Will. JT. Me. We're not all blood. But that's never mattered.

We're brothers where it counts.

JT leans back, typing something into his phone with a smirk.

"Well then," he says. "Let's handle Bat Shit."

CHAPTER TWENTY-THREE

Alex

The day crawls by, humid and sluggish, each second sticking to my skin. Will's out again, doing laps in the beater while Ashley runs through her usual unhinged routine. JT's working in the bar at one of the booths, headphones on, probably erasing someone's identity for fun.

I've been staring at my phone in the back office, fully convinced it's withholding information on purpose.

Then her name pops up.

[Legs]: Any updates on our favorite lunatic.

I lean back in my office chair, smirking before my fingers fly.

> **[Hex]:** Bat Shit's been busy. Still trailing your ex, desperate for a callback she's never getting. Hits his dealership, waits in the gym parking lot for him to come out, then drives off like it's all very casual.

She doesn't respond, so I continue—

> **[Hex]:** But she follows you too. Shop. School drop-off. Sits in her car just watching your life as if it's her favorite tv series.

A pause. Then bubbles.

> **[Legs]:** What does she do for work? How does she even have time for this full-time crazy gig?

I grin. Teed up.

> **[Hex]:** Credit card fraud. Identity theft. Bank scams. Classic amateur hustle.

> **[Legs]:** You're kidding?

> **[Hex]:** Nah. She's been using three maxed-out cards tied to someone named Carol Wansley. Real Carol lives in Arizona. She's got no idea her fake twin's been buying gummy hair vitamins and monogrammed loungewear for the last six months.

> **[Legs]:** Holy shit. So you're saying I'm being stalked by a broke, delusional con artist with thinning hair?

[Hex]: The thinnest. Extensions are struggling.

[Legs]: Stop.

[Legs]: You're gonna make me laugh out loud in front of a client.

The thought of her at work, trying to stifle a smile over my words, hits me in the feels.

[Legs]: You wanna stop by?

[Legs]: If you're around.

[Legs]: See the shop… officially?

I stare at the message, half-convinced it'll vanish if I blink. I never thought I'd be invited into her space. Not the shop. Not the center of the world she built with her own two hands.

Yeah, I want to see it. I want to see *her* in it.

My hand tightens around the phone. I'm already standing, grabbing my keys like I'm sixteen and she just asked me to sneak out.

Fuck yes, I want to see her shop.

[Hex]: You sure? I don't want to distract you while you're doing important arts and crafts.

[Legs]: Don't disrespect my profession, Alvarez.

[Hex]: I would never.

> **[Hex]:** You know I'd love nothing more than to watch you work with your hands.

> **[Hex]:** I'd let you paint every inch of my body if you wanted to.

> **[Legs]:** I think you may have it bad.

I smirk, already moving toward the door.

> **[Hex]:** If this is bad, baby... I hope I never feel good again.

She doesn't respond right away, but I can picture her reading it. Probably biting her lip, trying not to smile too wide.

Sable is opening the door.

And I'm walking right through it.

CHAPTER TWENTY-FOUR

Sable

> **[Hex]:** If this is bad, baby... I hope I never feel good again.

The words are still lingering on my phone screen, and I'm still hot from reading them when I hear it—

The low, unmistakable growl of a motorcycle rolling up outside.

My chest lifts. My pulse kicks up.

He's here. So quick.

I smooth the front of my shirt, completely aware that I'm not exactly dressed to seduce—dust on my leggings from sanding earlier, a fitted tee that's seen better days—but that doesn't stop the rush running through me. There's something about Hex that short-circuits every reasonable thought in my body.

Excited. That's the word. I'm excited. To see my *murderer boyfriend*, apparently. The one man who has made my life infinitely less terrifying just by existing. The juxtaposition that thought brings to my attention cannot be ignored.

The second I see him, my throat goes dry. I unlock the door just as he swings a leg off the bike.

He's wearing a slate gray T-shirt, snug across his chest, sleeves hugging just enough to frame the angel wing tattoo that arcs over his bicep. The muscles underneath look indecent. Black jeans hug thick thighs that I have very vivid memories of clutching. Worn boots. Heavy steps. That cocky smirk that says he already knows what I'm thinking.

"Hey," I manage, moving aside to let him in.

Hex steps into Thorne Revival with quiet purpose. His pace unhurried, as if my space has earned his respect. His gaze moves across the room, taking in the furniture, the soft light pouring through the front windows, and the paint-stained drop cloth I keep forgetting to fold.

"You did all this?" he asks, voice low, a little awed.

I nod, proud despite the nerves kicking around in my gut. "Yeah. The front room's mostly finished pieces for sale. The pieces I find on the side of the road or specifically buy to flip. No one sees potential in them until I drag them home and work my magic."

He moves to a refinished cabinet closest to the front window. It's a tall art deco beauty with soft blue lacquer, gold hardware, and a new marble top I nearly broke my back hauling inside. He moves his fingers across the edge, gently, as though the piece holds a consciousness he doesn't want to disturb.

"This one's beautiful," he murmurs.

I smile. "She was a disaster when I got her. Warped legs, chipped veneer, smelled like cat pee. But I could see it, you know? The beauty. Under all that mess."

He glances over at me and says, "My mom would've loved this."

A warmth blooms in my chest. "Yeah?"

He nods. "We didn't have much growing up, but she loved old furniture. Said if you couldn't afford something new, you could still find something with history and make it yours. She moved through junk shops like they held relics, not bargains. Picked pieces that had stories, not hefty price tags. Our cramped apartment barely fit it all, but she kept filling it with stuff like this. Things she cleaned up, polished, patched."

He looks back at the cabinet. "She gave everything a second chance like it cost her nothing... but it cost her everything."

My chest squeezes. There is something about the way he says it, soft but rough around the edges. Like memories, still living under his skin.

I clear my throat. "Reminding you of your mother... not exactly the vibe I aim for with men, but I guess I can roll with it."

He turns his head to me and he lets out a sudden, deep laugh, the kind that escapes before you can think to hold it back.

"You don't remind me of her," he says, stepping closer. "You remind me of how much she would've liked you."

I blink at that, not sure what to do with the warm ache in my throat.

He glances away, gaze settling somewhere far off. "She had terrible taste in men, though." There's an edge in his voice, worn down and honed sharp by time.

He lets the silence stretch before adding, "The man the detective asked about. Ned Stauder. That wasn't just some distant acquaintance to me."

I feel my breath catch, readying myself for what truth might fall from his lips.

He stares at the cabinet, avoiding my eyes, as though its stillness might anchor what's coming apart in him.

"He's the one who took her life," Hex says quietly.

The words land with a weight I don't know if I'm strong enough to carry.

"Drugs, money, whatever excuse made it easier for him to sleep. He watched her die that night. Orchestrated the clean-up of the whole thing like she was just another problem to erase. She tried to leave him. To pull us out of his orbit. He didn't like that."

My hand instinctively moves, resting against the edge of the counter beside me. I don't speak. I know better. I let him talk.

"He came sniffing around not long after. Said she'd gotten in too deep, made some poor choices. Said he'd take care of me and my brother. Said he 'owed her that much.'" His jaw muscles work. "What he really meant was we belonged to him."

He finally looks at me, eyes darker now. Not with rage but resolve. "I fought our way out. Bled for it."

I manage a small nod because anything more might unravel the delicate thread of truth he just exposed.

He draws in slowly, steadier now. "That's why I don't play games with people like Dillinger. Or men who think they can buy silence, buy survival. I know what happens when they think no one's watching."

His voice dips. "I watch."

I step closer before I even realize it, pulled by the gravity of him. I wrap my arms around him. A quiet moment stretches between us, the air shifting as his hand comes to rest gently at my back. Not pulling me closer. Just... letting me stay.

I hold him a little tighter.

Jesus.

Ned Stauder killed his mother. Swept him and his brother into that life, as if they were part of the damage control.

I can never begin to imagine growing up—let alone surviving—in that world, surrounded by men who deal in violence like its currency. But Hex did. And he got out, built something, protected his brother, and somehow, he's still capable of... *this.* Of warmth. Of humor. Of holding me with meaning.

I ease back just enough to look up at him. "Thank you," I whisper. "For telling me."

His eyes meet mine, and there's something unspoken there. A trust he didn't owe me but gave anyway. And it settles in my chest. It's an ache, but not the bad kind. The kind that lets you know someone just gave you a piece of their truth.

I offer a little levity, nudging the mood gently. "Most of my work is commissioned," I say with a nod of my head. "Want to see what I'm working on now, actually?"

"Lead the way," he says, voice stripped of any lingering edge.

I turn, and his gaze trails after me like a touch I can almost feel.

The workshop is as much in disarray as I probably look. Dust floats lazily in the air, tools strewn across my work bench. Self-conscious, I tighten my hair tie, and adjust my smudged reading glasses still perched on top of my head.

If he notices my mess, he doesn't seem to mind.

I lead him to the massive piece I've been pouring my heart into all week. A three-section antique armoire, early 1900s, with hand-carved floral detailing and cracked molding I've been painstakingly restoring with a scalpel and a prayer.

"It takes finesse," I explain, gently brushing a finger over one of the scrolls. "Too much pressure and you destroy it. Too little and you don't fix anything. You've got to repair it without erasing what makes it special."

When I glance back, Hex is looking at me in that stunned way people do when something hits too close to home.

"That's how it feels with you," he says quietly. "Like something delicate. Something I don't want to break by doing too much or not enough."

I swallow, caught off guard by how hard those words land.

He closes the distance, the eye contact burning with intensity. "I've been looking forward to seeing you," he says, voice rough and tingling through my torso. "I owe you a birthday redo."

I let out a dry laugh, my brow shooting up. "You mean the birthday where I found out my boyfriend's killed people while simultaneously being blackmailed with photos of me giving *very* enthusiastic head. Photos so graphic they'd probably get Ruin's End flagged by the county health department?"

His smirk is slow and shameless. "That one."

"Well, sorry to disappoint you, Big Guy"—I pat his chest—"but thirty-nine-year-old women don't exactly have wild expectations for birthdays, let alone *redos*."

His hands settle on my waist, guiding me toward him as though I've always belonged there.

"Could've fooled me," he murmurs. "And did you call me your *boyfriend*?"

My heart jumps. Maybe I shouldn't have said that? I just assumed I'm the only chick he's banging that he's exclusively told about his side hustle.

He's close now, closer than I should be letting him get when I still have voices in my head whispering, *you're being watched.*

There were photos.

A threat.

But nothing's come of it. No new messages. No new chaos. Maybe Hex really did take care of it.

What if he killed her?

I'm about to pull back—say something self-deprecating or joke about Ashley's radio silence being the result of her murder—but then his lips brush mine, and my body decides for me: shut up.

I let the kiss happen.

But he picks up on my hesitation.

Instead of deepening it, he slows. Softens. His hand comes up to tuck a loose strand of hair behind my ear, kissing my forehead, and lingering just long enough to steal my breath again for an entirely different reason.

When he pulls back, his eyes flick up to my hairline. "You always wear these on your head?" he asks, tapping the pair of glasses still perched there.

I smirk. "There are lots of little intricacies, ailments, and failing parts you've yet to discover, Hex. I'm a full-time restoration project."

"Good. Gives me something to work on between jobs." He grins—full and unfiltered—the kind of expression that says he's more than ready to rise to the occasion. "Learning everything about you."

Between jobs.

I roll my eyes, turning to glance around the shop. "I know it's a mess. I hit my stride and next thing I know, open stain cans are multiplying, hardware covers every surface, and I have no idea where I left my coffee."

Hex lets out a low chuckle. "Will would have a goddamn field day back here."

"Will," I repeat, intrigued by who he surrounds himself with. "So... your people. You're not doing all this alone, right?"

He leans against the nearest worktable, arms crossing over that just-right shirt of his. "Nah. Will and JT are my family. Will is not blood, but it doesn't matter. Our bond is closer than that. We've been through so much together."

I study him with curiosity as he moves about my space taking in the many different pieces in various states of repair.

"In my twenties, I fought underground," he says, dragging a calloused finger over a walnut nightstand. "Cage matches. No rules. No gloves. No spotlight. Just survival. I made more money getting punched in the face than I ever could doing something respectable."

"That tracks," I murmur, making him huff a soft laugh.

"But it went beyond money. It fed control. Fearlessness. After being jerked around by the guy running it all—Ned—I took everything I learned and decided to turn it into something good.

"We always talked about owning a bar, the three of us, so... I bought one." His tone shifts, softening with pride as he finishes his self-guided tour, meeting right back at me. "Built it into what it is now. Ruin's End."

He runs a rough hand through his hair and looks in the direction of his bar. "The regulars are more than just patrons. They're a community. People come to us when shit hits the fan. If someone's being harassed, threatened, needs protection... they know I'll handle it. Some pay in favors. Some pay in loyalty. Some just keep the lights on with their bar tabs."

He shrugs, brushing it off with the ease of someone who doesn't realize he's done something remarkable.

"Right, so you're basically the neighborhood justice league with a liquor license," I say with a tease as I look up into his eyes.

His lips curve. "Depends on the night."

I smile, leaning back against the armoire, watching him as he stands in the middle of my chaotic, dusty shop like he has always belonged here.

It's insane. All of it. But it doesn't feel wrong.

It feels... *safe.*

And maybe for the first time in a very long time, I'm starting to believe that's allowed. Like I deserve to explore it.

He leans down into me, lips brushing mine again, slow, tender—

But I touch his arm and push him a hair's breadth away. "Wait—" I breathe into the air between us. "What if she's watching again? Recording us? What if—"

He cups my face gently, thumbs stroking my cheeks. "Hey. JT's already shut Bat Shit down. She couldn't stream a cat video right now, let alone access your cameras or phone. And besides," he adds, voice lowering into something dark with confidence, "this time of day, she's probably busy following Andrew to the gym. Her schedule's not exactly hard to map."

I cringe internally at how well he knows her movements, but I'm grateful and ridiculously impressed. "You know that's disturbingly thorough, right?"

He smirks, eyes locked on me. "When it comes to protecting what's mine, I leave nothing to chance."

That declaration sends heat rushing through me, settling deep and warm between my thighs. My heart speeds up as I reach out, my fingers resting against his chest. "I believe you."

He exhales a long breath, relaxing at my admission. Then, slowly, his hand slides up to where I'm touching him and he covers my touch. I feel his heart beating beneath my palm.

I want this man so fucking bad.

He dips his head, brushing his mouth over mine. Not rushed, not forceful; a slow kiss that deepens as my body tilts into his. His other hand finds my hip, thumb sliding under the waistband of my leggings, palm dragging across the bare skin beneath.

A shiver races through my body.

Hex moves with a kind of composed assurance, reading me in ways I haven't learned to read myself. His fingers dip lower, between my legs, slipping easily between my folds. A groan rumbles in his chest when he feels how wet I am.

"Fuck," he mutters against my lips. "You're soaked."

I clutch at his shirt, hips instinctively pressing forward into his touch. "Hex."

Then he's backing me up, steering me toward the nearest table with a hunger in his eyes that nearly buckles my knees.

Just as he shifts me toward it, I blurt out, "Wait! Not that one. It's got a broken leg."

Hex stills, then withdraws his fingers with maddening slowness, dragging the moment out just to watch me come undone. I let out a breathy laugh, and he grins.

"Good to know." His voice is low, wicked. "Wouldn't want to give you more work."

Before I can say anything else, he grabs me under my thighs and lifts me straight off the ground like I weigh nothing. I gasp as I wrap my legs instinctively around his waist. Our bodies flush, he kisses me deeper now.

"What about this one?" he mumbles over my lips, eyeing a desk near the wall.

"No," I giggle, breathless. "That one's from the thirties, and I haven't sanded it yet. That's a splinter in the ass just waiting to happen."

He sets me back on my feet gently, though his hands linger on my body. "Maybe this isn't the best place for all I want to do to you."

I nod, still catching my breath. "I know. I'm sorry, this just... isn't ideal for fooling around. We might end up needing tetanus shots."

He doesn't move away. Doesn't step back. Just watches me, focused and still, committing every flicker of humor in my face to memory. Then he tilts his head and grumbles, "Take them off."

I blink. "What?"

"Your leggings," he says, dark eyebrows drawing together. "Take them off."

Heat floods my face. "You're serious?"

"If you don't, I'll do it for you." His voice is calm. Confident. A challenge wrapped in velvet. "And I won't leave them intact."

We're being serious.

I hesitate—just for a breath—and he's already on his knees.

His hands grip the waistband of my leggings, and in one swift motion, he yanks them down past my hips. The fabric drags along my thighs like he's peeling away resistance itself.

The breath leaves my body for good.

This man, a storm in human form whose gaze alone commands silence kneels. *For me.*

The sight knocks something loose in my chest. It's more than arousal. It's reverence. Worship. Power. *Mine.* Laid bare at the altar of my skin.

My legs go weak. My thighs clench. Heat blooms, deep and dizzying.

He doesn't rush. Just looks up at me, eyes dragging over every inch like he's savoring the shape of my uncertainty. Both knowing he's two seconds away from unraveling me.

And maybe I've already come undone. Because something about seeing him like this—shoulders broad, knees biting into the floor, gaze locked on me like a promise—ignites a fire I didn't know I carried. Unstoppable. Untouchable. *Dangerous.*

My hands tremble. He lifts my shirt. His mouth finds the flesh of my stomach. Everything fades.

"Hex—"

"You had your chance."

He brushes warm kisses down one thigh. Then back up the other. Then his tongue traces the damp spot in my underwear, a wordless vow made of heat and pressure.

A moan slips out.

Hex hooks his thumbs into my panties and pulls them down in one smooth, practiced motion. Before I can say his name again, his tongue is on me—slow, thick strokes—then his mouth seals around my clit.

I cry out, fingers clutching the edge of the desk behind me. His fingers slide inside. One. Then two. Curling just right. Pleasure builds fast, hot, and impossible to outrun.

He shifts. Lifts one of my legs over his shoulder, opening me.

His mouth returns. Sucking. Licking. Biting just enough to make me whimper. I'm seconds away from falling apart when he pauses, lips brushing my skin. The rasp of stubble makes my breath hitch.

"You ready to fly?" he asks.

I nod, thinking it's just a metaphor.

Then—still on his knees—he *lifts* me. In one ridiculous, glorious motion, he gathers both my legs and hooks them over his shoulders like a reverse piggyback.

I yelp, laughing, squirming as I scramble to adjust my balance. "Hex. Oh my God—"

Crossing the room with the ease of a man stronger than most. My legs tighten around his neck, thighs quaking from the weight of sensation already threatening to detonate.

He presses me to the wall, hands firm beneath my ass, mouth diving back between my legs like he never left.

The *angle*.

The pressure.

I reach up, bracing my palms higher against the wall—higher than I've ever stretched—body trembling with need.

He flicks his tongue just right on my clit and I shatter. My orgasm crashes through me, violent and raw. I bite back a sob, legs locking tighter, fingers dragging down the wall.

When he finally lowers me to the ground, my knees buckle. I glance at my fingertips, stained from the walnut I used earlier. My eyes dart up at the wall and see the mark I left.

"Looks like that one earned itself commemoration," I murmur, breathless.

Hex follows my gaze, eyes lingering on the streaks before meeting mine with a smug smile.

"Good," he says, voice rough. "Now every time you walk past it, you'll remember exactly *who* got you that high."

CHAPTER
TWENTY-FIVE

Sable

"I'm just saying," Demi drawls as I turn the wheel to round the corner toward the shop, "he dropped to his knees and there's still no ring? Girl, slip a cock ring on that man, declare him your emotional support orgasm, and lock it the hell down."

I choke on my iced coffee, nearly spilling it down my shirt. "It's been less than two weeks."

"Modern problems, modern proposals."

"Can you not?"

She grins wickedly and wraps her lips around her straw. "I absolutely *cannot* not. So? Have you committed full penetration yet? Was it everything I've built up in my head? Did he flip you over and smooth out your rough edges like one of your vintage cabinets?"

"*Jesus*, Demi."

She shrugs unapologetically. "I'm just living vicariously through your orgasms, babe. I've been in a dry spell so long my vibrator's begging for a vacation and a union rep."

I laugh despite myself as I pull up to the curb, shifting the car into park. The sound of the locks snapping free in the doors loosens something in me; breath rushes out, and the tension slips from my spine one vertebrae at a time.

"I'm doing my best to take it slow," I say, unbuckling my seatbelt. "But every time I see him... the depravity that goes through my mind is concerning."

Demi lets out a low whistle and snaps her fingers. "Lean into that!"

I pull the shop keys from my bag and sigh. "I mean, yeah, he's hot. Obviously. And apparently murder does something to my sex drive I wasn't prepared for."

Demi snorts. "We all have our kinks."

"But also..." I trail off, struggling to put words to the chaos in my head. "I just can't stop overthinking my side of it. I didn't want to wait—I'm thirty-nine, not nineteen—but the minute it ended, I started second-guessing everything. Even now, I'm questioning whether I've already rushed things."

"Rushed?" Demi blinks. "Sable. There are women who wait three years in a relationship before anyone finds their clit."

I crack a smile. "I don't know. Maybe it's why I've never been married. I jump into things. I don't demand more respect."

"No." She pulls off her sunglasses dramatically. "You've never been married because you stayed in a long-term situationship with a man who could find a new reason to emotionally disappoint you every fiscal quarter."

"That is disturbingly accurate," I say, chewing at a hangnail.

"Thank you. I've had a decade to solidify my thoughts on your relationship."

We're halfway to the shop when I stop cold, my stomach lurching. I grab my best friend's arm. "Demi."

The lock. Not tampered with or rusted through—destroyed. The deadbolt hangs crooked in the frame, metal warped like it took a hit from something brutal. Cracks web outward from the impact point in the glass, fine and splintered veins, with one jagged fracture slicing down the lower pane.

Her face turns from shocked to raged. "That bitch."

I pull my phone from my bag and text the only person I know who will have answers and zero chill:

> **[Sable]:** I think someone broke into the shop.

The reply comes almost instantly.

> **[Hex]:** Don't go inside. I'm coming.

I stare at the screen.

> **[Hex]:** 5 minutes.

Demi's eyes go wide. "Damn, he's on it."

A moment later, the low growl of a blacked-out Silverado curls around the corner, familiar in a way that makes my skin prickle. It slides to a quiet stop. A ghost by design.

Hex steps out of the truck, black shirt clinging to his chest, jeans hugging thighs built for murder.

Demi's jaw drops. "Oh, thank God you're here, Frank."

"Frank?" Hex questions, looking to me for some semblance of an answer.

I rub my temples. "She thinks you're The Punisher."

Hex lifts a brow. "Oh yeah? I can see that."

Demi claps. "SEE?! I knew you had Punisher energy!"

Hex lets out a quiet huff of laughter, shaking his head. Then he turns to her, nodding with a kind of unexpected grace.

"Hex Alvarez," he says, voice pitched low. He's polite, but far from soft. "Don't believe we've officially met."

Demi fans herself theatrically. "No, but I've heard plenty. You really should come with a warning label, sir."

He gives her half a smirk, then the shift is immediate. His expression darkens the moment he sees the broken lock. In one fluid move, he draws the gun from the waistband of his jeans, holds it low against his thigh, and turns to me with sharp intent.

"Stay behind me."

Demi edges closer, her voice tight. "Wait. He's got a gun. Do we seriously need to go in?"

"I have to know what happened. It's my shop," I whisper, following him in. "You can stay out here."

"Bitch, please," she mutters. "If you die, who's gonna narrate the sequel to your filthy little love story? No. I'll take a bullet for you. You've got multiple orgasms left to live."

I ignore the ridiculousness that is my best friend.

The front of the shop is a mess. A table's flipped, my vintage rug crumpled and crushed underfoot, and all the carefully placed details—sculptures, trays, bowls—have been tossed everywhere.

Hex sweeps through it methodically, clearing each space as we move behind him. His body tense. Protective.

When we make it into the workshop, air is stolen from my very lungs.

The three-piece antique armoire—the one I've spent weeks restoring, hours carving, gluing, and shaping with care—is destroyed. The center door lies in shards. One of the legs is completely split. Deep gashes cut through the delicate scrollwork I showed Hex just two days ago.

Something between a gasp and a sob escapes my throat. I didn't even know such a wretched sound lived inside me.

Hex turns immediately. "Shit," he says, stepping toward me, his voice suddenly gentle. "Sable, *fuck,* I'm so sorry."

Tears spring to my eyes as I crouch near the ruins. "This is commissioned work. It's already sold. I don't even know how I'm going to explain this to the client."

"I should've handled this better from the beginning," Hex says as he strokes a hand down his chin. His eyes sweep across the damage as though every wrecked piece is proof of his failure.

"Hex," I breathe, voice trembling. "This was never your—"

His head turns, and his brows pull together just slightly, eyes narrowed with intent. His jaw tightens, but it's not clenched in anger, but firm with conviction.

"It was always my problem," he says. "The second she made you feel unsafe, it became mine."

Demi, still crouched near a shattered drawer, throws a hand in the air. "Thank you! Now go full John Wick on this psycho. Fucking break this bitch's neck."

He ignores her. His attention is focused on me.

"I'm worried about you and your son's safety," he says, voice low but firm. "Close the shop for the day. Pick up Bash. Go home. Don't bring him here. Don't let him see this."

I nod, trying to breathe through the knot forming in my throat. "I will. I'll file a police report before I leave and call Andrew to explain what's going on. Maybe start the process for a temporary protective order."

Hex blows out a breath, the kind you release when the truth is on your tongue but better left unsaid. "You think a piece of paper is going to stop her?"

"It's a step," I say, sharper than I intend. "I have to try the legal way first. I'm not dragging Bash into something that could blow back harder because I skipped protocol."

His jaw ticks as if he doesn't agree, but he respects my wishes. "Andrew should file one too," he says after a beat. "Keep her away from both of you, and more importantly Bash. But I don't want you at your place tonight. Not alone."

Hex glances up at the corner of the room, eyes narrowing. "You've got cameras. I'll have JT pull the footage. If we're lucky, we can get a clear shot of her and hand it to the cops. Confirm everything with evidence."

Demi's eyebrows lift. "Wait, he can just, like... jump into someone's cameras? That's scary."

Hex expels something close to a laugh. "You have no idea how scary someone as smart as JT can be."

I blink at him, still in shock by everything happening around me. The chaos claws through my brain.

"I'll take the weekend away from the bar," he continues, wrapping a warm hand over my white-knuckled fist gripping my phone. "Will and JT can handle things. Come to the Hill Country with me. Just you and me, and the quiet. Space to breathe while we figure out the next step."

Demi steps up beside me, placing her hand on my back. "You should go," she says softly, surprising me. "You need to go."

I look at the wreckage around me. The shattered armoire. The ruined front.

And I nod.

I want peace. I want protection.

Andrew sits across from me at the kitchen table, a half-drunk soda between us. Bash is on the floor nearby, surrounded by colored pencils and a sketchpad, humming to himself while he draws some kind of superhero space battle.

The man I used to know intimately once told me he wanted to be a football coach. Said it with that same far-off tone he uses when talking about businesses he'll never start. I doubt he ever tried. He's a car sales manager now, which honestly tracks. He's always talked a big game. All vision. Paints a pretty picture with words. But there is no follow-through.

Maybe that's how he reeled in Ashley. He likely fed her promises he never meant to keep. Told her he'd give her the world. Maybe even promised he'd leave me.

Just words.

That's the thing about Andrew. He's good at sounding sincere. Good at giving just enough to be believed. But when it comes time to act, he always falls short.

I walk him through everything. My voice is quieter than usual, careful not to alarm Bash, even if the tightness in my chest still hasn't let up since I saw the destruction in the back of the shop.

When I tell him about Ashley, about the photos—to which he gets all awkward and grimaces at the thought of me with another man—the texts, and what she did to the armoire, his face goes pale.

"I didn't realize it got that bad," he says, rubbing a hand over the hair along his jaw. "I mean... yeah, I knew she was intense, but I didn't think she was capable of something of this caliber."

I arch a brow. "She's unstable, Andrew. She's stalking me. And she's been parked outside my shop day after day. Following me. She's following you too for God's sake."

"I didn't know," he says again, shaking his head. "I swear—she and I—we only hooked up once. Before we split. I... I regret it, Sable. I was in a bad place. I know that's no excuse."

I let that hang in the air. I've already done all the yelling, the crying, the untangling. I'm past it. This isn't about punishment. It's about protection. For my entire family. Andrew included.

He glances toward Bash, then back at me, voice hush. "I'll file the temporary restraining order. Whatever I need to do."

"Thank you."

Andrew blows out a long breath and scrubs his hands down his jeans. "I'll take Bash out to my parents' place for the weekend. Get him out of town, let things cool down." He turns his attention toward our son. "Hey, buddy. Want to go see Grandma Lynn and Grandpa Dale at the lake house?"

Bash jumps up, his face brightening at the idea. "Can I bring my tackle box?"

"Of course," Andrew says, ruffling his hair.

That small joy—the idea of my son casting a line off the dock, blissfully unaware of the storm circling the adults—is enough to soften the knot in my chest. A little.

Andrew stands, hesitating, like he wants to say something else but isn't sure if he's earned the right.

"For what it's worth... I'm really sorry, Sable. About all of it."

I nod. "I know."

But that's all it is. An apology. No solutions. No help. Regret wrapped in good intentions and not much else.

And maybe for once, I'm finally starting to see him clearly. Not just as the man who failed me, but the man who fooled both women.

He shifts his weight, one foot toward the door, the other still planted like he's trying to root himself back in this house.

"I don't know," he says slowly, "maybe we can... figure something out. Down the line. You know. Be a family again."

I stare at him.

Is he serious?

Now he wants to dangle hope? After his mistress has stalked me, after showing up empty-handed while I cleaned up his messes, raised his son, paid his bills, kept the whole damn operation afloat while running on nothing but caffeine and grit?

"You think this is *salvageable*?" I ask, not even trying to hide the disbelief in my voice.

He shrugs, eyes doing that thing where they soften just enough to pass for sincerity. "People change."

I want to hold hope that's true. That people can turn themselves inside out, choose better, be better.

But some don't. Some just get better at hiding the same rot. They wear your patience like a borrowed coat and call it love. Never again.

"Clearly, I'm seeing someone," I say.

That gets his attention. He blinks, sharp and quiet, like he wasn't expecting it.

"*Oh.*"

"It's turning into something serious," I add, because I don't need to explain what is going on between Hex and me. "He's good for me."

Andrew doesn't speak, but the disapproval rolls off him in waves. His expression manifests into the same look that used to make me shrink, explain myself, try to smooth things over.

Not today.

Hex has a past, but he owns it. He doesn't hide behind charm or delay responsibility until his woman's already breaking.

He's gray in a thousand ways, sure, but he's green in all the ones that count.

Green in how he shows up.

Green in how he listens.

Green in the way he looks at me, like I may just be enough.

Andrew? Red.

Red in his absence.

Red in his promises.

Red in every emergency he created and left for me to clean up.

And for the first time, I don't feel the need to explain that to him.

"Please let me know when you file the restraining order."

CHAPTER TWENTY-SIX

Alex

When the evening rolls in, Ruin's End becomes a blur of bodies, booze, and momentum that doesn't let up.

The bass thumps low from the speakers. The scent of spilled whiskey, lime, and anticipation settles over the bar as usual. The air's electric, bodies pressed shoulder to shoulder, and somewhere in the mix, someone's about to get too drunk, too bold, or too stupid.

Not my problem tonight.

I'm behind the bar with Will, who has his sleeves rolled up and a bottle in each hand. He takes three orders at once without breaking a sweat. He's wired differently. Got his shit together. Has the kind of hustle that earns you your place. He cleans with conviction, pours with precision.

He slides a vodka soda across the bar, then leans in slightly, keeping his tone casual. "She had a... surprise visitor today?"

My jaw flexes. "One of those rare bats. Real dark, nasty mouth on it. The disruptive type."

He winces. "Shit. One of those." He starts wiping down the bar even though it's already spotless. "I should've kept eyes out for an infestation."

"Not your job, Will," I mutter, tossing a coaster onto the counter a little too hard. "You work enough as it is."

"Still," he says, voice low, "I could've kept the roost clear."

"You don't owe her that," I say. "You don't owe me that."

From down the bar, Larry, a retired mechanic, rests his beer gut against the bar, anchoring him as he nurses his third Coors. Always smelling faintly of motor oil and menthols, he pipes up from his usual stool. "Did I just hear the word 'roost'? Don't tell me Hex is playing house now."

Next to him, Travis, proudly sporting a pair of mirrored aviators indoors and a mullet that looks hand-sculpted by gardening shears, lets out a sharp whistle. "So, when do we get more posts from you two? Been a while since we saw her on the feed. Maybe she came to her senses?"

"Yeah, baby," Connie chimes in, raising her margarita. She's parked at the corner with her ever-present leopard print hoodie zipped halfway over a rhinestone-studded tank top. Her slippers are fluffy, pink, and criminally bold. JT lets her in regardless of what she's wearing because she brings him cannabis-infused treats. "Give the people what they want! Some small-town PG content is all I'm asking for... or more if you're willing." She winks and tips her marg in my direction. It sloshes out, and I feel Will's eyes home in on the mess.

I grab a rag and chuckle, trying to shake it off. "You all spend more time on my social page than I do."

"You got the most exciting love life in this zip code," someone calls out.

Will snorts. "That's not saying much."

"Hey, speak for yourself," says a woman nursing a paloma. "I personally look forward to Sable appearances. She makes you tolerable."

"Thanks, Jules," I say dryly. "Glad she's improving your experience."

"She makes you smile. That's worth tipping a little extra."

Will raises a brow at me as he passes. "Sable coming in tonight? This place might riot."

I dry my hands on a bar towel, still running hot under the surface. "I'm taking her out of town. Hill Country. Just for the weekend."

Will glances up. "A getaway?"

"Something like that." I flick my gaze toward the door. "She needs a break. From the bats."

He nods, catching the meaning. "You too."

"Yeah." I pause, pressing my palms into the edge of the counter. "Even I'm getting tired of chasing them off."

From down the bar, the same camo-hat regular pipes up again. "Bat problem? You know what you need for that? Shotgun. Buckshot spray. Ain't gotta be a good shot if the spread's wide enough. Those fuckers are fast."

Will and I both stop and look at him.

He takes a sip of his whiskey, completely serious.

Will shakes his head. "You know... not the worst suggestion."

I grunt. "We'll call that Plan Z."

Will chuckles and nods toward the register. "I've got the bar. Macy's coming in at seven."

"She ready for a Friday?"

"She's got it. Cute, edgy, but sharp. Dreads, ink, piercings." Will trails his eyes over our regulars. "She fits in. More importantly, she slings drinks clean, fast, and with zero drama. Doesn't blink twice at a busy shift."

I give him a look. "You trust her already?"

He shrugs. "I trained her myself. Girl knows her pour counts better than most of the guys we've had here for two years. Hustles harder too."

I nod. "Good."

Will slaps the towel on the counter. "Go. Relax. You look one bourbon away from making a mistake."

"You're not wrong."

"Tell Sable the bar says hi."

From a nearby table, one of the younger guys grins. "Yeah, when are we getting more posts of her anyway? She dropped off the grid or just hiding from us?"

Another voice chimes in. "She's too hot for him, that's why. He's keeping her off the feed to maintain the illusion she still exists."

The laughter rolls easy, and I shake my head, a reluctant smirk tugging at my mouth. "You all need hobbies."

"Watching your love life is our hobby," someone calls back.

"Told you." Will leans in with a crooked smile. "This place might riot if she doesn't make another appearance soon."

JT steps out from the back, hoodie slung low, phone in hand, face grim. His eyes cut straight to me.

I know that look.

I move out from behind the bar, wiping my hands down my jeans as I follow him toward the stockroom. It's quieter here, but only just. JT slides his phone into his pocket, arms folded, jaw clenched.

"What is it?"

He leans against the shelf. "Stauder's sniffing. Not the cops—yet. But there's pressure. Someone in Brandon Dillinger's circle started asking questions about that Friday he was here."

My spine goes tight.

"He was nothing but a fucking problem," I say. "And a rapist."

I drag a hand down my face, making sense of the pressure. I think out loud, "But Ned only cares about profit. If Dillinger helped launder money through Stauder's shell companies and is now missing, their dirty money flow has gotten sticky."

JT nods. "Exactly. And I've got eyes on Ned. He's pissed. Texts between him and one of his guys say he suspects you had something to do with it. He's not dumb."

"But he doesn't have proof." I cross my arms, mind already spinning. "Cameras were down. Alibi's solid."

"But Stauder's boys are getting twitchy," JT points out. "You know they don't care about proof."

Will joins us, wiping his hands on his ever-trusty rag. "So what's the play?"

I exhale with force. "This is the worst time to leave. But I'm not going far. If anything shifts—if anyone from Stauder's crew so much as breathes near this bar—I want to know."

"We got it," Will says without hesitation.

"I mean it," I say, tone hardening. "You see someone shady? You don't wait. You call me. I'll come back."

JT raises a brow. "You sure about going?"

"No," I say honestly. "But I gave her my word. She needs a break. She needs to feel safe. And after what Ashley did to her shop... this weekend isn't optional."

Will gives a rare, serious nod. "She's good for you, man."

JT smirks. "Yeah, she might actually help you sleep with both eyes closed."

I crack my knuckles and grab the duffel I left in the office. It's not packed light. I've got extra clothes, my Glock, the backup piece, burner phone, and enough cash to disappear if anything were to go sideways while away.

Sable doesn't need to know that possibility exists. Not yet.

I take one last look around the bar. The regulars are loud, laughing, a couple of them dancing near the jukebox. Business as usual. Exactly what I want.

"You good?" JT asks as I start for the door.

"I've got something to protect," I say without hesitation.

He grins. "Then go protect her. We'll handle it here."

I pause, turn. "And if Ned's people make a move?"

JT's face goes hard. "We move faster."

Good.

I push through the back door and head straight into another restless Friday night.

The road winds through rolling hills, draped in soft spring green, dotted with bluebonnets and wild poppies that hold the remaining sun in their petals. The truck hums beneath us, tires kissing the asphalt in a steady rhythm as the clutter of town falls away behind us.

Sable hasn't said much since we pulled out of her driveway. Her hands sit quiet in her lap, fingers twisting the edge of her shirt sleeve. Her body's here, but her mind's still caught in the shop mayhem or the conversation she had with Andrew.

"You good?" I ask, keeping my eyes on the road, letting the question remain light.

She exhales, long and low. "I don't know. I think so. Maybe."

I glance at her.

She's staring out the window. "It all just got so out of hand. I'm not trying to start a pity party, but... damn, Hex. I've been trying to do everything right. I put myself through school. I built my businesses from the ground up. I worked my ass off to make my life into something that mattered—"

She pauses, and I don't fill the silence.

"But, somehow, I still ended up with a love life that compares to a car crash. Or maybe a really shitty reality show. And I can't say I regret it. I got Bash out of it, and he's everything. But... why does it feel like I keep getting the shit end of the stick no matter how hard I try?"

"Because life's an unfair bastard," I say, keeping my eyes on the road. "Doesn't matter how good your intentions are—sometimes you're just the one it decides to take swings at."

I watch color bleed through the crisp blue sky outside the windshield as night approaches. Long strokes of rust and lavender pour across the Hill Country horizon. We haven't passed another car in ten minutes. It's just us and the winding two-lane roads that snakes through fields of mesquite and passes low stone fences that haven't held a damn thing in decades. Everything out here has been weathered slow. Nothing forced. Nothing fake.

Sable props her elbow against the passenger door, cheek resting in her hand. Her other hand picks at the fray in her jeans where a hole has formed—absently, the way people do when they're trying not to think too loud. The soft light of evening slants across her profile, catching in the curve of her jaw, the loose strands of dark brown hair she didn't bother to tie back. The exhaustion etched in her posture, her eyes, her lips, mimics the one I'm all too familiar with. The kind of fatigue that lives in your bones.

"My dad left when I was eighteen," she says, voice barely above the hum of the road. "Just... gone."

I keep my eyes on the pavement. I listen.

"My parents split, and he decided the version of me that didn't need him anymore wasn't the version he wanted in his new life." Her laugh is quiet and bitter. "Independent daughters with opinions don't fit well in starter families."

She looks at me, almost wincing, as though realizing too late that her honesty might paint her in a way she's not ready to wear. But it doesn't sound angry to me. It's real.

My fingers tighten around the steering wheel. "We both had to grow up at eighteen. I took on my little brother when my mom died. I didn't really get a say."

Sable turns fully to face me then, pulling her leg up into the seat, one arm curled around her knee. Her eyes are wide, glassy at the edges, catching every bit of light. "God, I shouldn't have brought that up. My story is melodramatic compared to—"

"No." I shake my head, jaw set. "Don't do that."

"But—"

234

"Don't," I say again, softer this time. "Your story means something. All stories do. Doesn't matter if they're brutal or quiet or messy or clean. They're real. And I've got the feeling no one's really listened to yours in a long time."

She doesn't speak. Just stares, caught in the space between understanding and denial. Hearing me say it is one thing but believing that I mean it is something else entirely.

The truck cab goes still. The road, tires, and evening wind are the only sounds enveloping our space.

"I think I've spent most of my life taking what I can get," she says finally, voice cracking at the edges, "then holding on for dear life. Because I figured if I didn't, I'd end up with nothing. If your father can so easily walk away, any man can. I just kept doing more and more in an effort to try and get people to want to stay."

She shifts, swallowing hard, fingers curling tighter against her knee.

"I don't want to do that with you," she adds. "But I don't know what this is. And honestly? I'm off to one hell of a start."

I glance at her, eyes dragging over the way she's drawn in on herself. There is so much fire in this woman, who keeps waiting to be told she's too much of something. Or not enough of something else.

"Maybe we don't need a name for it yet," I say quietly. "You just show up. I'll meet you there."

She lets out a shaky breath, like she's still bracing for the catch.

So.

"I don't want what's easy, Sable." I lean onto the center console, voice steady. "I want what's *real*. The kind of real that's messy. Unfinished. Still figuring it out."

I watch her closely as I continue, "You don't have to earn me. You don't have to hold your breath or shrink yourself down just so I'll stay."

Her head tips slightly, eyes glassy but focused on me.

"You show up with all your sharp edges and I'll keep showing up with steady hands. That's the deal."

She blinks, slow.

I reach out, my hand resting over hers, thumb brushing that tight curl of her fingers.

"I don't need you perfect. I just need you. And you've already given me more of that than most people ever do."

Her mouth pulls tight, ensnared within a fragile space between laughter and tears, unsure which emotion will win. She presses her lips together and blinks hard. "You're gonna ruin me if you keep saying those kinds of things."

I smirk, but it's softer now. Quieter. "Pretty sure we're already ruined, Sable."

She glances at me, breath hitching.

I squeeze the delicate hand below mine. "The point is finding someone who'll walk out of the ruin with you."

The air in the cab shifts. Not fixed. But less sharp and easier to breathe.

Outside, the land opens wide around us. Rolling hills unfurl under a cotton-candy sky, dotted with wind-gnarled oaks and ranch gates rusted with stories. It's quiet in a way that feels earned.

And for the first time since we left, Sable exhales the kind of breath you don't fake. The kind that says she's finally letting some of it go.

CHAPTER TWENTY-SEVEN

Sable

The house greeted us with a hush so profound, it felt as if the world had paused at its threshold. Beyond the creaking door, silence pooled the way it only can in a place this remote.

I take a step inside and just... stop.

The place smells of cedar, leather, and something warm and lived in. Vaulted ceilings with exposed beams stretch overhead. The walls are all-natural wood and stone, textured and imperfect in a way that feels honest. Everything's rich but minimal—thick rugs underfoot, a leather sectional that belongs in a whiskey ad, and a fireplace that demands attention even when it's not lit. There's no TV in sight, just the peace of good design and windows that pour the Hill Country right into the room.

"This is..." I trail off, turning in a slow circle. "This is insane, Hex."

He drops the keys in a dish near the door and glances over at me. "Good insane?"

"The best kind."

He reaches for my overnight bag and heads down the hall. "Bedroom's this way."

Hex disappears down the window lined corridor with my belongings. I trail behind him, feet sinking into velvet carpet, stepping into a room that whispers bedtime stories with a wicked twist. The bed is massive, all dark wood and soft linen. Windows frame a sweeping view of the enormous trees outside—towering oaks and knotted cedars with branches that twist like old hands.

He sets the bag at the foot of the bed. "Hope it's not too presumptuous that I figured we'd share a room."

I lift a brow. "After whisking me out to the middle of nowhere with your arms, your bourbon, and your woodsy candle smells? I'm all yours."

He chuckles, shaking his head. "Fair."

I fold my arms across my chest and square my stance near the foot of the bed. "Okay. Here's the deal. If we're doing this, I've got needs."

Hex glances up from where he's unzipping one of his bags. "Needs?"

"Air conditioning at sixty-eight. Non-negotiable. I wake up in night sweats more often than I care to admit."

He stands, tossing a hoodie onto the nearby chair. "Done. I sweat too."

"I need the side closest to the bathroom," I say, circling around the bed, pressing my palm against the mattress to test the give. "Because aging is brutal, and I get up to pee. Twice. Minimum."

"Understood."

"And I sleep in a fortress of pillows." I reach for the tote of pillows I brought in and start stacking them on my side. "One between the knees, one behind the back, one I hang onto for dear life. Helps with the aches and pains. Don't judge."

"I wouldn't dream of it."

I pause with a pillow tucked under one arm, eyeing him. "Also, sometimes I wake up talking. Or snoring. Or both. Getting older isn't exactly a seductive transformation."

He crosses the room at a casual pace, posture loose but attentive, and rests his shoulder against the doorframe. "I think that's cute."

I shake my head, a short, embarrassingly *me,* snort escaping before I can stop it. "You're only saying that because you haven't heard it in action."

He smiles, easy and steady, then steps forward and grabs one of my pillows, fluffing it with an exaggerated seriousness. "Well, I guess we'll both find out soon enough."

I press the back of my hand to my forehead in mock despair. "You're not ready."

He shrugs. "Try me."

Sliding the pillow onto the bed, he brushes past me in the process. "You're talking to a man who wears compression socks on long drives and cracks his back every time he gets out of bed. I've started stretching before sleep, chasing peak performance in the sport of unconsciousness.

So, trust me when I say our *boats* look so similar they might as well be the same."

I laugh, and it surprises me how good it feels. The tension between my shoulders starts to loosen, inch by inch.

Since our conversation in the truck, my realization grows, strengthens with each passing moment—he gets it. Aging jokes and sleep quirks aside. He accepts my guardedness. The weariness that has built up after years of being the one who holds everything together. The understanding from him makes me think I don't have to do that with him. I could let go—really let go—with someone.

The idea of dating, of getting close enough to let someone see the raw, uncurated version of me... it's always felt like a risk I couldn't afford. But standing here, with him, in this quiet house tucked away from the world, that risk doesn't feel quite so terrifying.

Getting intimate again—truly intimate, walls down, breath for breath—doesn't feel impossible anymore.

It might actually be good.

Really good.

We head back out to the kitchen that glows soft in the overhead light. It's clean, serene, and warm in a way that doesn't feel accidental. I halt near the island, eyes drifting over the exposed shelving, the dark slate countertops, the old butcher block built into the cabinetry. Every detail looks custom, handpicked by someone who knew exactly what kind of peace they were trying to build.

"This place is..." I turn slowly, taking it in again. "It's an escape?"

Hex pours two glasses of water from a filtered carafe chilled in the fridge, then leans against the counter opposite me. "Peace is hard to come by. Took me a long time to afford the kind that doesn't come with strings attached."

"Did you grow up in Stillwater Bend?" I ask, curious to learn more about him.

He shakes his head. "No. Town called Red Bluff. About fifteen miles south."

"Close enough to count, but far enough to keep secrets," I say quietly.

He doesn't laugh, just nods.

"I never knew my dad," he says. "JT's my half-brother. His dad stuck around for a little while longer than mine, but men never really stayed in our house. My mom had a thing for the wrong ones."

His jaw tenses, and I know where this is going before he says the name.

"The worst of them, Ned Stauder."

I set my glass down and lean against the island, facing him.

"She worked at a diner. Waitress. He walked in one night, and said he'd change her life." He huffs. "He did that alright."

My heart's already sinking, but I ask anyway. "How did she die?"

"She OD'd. When I said he orchestrated everything, he had his guys stage the scene so it couldn't be traced back to him. Cops took one look and wrote her off as a junkie that didn't matter." His nostrils flare as if reliving the memory. The injustice. "But she'd never touched anything before him. Not one pill. Not one line."

I allow a beat to pass, processing something I have no real-life understanding of.

"JT was ten. Bash's age," he says, the smallest hint of a smile tugging at his mouth as if he let in a fleeting memory of his brother back when things were still innocent. "I did what I had to. Took care of him the best

241

I knew how at eighteen. But we didn't have shit. No money, no support. Then Ned showed back up. Said there were ways to make cash fast."

I'm engrossed by his words, but hearing this story from his mouth makes my stomach twist.

Not just because of what he lived through—though that alone is enough to wreck me—but because of the calm strength in how he tells it. There's no dramatics. No self-pity. Just a man who was forced to grow up too fast and never looked back.

"Fighting," he says, voice low and flat. Almost hollow. "Started in garages that turned into cages. Concrete floors. Fluorescent lights buzzing overhead. Just fists and the will to live to see another fight. Another dollar. If there were any rules, they changed depending on who had money riding on it."

His gaze is far away now, locked on a point behind me.

"Word spread. Bets got bigger. Rounds got bloodier. I kept winning, and every win meant more cash in Ned's pocket. He called me his golden investment."

He stops cold, jaw clenched, throat moving with the effort of choking down whatever's clawing its way up.

"One fight... the worst one." His eyes flicker. "They imported a guy for the job. Hands wrapped in steel-threaded tape. Illegal as hell. Didn't matter. Nobody monitored anything. Or if they did, they got paid to keep their mouths shut."

His posture falters for a second, the kind of movement that says pain still lives under the surface. Maybe it always will.

"He hit me in the ribs first. I felt something give—heard it, actually. Then he went for my face. Broke my nose. Split my cheek wide open.

Nearly lost my left eye. I was choking on my own blood before the first round ended."

I cover my mouth, stomach turning. He keeps going.

"They dumped me in a warehouse after. Left me on the floor, half-conscious, bleeding out. Cold concrete under me, blood soaking through my shirt, pooling around me like it meant nothing. Like I meant nothing."

A beat of silence.

"But I lived," he says simply. "And I made a deal."

I swallow hard. "A deal?"

I watch his profile as he speaks, the hardness in his jaw, the calm behind his eyes. He's beautiful in a way that shouldn't make sense for someone with blood on his hands. A man who's dangerous by necessity, not by nature. And yet, here he is—offering me the truth. Peeling back the layers with nothing to gain from it.

"I told Ned I'd fight him again. Same guy. No medics. No rules. Just me and him. Everyone would be betting against me after the beating I took. And if I survived a second time, he'd get his pay out and clear everything. JT and I would walk. No debt, no favors. I keep my fair cut. He never speaks my name again."

My voice barely comes out. "And he agreed to that?"

Hex nods once. "He didn't think I'd survive. That's why he said yes. Even made a few bets against me."

"But you did."

He holds my gaze, the weight of truth in his eyes. "Barely. Took everything I had to stay upright. I could feel bones grinding. Thought my lung might've collapsed. Will and JT found me after. They helped patch me up the best they could. Took months to heal. But I did it."

He pauses and glances around the kitchen, eyes landing on the windows that open out to the dark stretch of trees. "Used the winnings to buy this place. Built something that couldn't be taken from me. Got out of Red Bluff. Got JT and I out from under Ned."

"And bought the bar."

He nods again. "Bought it not long after. Took every cent I had left. Poured it all in. Turned it into Ruin's End." His mouth curves into something that's not quite a smile, but close. "Made it a safe place for good people who really needed help."

There's a vulnerability in that I wasn't expecting. And something in me aches.

He protected his brother the way I protect Bash. On instinct. Without question. He made sacrifices I can't even begin to imagine. And while the choices he made afterward, for others in need, might be morally gray—or pitch black—there's no denying the heart behind them.

I feel it in my chest, low and warm and terrifying. Because it's been a long time since I let myself feel this much for someone new. And even longer since I've looked at a man and thought—

He might understand me. Not just tolerate the disarray or the walls but actually *see* me.

And still choose to stay.

Because he fights.

I step closer, the sound of my boots soft against the tile. The air between us shifts, filling with something unspoken that's been building since we crossed the county line.

My fingers graze the edge of the counter as I come around, grounding myself before reaching out. I rest my hand near his, close enough to feel the warmth radiating from his skin but not touching.

"You've been through hell, Hex," I whisper, the words slipping out with my breath.

Then I close the distance between us, stepping into his space with the ease of someone who knows exactly where they fit. My arms wrap around his solid frame, folding into the kind of embrace that says, *I see you too. I'm not going anywhere.*

His chest rises against me, then stills, and for a second, I'm sure he's forgotten how to breathe.

He doesn't tense. Doesn't pull away.

With a crawling calm, he leans back just enough to look down at me. And the look he gives me isn't one I've seen before. It's not the kind that makes your stomach flip or your pulse jump. It's quieter. Still. Like I've reached some place in him no one else has, and he's finally letting it be seen.

No fire.

No flirtation.

Just recognition.

The kind that settles deep in your bones.

And right there—in the soft hum of the kitchen, in the warmth of his arms and the steady, unshakable way he's looking at me—every hesitation I've carried about what this might be between us... falls away.

The night grows legs. We snack on a few things he has at the house and move to the back patio. The air is cooler now, darkness stretching out for miles. He pours bourbon for us and nods toward a big, worn chair nestled in the corner.

"That's my spot," he says. "Best seat in the whole house."

I settle in the chair across from him, quiet between us, twilight stretching soft and blue over the hills.

"I don't want her dead," I confess suddenly. "Ashley. I mean it."

He nods. "I know."

"I think... I want to believe she's redeemable. She's not evil. She's just... lost. Hurt. And she hurts people because that's what she knows."

"You've got a generous heart, Sable"—he tilts the glass, letting the amber roll with the light—"but deep down, you know people like that don't change. They learn how to pretend better. Then they hurt again. Hurt worse. And usually, the people trying to save them are the ones who bleed." He lets a moment pass before adding, "Tell me that doesn't sound familiar."

I shift, the words settling under my skin. Not harsh. Not meant to be. But heavy.

"Her and Andrew are perfect for one another," I murmur. "It's so fucked up."

He looks over at me, eyes steady. "I know. And the fact that it bothers you says a lot about you—about the kind of person you are. You need things to be fixable. Believing in redemption feels safer than accepting some people just... won't ever choose it."

He's not wrong.

The truth of it slides between my ribs. It's gentle, but sharp enough to make me feel exposed. Andrew's excuses, my father's absence, wearing myself down to threads just to hand someone another chance.

I sip my bourbon, the warmth of it trailing down my throat, centering me. My eyes drift toward the trees, thick silhouettes swaying in the evening breeze. I focus on them. On the quiet. On the way this place seems to hold space for people like us. People worn out, still trying.

Hex doesn't press. He just lets me sit with my thoughts.

And maybe that's what softens me most.

After a minute, he adjusts in his seat, voice lower now. "Come here."

I glance at him.

He pats the chair next to him. It's worn-in, oversized, the kind of seat that invites comfort. I move to him, drawn in by something instinctive, curling into his lap.

"This really is the best seat."

His arms close around me, a barrier against everything else, and for once, I let someone just hold me.

His chest is firm and warm against my cheek. I feel the steady beat of his heart, the measured rhythm of his breathing. One of his hands finds the nape of my neck, fingers sinking into my hair. The other rests just above the small of my back.

The silence stretches again, but this time, it's not empty.

It's filled with care.

Hex doesn't try to change my mind about Ashley. Doesn't drown me in comfort or reach for the right thing to say. He just holds me as if I'm something worth keeping, even when I have nothing left to give. Even when I'm tired. Frayed. Not strong, not shining. Just... me.

And somewhere between the hum of the crickets outside and the warmth of him wrapped around me, the thoughts start to drift.

I stop bracing. I stop replaying.

Eventually, I stop thinking altogether.

I just sleep.

CHAPTER
TWENTY-EIGHT

Sable

P ale golden light stretches across the ceiling in soft ribbons.

I'm in bed.

Barefoot, but in yesterday's clothes, and stretched across crisp sheets that carry the scent of cedar, laundry soap, and something distinctly him.

It takes me a second to register how I got here.

The last thing I remember is bourbon on my tongue, the slow thump of his heartbeat beneath my cheek, the sound of crickets, and the occasional rustle of leaves. I must've fallen asleep on him out on that oversized chair. And he—*God*—he must've carried me to bed. Didn't wake me. Just let me sleep.

My heart folds in on itself a little.

I glance to my right. The other side of the bed is empty, but the warmth lingers in the rumpled sheets, a silent trace of where he'd been. There's a faint indentation on the pillow, and I swear, I can almost remember it. A dream-like impression of arms around me. Of being held. Of not waking once all night.

Which is insane.

I always wake up. *Always.* Usually twice, thanks to my bladder and the lovely curse of being a woman nearing forty.

I blink again and smile, dazed and soft.

"Damn it," I murmur to the quiet room. "I missed our first night actually sleeping in the same bed."

I press my face into the pillow, indulging in the kind of childish pout reserved for teenage crushes, even as the ache in my back from sleeping in jeans pulls me back to reality. Definitely not a sexy wake-up moment.

Somewhere in the distance of the house, I hear faint movement. A low clink of glass or maybe a cupboard door closing.

I throw the covers off and pad across the cushioned carpet toward the bathroom.

When I catch sight of myself in the mirror, I stop.

Jesus.

My mascara's done some kind of modern art beneath my eyes, and my hair looks freshly humiliated by a gust of wind.

I quickly run a comb through it, then brush my teeth using the travel kit I brought. A minty reset helps, but when I blink up at my reflection again, my eyes feel... wrong. Dry. Burned. Almost crunchy.

Contacts. *Fuck.*

I peel them off my eyeballs with a dramatic wince and hurl them into the trash with all the flair of banishing a demon. From the side pouch of my cosmetics bag, I dig out the glasses I always mean to wear before bed but never do. They're slightly crooked from being crammed in a case too long, but they'll do.

I take one more breath and stare at myself again, hands pressed to the edge of the counter.

"Don't overthink it," I whisper to the woman in the mirror. "Just... don't."

Because for once, there's nothing to fix. Nothing to manage. Just a man in the kitchen who let me sleep in his arms, carried me to bed without making a thing of it, and left the morning to start gently.

And for me?

That might be scarier than anything.

The floors are warm under my feet as I tiptoe toward the kitchen, trying not to make a sound. Not sure why I'm sneaking. Maybe it's because I don't want to interrupt the calm, or maybe it's because I'm hoping to catch an unfiltered, unguarded glimpse of him.

And *oh, do I.*

Hex is standing at the stove, flipping pancakes with the kind of focus that suggests he takes his breakfast as serious as his bourbon. He's shirtless and I watch as his broad back flexes with every movement. And those thick arms are some kind of walking thirst trap with a spatula. Gray sweatpants hang loose and low on his hips, just enough to make me rethink every responsible thought I've ever had.

Arguably the sexiest man I've ever seen... making pancakes.

My ovaries write a strongly worded letter to my self-control.

"Morning," I manage, voice a little hoarse.

He glances back over his shoulder and smirks, unapologetically slow about it. "Well look who's up. I was just about to come check if you were still breathing."

"I didn't want to leave the bed, in hopes you'd come back to it," I admit, leaning on the counter, arms crossed.

I'm trying to seem chill and not like I've forgotten how basic motor functions work.

"You like my bed," he says, flipping a pancake with ease. Not a question. "Where I might add, you were fully clothed and drooling on my pillow."

I hard blink, or just shut my eyes as if it will expel the embarrassing thought. "I drooled?"

He grins. "Only a little. It was cute. You make this little sound when you're really out. Kind of a cross between a sigh and a grumble."

"I do not grumble in my sleep." I inhale all the air in the room and hold it.

"You sure?" A dark eyebrow arches.

I let it out and let the embarrassment go with it.

"You're on thin ice, Pancake Man," I say with a wink.

He plates a cake with ease and turns, leaning a hip against the counter. "What can I say? I just happened to have all the ingredients. No whipped cream though." He grins. *That grin.* The one that curves a little wickedly at the edge.

Heat rushes straight between my legs at the memory of the bar... of the *lunch-that-wasn't.*

I blush. Hard. Then clench my thighs as if that will hold the wetness in.

Hex's eyes flick down for a half second before lifting back to mine, amusement dancing at the corners where I notice the hint of a wrinkle.

"Shame," I say, playing it cool, "whipped cream really turns things into a good time."

His smile deepens. "Next time, I'll plan ahead."

I shake my head, taking a seat on a barstool and pretending not to be weak in the knees.

He tilts his head.

"You suppose to be wearing glasses all the time?" he asks. "This is the second time I've caught you with them."

"No," I mumble. "Just... my contacts betrayed me."

He steps in to crowd my space, and that makes my pulse tick faster. Then he reaches up and plucks the glasses off my face with ease.

"Hey—"

He slides them over the bridge of his nose and squints out the window. "Damn! You're fucking blind, Sable."

The glasses are so crooked on him, I can't help but laugh. He's giving smoldering librarian who moonlights as a barroom brawler. "Give those back before you hurt yourself."

"Do you need to register these as a visual disability?" he teases, handing them back.

I slip them on, cheeks still warm and smile feeling permanent. "Don't knock it. They give me depth perception. And yes, I can't drive without some sort of correction."

"Well, now that you can see, have a go at these pancakes." He passes me a plate. "Get ready to be impressed."

I raise an eyebrow. "I hope you don't expect me to eat ten of these. That was a one-time thing."

A waft of hazelnut reaches my nose, steam curling from the coffee mug he sets beside my plate. "Nah, just two. Maybe three. I like knowing I can out-eat you. It's humbling... for you."

I take a bite, instantly impressed by the vanilla and hint of cinnamon caressing my taste buds. "You wish."

Hex leans in, eyes flicking down, then dragging back up with unhurried purpose. "I don't have to wish. I know I'm good at eating."

Oh, we're not talking about food anymore.

"You've felt it firsthand. Twice." He doesn't break. Doesn't smirk or wink like an amateur. He just *delivers* the line, calm and lethal, fully aware of what it does to me.

Heat pulses through me so fast I almost forget to chew.

"If we're keeping score..." he adds, "I'm ahead by one. But I'm happy to selflessly give you your third to keep my lead."

My mouth goes dry. My thighs press together like they're answering a call before my brain has even realized it.

"*Jesus,*" I murmur, almost to myself. "You're real slick, huh?"

He shrugs. "I'm good at what I do. And you, Legs, like it slick. If you didn't, you wouldn't be squeezing so tight under the counter."

I shoot him a glare, or try to, but my smile betrays me. I'm blushing. Burning. Ready to melt into this stool.

We eat the rest of breakfast in silence, but the air vibrates with tension. His eyes keep finding mine. And every time they do, my body responds, waiting for the next move.

When I finally push my plate back, Hex is up and already rinsing his, grabbing for mine too.

"I got this," he says. "Go get dressed. Something comfortable."

"Where are we going?" I ask.

He dries his hands, gaze drifting to the window, measuring the daylight. "Somewhere close. Somewhere you'll like. Thought we'd take advantage of spring before the sun turns everything worth doing outside into a trip to hell."

I eye him, curious. "That's not an answer."

"That's all you're getting." He tosses the towel he used over his shoulder.

I start walking out of the kitchen but stop to look back at him. "If I get my third today, don't expect me to be surprised."

Hex grins that stupidly sexy grin, eyes stroking me with heat. "I don't want surprised. I want you begging."

I disappear into the hallway before he can see what his words do to me.

We return from our day out just as the sky starts blushing into dusk, the air still comfortably warm and soft around us. My hands are only half-full. Hex insisted on carrying the heavier bags, leaving me with the jar of wildflower honey, a sage colored linen sachet I didn't need but wanted, and a half-melted chocolate bar from a roadside market that we'd already cracked open somewhere between enjoying ourselves and too much laughter.

The sachet smells of cedar and bourbon, something earthy and sweet that reminded me of him the second I picked it up. I didn't even hesitate to buy it.

"I want my sheets to smell like this," I'd told him in the little shop, turning the sachet over in my hand and raising it to my nose. *"Smells like you."*

He'd leaned close, voice low enough to make the shopkeeper pretend she wasn't listening. *"I'd happily rub myself all over your sheets to make that happen."*

The thought of this beautiful man spread out all over... *"I'll take that too."*

So now, walking back into his house with that scent tucked under my arm, I already feel a little more tethered to him. Like the day threaded something unexpected between us, something I want to keep for an indeterminable amount of time.

I pause in the entryway, reluctant to let the last few hours go.

Hex nudges the door shut behind me with his boot, sets the bags down, and slides his arms around my waist.

"Thank you," I murmur, resting my hands against his chest. "For today. I can't remember the last time I let myself just... *be.*"

He kisses my forehead and doesn't move. Warmth from his breath brushes against my skin, as if staying there could freeze this moment in time. "You make it easy."

I lean back to look at him, and he must see a softness return to my face because his expression shifts. It's the permission he needs, letting him know the stress of the week is coming to an end and I'm ready to relax. His eyes dip past my lips and toward my breasts. His fingers curl into my waist. "Been thinking about how I want to give you number three since breakfast," he says quietly.

I let out a breathy moan as his warm mouth moves just under the lobe of my ear. "You really don't let things go."

My feet leave the floor as he lifts me without warning, arms secure beneath my thighs. "Not when it's something I want this bad."

I wrap my arms around his neck, letting myself be carried, not just in the literal sense. He is picking up the weight of my body, sure, but also the weight of my stress, the weight of my trauma, and handling it with such care, I cannot help but be stolen away by this man. There's something grounding about being held like this, about the confidence in his touch. I've needed this for so long.

Inside the bedroom, the light is low, a hush as the evening begins to settle. He sets me down gently at the foot of the bed, but when I move to reach for him, he grabs my outstretched hand. He sits instead, pulling me into his lap and guiding my legs around his hips.

Hex's hands stay grasped onto my body, steadying me. "Before we do this," voice low as it slithers over my skin, "I've got a condom. I got tested a while back. Haven't been with anyone since."

I nod, threading my fingers behind his neck and into the short hair I've been dying to feel again. "I have an IUD. I got tested after I found out about Andrew. I'm good."

His brow lifts. "You want to skip the condom?"

"*Abso-fucking-lutely.*"

But even as I say it, something must flicker across my face, because his hand comes up to brush my hair back behind my shoulder.

"You sure you're ready?" he asks. "We can take things slow. I noticed your hesitation when I told you to take your leggings off the other day."

I bite the inside of my cheek, stomach tightening.

Of course he *saw* me overthinking.

Because even when I swear I'm playing it cool, that nervous static still hums beneath my skin. I want this—God, I want *him*—but my brain?

It doesn't always listen to my body. Not when it comes to sex. Not when it comes to letting go.

"It's not that I don't want to." I try to smile, soft and wry, like I can pass it off as casual. "I'm thirty-nine, for fuck's sake. I should be past this."

But the truth rushes in before I can stop it.

"I've never fully let go," I admit, the truth catching in my throat. "Not even with Andrew. Ten years, and I still held a part of myself back every single time. There's always been this voice in my head. A tight grip I can't unclench."

A calloused thumb brushes against my cheek. "What does it say?"

"That I'm not enough." The answer tumbles out of me as if the dam finally broke. "That if I let someone see *all* of me—my need, my mess, the way I lose myself in pleasure—they'll pull away. That I'll get left." I pause, a wave of shame threatening to rise, but I ride it out. "I stay in control. I make jokes. I stay sharp. I prove I'm worth keeping around in all the ways that don't risk breaking my heart."

I place my hand gently on my chest, then slowly lower it down my body, feeling the heat beneath my skin. "But I know that version of me—the one who can let go—exists. I feel her when you touch me. When you look at me like I'm already known." My voice softens to a whisper. "You get me so wet it scares me. The way I crave you... it's like my body knew you were coming. And now all I want is to finally exhale. And breathe you in."

Hex leans in until our foreheads meet, his voice caressing my lips. "Then that's what we'll do. We'll breathe. Together. I want you to be completely comfortable. Confident. That comes from trust."

I nod. "I do trust you."

"No." He draws the word out and tilts his head, gaze never breaking from mine. "You say that. But I've learned something about trust, Sable. It's not about words."

He pauses. With two fingers, he lifts my chin. "I'm not gonna tell you I won't hurt you."

The words instantly bruise.

They knock the air out of me, faster than I can hide it. My heart stutters. Every old wound flares hot. The abandonment. The rejection. The hollow ache of promises that meant nothing.

Not again. I can't do this again.

I start to pull back, my hands pressing against his chest like I'm about to climb off, save myself before I fall. Before he can leave me half-broken, trying to pretend I'm fine.

But his hands don't let me go.

Hex catches my ass in a firm grip, dragging me forward until I'm flush against him, straddling the unmistakable hardness of his length.

A small whimper escapes my lips.

He doesn't even flinch, doesn't apologize. He just holds me there, locked to him. And when his voice comes again, it's steel wrapped in velvet.

"What I mean is... I won't *say* it. Because saying it doesn't mean shit. But I'll *show* you. Every day. Over and over." His eyes burn into mine. "Trust is earned through action. Consistent. Constant action."

And then—*God*—he grinds his hips up just enough to remind me what's pressed between us.

Hard. Unapologetic. Undeniable.

"That?" he growls. "That's for you. *Only* you."

Heat floods through me so fast I nearly moan. My confidence cracks open—just a little—but it's enough. Because this man, this walking inferno of control and chaos, is hard beneath me, from *me*. From *this*. From all the messy, guarded, terrified pieces of me I thought no one could ever fully want.

His gaze softens, but his grip on my ass stays firm. One hand trails up my back—*slow*—dragging his fingers along my spine in a delicate path that's so intentional, it feels like worship. He palms the base of my skull, threading his fingers into my hair and lightly gripping the strands in a fist as he positions me closer, lips brushing mine but not yet kissing.

"You scare the hell out of me," he says, breathing the words into my mouth. "But not because I think you'll break me. Because I know I'll burn the world down before I let anyone else harm you."

The words settle deep on my lips, molten and possessive.

And just like that, the fear doesn't vanish—but it quiets. Because he's not asking me to be fearless. He's asking me to believe I can trust him through the fear. To let go. To *feel*.

And with the way his body moves against mine, his heat, his promise, his brutal honesty—I just might.

"I'll never ask you what you want." He begins to press kisses down my neck.

The words catch me off guard. I blink, unsure I heard him right. "Why not?"

He keeps descending, mouth moving across the hollow of my collarbone and every nerve below my waist strains for his attention

"That's my job," he murmurs, dragging his lips back to my mouth, voice like a drug. "To figure it out. To know you—and your body—better than you do. To listen. To take what it tells me and give it back to you until you can't remember how to breathe without me."

A flush blooms hot beneath my skin, rising in waves I don't try to stop. My hips move instinctively, pressing myself into him, needing friction. Needing more.

Is this what it feels like to be wanted completely? To be known before we've even fully connected?

His fingers release my hair and slide to the back of my neck. His eyes never leave mine, drinking in every flicker of reaction like it's gospel.

"I want to learn every inch of you," he says, as the hand on my ass scoops me further onto his hard cock. "Every sound you make. Every place that makes you come. I want to make you feel so good, you forget every man who didn't give a fuck about learning you at all."

It hits me like a current. The way he says these words. The conviction in every syllable. This isn't a man trying to impress me. This is a man telling me the truth. Declaring it.

And I can't speak. Can't look away. Can't pretend I'm not trembling in the most delicious way.

This isn't just lust. It's restoration.

"And if it helps," he adds, his mouth curving into that devastating grin, "I'm happy to guarantee an orgasm every day as reinforcement."

A laugh bubbles up—light and choked and desperate all at once. My heart's pounding. My thighs ache. And somehow, through it all, my sanity is still holding on by a thread.

But if he keeps looking at me like that, if he keeps talking to me like I'm the only thing in this world worth worshipping...

He taps my hip, then leans back on his hands. "Stand up."

I slide off his lap and step back, pulse pounding beneath my breasts but not out of fear. Anticipation. Desire. Something much deeper.

He stays seated, legs spread comfortably wide, and my eyes fall to the straining bulge beneath his jeans.

"Take off your clothes," he says. "Slow. I want to watch."

The words have my eyes snapping to his. I feel exposed, even fully dressed. But I don't look away.

This is what trust looks like. Not a dramatic declaration. A choice. One piece of clothing at a time.

My hands go to the hem of my simple cotton T-shirt. I creep it up past my stomach, then ribs, revealing a neutral-colored bra that pushes the girls up, but is more suited for not showing lines than a striptease. I let the shirt fall to the floor. Not trying to do too much. Just what he asked of me. His eyes follow every motion like they matter. Like I matter. And comfort stokes the fire in my core. My limbs begin to feel less and less tense, relief from the ache of overthinking.

As I reach for the button on my jeans, he pulls his own shirt over his head revealing that chest built of packed muscle and rippling abs that I *must* take the time to count with my tongue. We match each other move for move. I'm still nervous—self-conscious in a way I can't explain—but each time he mirrors me, something settles. Like maybe he doesn't notice the stretch in my stomach from carrying Bash, or the softness in my thighs that never truly left. Or maybe he does, and he just doesn't care.

Bra. *Gone.*

He lifts up and his pants drop next.

My jeans slide off in a sluggish shimmy down my thighs, that makes me giggle.

He stands, letting his boxer briefs fall, and I'm stunned again by the sheer presence of him. Not just the size, not just the body... *him.*

I take a deep breath and hook my thumbs in the waistband of my underwear. I glance up and his dark eyes are still locked on my face.

"I want all of you," he says simply.

So I give it to him. One step at a time.

I stand exposed, heart galloping beneath my ribs, the cool air teasing my skin. A charge of trust rushes through me. Then the tension hits.

"Now what?" I ask, breath caught somewhere between nerves and need.

Hex doesn't miss a beat. His voice becomes gravel and fire, pebbling my nipples to hard points. "Now I get to fuck you. And worship every inch of that beautiful body."

God.

He's all sharp lines and raw strength, every muscle taut beneath inked skin. That angel tattoo sweeping down his arm draws my eye across his bicep, over his forearm, ending at his large hand wrapped around himself. The contrast of that softness—the reverence in the way he strokes—makes even more heat bloom between my legs.

Something about it makes me proud. Not just to be wanted like this, but to feel like I deserve it.

I move toward him.

He reaches for my hips, drawing me closer. His mouth finds the swell of my breast, lips warm and sure, and I gasp as he sucks one erect nipple into his mouth. Then moves to the other. His tongue swirls, teasing, then teeth drag just enough to make me squirm.

My hands find his shoulders first—broad, solid—and then my fingers slide into his hair, gripping at the nape, holding on as my body starts to respond faster than I expect.

A large hand glides between my legs, then delicately brushes my lips and strokes through my wetness before one thick finger pushes inside me. Then another joins it. I gasp at the pressure, the stretch, the way my body welcomes it.

"You're tight," he groans against my skin, voice muffled. "You're gonna need another to fit me."

After a few more caresses, a third finger pushes in and my breath stutters. He moves them with care at first, then purpose, sweeping in and out, dragging against every spot that makes my legs weak.

My head falls back, hips rocking forward. "Hex—" I choke out. "I'm close... I'm gonna come. Stop."

His voice is velvet and a growl all at once. "There will be more."

My breath is ragged now, falling out of me in huffs as if I can't catch a deep enough inhale. "I've never had more than one during sex."

He lifts his head, eyes on fire. "That's because you've never been with me."

Then his fingers curl again, and he whispers, "Go ahead and come on my fingers, darlin'."

CHAPTER
TWENTY-NINE

Alex

T he first tremor starts deep inside her. I feel it before I see it. Tight, fluttering pulses clenching around my fingers. Her breath catches, a jerk running through her as her body moves before her mind can catch up.

That's it. She's coming.

I slide my fingers free, slick and glistening, and grip her hips, guiding her forward. The head of my cock finds her center. She gasps, one hand flying to my shoulder, and I pull her down onto me. Inch by slow inch, She stretches for me. Takes. Welcomes.

Fuck.

I fit inside her like she was made for this. *For me.* Her walls pulse around me, still trembling from the orgasm I gave her, and I'm barely in before I'm clamping down on every bit of control I've got not to lose it.

I feel like a virgin again. First time. First thrust. First taste of heaven.

Sable drops her head, lips parted on a breathy moan I know I'll hear in every dream from now until the day the good Lord puts me in the ground.

I slide my hands up her spine, palms wide, firm. Memorizing her bare skin under my fingers. She's warm, soft, and so strong. I kiss the swell of her breast as she moves against me. Then the other, tongue circling her nipple. I suck—once, then harder—earning a beautiful hitch in her breath when I push just a little harder than I did before, testing her.

She's not thinking anymore. She's moving on pure want. Clutching at my shoulders. Hips rolling. Desperate for an anchor.

I look up, and *goddamn.* Flushed. Radiant. Her body glistens with the beginning of sweat. Every part of her says *mine.* She's every version of divine I never deserved. And something primal surges in my chest.

Sable's nails rake my back, a sharp, welcome sting. "You're so big," she whispers.

She's not talking about my size. It's about the way I fill her. Stretch her. Claim every inch of her from the inside out.

And hell yes, I'm proud of that. Proud of the way she yields. Of how her body speaks truth her mouth never could.

I let her ride me. Because it feels good. So fucking good. She's tight and wet and so damn responsive it nearly breaks me in half. I grip her hips, guiding her just enough to help her chase the edge.

But I want more. I want all of her. Every damn angle.

"Turn around for me," I say, voice rough from holding back. "Lay down. Stomach on the bed."

She moves with a kind of surrender that feels sacred, not because she has to, but because she wants to. And fuck does she move. She lays out for me like a gift—body stretched long, ass lifted just right, one knee bent just how I want it.

Air catches in my throat.

Fuck, she's perfect.

Her pussy is slick, pink, glistening with everything I want. Open. Mine.

I kneel behind her, hands smoothing over her ass, spreading her slow. Leaning in, I lick her from her clit to that sweet, soft pillowy opening. Dipping in, tasting all of her.

She moans—sharp, high. Her body jolts under my hands.

I do it again. Slower. Deeper. Tongue circling her bud, teasing her just enough to make her hips twitch like she's deciding whether to run or beg.

I grab both cheeks, holding her in place, licking again—and again—until she's squirming, panting, muttering my name like a prayer.

Sable's right on the edge again. I feel it.

And I want her to break on me.

I press the tip of my cock against her again. One long thrust, and I'm buried deep. She cries out, back arching. I nearly come right then.

My hand slides under her bent leg, angling her just how I want her. I reach between her thighs, fingers circling her clit with the precision of someone who has known this beautiful woman's body forever.

I thrust again. And again. Deep. Measured. Claiming.

Her breath stutters. Her pussy clenches around me like a vise.

I growl low in my throat, my own orgasm building hard and fast behind hers.

"Hex," she moans, voice broken and needy.

I thrust harder, fingers moving faster. "Come for me."

And she does. Her walls lock around me, pulsing, drawing every last ounce of control from my body.

I follow with a guttural sound, burying myself as far as I can go while she milks me dry. She moans louder, her entire body shuddering. We fall apart together. Raw. Spent. Full.

She lets out a shaky breath, face buried in the pillow. "*Holy shit,*" she whispers.

I chuckle, breath still ragged, and press a kiss to the center of her back. "This is just the beginning. I've got you all night."

And I mean it.

We wrap ourselves in one another, in heady conversation. Then, after we raid the kitchen for cold grapes and half a granola bar, both of us laughing, drunk on skin and heat, we come together once more. We never stray far from the bed, never need to. It's all right here: warmth, hunger, the unspoken truth of what's building between us.

Eventually, I've got her wrapped in my arms, her head tucked under my chin, her bare leg thrown across mine. Neither of us quite ready to sleep. The room is still and thick with the scent of sex, sweat, and the sachet that she said smelled like me on the nightstand. I could stay here forever.

A buzz disrupts our peace.

My phone, buried in the pocket of my jeans on the floor. One long, vibrating pulse.

I groan, stretch an arm to the floor, and dig it out. The screen lights up.

1:30 a.m.

Will.

My stomach sinks.

Sable stirs against me as I answer, "Yeah?"

His voice is tight, rushed. "They jumped JT."

I jolt up, reaching for my jeans again. "What happened?"

"He was out front. I barely got there in time to pull them off him. He's in bad shape, Hex. I wouldn't have called otherwise."

I'm already on my feet, phone pinned to my ear, one leg back in my pants. "Who was it?"

"Stauder's guys. Jim and Tanner. Said they were looking for you, but JT was the next best thing. They said Ned's done playing. Said you're no longer in the clear. That you owe him."

My jaw locks as rage climbs my spine. "The fuck I do."

Will exhales hard, voice thinning and bracing for impact. "He said if you didn't sit down and talk... he'd go after something else. The bar is my guess."

I glance toward the bed.

Sable's sitting up now, the sheet pulled to her chest, wide, alert eyes locked on mine. She's already piecing it together.

My chest burns with the kind of fury I haven't let loose in years.

He touched my family.

And now he's threatening my home or worse, something I hope he won't find out about, but I know how easily it will be to sniff out Sable.

He has no fucking idea what he's just done.

I let Will know I'm on my way. Stillwater's forty minutes out. I'll drive it faster.

"Does he need to go to the hospital?" I ask as I shove my feet into my boots.

"I don't think so," Will says, voice tight. "Some deep cuts. One of them had a knife. But JT held his own. Took a beating, though."

I clench my jaw. "No cops?"

"No time. It happened fast. But once people inside realized what was going on, the bar patrons jumped in. Ran 'em off. Place cleared out after that. I've got him in the back office now. I'm keeping pressure on the worst of it."

"I'm on the road in five," I growl and hang up.

Behind me, I hear rustling.

I turn to see Sable out of bed, already pulling on jeans and a hoodie. "What are you doing?"

She looks at me like it's obvious. "Coming with you. Those phones aren't exactly soundproof, Hex."

Her movements are determined as she quickly stuffs her items back into the bag she brought.

"We'll go back," she adds, grabbing her shoes. "Make sure your brother's okay. I can help."

Something lodges in my chest—part shock, part something I'm too wrecked to name right now. But it roots itself deep.

We move fast, grabbing everything we brought and locking the house down. She tosses her bag into the truck, barefoot for all of two seconds before slipping into sneakers. I throw it in reverse, and we're gone.

The Hill Country stretches out in shadow and silence. The cab is dark, quiet except for the low rumble of the engine and the occasional groan of gravel under the tires. My knuckles flex on the wheel. We're tearing through narrow roads flanked by thick trees and fence posts older than the highway system, and all I can think about is JT. Bloodied. Alone. How long he suffered before someone helped him.

I recognize the moment it happens. When something turns in me.

Not rage. Not panic.

Something colder.

Darker.

A kind of clarity that only shows up when you've bled for people and buried parts of yourself to keep it from breathing. When vengeance stops being an idea and starts feeling like religion. Like ritual.

It comes in the overwhelming need to tear those involved apart one nerve at a time. To take the softest part of their fear and stretch it until it screams. By the end, they'll regret every breath they wasted walking on this earth.

If Ned were to touch JT—if he laid a finger on him himself—

No.

My grip tightens until the leather creaks.

And if he ever looked at Sable—if he ever *tried*—

The thought burns straight through me, sharp enough to taste. Red washes over my vision. I see her under him, crying out, and the image alone nearly blinds me. I wouldn't just kill him. I'd make it slow. I'd carve pain into his spine so deep he'd forget his own name before he forgot her face. I'd make his death art.

I breathe through my nose. In. Out.

I'm not afraid of what I'd do.

I'm afraid of how easy it would be.

And I wouldn't regret it. Not for a second. Not even if it cost me everything.

Everything but *her*.

I glance over, wrath wrapping around my chest.

Silver light grazes her skin. She's asleep. Head tipped toward the window with one hand curled loosely in her lap. Her mouth parted, breathless and beautiful, suspended in everything we are becoming.

She came with me. No hesitation.

I tighten my grip on the wheel, jaw locked as the dark highway eats up mile after mile.

She has no idea how far I'd go for her. No idea what kind of man she's in bed with now.

And God help the bastard who gives her a reason to find out.

I'd burn the whole fucking town of Stillwater Bend to the ground for this woman.

And if Stauder so much as breathes near her, I'll show him exactly what kind of monster he helped make.

CHAPTER
Thirty

Hex

Thirty-two minutes.

I keep one hand on the wheel and one eye on the clock the entire damn drive. I pull into the back alley of Ruin's End. Sable still asleep in the passenger seat, the second the truck eases to a stop, she jostles awake.

"Sorry," she mumbles, stretching lightly. "My body's not used to staying up this late. Or"—she pauses with a sly grin—"that many orgasms in one night."

That pulls a smirk out of me. I reach over and squeeze her knee. "You can go up to the loft and crash in my bed if you'd rather not deal with this right now."

She shakes her head as she unbuckles. "I want to see JT... if that's all right."

It's more than all right. I nod and we get out, boots on pavement, night air thick with the noise of cicadas buzzing around us.

Inside, the bar is quiet. Patrons have all left. Only the hum of fridges and the faint clatter behind the bar echoes across the space. Macy's going through closeout, cleaning down the taps. It's barely been two weeks and her first full weekend, but she moves like this is her hundredth night here. Will's influence, no doubt. He favors tight, clean systems and has zero tolerance for laziness.

She glances up, nods once at me, then does a double-take when she spots Sable behind me. There's curiosity there, but no time. I lead Sable through the hallway toward the office, already bracing for what she's about to see.

A sick bloody trail smears along the floor, telling a story I don't want to read.

I glance back at her, expecting to see her falter.

She doesn't. Not even a flicker.

I first notice Will through the office window, jaw tight. I open the door and look to my younger brother. JT's propped up on the beat-up couch, shirt off, torso wrapped with a bar towel, face swollen and bruised to hell. There's dried blood crusted at the corner of his mouth. One eye already purpling shut. His knuckles are split open, and there is a patchwork of cuts across his upper body.

My fist connects with the drywall before I can stop myself. The crack ricochets through the room, sharp enough to rattle bone. I feel the skin tear and know the familiar bruise I'll feel later.

"*Jesus*," I mutter when I see him. "JT—"

"I'm good," he rasps, each word scraped out with pain. "Will patched me up."

Will wipes a spot on his hand that's crusted with blood. "Bleeding's clotted... *mostly*. He needs rest."

I can barely think. Rage is hot under my skin. I want to turn around, get back in my truck, find the bastards who did this, and tear through each fucking limb with a dull knife.

But Sable steps forward, calm and poised, a world away from the woman who came undone in my arms not even an hour ago. She lays a hand on Will's arm.

"Mind if I take a look?" She asks softly.

Will glances at me, then back to her, something in his expression relaxing. He steps aside without a word. I'm in awe of her ease around my brothers.

Sable kneels in front of JT, focused like a switch flipped, and she's pure instinct now. Pure care.

"I've got a ten-year-old," she says, voice soothing without trying. "He doesn't get stabbed in fights—*thank God*—but I've learned how to clean and bandage things right. Especially the ones that don't get stitched but probably should." She winks at JT. "Boys like to play rough."

JT gives a weak huff of a laugh. "Don't I know it."

She lifts the towel with steady hands, as if the gore does not faze her. When she sees what's underneath, there's not a crease of fear to be seen. With narrowed eyes, she shifts into gear.

"You did good," she tells Will, inspecting the wound. "Cleaned it, slowed the bleeding."

Will blinks in surprise, rubs the back of his neck, and mumbles, "I just... disinfected what I could."

"Well, you probably did better than most in this kind of situation," she says without looking up.

She glances up, her eyes immediately locating the first aid kit as if she's been here before. Reaching over to the filing cabinet, she grabs the opened kit, and starts working. Gloves snap into place as she pulls out antiseptic wipes and clean gauze. She cuts open a packet, speaking like she's a nurse to a wounded soldier, "This'll sting," and gently wipes along the edge of one of the stab wounds.

JT hisses but doesn't pull away. His fingers dig into the couch's fabric.

Her instincts aren't performative—they're bone-deep. Pure maternal. The kind of care that comes from somewhere raw and embedded. The kind I didn't know I was still starving for until I watched her kneel beside my brother, steady hands and steady voice, as if she were born for moments like this.

And I've never wanted someone more.

Sable takes her time. Every wound is cleaned twice. She pats each area dry with gauze and talks to him the whole time in a low, calm voice that reminds me of our mother.

"You're lucky," she says, finally looking him in the eye. "I think they'll scar, but they look shallow. I'm no doctor, but I'd say the bruising is going to suck, but you'll heal."

She grabs fresh gauze, antibiotic ointment, and surgical tape, then begins wrapping his torso with smooth, practiced movements.

"Bash wanted to learn skateboarding when he was six. YouTube's great for a crash course in quick repairs. Did you eat today?"

"Burger earlier," he says, clearly trying not to wince as she tightens the bandage.

"Well, you're getting broth and a damn hydration packet when we're done. Sit tight."

JT stares at her in awe like she just blew in on angel wings, with a first-aid badge and a promise to cure all his mommy issues. "You always like this?"

Sable doesn't look up. "Only when my kid or the people I care about get hurt." She glances toward me, then back at JT. "You're officially in that group by proxy."

JT leans his head back and grins through swollen lips. "If I were older, you could've been mine."

Sable lets out a snort, grabs another piece of tape, and says, "Sweetheart, while you were still swimming in your daddy's nuts, I'd already been fantasizing about doing scandalous things with the original JT. Justin Timberlake."

Will coughs to cover a laugh from the corner.

Sable stands and brushes off her hands. "So... that's a no from me."

JT's still grinning, even though I know his whole face must ache. "Fair enough."

I'm still watching her, stunned. I know I must be looking at her the way you look at something you thought only existed in fairytale stories.

She handled it all—blood, bruises, pain, humor—without breaking stride. Didn't blink at the mess. Didn't shrink at the gore. She came in, took control, made things better, and somehow didn't make a show of it.

Sable's not just good in a crisis. She *becomes* the calm in it. Like the storm bends around her instead of touching her, like chaos itself doesn't dare disrupt the steadiness she brings.

Being in my bed, writhing beneath me and whispering my name in the dark was a bonus. But having her in my life—in *my world*—is becoming a need. To have her threaded through the parts of me I've kept sealed off. Not because I thought no one could handle them, but because I never believed anyone would try.

But she would.

She already is.

The depraved thrum in my chest for wanting her, needing her doesn't feel like lust. It's been something I've been missing since the moment my mother's body went cold. Something sacred. Something I'd kill to protect.

Hell, something I *will* kill to protect.

Standing there in the bloodstained office of my bar with drywall dust on my knuckles and my brother busted to hell, all I can think is:

What the fuck did I do to deserve this woman?

JT refused the bed upstairs, no matter how many times I offered it. Stubborn little bastard kept waving me off, half-sitting, half-sinking into the office couch.

"I'm fine," he said, more annoyed than weak. "Stop hovering, man."

Will even offered to take him to his place, but JT gave him a hard "fuck no" without missing a beat. Said he wouldn't subject himself to staying in the *House of OCD* for even one night. I didn't argue after that. Just tossed him a blanket and made sure the office door locked from the inside.

Now, upstairs in the loft, I watch Sable climb into my bed with the ease of someone who belongs there. With one graceful movement, she shucks off her pants, bare legs brushing the sheets as she slides beneath the covers.

She's quiet. I don't think she's questioning her choice to be with me, she's likely bone-deep tired. I see it in the way she moves, her limbs slower, heavier. In the way her eyes press shut just a beat too long when she blinks.

I stand near the edge of the bed, watching her in the soft lamplight. She's curled on her side, her hair mussed, her breathing slow but not quite restful. Her body looks like it's trying to relax, but her face... her face still holds the tension of this late hour.

I reach for the hem of my shirt, ready to strip off everything the night dumped on us, but I stop when she slides to the edge of the bed.

The motion is slow, intentional. Not for show.

For *me*.

The blanket falls from her lap. Then she positions herself to kneel in front of me on the mattress's edge.

She doesn't say anything. Doesn't ask to help me.

She just looks up at me with those tired, beautiful brown eyes and lifts her hands to the bottom of my shirt.

Her fingers graze my skin—light, curious—as she pushes the fabric up inch by inch. I raise my arms, letting her take it off. Her knuckles brush scars and hardened muscle on the way. The shirt lands somewhere behind her, forgotten.

Sable's hands coasts over my torso like she's *studying* me. Not mapping the damage but *honoring* it.

Pressing her palm flat against my stomach, she trails upward, over the dip between my ribs. She runs her delicate fingertips across the old burn mark on my side, a faint keepsake of a fight I don't remember winning.

She traces one of the deeper scars near my underarm, a questioning look taking over her features.

"This one?" she murmurs.

"Knife. Big one."

She nods like it makes perfect sense and doesn't blanch at the idea of someone stabbing me.

Her thumb skims higher, over my chest, to the black and gray wings inked over my shoulder.

"Tell me about the angel," she says softly.

I exhale, every muscle in my body drawn tight... except where she touches me. There, everything melts.

"It was a story my mom used to tell. Back when we were living in a place that smelled like mold, and I couldn't go to school without the poor showing. Back when I thought surviving meant keeping my head down and staying useful."

Sable adjusts herself, circling her hand around my wrist and pulling me to sit on the bed with her. She curls back up on her side and I face her. I stay sitting up, legs half off the edge, not ready to settle. The hand she used to pull me in cradles the knuckles that carry the busted skin from earlier.

"She told me of an angel," I say. "Not the kind you pray to. Not soft or glowing or merciful, like they preach of."

Her gaze doesn't leave my face as I speak. Not once.

"This angel... she doesn't save the worthy. She saves the *ruined*. The ones who stop trying. The ones who stop believing they deserve anything good. Not because they are bad, but because they've spent too long in the wrong situations."

She lifts my hand to her mouth and kisses the broken flesh. Every knuckle. Slow. Like it matters. Like *I* matter.

I pause, jaw tight.

My voice drops with the weight of emotion. "Mom said the angel watches, waits for the one person too tired to ask for help. Too proud to beg. Too damaged."

Sable intertwines her fingers with mine.

"But this particular angel doesn't show up to save you. She is meant to stand beside you. And if you truly want out of hell, she'll walk the path with you."

She's still holding my hand.

But the other one—the one she held to my chest moments ago—moves again. It coasts over the line of the tattoo, tracing the blade in the angel's hand, the feathers of her wing, the shadow etched into her face.

"She's beautiful," she whispers.

"She's you," I say.

Her lips part, but no air escapes. Glassy brown eyes dart to mine, searching for an answer.

I don't say it to charm her. It's true. I've spent most of my life waiting for the world to take something else from me, and this woman somehow showed up instead.

And I think she knows it. Because instead of speaking, she sits up, leans in and presses her mouth to the center of my chest. Right over my heart.

She stays there for a long moment, before pulling back.

I try to force a smile, "You always this drawn to tattoos?"

She lets out a soft chuckle, one shoulder shrugging as she lays back down in the sheets. "Not usually. Just yours. I mean, I admire creativity, of course. But I've never gotten one."

That catches me off guard. "You? Artistic as hell and never thought to design your own piece?"

Her smile falters just a touch, turning inward. "Trust me, I've tagged along to plenty of Demi's appointments. I just could never decide what to get. What would mean enough. What would last. Kinda strange, right? I mean... a tattoo lasts forever. But the depth of the meaning has to also."

I nod, something tightening in my chest. "Nah, it makes sense."

She lifts a hand, brushing her fingers against the edge of the sheet, thoughtful. "I've never really had something that felt permanent. Nothing with roots. No person, no place I could feel sure of." Her voice softens. "Certainly nothing I felt brave enough to mark on myself." A beat, then she adds, quieter still, "Maybe one day I'll do something for my son. That's the only person I've ever felt might stay."

The room stills.

I slide closer, resting my hand on her thigh over the covers. "You think you can bring me peace and not expect me to crave you like madness?"

A weighty blink and then the cutest fucking smile washes over her face. She tilts her head, shuts her eyes, and lays back on the pillow.

Dipping my head, I place a kiss on her lips and watch as the muscles on her face relax with each passing beat. She's close to sleep. Still breathing steady. Still here.

"You're it for me, Sable."

And I don't move. Not for a long time.

Pulling her into me, her skin is warm against my chest, and the ache in my ribs dulls just enough to let me breathe.

But I don't sleep.

Can't.

JT's busted face plays behind my eyes every time I close them. Stauder's threat still echoes in the back of my skull. And this woman—this rare, unexpected woman—is lying here in my bed, carving forever into my heart without even realizing it.

Eventually, I slip out of bed. Quiet. Careful not to wake her.

I walk to the kitchen, open the drawer near the sink, and pull out a black felt-tip marker.

Sable's still curled on her side, deep in sleep. I sit on the edge of the bed and lift her arm, holding her hand so she doesn't stir.

Then I draw.

An angel wing. Not finished. Just the outline as if emerging from her skin. Each feather sketched in soft, rising arcs.

It's fluid, feminine, and strong—wholly Sable.

I don't know what she's going to think when she sees it in the morning.

But if there's any justice in the world, she'll feel what I feel looking at her now.

I don't sleep. Just lay next to her, staring at the ceiling, one hand on her hip holding what's mine, heart full of fury and something dangerously close to love.

CHAPTER
THIRTY-
ONE

Sable

My body wakes up before I want it to. Not from an alarm. Just a habit. It always does this when I have nowhere to be. Snaps right back online no matter how little sleep I give it. I got maybe three and a half hours tops.

The room is still dim, soft morning light starting to leak in at the edges of the dark curtains. I stay still for a second, soaking in the quiet.

Hex is next to me.

Asleep.

And for once, I get to see what it's like to have him laying in bed with me. Not tense, not watching or protecting. Just breathing. Laid out beside me, one arm slung across his chest, the other still resting near where I must've curled in close sometime in the night.

His face is softer in sleep. His mouth, his jaw, far less sharp. His lashes are long, and the lines near his eyes have eased. There's peace here he likely never lets the world see.

My gaze drifts lower, over muscles I've already touched, already begun to claim. But with nothing in the way now, I catch the smaller things: faint scars scattered across his skin, the kind only noticed when you're close enough to memorize them. I catalogued his ribs before sleep took me, but not the round bullet sized mark inside of his forearm. Or the scar running along the side of his head buried deep in dark hair. Those perfect lips and the divot that hooks just above the right side of his upper lip.

I reach out, careful not to wake him, and trace a white line on his exposed thigh with my fingertip. Faint. Raised. Old. My heart clenches in my chest, heavy with anguish.

And that's when I see it.

My arm.

I pull it closer and blink, realizing it's not just a smudge or a shadow. It's a drawing. An angel wing inked in clean, perfect lines from shoulder to elbow. The delicate feathers emerging from my skin, curve with my movement.

I scoot up enough to look the art, brushing my fingers over it, afraid to smudge it but needing to feel it's real.

Somehow in the calm the early morning hours offered after a tumultuous night, he drew this. Warmth wraps my heart, realizing just how much my body trusts him that I didn't wake in the least.

I smile, something full and bright blooming in my chest. The story he told me slips to the forefront of my mind. His mother's angel.

I don't know what to do with the emotion that it makes me feel. But I know I'm not ready to let it go.

My fingers trace the wing once more, and I want him to feel how much it means—how much he means—in every touch, every kiss. Shifting closer, I nestle back into the space beside him, careful with the covers. My lips hover near his. I press a kiss to his mouth: gentle, testing, sweet.

His eyes don't open at first, but the scratch in his voice is low and rough from sleep. "You do that again," he says, "you're gonna get a whole lot more than kissing. You've already woken the beast touching my thigh the way you did."

I grin, lips brushing against his again. "It's almost like that was the point."

He opens his eyes at that, and the look he gives me is pure fire and soft affection tangled into one. His hand slips under the covers, palm spreading across my hip.

We don't rush. Just a slow build of touches, kisses, hands exploring skin we already know but want more of. He pours himself into me with the kind of reverence that says I matter, and I return it, showing him that I see him. I see all the strong, broken, beautiful parts that make up the man beside me.

Forty-five minutes pass in a haze of warmth and whispered things I'm not ready to call love out loud but feel deep in my bones.

Eventually, the guilt catches up with us.

I press my forehead to his chest. "We should check on JT."

He groans, dragging a hand down his face. "Yeah. We should."

Neither of us moves for another full minute.

The moment sinks into my skin with the same quiet permanence as the drawing on my arm.

The loft is quiet, the scent of coffee already drifting in from downstairs. Maybe Will's back. It couldn't possibly be JT.

But then my phone buzzes.

I almost ignore it, but habit wins. I reach for it at the edge of the nightstand and see the sender's name in bold: **Brenda Melrose**.

My stomach drops before I even open it.

It's the client with the custom armoire Ashley destroyed.

The message is polite, professional. She's asking if everything's still on track for delivery next week and includes an innocent, attached photo of the space it's meant to go in. I stare at the picture of a room that now has no piece of furniture to fill it. That beautiful, one-of-a-kind cabinet is splintered in the middle of my shop.

My chest tightens.

I slide the phone face down on the nightstand and sit up, the covers falling from my chest. I'm already thinking through supply chains, salvage leads, restoration timelines. I'll have to find something comparable. Fast.

Hex shifts behind me. With a large hand he hooks me, dragging me over to him. "You okay?"

I nod, but it's more muscle memory than truth. "I need to get back to the shop. It's the client expecting the piece that... doesn't exist anymore."

He sits up too, the lines of sleep giving way to something sharper. He doesn't argue for me to stay, but I can feel it in him. He's working something out behind his eyes.

"I'll be okay," I say, more gently this time. "I just need to start sorting things."

He moves without a word, walks across the loft to the dresser, opens the top drawer. When he turns back, he's holding the Sig he taught me to shoot with.

My stomach flips.

He presses it into my hands, his fingers curling around mine for a beat longer than necessary. "Keep it on you," he says. "At all times."

I swallow hard. "Hex—"

"I need to know you're not out there with no protection when I can't be with you." He lifts his eyes to mine. "It's not about being scared. It's about being smart."

I nod, fingers closing around the grip. "Okay. I will."

We've only known each other a couple of weeks. Two weeks. Sixteen days. I used to tell myself I'd wait months before introducing Bash to someone new. That I'd need time. Enough time to be sure, to test the waters, to make certain I wouldn't confuse him or bring someone into his world who wouldn't stay.

But I am certain about this.

The pull to stay here, in this soft bubble we've built, is strong. But life's already knocking. Really fucking loud, with all the glory of its messy impatience.

Even so, something in me won't let the truth of this time we've spent together pass by like a fluke.

I take a deep breath before saying: "I want you to meet Bash."

That gets his attention. His eyes flick to mine with what can only be described as surprise. He blinks. "Yeah?"

I nod, the weight of what I've just said hitting me full in the chest now that it's out.

"He'll be back tonight, all wound up from fishing with his grandparents, talking a mile a minute, probably sunburned and sticky from too much lake water and not enough sunscreen," I say, wrinkling my nose. "But... maybe sometime this week you could come over. Have dinner?"

His whole expression changes, seeming to melt him. "Yeah. I'd like that."

I smile, but something inside me stirs. I'm nervous, but uncharacteristically hopeful for the first time in a long time.

I've never felt anything like what I'm experiencing with Hex before. Not this kind of steady. Not this kind of safe.

And it's not just the way he makes me feel in bed—though, Lord knows, that's top notch—or the way he looks at me like I'm something rare he refuses to mishandle. It's the way he stepped into my world, saw my yard and my life, saw Bash's life, and didn't hesitate to add to it. A playscape, quietly built. A promise, unspoken but solid, that he plans to stick around long enough to see my son play on it.

It's the way he told me to share his truth with Demi without blinking. No flinching, no conditions—just trust in me, and in her, because I trust her.

And it's the way he handed me a gun this morning—no fear, no ego. Just the quiet conviction that I deserve to be protected, even if he's not standing beside me.

That kind of trust? That kind of care? I've never had that before.

Hex is different. He's real in a way most people aren't.

And when I said I want him to meet Bash... I meant it.

Because if I ever want my son to see what it looks like when someone shows up to treat a woman right, I want him to see Hex.

I hold his gaze, still sharing a quiet smile. I hope he sees what my invitation really means. It's not just dinner. It's a door fully open to him. One I never thought I'd let anyone walk through again.

I get dressed, pack up what little I brought for the weekend, and before we leave, I stop by the office to say goodbye to the boys. JT's still on the couch, bandaged and bruised, but cracking jokes. Will is back and gives me a nod and a soft thank you.

Then Hex and I head out.

The truck ride is quiet but not strained or awkward. My hand rests on the center console. His is right beside it. Every few minutes, his fingers brush against mine like a subtle check-in.

When we pull into a spot near the front of my shop, the air feels different. The glass has been swept, the door secured with plywood, but I know what waits for me inside. Furniture toppled, tools scattered, pieces ruined.

Hex kills the engine and walks me in, stalking every shadow, eyeing every corner.

I step through the door and pause. The familiar smell of sawdust, finish, and something older hits me square in the chest and I do my best to choke back tears.

This place is mine. My hard work. My freedom. And it's a fucking war zone.

"I hate this," I whisper.

Hex doesn't say anything. He just steps beside me and starts picking up furniture and strewn tools. A broken clamp. A knocked-over stool. He doesn't need direction. He just helps.

We work in silence for a few minutes. He moves through the space with careful hands, as though he understands it holds more than just objects. It holds pieces of *me*.

Then his phone buzzes.

He pulls it from his pocket, glances down, and frowns. "It's Will."

I pause, wiping dust off my palms and onto a nearby rag. I feel the shift immediately.

Hex listens for a few seconds, jaw locking up again, then hangs up.

"One of Stauder's guys just dropped a message off," he says, voice edging back into gravel. "Told Will where I'm supposed to meet him."

His cautious energy recalibrates—calm, focused, lethal. He's already halfway out the door in his mind, scanning threats I can't see.

All I see is him. And the sudden, terrible thought hits me, that I might lose him before I even get to tell him what he's starting to mean to me.

I close the distance between us, every bone in my body aching to pull him back, to run away and hide, to pretend the world can't find us here.

"You need to go," I say instead, my voice steady, but my heart anything but.

He nods, then cups my cheek in one hand, his thumb dragging over my lips like he's memorizing the texture. "Lock the doors behind me. Don't open them for anyone but me or someone you know well. Keep that Sig on you. And text me the second you get home tonight."

"I will."

Leaning down, he kisses me with an indescribable fervor. Like he's pressing a piece of himself into me, just in case. Like he knows he's walking into a den of vipers who don't care who they take from this fucked up world.

And I let him. I take the kiss like he's promising his return.

When he pulls away, I hold his eyes. "Be careful."

"I'm not the one you need to worry about." *As if that were possible.* He says the words, wearing a smug look that hints at the unhinged side of him I pray to God I never have to see in action.

The door closes behind him. A simple sound, a whoosh of warm air. *This is what the world falling out of alignment feels like.*

I stand in the center of my shop, pulse pounding in my ears, staring at the space he left behind.

And suddenly, I can't breathe.

Not because I don't trust him. Because I do. I trust this man with my body, with my soul, with my damn life. But trusting him to come back in one piece? That's a new kind of fear—one that sinks its claws in deep.

He's not invincible, no matter how solid he feels under my hands. I've seen the scars. Heard the violence of his past. I know what kind of danger lives along the edges of his life.

I want to scream after him. Beg him not to go. Tell him that I'm falling for him so fast it terrifies me. That I can already see the hole he'll leave behind if he doesn't come back.

But I don't.

I put on the face I've always worn when everything feels like it's about to break. I square my shoulders. I lock the door like he told me to. I keep my hand close to the Sig.

And I pray that after all the things that didn't kill him, Ned Stauder won't be the one who finally does.

CHAPTER
THIRTY-TWO

Alex

The door yields under my hand. I let it close behind me with a soft thud. The air carries the tang of lemon cleaner and the faint trace of bourbon, remnants of countless spills and wipe-downs. Everything is in its place at Ruin's End, yet there's a quiet that feels almost reverent, as if the walls themselves are holding their breath.

Will's behind the bar, sorting through a short stack of mail and receipts. He doesn't look up right away.

JT's probably still in the back, stretched out on that busted couch he refuses to give up. Told us again this morning to fuck off and let him sleep until the bruises stopped screaming.

Will finally looks up at me. "That was fast."

"Did what I could. Helped Sable sweep up. She's still got a hell of a mess in there." I pause, letting my hand settle on the edge of the bar. "Who was it?"

Will gives a quiet nod, then sets aside what he is doing. "Devin." He walks around the bar and stops in front of me. "I've seen him before. Short guy, too many teeth crowding their way to the front, shoulder holster he thinks nobody sees."

"What'd he say?" I prod.

Will reaches into his back pocket and hands me a crumpled slip of paper. I smooth it out. Nothing but an address and time.

"He said you'd know what it meant," Will says. "Said you'd be smart enough to show up."

I stare at the paper, memorizing the information. One of his warehouses I'm familiar with. I fold it once and slide it into my back pocket.

Footsteps shuffle in the hallway behind me. I hear the creak of the floorboard outside the office.

"I'll go with you," JT calls out, voice low and rough.

I don't turn. "No."

"I'm fine."

"Not even fucking close to fine," I snap, turning on the heel of my boot to face him.

JT's leaning on the doorframe, arms crossed over his chest, chin raised in quiet rebellion against the pain visibly blooming across his features. The swelling's gone down, but his eyes are still swollen and bruised, and there's a long, healing cut along his jaw that already looks like it needs to be rebandaged.

He's not limping, but he's stiff. And pissed.

He stares me down, teeth clenched, that fire burning just behind his gaze. He wants to move. To fight. To feel useful. I know that feeling too damn well.

"You're just beginning to heal," I say, quieter but firm. "And if this goes sideways, I'm not putting you in the middle of it."

JT's jaw ticks. He looks at the floor, then back at me. "Man, I hate this shit."

I nod. "Yeah. Me too."

Will steps out from behind me.

"Then I'll go," he says.

I shake my head immediately. "Not happening."

"Hex—"

"No." I grab his shoulder to draw his attention to my words. "You've stayed clean where Stauder's concerned. You think that's luck? He hasn't touched you because you're not on his radar. Let's not change that."

Will crosses his arms, feet braced shoulder-width apart. "You're not walking into this alone."

I narrow my eyes. "You don't think I can handle him?"

Will huffs one short, dry laugh. "I know you can. Doesn't mean you should have to. And he definitely won't be alone."

I stare at him for a beat, rolling my neck to relieve some of the tension I'm having a hard time releasing. "You don't get it. If he gets even a scent of what you're capable of, he'll find a way to use you."

"You don't get to protect me from choices I've already made. I live this life." His voice doesn't rise, doesn't shake. "We stand together. That's always been the deal."

I study him. He's not built as big as me, but that never mattered when we were younger, barefoot in dirt lots, fists flying, blood on our lips. He preferred precision. I preferred brute force.

That hasn't changed.

He's the kind of man who folds his shirts with crisp corners, keeps his shoes spotless, and straightens crooked frames on other people's walls. Every detail of him is curated, controlled.

To anyone else, Will is the pretty boy. Too put-together. Too calculated. But that's the trick. That's what makes him lethal. He's wiry and fast, sharp as a blade and just as deadly on impact.

A polished shell hiding something far less civilized.

But he'd rather handle the aftermath. Clean the blood, stack the bodies, and return order like it was never broken.

Will doesn't make threats. He doesn't posture. He waits, patient as gravity, until certainty sharpens into intent—then moves.

I nod once, slow. "We do it my way."

"Always."

Behind him, JT shifts against the doorframe, arms still crossed, but his eyes are softer now. There's frustration in them, yeah. But he's not trying to argue anymore.

"We are getting out of this," I say, looking between them.

Will nods once and slings his jacket on.

I should be thinking about our plan. I should be visualizing exits, angles, contingencies.

Instead, my mind is on Sable. Her voice. The angel wing I drew on her skin. Her son's name on her lips.

I've got plans this week. Meet her kid. Sit at her table.

But there's no guarantee I walk out of this in one piece.

Stauder never deals straight.

And whatever's waiting at that warehouse...

It's not just a conversation.

The warehouse hasn't changed.

Same rusted panel doors. Half the overhead fluorescents dead or flickering. Paint peeling from the beams the way old skin flakes from a sunburn. There's still blood on one of the support columns near the far wall. Mine, maybe... or someone else's.

Back in the day, this place hosted underground fights. Not the flashy kind with cameras and pay-per-view. It wasn't fucking *entertainment*. It was a meat grinder with a crowd. Bare fists. Broken ribs. Bets passed hand to hand in blood-soaked bills. Beaten bodies dragged out the back before they got cold and became a problem. If you won, you got paid. If you lost, you got stitches... that is if anyone gave a shit to patch you up.

Stauder owns half the warehouses off Jackson. Paper says storage. Reality says drug pipelines, weapons drops, unlicensed contraband in crates labeled *organic produce*. He kept the law at arm's length with hush money and made sure bodies were too mutilated to identify.

Cops didn't ask questions. Not when their kids' college funds came from envelopes dropped in mailboxes with no return address.

Will walks in beside me, eyes sharp and scanning the scene in front of us. No need for chit chat.

Five men stand and sit near a folding table in the center of the space. Makeshift chairs. A single fan humming in the corner. All of it too familiar.

Then I see him.

Tanner.

Five-foot-nothing, greasy hair slicked back with spit and cockiness, scraggly goatee that looks glued on in the dark. He's laughing with one of the others, some smug-ass look on his face, until his eyes meet mine.

The little fuck who touched my brother goes still.

I walk.

Each step a countdown.

Will doesn't move to stop me.

"Morning," Tanner says, lips curled like he knows something I don't.

I don't answer.

I bury a right hook so deep into his jaw I feel his teeth crunch like gravel underfoot.

His head snaps back, body crashing into crates. Blood hits concrete in a lazy splash.

"That's for JT, you piece of shit," I snarl, shaking out the sting. "Say another word, and I'll make you gargle what's left of your fucking molars."

Tanner groans, slouched on the floor, hands over his busted mouth.

"Now, now," a voice drawls from behind us. "Let's not get messy before the pleasantries."

Ned Stauder steps into view.

Close to sixty with weathered skin comparable to cracked leather. He's lean, relatively still fit for his age. He's not much to look at in a fight... but that's the con. The danger isn't his hands, it's his *reach*.

His men flank him. Broad. Armed. Faces blank like they've been taught how to kill with no witnesses and even less guilt.

Ned lifts a hand. His muscle pulls back. Obedient dogs waiting on the kill command.

"You done swingin'?" Stauder asks, voice lazy but with an undeniable edge behind it.

I run my other hand over my busted knuckles, blood already drying in the creases. "For now."

He smirks, slow and crooked, clearly enjoying the advantage of catching me off guard. "Good," he says. "Let's talk."

He nods toward a couple of plastic chairs flanking the folding table, cheap and creaky, one with a cracked leg that's secured with electrical tape.

I don't move.

Will doesn't either. He plants himself by my side, arms folded across his chest, gaze locked on the men standing behind Stauder. Watching their hands, their spacing. Every inch of him is calm.

Stauder shrugs, unbothered. "Suit yourself."

He circles the table with the ease of a man preparing to deal cards, not leverage someone's secrets. In one hand, he holds a plain manila folder. He sets it down, drawing my attention, then taps the cover with one nicotine-stained finger.

"You know Brandon Dillinger's gone missing," he says. Not a question.

I draw a lazy gaze to meet his. "I've heard."

"Cost me a lot," Stauder continues, beginning to pace. He takes measured steps that scratch across the concrete floor. "His... *partnerships* kept certain doors open. Made certain people look the other way. Now his company's crumbling, bleeding money, and I've got a goddamn detective sniffing around the carcass."

He glances at me, one brow lifted.

"You know Bryant?"

"I know the name."

"Then you know he's a fucking bloodhound."

Knowing exactly how far my reach is, Stauder stops pacing and plants himself just outside my striking range. He clasps his hands loosely in front of him, gaze steady but sharp and testing.

I don't move a damn muscle.

His face is calm, but I can see the calculation behind it. The tension riding just beneath the casual swagger. He's not here to make peace.

He's here to own me again.

"And you wanna know what I find interesting, Hex?" he says, voice quiet but cold. "Brandon met with you just two days before he disappeared. Strange coincidence, don't you think?"

"I don't know a fucking thing about it," I say.

"You think a bar and a few dim-witted loyalists erase the years you spent breaking faces for me?" He chuckles, shaking his head. He leans on the table with both hands. "Don't insult me.

"You really think you're clean now?" he asks. "You think you get to wash the blood off just because your whore's got a kid and a mortgage?"

Rage spills over my patience at the mention of Sable. I lunge, but Will puts his arm out effectively stopping me.

Ned widens his grin, enjoying his provocation.

"You were nothing, Hex. Raised in piss and poverty. Wild. Angry. Your mom? Strung out and seeing angels. You made your living off my name. Off my money. Off my fights. Then when I looked to you to deal with Dillinger's little girl problem? What do you do?" He slams a hand on the table. "You fuck it all up. Like I've done nothing for you!"

He breathes out, slicks his thinning hair back with his palm and gathers himself, then looks up with a grin. "But see, I've got footage. From outside that condo. That genius little brother of yours must not have swept far enough. One of my guys caught you and that pretty piece of ass in walking distance from the building."

I'm trying so fucking hard not to lose my shit, but I don't say a word.

"Oh yeah," he says, shaking his head. "I learned a lot about her. Real interesting woman. Cute shop. Nice little house. Son about the age JT was when your mama got so doped up she saw Jesus."

I clench my fists so hard, my wrists begin to ache from the tension.

Will steps closer, body taut. "Don't," he warns.

My pulse is in my goddamn ears.

Ned knows he's struck something deep.

"You don't get to pretend to be human now," he says, like it's gospel. "You're a dog. You're *my* dog. And dogs don't get to play house."

I sidestep Will and get right into this human shitpile's face. "What the fuck do you want, Ned?"

Ned licks his bottom lip, like he's tasted victory before and he's about to enjoy it again. "The way I see it—you owe me. You cost me Dillinger. Cost me access, money, movement. I'm not here to bury you, Hex. I'm here to give you an out."

He steps closer, showing me how fearless he is. I take long and slow breaths into his face.

Big fucking mistake.

"I've got a fight lined up. Two weeks. Big stakes. Underground stream. You fight for me. You win. All debts cleared. Simple. Or—"

I turn and start walking. Will turns with me, already in step.

"I take a trip to Hawthorne's house," Ned calls out, voice ricocheting across the air, fueling the inferno inside me. "Maybe drop a package in the kid's backpack. Or maybe I just watch. Follow. Wait till you're not looking,"

I freeze.

Not from fear.

From fury so sharp it turns surgical.

My fists curl so hard the broken skin on my knuckles has blood welling like a warning. I could be across the concrete in seconds. I could break his jaw, his ribs—fracture something essential before anyone gets a hand on me.

And for a second, I want that.

I want it so bad my teeth ache.

I want to hear the crunch.

I want to see him bleed.

I want him to understand what it feels like to beg for breath he doesn't deserve.

But then it hits me—

There are too many men between me and him. Even with Will's help. Armed. Ready. They wouldn't just hold me back. They'd take me out.

And while I'm bleeding into the pavement, Sable and Bash would be alone. They would be vulnerable. The angel wing I drew on her skin this morning would mean nothing if I'm not alive to protect what it represents.

They'd be wide open. Unprotected.

He *wants* me reckless so he can gut the rest of my life without lifting a fucking finger.

I shift my weight. Roll my shoulders back. Quiet. Controlled.

"I'll be there."

But make no mistake—

I've already made the decision.

I will destroy him.

And it won't be with fists.

It'll be slow.

Painful.

And so permanent, even the devil will flinch when he sees what's left of Ned Stauder.

CHAPTER THIRTY-THREE

Sable

An email pings on my phone just as I'm elbow-deep in sticky-as-fuck honey glaze.

I nudge the screen awake with my pinky, squinting through the faint smear of olive oil across the glass.

Temporary Restraining Order Hearing Confirmed.

My stomach sinks. It's scheduled for the end of next week. A judge will decide whether the temporary order on Ashley becomes permanent. She's been notified.

Of course she has.

And now I get to spend the next ten days waiting for whatever unhinged bullshit she's planning in response.

Perfect.

I need to talk to someone before I spiral completely.

I nudge the phone again and use a voice command to immediately call Demi.

She picks up on the second ring.

"Tell me you're calm," Demi says instead of hello.

"I just softened butter with my body heat because I forgot to take it out of the fridge and I'm thirty seconds away from torching this bird. So no, I'm not calm."

She snorts. "Jesus Christ. Are you seriously roasting him a whole chicken, channeling full vintage housewife vibes?"

"I didn't plan this. The grocery store ran out of rotisserie, and I panicked, okay?"

"You're feeding a man dinner. You're emotionally naked. You're domesticating."

"I'm not domesticating, Demi. I'm stress-cooking. It's a clinical condition." I mutter, grabbing a paper towel with my wrist because my fingers are coated in syrupy garlic goo.

"Well, call the CDC, because it sounds contagious. You got the 'future-wife shakes,' and it's terminal."

I whack another garlic clove harder than necessary, the papery skin exploding across the counter. I can't remember how much I already added.

It's probably too much, but what's a little more?

"You're not helping."

"I am *absolutely* helping," she says. "I'm just saying, roast chicken is how you lock a man down. That and an outfit that says, 'I bake and I swallow.'"

"Jesus, Demi!"

"What? I'm giving you the tools to get what you want."

"You're giving me heart palpitations."

"Oh, sorry," she says, mock-serious. "Would it help if I told you that it won't matter if you burn the chicken or give him salmonella, because he's already so obsessed with you he'd die with a boner and a smile?"

"DEMI."

"SABLE. I'm telling the truth. That man would eat ketchup on drywall if you served it with that little 'I tried' look on your face."

I groan and bury my smile in my arm for a second before muttering, "I'm *trying* to create a warm, welcoming environment. Not a fucking last supper."

Hex has FaceTimed me every night this week. He calls at closing hour, keeping me on the phone while I lock-up, just to be sure I make it out and home safe. Always with that low voice and sincere presence, checking in without pushing.

Tonight's different though. He's not on a screen. He's coming over.

To meet my son.

I told Bash about him last night. About the man who I've been spending time with more than just a little. The one who put in the playscape in the backyard. The one who is pretty serious.

The moment I said playscape, Bash's whole face lit up. He didn't say much though about Hex—he's cautious with new people, especially when it comes to his mom—but I caught the excitement in his face. Hiding under that stubborn little smirk of his.

"Demi," I say, pressing the phone between my shoulder and cheek as I grab the pan for the carrots. "If this chicken turns out terrible, I swear to God, I'm setting the oven on fire and blaming you."

"You'd be doing the world a favor," she snorts. "That oven's unstable."

"No, Ashley's unstable," I groan, then immediately regret the words. There's a pause on the other side.

"Got the email, huh?" She knows I've been worried since the moment I filed the temporary order last Friday.

"Yeah."

"I'll bring wine to court," she says. "And maybe a stun gun. You know, just in case."

"I can't tell if you're joking," I say, using the back of my forearm to swipe at my temple.

"I can't either."

I smile despite myself, then glance at the oven clock. "I've gotta go. The chicken's probably dry. I forgot the salad. And I'm sweating through my bra."

"That's called pheromones. Men love that shit. Makes them feral."

"*Goodbye, Demi.*"

"Godspeed, Chicken Queen. Don't forget to baste the bird *and* your man."

Outside the kitchen window, the playscape catches the evening light. It's sturdy and simple, but it looks safe. Something that could last. It makes me smile.

I hang up with Demi just as the oven beeps and my phone buzzes again.

Hex is on his way

By the time Hex knocks, I've washed the glaze off my arms, swapped my sweaty bra for a clean one, and wrestled the carrots onto a serving dish that kind of hides the fact they're still mostly raw.

I open the door to dark jeans, a fitted henley, and that tattoo just visible at the collar. He smells of cedar and clean laundry, and I already know I'm in trouble because my entire body softens just seeing him.

But before I can get lost in his presence, Bash barrels around the corner.

Hex steps inside, eyes catching mine for a half-second—just long enough to give me that grin that does very inappropriate things to my lady bits—then he crouches, meeting Bash eye to eye.

"You must be Sebastian."

Bash narrows in on him, skeptical but not rude. "Are you the one who put my playscape in?"

Hex nods, one knee up, resting his forearm casually over the top. "Sure am. You test it out yet?"

"Yeah," Bash says. "It's solid. I jumped from the top and didn't even roll my ankle."

Hex laughs, deep and genuine. "Well, shoot, I must not have picked out one big enough for you, my man."

Bash glances up at me. "Mom says I shouldn't be jumping off of it."

Hex tilts his head, mock serious. "Your mom's right. But you could use the rope and swing off it, Tarzan style."

I raise an eyebrow. He flashes me a quick wink, subtle enough that Bash doesn't catch it, and something low in my stomach clenches hard.

Watching the two of them like this—Hex grounded and patient, Bash trying not to look completely thrilled—is disarming. There's no awkwardness. No forced politeness. Just two people figuring each other out as if they've done this before in some other life.

We settle at the small kitchen table I salvaged from a yard sale last spring. It used to be chipped and waterlogged. I stripped the finish, sanded every inch of it down, and painted the legs a pale matte green. It's still a little wobbly, but it holds.

Bash immediately scoots into the seat next to Hex.

"I usually sit there," he tells him, pointing at his usual spot, "but you're bigger. And in case there's a fire or something, I feel like you'd probably be better at saving us."

Hex doesn't miss a beat. "That's fair. I've got long legs and good reflexes. You sit tight, I'll handle the escape route."

Bash considers that for a moment, then nods with the authority of someone far too small to be that certain. "You're kind of a big guy. You ever kill anyone?"

"Bash!" I hiss, nearly choking on air.

He shrugs, totally unbothered. "It's a fair question if you're going to date my mom."

Hex turns toward him, completely unfazed, his mouth twitching with amusement. "No kills, *officially.*"

"Whoa." Bash lights up, excitement and what I could only assume are a million questions bubbling inside of him. If Hex is being serious or not goes right over his head.

"Okay," I cut in, placing the tray of chicken on the table with hands that aren't as steady as I'd like. "Let's redirect that curiosity to dinner, please."

We start to plate up. Barely halfway through chewing a mouthful of carrots he's pretending not to hate, Bash looks up at Hex again.

"You play video games?"

Hex sets his fork down and leans back in his chair slightly, giving my son his full attention. "Used to. Not much anymore. My little brother JT's the real expert."

Bash perks up at the mention of a little brother. "Is he my age?"

Hex shakes his head. "Twenty-four. And yeah, he's always trying to get me into whatever's new. But I'm trash at anything that requires more than two buttons."

Bash grins. "You'd like Death Strike. You get to throw knives and sneak up on people and there's, like... a lot of blood."

I shoot my son a look that could flatten buildings. "Bash."

He shrinks just a hair. "I didn't say I play it. I said he'd like it."

Hex chuckles, then shifts his attention back to Bash, this time with a little more weight in his tone. "Your mom's not wrong about the violent ones, kid. Some of them get in your head more than you think."

Bash frowns. "Yeah, but they're not real."

"They're not," Hex agrees. "But your brain doesn't always know the difference. You feed it too much violence, and it starts to think that's normal. That it's okay to react like that in real life."

Bash pauses, his young brain turning the thoughts over.

"JT used to get real worked up after certain games," Hex continues, picking up his fork again. "Couldn't sleep. Always wired. Once, I had pulled the plug on his console and made him go outside. He pouted for a whole day, but then we ended up building a dirt ramp for his bike and he forgot all about the games."

Bash is silent for a beat, clearly trying to picture that. "I guess... I'd rather have a ramp."

Hex smiles with sincerity. "Smart choice."

And that's it. Nothing preachy. No lectures. Just that secure voice, calm and real, and somehow it lands with Bash in a way that sticks.

The chicken flakes apart in dusty threads, and the carrots snap under my fork, defiantly uncooked. I push most of my offerings around my plate, chew thoroughly what I can muster, and wash it down with a sip of tea.

But Hex?

He eats every bite. No weird faces. No choking.

Either he has no taste buds or the best manners I've ever seen on a man who could bench press my vehicle.

He leans back slightly in his chair, glancing at me between bites. "It's really good."

Bash nods around a mouthful. "Better than Nana's meatloaf. Don't tell her I said that."

He's only saying that because of Hex. Bash is the pickiest eater and challenges my patience on the daily when it comes to food choices. I press my napkin to my mouth to hide my grin.

Watching them like this—Bash leaning into Hex's space, Hex meeting every question with patience—something tight in my chest finally loosens. The walls I've spent years building, brick by careful brick, don't feel quite so necessary anymore. Not with him.

Bash stretches out beside him, questions still piling up, each one a quiet prod to see if Hex will flinch.

He hasn't yet.

And I don't think he will.

CHAPTER THIRTY-FOUR

Alex

Bash reminds me so much of JT at ten, it's fucking eerie. Too smart for his own good, already picking apart the world and trying to understand where he fits in it. He has that mix of curiosity and confidence that makes you want to see what he turns into when he's older.

After we finish eating—and I power through every dry-ass bite of that chicken with the performance of a man at a five-star restaurant—Bash slips away and returns with a tablet.

"Wanna see what I built?"

"Yeah," I say, leaning forward. "Show me."

He slides back into the seat beside me with easy familiarity, his skinny elbow bumping mine as he tilts the screen so I can see. It's some kind of elaborate fort-meets-labyrinth hybrid, pixelated but impressive. He's already got traps set up and little signs posted for imaginary intruders.

"I've been working on this for a week," he says proudly. "It's not done yet, though. I still need a booby trap floor and maybe a lava moat."

"A lava moat is always a good move," I say dead serious. "You got guard animals?"

"Working on a pack of fire wolves."

"Smart."

That gets a grin out of him, big enough to make me forget how skeptical he looked earlier.

I nod along as he explains the layout, but I can't help stealing glances across the table. Sable leans against the counter, arms crossed, watching us. There's this soft look on her face. Like she's at ease. Like we fit.

I don't think she even knows she's smiling.

"Mom," Bash says suddenly, practically bouncing off his chair. "Can we go outside? I wanna show Hex the playscape!"

Sable straightens. "I don't know... I think Hex might be a little too big for it."

I grin and turn toward her. "You better be talking about my stature, darlin'. 'Cause I'm all kid inside."

She tries to hide her laugh but fails miserably. "You break it, I suppose you'll have to buy us a new one. And I'm not talking plastic, Hex. We want the deluxe cedar model with the rock wall and the wave slide next time."

Bash's eyes go wide. "With the lookout tower?"

"Exactly," Sable says, shooting me a playful warning look accompanied by a sexy wink.

I hold up my hands. "Deal. But only if I fall through the floor or get attacked by fire wolves. Otherwise, no promises."

Bash's already halfway to the door, barefoot and buzzing with excitement. "C'mon, let's go!"

I stand, stretch, and glance once more at Sable. "You coming?"

She shakes her head, still smiling. "You two go ahead. I'll clean up."

I want to tell her to leave it. I'd rather we all go out and make fools of ourselves climbing plastic towers and dodging imaginary danger. But I know this moment matters too—her watching from the kitchen window, seeing us together.

Night has fully settled by the time Sable steps onto the back deck, barefoot, her hair tousled in that careless way that suggests her thoughts have been busy. Bash is hanging upside down off the monkey bars, narrating some epic ambush plan with his imaginary fire wolves.

"Hey, bud," she calls gently. "Time to start wrapping it up. School tomorrow."

He groans with full end-of-the-world agony. "But I'm not even tired."

"You say that now, but I guarantee the minute you're in bed you'll be out like a light."

He drops down with a dramatic sigh, then looks up at me. "Are you coming back?"

I glance at her, waiting for my cue. She meets my eyes, something warm flickering in those beautiful browns.

"Hex can come over any time he wants," she says, voice soft but certain.

I almost offer to head out right then, to give them space for bedtime routines and all the rest of it.

But before I can get the words out, she adds, "Stay. It'll only take a few minutes."

So I nod, watching as she disappears inside with Bash, who's already negotiating for one more chapter of whatever space-dragon book they're reading together.

I move into her living room and settle on the couch. It smells like her, coconut and vanilla and something warm, like clean cotton and sun.

I lean forward. *Inhale.*

Lean back. *Exhale.*

Rest my hands on my knees. Breathe again.

It's too quiet.

Not outside. Not in the house. In me.

Stillness doesn't sit right in my chest. Never has. It means there's time to think and remember. And I've spent years keeping myself busy, keeping sharp. Muting it out.

But here, in this house that smells like peace, I feel it.

The guilt. The history. The hands I've used to hurt people.

I look around at the throw pillows and the faint glow of the hallway they disappeared down. Maybe Ned is right. This was never meant for someone like me.

Men like me don't end up in houses like this. They don't get good women or quiet mornings or kids who smile at them like they're safe.

We end up with regrets and criminal records and blood under our fingernails that soap can't touch.

I've done bad things that don't balance out with the good in her life, even with the right intentions. Things I wouldn't want her to know. Things I don't want to say out loud, because if I do, maybe she'll look at me and see what I am, not who I'm trying to be.

And she'd be right to walk away.

The couch shifts under my weight. I stare at the blank TV screen like it might give me an answer. Nothing. And the familiar ache creeps in to say:

You don't get to have this.

You're not meant for soft things.

Give him an angel and he'll find a wing to break.

Eventually, her faint footsteps on the hardwood return, leisured like she's letting the moment stretch. She ambles into the room bathed in the kitchen light, wearing an oversized sweatshirt and a sleepy-kind-of peace.

Sable drops down beside me without a word, tucking her legs up and curling into my side. She presses her face into my chest and exhales, then pulls back just enough to kiss me. Her lips linger like she wants me to know this one really means something, but also like she knows I need this kiss to stay upright.

I run a hand through her hair, brushing it back from her face. "You relieved?"

She smiles. "Immensely. I worked that up in my head to be a lot more stressful. You were amazing."

"Bash is amazing," I say. "Kid's sharp."

"You were too."

I pull her closer than I probably should. Her hand presses against my chest, her thumb moving in small circles over my shirt. She notices my hesitation—of course she does. We are attuned.

"What is it?" she asks.

I pause, but I don't dodge. I don't lie. Not with her.

"I want to give you a good reason to choose me," I say. "You've rebuilt your life. You're this grounded, bright, capable woman who doesn't flinch when shit goes sideways. And I'm... a man with too many bruised knuckles and a past I still haven't figured out how to carry without it bleeding all over the future."

She stays quiet. Just listens.

"I used to tell myself the violence didn't stick to me. That it didn't count if I was doing it for the right reasons. But it gets inside you. Makes a home in the worst way. And the scariest part? Some days, I don't even know who I'd be without it."

Her thumb pauses on my chest.

"I want to be better for you. I am better with you. But there's still this part of me that thinks one day you'll wake up and realize I was just a detour. That I don't belong here. Not with you. Not in a house that smells like pancakes and laundry."

I lift a hand to her jaw, tilt her face toward mine so I can see her eyes.

"I'm falling in love with you," I say, quiet but certain of my words. "Fast. And I can't stop it. Even if I'm not the kind of man you were supposed to end up with."

She pauses—just for a breath—but it lands heavy in the space between us.

Then she pulls back, just enough to look at me, eyes level with mine and clear.

"There was never a blueprint for that," she says softly. "Not for me."

I blink. Her thumb strokes across my cheek like she's memorizing my face. Her voice drops lower. "For a long time, I thought love had to look a certain way. Tidy. Predictable." She shakes her head. "But that wasn't *love*. That was survival. And I'm done just surviving. I realize I need a different kind of safe. And that the safe I used to look for wasn't the same as *good*. And it sure as hell wasn't *enough*."

She leans in to brush her warm mouth on mine.

"I want you. All of you. Not just the protector. Not just the man who shows up for me when things are messy. I want the man who thinks he's too fucked up to be loved. The one who," her eyes hold mine, "may not know how to sit still and be cared for."

Her words hit me straight in the chest. I open my mouth to say something, but she's already moving.

She shifts to straddle my thighs. My breath catches as her fingers find the hem of my shirt, slipping beneath it, palms grazing my stomach like she's trying to touch every inch I've ever tried to hide.

"You don't have to prove anything," she whispers. "Not with me."

Her hands move to my belt.

I still. Every nerve in my body goes tight.

"Sable..."

But she's already unfastening the buckle, already lowering her mouth to my neck with a kiss that's equal parts adoration and hunger.

I reach for her, but she catches my wrist midair and presses it gently back to the couch cushion.

"Let me," she says.

Two words, and I swear something inside me fractures.

Because no one's ever said that to me. Not like this. Not without expectation. Not without the edge of control.

She slides down to the floor, kneels between my knees, and unzips me. Her hands caress me like I'm not something to be handled but something to be praised. Her fingers are sure, freeing me from its fabric constraints.

My heart hammers. Nerves and anticipation mixing. Like I've never had this done before. Like I've never been the one given to.

Her mouth swallows my hard cock. Hot. Wet. Uninhibited.

She doesn't look away. Not once. Her hands brace my thighs as she takes me deeper, tongue dragging with purpose, lips soft but firm. Her tongue swirls where my head dips and meets my shaft. I pant out a groan. My eyes roll back at the rhythm she sets. It feels like worship and undoing all at once, and I feel it deep within me.

I clutch the couch, breath ragged, every part of me on fire.

"Sable..." Her name falls from my mouth like a sin I was born to repeat.

She hums low in her throat—*fuck*—and I feel it all the way down into my balls.

My vision blurs. I close my eyes and lean my head back. I clench my jaw. She pumps her mouth faster, taking me in, then adding in her hand like she's trying to drown out every ugly voice I've ever carried inside with the pure pleasure she's creating.

And I let her.

I let her.

My balls tighten. And I come undone with her name on my tongue, my hand tangled in her hair, and my claim in her, coating her mouth.

She pulls back slowly, wipes the corner of her lips with the pad of her thumb, and looks at me like she sees me.

Not the fighter. Not the protector.

Just me.

I'm still trying to breathe when she climbs back into my lap, straddles me like the world hasn't just shifted beneath our feet. Her forehead rests against mine, our breath mingling.

"I choose you," she whispers. "I want to give you the right place to land. The place you've always deserved."

My chest splits open. I feel myself let go. I feel all of it. For once I'm able to loosen my grip on everything I've held tight.

I love this woman.

And right now, that's everything.

We sit there like that for a long minute. Her fingers tracing lazy patterns on my skin. My hands tucked under her thighs, holding her there.

And then she speaks, voice soft but certain. "I have the court hearing next Friday."

Her head stays resting against mine, but her body goes tense. Like she's expecting me to falter. Or pull away. As if her problems could be too much.

"I've been trying not to spiral," she murmurs, "but I keep thinking Ashley's going to pull something before then. She's been too quiet. It's making me jump at shadows."

I wrap my arms around her body, tighter this time. Protective.

Next Friday isn't just her hearing.

It's the night Stauder expects me to show up and fight. The fight I haven't told her about yet.

"I've got you," I say, low into her hair. "No matter what."

And I mean it, with everything in me. But the weight of it isn't lost on either of us. Because that promise doesn't just mean Ashley. It means Stauder too.

Next Friday's already circled in blood.

CHAPTER
THIRTY-
FIVE

Sable

I 'm stuck in the car line, engine vibrating beneath me with the same restless energy crawling under my skin. Inching forward, I pretend I'm not clenching the wheel hard enough to leave marks. I try not to check the clock again and spiral into what-ifs. But my stomach's already tying itself into knots, and no amount of deep breathing is undoing them.

Today's the hearing to make the restraining order against Ashley permanent. If it goes through, it won't just protect me, it'll protect Bash, and Andrew, too. It'll put something legal and solid between us and the woman who turned my life into a nightmare.

I should feel empowered. I should feel ready.

Instead, I just feel... exposed.

Lately, the only peace I've found is in the quiet hours with Hex. When Bash is asleep. When the shop is closed and the bar's lights have gone dark. Sometimes he shows up late—so late it's almost morning—slips under my covers with that big, warm body of his, holding onto me. A need so quiet it barely breathes. He never stays long. He's always gone before Bash opens his eyes. But for those few hours, I forget everything else.

We've hooked up a few times during that stretch. *God, the way he touches me...* it feels... almost sacred, like he memorized me in another life. His hands move with certainty, always finding what I need before I ever have to ask. I can still feel the drag of his mouth against my neck, the way he whispers my name. There's something unspoken in the way he moves with me, as if he's trying to etch the moment into memory before it slips through his fingers. As if part of him is already halfway out the door.

That's what's been bothering me.

The way he's been quieter lately. Not distant, not with me—if anything, he's more attentive, more intense—but there's a weight behind his stare that didn't exist before. Something unsaid. Last night, his arms wrapped around me, but his head lived somewhere else entirely. I could feel it.

Something bigger than what he is telling me happened in that conversation with Stauder. He didn't speak much about it—just said it's nothing I need to worry about—but I'm learning that tone. That careful brush-off. Hex hasn't lied yet, not really. But he shields. He protects. Even when it means carrying too much on his own.

And I let him.

There was blood on his knuckles when he returned after speaking to him. I watched him from across the shop, that unreadable stillness he wears like armor. He didn't say who's blood. I didn't ask.

That's the problem, isn't it?

I haven't asked.

I don't know what that makes me... apathetic? Complicit? Stupid? Or maybe... maybe I know exactly what it makes me.

Someone who's tired of being good. Someone who's learning that good doesn't always keep you safe.

But what if he goes too far one day? What if I wake up and realize I let my son get close to a man who doesn't draw the same lines I do?

Or worse... what if I'm already too far gone to care?

He says he protects people. That he only hurts the ones who deserve it. But that's a line you draw in sand, not stone.

What scares me isn't that he's dark.

It's when he looks at me with those eyes like I'm the only thing anchoring him to something decent...

And all I can think about is how badly I want Hex beside me today. Not just in spirit, but standing next to me, hand in mine. Even if he won't be. Even if whatever's weighing on him keeps him away.

A car horn startles me. I blink and realize I've let the gap grow too wide between me and the car in front. I idle forward and spot Bash's teacher at the curb with the line of kids starting to emerge. My heart gives a little jump.

But she doesn't wave for Bash to come forward.

Instead, she steps up to my window, her expression polite but puzzled.

I roll it down. "Hey, everything okay?"

"Oh, yes," she says with a small smile. "I'm just surprised to see you, Ms. Hawthorne. Sebastian has already been picked up."

I blink. "What?"

"One of his approved pickups came through the line. Demi Kincaid? She had her ID, and we checked the list. You wrote her down as authorized."

My blood runs cold.

"Demi?" I repeat, more to myself than to her. "She picked him up?"

The teacher nods, trying to assure me this is all routine with an all too big smile. "Yes, a few minutes ago. ID matched, everything looked great."

That doesn't make sense. Demi's never picked Bash up. She's only on the emergency pick up list in case I'm with a client or Andrew can't get away from the dealership. She wouldn't even know how the car line works without calling me first in a panic, asking where to go, what lane to be in, how to not piss off the line monitors.

Something's wrong.

My fingers fumble with my phone. I scroll fast, my hands shaking now, until I land on a photo of Demi from her birthday last year. She's mid-laugh, one eye half-closed, holding a mimosa. Not flattering, but unmistakably her.

I flip the phone toward the teacher. "Is this who picked him up?"

She leans in. Then her face shifts.

"No," she says slowly. "That's not her. The woman who picked him up was blonde. But her ID said Demi Kincaid." She doubles down, acting as if she didn't just make a colossal fucking mistake.

The words don't compute.

All I hear is... *blonde.*

My lungs constrict for a second as if they forgot how to function.

My heart is hammering so loud I can barely hear her when she says, "Do you want me to call the school resource officer?"

"No," I say too quickly. My voice is tight, too bright. "It's probably just a misunderstanding. Demi must've dyed her hair or something. I'm sure it's fine."

I give her the best fake smile I can muster and roll the window up before she can ask another question.

My fingers are already moving, but I don't call Demi.

I call Hex.

It barely rings once before he answers. "Hey—"

"She took him," I say, but the voice that comes out feels borrowed "Ashley. She took Bash."

Saying her name makes my throat close up.

"What?" Hex's voice shifts immediately. No more softness. Just steel. "Where are you?"

"At the school. Car line. His teacher said Demi picked him up. But it wasn't her. She had an ID with her name, blonde hair—but it wasn't Demi. Hex, it was Ashley. I know it."

He doesn't hesitate. "I'm on my way. Send me your location. I'm getting JT on her now. We'll find them."

"I should've come earlier. I could've prevented this—"

"Stop. None of that," he snaps, low and firm. "She's the one who did this. Not you."

My breath stutters out of me. I'm already picturing the worst. Bash in some strange car. Ashley's voice in his ear. Her hands on him. My stomach twists so hard I nearly gag from the nausea.

"I should've known she'd try something today," I whisper. "I felt it."

"And now we know," Hex says. "And I swear to you, we'll get him back."

I nod, even though he can't see it. My fingers fly to share my location, heart in my throat. The sound of Hex's truck roaring in the background is the only thing keeping me from falling apart.

"JT's already moving," he tells me. "We'll get her location as well. Just sit tight. I've got you."

But I'm not sure I can sit still. Not with every part of me screaming to run. To fight. To tear the world apart until my son is back in my arms.

Because Ashley didn't just take him.

She declared war.

"I've got her location," Hex says, still on the line. "She's at the park off Meadow Ridge. Two blocks from you. I'm ten minutes out."

My heart lurches.

The park.

That's where Bash always wants to go after school when the weather's good. There's a little trail he likes to run, a jungle gym he's too big for but still climbs anyway. Our spot.

"Do you have the gun?" Hex asks, his voice clipped now. Controlled. "The one I gave you?"

I pop the glove compartment open with trembling fingers. The case is there, black and smooth, tucked between a wad of tissues and an expired insurance card. I snap it open. My name's on the registration card tucked inside. Hex made damn sure everything checked out as legal, registered, proper. *Safe.*

He never gave me that thing lightly.

I wrap my hand around the grip, the cool weight of it anchoring me.

"Yeah," I say, voice flat. "I've got it."

"Don't do anything," he says quickly. "Wait for me."

"I can't wait," I bite out. "She has my son, Hex."

Silence on the other end. But it's not because he disagrees. It's because he knows.

He taught me what to do when the decision's already made. When waiting isn't an option.

I hear him exhale. "Call the cops. Tell them what happened. Keep your phone on you. Sable—don't hesitate."

I nod. "I won't."

And I hang up.

I dial 911 with one hand, the other snapping the case shut and stuffing it into the glove box. I slip the weapon into my purse and secure it the way he drilled into me: barrel down, safety on, no room for error.

When the dispatcher answers, my voice is surprisingly steady. "My name is Sable Hawthorne. My son Sebastian was just abducted by a woman named Ashley Vaughn. She used a fake ID to pick him up from school. We have her location. She's at the Meadow Ridge Park. I'm on my way there now."

I rattle off the make and model of my car, my plates, the color hoodie Bash wore when I dropped him off at school this morning. I know what to say.

As soon as I end the call, something shifts inside me. The panic that was clawing at my throat settles into something colder. More focused. I pull out of the school lot and head toward the park. My pulse is a war drum, pounding out every second I've lost, every second she's had him.

I run through everything Hex ever taught me. Every scenario, every control point, every hard-earned lesson he drilled into me at the gun

327

range. How to stay alert. When to speak. When to stay quiet. When to stop waiting for someone else to save you.

This is one of those moments. A situation where the decision is obvious.

But beneath the focus, under the steady breath and the clinical movements, something older and darker pulses through me.

Not panic. Not fear.

Rage.

Cold, righteous rage.

The kind I've buried for years under calm smiles and crisis plans. Under the belief that if I just fixed everything fast enough, maybe the world wouldn't fall apart.

But I'm not fixing anything today.

I'm choosing.

Choosing to be the kind of woman who doesn't wait for permission to protect what's hers.

I used to think I had to be good.

But I'm not scared of the dark anymore.

I'm in love with someone who lives in it.

And right now, I don't want the light.

For once, I'm not scrambling to find the line between right and wrong. I'm standing in the middle of it. Gun in my purse. Steel in my spine.

I don't care how this ends. I only care that it does.

I want my fucking son back.

CHAPTER THIRTY-SIX

Hex

I'm preparing to fight tonight. Gloves on, tape tight, and Will and JT trading strategy as if this is any other Friday. I bounce on my toes in the gym, working through the motions while my mind stays split: half on the ring, half on Sable.

Then the phone rang.

Sable.

I don't need to hear more than three words to grab my shit and haul ass out the doors.

"*She took him.*"

Ashley fucking Vaughn.

She's crossed into a place she won't return from.

I fling myself behind the wheel and fly out of the lot. I'm doing sixty through a residential zone, praying I don't see red and blue in my rearview. Not until I get there. Not until I know they're safe.

The path narrows to a single point. Sable. Everything else—my fight, Stauder, whatever bullshit he's about to pull tonight—it can burn.

Sable's voice rattles in my head, strung so tight with fear I could feel it cutting her in half. She tried to hide it. She always does. She thinks being strong means going at it alone.

But I heard her. And the second she said Ashley's name, I stopped breathing.

JT's got eyes on the traffic cams. He's working her plates, scanning for every blonde in a ten-mile radius of that park. Will's holding down the bar. I told them I'd call if I needed backup—didn't need to say it, but I did, as if the words themselves could ward off disaster.

But right now, it's just me. This truck. The engine roaring as I punch it through a yellow light with half a second to spare.

My knuckles whiten around the wheel.

Sable's got the Sig. We checked the boxes: Registered in her name and a concealed carry permit in case some asshole cop decides to ask questions. I trained her how to hold it, when to draw, and how to move.

Because I knew there might come a day when she would have to use it.

God, please don't let that day be today.

She's already on her way. I don't blame her. Bash is out there. That sweet, scrappy little kid who's already been through too much. I'd be doing the same thing. Hell, I am. But Sable walking into that park alone with Ashley somewhere out there?

My fucking nerves are burning.

330

Seeing JT the other night—bloodied and broken—felt like a knife twisted in my gut.

But Sable—*fuck*, Sable. If she gets hurt trying to protect him... It will destroy my very being. I'd never forgive myself.

I slam my palm against the steering wheel, sharp and loud. The echo ricochets through the cab.

"Come on," I grit out, leaning into the next curve, tires squealing as I take it a bit too fast.

I see the park coming into view.

Almost there. Hold on, Sable. I'm coming.

CHAPTER THIRTY-SEVEN

Sable

T he second I pull into the parking lot, I see him.

Bash.

He perches at the edge of the bench, folded into himself the way he gets when his nerves take over. Ashley sits too close, arm draping over his shoulders, staking a claim she has no right to.

My focus locks on them before I'm even fully out of the car, my hand clutching my bag like it holds a live wire. A jogger cuts across my peripheral and that's when I notice there are a few people scattered around—someone walking a dog, a woman at the playground with a stroller—but no one close. No one watching.

My chest seizes.

Bash's eyes find me before hers do. Recognition flickers across his face. Relief softens the crease between his brows but it doesn't last long. He pushes off the bench on instinct—only for Ashley's arm to tighten around him, bicep flexing as she pins him in place.

She turns her head and sees me.

The air between us shifts. Her smile stiffens. Her back goes rigid. Her hand clamps down harder on my son.

My feet are moving closer.

Each step feels heavy and slow, but I'm closing the distance fast, every cell in my body vibrating with fury and fear. I don't reach for the gun yet. Not with Bash that close. Not with her hands still on him.

Her fingers move through his hair with a softness she hasn't earned, her entire body leaning into a lie she's desperate to make real.

My stomach turns. Another wave of nausea rolls through me.

Bash has the quiet panic of a trapped animal all over his face. He's wide-eyed, silent, and his shoulders are drawn up tight. His little hands are pressed against his knees, fingers twitching, pleading with his eyes for permission to bolt.

My baby.

"Let him go, Ashley." I demand through gritted teeth.

A fake innocence clings to her as she feigns surprise at my arrival. But her eyes betray nothing but the same smug glint from the bar. The same knowing smile she wore, convinced she held the upper hand.

"I'm just spending a little time with him," she says lightly, brushing hair from Bash's forehead. He flinches. Her voice is sweet, almost sing-song. "We were talking about how different things would be if you weren't around."

Bash stiffens. I see the sudden jolt in his small frame, a silent hit from something he clearly feels.

She's messing with his head.

"Don't do this," I say, keeping my voice low, even. *Don't let her rattle you.* "He doesn't understand what's going on. He's scared."

Ashley tilts her head, that condescending angle saved for things found to be ridiculous. "Is he?" she says, all wide-eyed mockery. She picks at the shoulder of his shirt, brushing away some imaginary lint, the way a mother might. But she's not. She never will be. "Or is he just confused because everything's been so unfair?"

My jaw clenches so tight my teeth hurt.

"You want to come at me? Fine. Come at me. But involving Bash—what the hell is wrong with you?"

She rises slightly from the bench, just enough to shift position, but not enough to let him go. Her arm stays firm around him, the way someone might hold onto a possession they know they're not supposed to have.

"You don't get it," she says, her voice hardening. "You never did. I didn't just want Andrew. I *loved* him. And he never even gave me a chance. Because of *you.*"

I step closer, hands trembling at my sides.

"Ashley, my relationship with Andrew is over," I say, careful with every word. Bash is right there. He's listening. "Whatever this is in your head—it's not real. It never was."

Her laugh breaks apart, brittle and jagged.

"He wants you," she hisses. "Always has. Perfect Sable. The one with the business, and the brains, and the beautiful little boy."

Her hand slides over Bash's hair again and I see his lip tremble. A flicker of panic flashes in his eyes. I go cold. Ice in my veins. Cement in my limbs. Rage in my bones.

Her hands don't ask. They take. Wrapping around him with the confidence of someone who already owns the ending.

"You ruined him for me," she whispers, each syllable laced with veneration and resentment in equal measure. "He told me you were the best woman he ever knew. Do you know what that does to someone? Hearing that? After he's already been inside you?"

Every muscle in my body goes tight at what Bash might hear.

"Let. Him. Go."

Her eyes don't see me. They're blown wide and wild, staring straight through me at some imagined elsewhere. A world she's rewritten in her favor. One where I never existed. One where she got the man, the house, the child.

"I could've given him a child, too," she murmurs, voice thin and trembling. "I would've given him everything. But you're in the way. You and your son—"

Her hand creeps lower.

Bash jerks in her grip, a soft, startled sound escaping him like he still doesn't understand what's happening. But I do.

She's about to do something I can't come back from.

Something *she* won't come back from.

The sound that comes from her chest next is feral. A broken screech of something unraveling all at once: pain, delusion, and desperation snapping free.

His eyes go wide—round and confused.

Her fingers wrap around my son's throat.

And the world *stops.*

One heartbeat.

His mouth opens but no sound comes out. He flails.

He slaps at her wrists, weak and panicked.

And something inside me tears open so violently I swear I feel it shoot through me like fire.

There's no time.

My hand dives into my purse, fingers finding the grip. I yank the pistol free, fast but controlled—*just like Hex taught me.*

My thumb releases the safety.

His voice is in my head, steady and sure:

Breathe. Line it up. Look past the fear. Find the shot.

Ashley angles forward away from Bash, back exposed. I have a path. A clean one.

White-knuckled hands around his throat, she digs her fingers into the softness of his skin. His face flushes dark. I don't even know if he sees me anymore. If he knows I'm here. If he knows his mom is watching this happen, helpless.

No.

Not helpless.

I raise the gun.

Every version of myself—the businesswoman, the mother, the fixer—breaks apart. All that's left is the part of me that would bleed the world dry to save him.

And it's enough.

My finger finds the trigger. I sight down the barrel.

Take the shot, Hex whispers.

I pull the trigger.

CHAPTER
THIRTY-
EIGHT

Hex

My boots hit the pavement before the truck is fully in park.
I break into a sprint. A shot rings out.

My chest seizes. I know that gun. I know who pulled that trigger.

I cut across the grass, heart hammering against my ribs as I round the edge of the playground.

Sable is standing ten feet from a bench, both hands gripping the gun just the way I taught her. Elbows locked, knees slightly bent. Not trembling. Steady. But her face is ghost-white, frozen in that moment after action, when your brain hasn't caught up to what your body just did.

Ashley's torso rests heavy on the bench, one leg folded beneath her, the other rooted in place—abandoned in a moment that came too fast to outrun. Her head lolls at an unnatural angle against the metal armrest. Blood blooms from her back in a quick, dark patch.

Dead.

Bash is coughing, choking back sobs as he scrambles away from her collapsed body. Purple marks darken around his throat. At the sound of her son's pain, Sable drops the gun and gathers him against her, clutching him tight as if the world is still poised to take him away.

They fall together into the grass, a tangle of arms and hair and broken sounds.

She's saying something—I can't make it out yet—but I can feel it. Her whole body is shaking. Her fingers thread through Bash's curls, palm firm against his back, rocking him in a rhythm meant to block everything else out.

I slow my approach, but only just. Eyes scanning the perimeter.

People saw. A jogger's already on the phone. A woman with a stroller is pointing, talking fast to someone off-screen. Good. Let them talk. Let them tell the story. Because what happened here? It's *justified*.

I reach them as Bash hiccups and sobs into her chest, and she looks up at me.

Her face—*God,* her face.

Not scared of consequences. Not yet. But wrecked. Shattered. Red-rimmed eyes locked in a stunned gaze, her parted lips trembling on the edge of a breath she can't fully find.

"She had him," she says, voice raw. "She had her hands on his throat."

"I know, baby," I breathe, crouching beside them. "You did what you had to do."

She nods, once, wanting to believe it. But her eyes keep darting back to the bench. To Ashley. To the red spilling down her blouse. To the silence where there should've been more screaming.

Sable's not used to death.

I am.

She wanted to handle this the right way. Courts. Restraining orders. Logic. Paper trails. She dotted every *i*, crossed every *t*, begged the system to see the truth.

But the system doesn't always get there in time.

She did. The moment forced her hand.

Even if it broke something inside her.

The sirens are close now. Maybe five minutes out. But there's enough here. Witnesses. Bash's bruised neck. Her legal weapon.

I watch her cradle her son, one hand still trembling, eyes far away. The gun lay in the grass where she dropped it. There was no panic, no concealment to question.

I know she's thinking about the fact that she killed someone.

Maybe imagining how close she came to losing Bash.

And I can't fix that for her.

But I can be here when it lands.

I kneel beside her and curl an arm around both of them, pulling them into me, letting Bash's sobs soak through my shirt, letting Sable collapse against my chest.

"I didn't want this," she whispers.

"I know," I murmur into her hair, holding her tighter. "You wanted this to end the right way. But it didn't. It ended the way it had to."

And God help anyone who tries to take her down for it.

The moment we cross the threshold of Sable's house, it feels different. The air hangs heavier, charged with the energy of what she just lived through.

Sable moves in a haze, holding Bash to her chest, his arms wrapped tight around her neck. His face is tucked into her shoulder, tear-streaked and red, but he's calm now. Tired. Worn out.

The paramedics checked him. He's okay. Bruised, shaken, but physically okay. Recommended, in time, to speak to a professional to work through the event.

They said the marks on his neck would fade in a few days. But we'll all remember those marks long after they are gone.

Andrew's already pulling into the driveway and hopping out of his truck. I hold the front door for him. He gives me a slight nod and the second he steps inside his eyes go to Bash.

"Bash," he breathes, voice cracking, and in three strides he's there.

Sable lets him go, and Bash doesn't hesitate, drawn forward to the man he knows. His dad.

Andrew sinks to the floor, clutching his son to his chest, his head bowed low, fingers splayed protectively over Bash's back. His shoulders shake. No words. Just that raw, helpless grip of a father who realizes how close he came to losing his child.

I back off, giving them space.

I send JT and Will quick texts of what happened, but I don't wait for a response. My eyes find Sable.

Frozen in the entryway, her hands hang limp at her sides, her body suddenly foreign in the absence of adrenaline. She doesn't look at me. She looks at Andrew and Bash curled up on the couch, whispering. Her eyes drink them in with the quiet desperation of someone trying to remember what safety looks like. Someone trying to believe it's real.

I step to her. Wrap both arms around her without a word.

Sable folds into me immediately, her head pressing against my chest like her body's just given up the fight. My hand finds the back of her head, fingers sliding into her hair, anchoring her there. I press a kiss to her temple.

"I'm not leaving you," I murmur. "Not tonight. Not tomorrow. If I have to move into this house and post up twenty-four-seven to make sure nothing like this ever happens again, I will. I'm not going anywhere."

She doesn't respond.

Just breathes. Shallow. Fragile.

Then, finally, she speaks. "I don't feel bad."

I pause.

"I don't feel *anything*," she says, a little louder this time. "Not guilt. Not shame. Just… relief. And I don't know what that says about me."

Her voice breaks near the end of her words, but tears don't fall. They just swell in her eyes, turning them glassy and wide.

I pull back enough to cradle her face in my hands.

"It says you're a mother," I tell her, my voice low, steady. "It says you protected your son. That you made a choice no one should ever have to make. But you made it. You survived it. You gave him a chance to grow up."

She stares at me, eyes rimmed in red, torn between wanting to believe me and punish herself.

"You didn't do anything wrong, Sable," I say. "You stopped someone from doing something evil."

Her shoulders tremble.

And then she's back in my chest again, arms around my waist, clinging like she might come undone if she lets go.

I hold her as long as she needs. We don't move. We don't speak.

Then, eventually, she whispers, "Can we go outside?"

"Yeah," I say. "Yeah, baby. Come on."

I guide her gently through the front door. The sky is soft with the beginning of twilight, the street quiet, calm. She sits down on the steps of the porch, barefoot and pale. A breeze lifts strands of hair off her face.

I sit beside her.

The porch light clicks on behind us, spilling gold over her skin.

She stares at the angelonias beside the railing. Soft purple and white petals color the edge of her house.

"They're blooming," she murmurs, more to herself than me.

"Yeah. They're strong," I say. "Took root fast. Didn't need much."

She nods slowly. Doesn't look at me.

Just breathes.

And then, barely audible I hear:

"I love you."

It's not grand. It's not tearful. It's solid. Like a truth she's known longer than she could admit. Like the words finally caught up to the feeling.

I glance over at her, but I don't speak. I don't need to. Wrapping my arm around her and pulling her into my lap, I kiss her temple again and repeat the words back to her.

My phone buzzes in my pocket.

I don't look. It's likely Will or JT trying to figure things out. The fight at Stauder's warehouse starts in less than an hour.

Too fucking bad.

This is where I'm needed, and this is where I'll stay.

CHAPTER
THIRTY-
NINE

Hex

I kill the engine. The morning air's sharp enough to sting my lungs as I head for the back entrance of Ruin's End. Just the one missed call. No texts. That alone would be enough to set me on edge... but not hearing from *either* of them the rest of the night?

That's a problem.

The bar should've closed out around two. They knew damn well I didn't show up to fight. I told Will. Told JT. And still—nothing?

Unlocking the steel door, I step into the quiet hush of the bar.

The whole place holds the echo of someone who walked off mid-close out.

Chairs are up. Bar top's been wiped down but there's no reflection in the grain, the way Will gets it. The bottles are all in their places behind the counter, but not aligned by label and height.

I track around the bar. No prepped limes in the fridge. No folded clean bar towels in the bin under the register. Half-assed rinsed mats.

By the time my eyes track the mop bucket near the entrance, the handle leaning against the counter, I'm sprinting toward the loft.

Not Will clean.

Something's wrong.

I move fast, sneakers heavy on the stairs. If I'm not here, JT's usually crashing up top.

I push the door open and there he is.

JT—sitting at the kitchen counter, elbows on the cold stone, face in his hands. He looks up when he hears me and damn near jumps out of his skin.

"Hex," he says, voice hoarse. "Shit."

"Where's Will?"

The bathroom door creaks behind me, and I whirl around.

Will steps out.

And I stop breathing.

His lip is split and swollen, dried blood tracing the corner of his mouth. His left eye is black and puffed near shut. Bruising creeps from his jaw down his neck, the shape of fingerprints stamped in deep red ink. One side of his shirt is ripped, exposing scrapes and swelling along his ribs. His knuckles are busted open—barely scabbed and raw—and he's limping.

Will—tall and lean, normally a goddamn pretty boy with those light brown waves and bright blue eyes—is wrecked.

I don't even realize I'm moving until I'm in front of him.

"Man," I breathe, staring him down, chest splitting. "Did they come after you?"

Will gives me that sideways grin that's more pain than charm.

"No," he says. "I went to them."

"What?"

"I might look like shit, but I won." He says with a crooked smirk.

My brain stalls. "You what?"

Will limps over to the kitchen, drags a stool out from under the counter with his foot, and drops onto it, wincing like hell but still smug underneath it all.

"Ned let me stand in for you," he says, glancing at JT. "He agreed. I knew if I told you, you'd never let me. So, we didn't. We went. Took care of it."

"You—" I run my hand down my face, heart thudding. "Jesus, Will."

"I did good," he says. "Real good. They sent a fucking tank in human skin. He opened wild—tried to break my ribs in the first round. But he was slow. Too heavy. I kept it tight, kept him moving. Let him believe the fight left me. When he charged, I took his knee out from under him and went for the jaw. Spit blood for two rounds but didn't go down. Got him flat by the fourth. Broke his orbital. Won it." He smiles again, grim satisfaction in it. "Didn't bring in what you would've, but Stauder accepted it. On the condition of one clean-up job. Of his choosing."

I stare at him. "Will—"

"Our debt is clear," he says.

"It's not our debt. And once he sees what you can do, you won't be free of him," I warn.

Will shakes his head slowly. "Of course it is *our* debt, Hex."

I look between him and JT, my chest cracking wide open. "I left you. I left you both. And you did this alone—"

"We're never alone," JT says quietly. "You taught us that."

"You think we'd let you carry all of it?" Will leans forward, voice softer now, but firm. "You think we haven't learned anything from you? All that training, all that discipline. We've watched you for years. You don't get to act like we're just your shadows. Sable needed you, man. And you needed us. So we showed up. We handled it."

"You don't know what could've happened," I snap, voice cracking at the edges. "You think I don't want you to fight because I don't think you're good enough? I don't let you go in there because I'm fucking terrified of losing you."

Silence stretches thick between us.

Will nods. "And Sable? She did what she did because you showed her how, didn't she? You gave her that strength. That knowledge. She saved her son. You made that possible."

His voice goes quiet. "Let us do the same for you."

I fold.

I rub a hand over my jaw, eyes burning. "You're both still fucking idiots."

Will grins, lopsided and bloody. "But *living* idiots."

I shake my head. "Yeah. And I'm gonna be paying for that clean-up job for the rest of my life."

"Damn right you are," JT mutters.

We all laugh. It's shaky, bitter, but real.

And when the laughter fades, and everything settles again into that heavy kind of silence—the one you only earn after a fight—I glance toward the door. Toward the road that leads back to her. Back to Sable.

Something shifts inside me, a magnetic pull locking into place and swinging home.

Because now more than ever, I know what it means to be surrounded by people who show up when it counts. When the fists are flying, when the blood's fresh, when the weight feels too damn heavy for one set of shoulders. And somehow—somehow—they still show up for me.

I used to think I had to protect everyone. If I could just take the hits, carry the weight, bleed first, then maybe nobody else would have to. Maybe I could out-suffer the world for all of us.

But that's not how this works.

I watched Sable put herself between her son and death. She pulled the trigger with no one there to give her permission. I watched her survive something she never asked for and never should've had to face.

And she did it because I showed her how. Because I wanted to be in her life and teach her what to do when a hard decision presented itself. Show her that she didn't have to stick around and patch up every broken thing just because she knew how. Fixing things didn't make them right. Sometimes the strongest thing she could do was confront it head on before the damage turned permanent.

She didn't need saving. Just someone to remind her she could save herself.

And Will? JT?

They fought. For me. For us.

They walked into the lion's den because they believed in what we've built. Because they knew I couldn't be in two places at once, and they decided that they would protect me.

They made a call I've never let myself make. And they did it without asking. Without fear.

Because I taught them to.

And that's what tears me up most. Not that they fought without me. Not that Will took hits meant for my back. But that I've been too fucking scared to let them show me what they've become. Because I know loss. I know the cold grip of it. I know what it means to bury people you swore to protect. And that fear kept me from trusting that they're not boys anymore. They're men. Fighters. Brothers in every way that counts.

And they made sure I didn't lose the one person I can't live without. Sable.

She's waiting for me now. Probably sitting at that kitchen table, hands wrapped around a mug that's long gone cold, wondering what comes next. Wondering if I see her differently. If what she did changed the way I look at her.

It didn't.

If anything, it made me love her more.

Because I know what it costs to make the hard choice. To do what needs doing and carry the weight of it afterward.

She did it anyway.

So yeah, I'm going back to her.

I'm going to walk through that door and wrap my arms around her and let her know, without question, that she's not alone. Not anymore. Not ever.

CHAPTER FORTY

Sable

*I*t's been two weeks.

I keep saying that out loud, chasing meaning in the rhythm. Maybe the right number will rest everything: my body, my brain, the way my stomach clenches when the wind hits just right. Sometimes I think screaming might make the ingrained paranoia of the past six months go away. Strip it like bubbling paint.

The shop stayed closed for a few days after everything. I needed time. Bash needed it more. Andrew agreed to let Hex take us out to his Hill Country place for a week to get out of town, breathe different air, and change the view.

It helped.

Hex never strayed far from my side. He hovered without hovering. Tentative, gentle, in a way I never expected from a giant, rough-edged fighter. One who handled Bash with glass-blown care and treated me as if every fractured piece deserved to be rebuilt.

The time we spent together changed the three of us. We played card games until Bash got too competitive and declared himself King of Uno. Hex rigged a gaming system in the living room; a setup so elaborate, it looked ready for permanent teenage residency.

One night, we dragged every blanket and pillow we could find into the middle of the floor and made a pallet. All three of us stayed there: me curled on one side, Bash sprawled down the middle, Hex capping the other end. I woke up at three in the morning, to pee of course, with Hex's hand in mine and his other arm tucked under Bash's shoulders.

Sleep came fitfully, broken by sudden starts. A vivid dream yanking me from sleep. His arms were always there to reel me back in and calm me down. Nothing in my life ever came close to feeling that safe.

One afternoon while Bash was in the other room FaceTiming his dad, Hex and I ended up on the couch, legs tangled. I had my feet in his lap, a glass of wine in one hand. He had bourbon, untouched, resting against his thigh. He hadn't taken a sip in twenty minutes. He was just... there. Calm. Still. Dangerous in every other setting but this one.

And for some reason, that made the question rise in my throat like it had been waiting there for far too long.

"Do you want a kid?" I asked, my voice smaller than I meant it to be.

He turned to look at me, not surprised, just thoughtful. Like he'd been expecting it.

"You offering me yours?" he asked with a smile.

I laughed under my breath. *"I'm serious."*

"*So am I.*" He set his glass down, leaned forward with his elbows on his knees, eyes locked on mine like he wasn't afraid of the weight that came with the question.

God, I wish I could've made it casual with him. But it just wasn't. Not anymore.

"*I don't think I want more,*" I said quickly, before I could talk myself out of it. "*Not because I don't love being a mom. I do. But I'm not nearly as young anymore. Bash is everything, and I gave everything to have him. My body, my sleep, my entire damn sense of self. And now that I'm here,*" I motion between us, "*I don't know if I want to go back to diapers and bottles and sleep schedules.*"

I looked away, maybe a bit remorseful, admitting that to him and myself. "*I'm not saying it's a forever no. But I don't feel a yes in me either. And I needed to say it before this thing between us gets even deeper than it already is.*"

He didn't flinch. Not even a twitch.

"*You think that'd be a deal breaker for me?*" he asked softly.

"*I don't know. You're younger. You've never had a baby that was yours, and I—*"

"*Sable.*" His voice landed with strength. Not loud. Just certain "*I didn't fall in love with the idea of starting a family. I fell in love with you. And I don't need a biological stamp on a kid to feel the fulfillment of fatherhood.*"

Tears pricked behind my eyes. Not because I was sad, because for the first time, maybe ever, I believed someone wouldn't leave when I showed them the parts of me that didn't bend.

"*I just didn't want you to wake up one day and resent me for it,*" I whispered.

He leaned across the couch, brushed his thumb beneath my eye even though no tear had fallen yet. His voice went soft again. *"You gave me something I didn't think I'd ever have.* You. *That's all I want."*

It wasn't a grand declaration. No fireworks. No dramatic music swell. But when he said it, I believed him.

Mornings were slow and warm and a little ridiculous after that. Hex made pancakes every single breakfast. Thick, fluffy stacks crowned with whipped cream, as if the meal were a sacred ritual. He'd hand me my plate with a smirk, eyebrow raised, leaning close under the pretense of small talk, then murmur filth that made my knees weak. Always quiet. Always with a straight face.

"Next time I put whipped cream on something, I want it to be those beautiful tits, not breakfast."

And in seconds, my thighs would press together, warmth blooming between them while I tried to act normal and butter my pancakes. He'd just smirk and sip his coffee, utterly unbothered by the fact that he'd wrecked me for the rest of the morning.

Hex, in time, told me everything. The same day Ashley took Bash, he stood only hours away from a fight that could've ended him. A fight arranged to settle debts and keep Ned Stauder from circling us like vultures.

He didn't hold anything back. Not the threat, not the consequences, not the part where Will stepped in and bled for him. It should've gutted me to know danger still surrounded us, that something as simple as loving Hex came with risk. But it didn't. Not really. Maybe it came down to my belief in him. Or maybe in myself, and what I'd do to protect the people I love with everything in me.

Either way, the fear didn't sink its teeth in the way it once would've. I knew danger wouldn't just vanish from his life. He wouldn't stop helping people who needed him.

And the strangest part of it all... how okay I felt with that.

Returning to Stillwater Bend wasn't the crash landing I'd imagined. Mostly because Demi waited for me with snacks, six candles she swore had cleansing properties, and a ridiculous amount of restraint.

She's toned herself down, for now. No outlandish comments in front of Bash. No loud proclamations about justified vengeance. Just a quiet whisper, buried in the corner of the shop, meant only for me:

"The Lady Punisher rides again."

I snorted into my coffee.

Now, two weeks later, I'm finally back in a rhythm. *Sort of.* Bash is back at school. My doorstep no longer feels haunted. And Demi—well, Demi is back to her meddling self, which is apparently a sign that the universe is healing.

She's currently trying to lure me out of the shop with vague promises of *"a surprise that will definitely change your life."*

Andrew just picked up Bash for the weekend, and the moment they pulled out of the back of the shop, the door cracked open, Demi peeking around it with the shameless timing of someone who might have been crouched outside waiting for her cue.

"If this is another half-priced Brazilian," I warn, grabbing my bag where the gun Hex gave me now permanently lives, "I'm not interested."

She raises a perfectly arched brow. "Not even if I hold your hand while you get yours?"

I blink. "Why would I get one?"

"Confidence. Smooth skin. Battle readiness," she says, deadpan.

I squint at her. "You're hiding something."

She clutches her heart. "How dare you. I would never—okay, fine, yes, I'm absolutely hiding something, but it's for your own good. And no, it's not another waxing appointment. That counted as a one-time coupon situation. And trust me, lesson learned. The rash I got definitely factored into the two-star rating I gave them on Google."

"Does Hex know about this?" I prod her.

"Hex *planned* this." She immediately squeaks and holds her hand up to cherry lips that match her hair.

I stop dead in my tracks. "He what?"

She grins. "Oops. Forget I said that."

"Oh my God. Demi—"

"Shh. Lady Punisher, *relax*. Just trust me. If I were going to kidnap you for something reckless and entirely inappropriate, I would've brought tequila and a shovel."

I stare at her. "I don't even want to know what that means."

"Then stop asking questions and get in the car. It's not a far drive."

I sigh, half-exasperated, half-suspicious. But there's a flicker of warmth in my chest now. Something stirring beneath the anxiety, the rebuilding.

"Where are we going?" I ask again, trying to peek at her phone to see if she has GPS turned on.

She just grins. "Let's just see if I'm really banned for fucking life."

I blink. "Wait—Ruin's End?"

She shrugs. "I mean, *you're not*. I'm the one who threatened to throw a chair at that bartender with the nice arms and emotional constipation. But who's keeping score?"

"You're definitely on some sort of list," I mutter as we pull into the lot.

As soon as we round the corner, JT looks up from where he leans on the window checking IDs, that lazy, crooked grin tugging at his mouth.

"Well damn," he says, smiling warmly. "Look who just made this place hotter by twenty degrees."

I snort, cheeks flushing. "You always this smooth?"

He shrugs. "Only when I mean it."

"Keep dreaming, kid." I wink and pat him on the shoulder.

Demi loops her arm through mine, smug as hell. JT follows in behind us.

Inside, the bar hums with early-evening energy. The music is low, voices rising, and glasses clinking. We barely cross the threshold before Will clocks us and recoils, a full-body flinch, as though a bar rag just flew out of nowhere and slapped him.

"Absolutely fucking not," he says, pointing dramatically. "Sable, you're welcome. But the pitbull has to go."

Demi flips him off with flourish. "I missed you too, High Lord."

He scoffs. "I still have frosting-related trauma, thanks to you."

Before I can respond, three or four patrons—clearly regulars—perk up in unison, the kind of synchronized curiosity that only comes from weeks of silent eavesdropping.

The first one, a tall, wiry man in a neon green trucker hat with *"Ask Me About My Ex-Wives"* written across it, leans forward with a shocked expression. "You're Sable? *The* Sable?"

Next to him, a woman in a biker vest covered in glittery patches and exactly three feathers braided into her gray hair squints dramatically. "Hot damn, I thought he made you up. Like that guy from Fight Club but with tits."

"Girl, we've had a pool going on what you looked like. Thought you might have been some AI bullshit." A third guy, all of five-foot-five with a mustache that deserves its own introduction, elbows the first man. "Told ya she was real."

"She's real!" someone in the back yells. "And fine as hell! Pay up, Denny!"

Then ZZ Top Beard himself slaps the bar, proudly sporting a *"WWHD—What Would Hex Do?"* tee that looks homemade and hasn't been within spitting distance of a washing machine since 2019. "Queen of Ruin's End right here!"

I nearly double over laughing. It's too much. Too chaotic. Too perfect. I snort, and everyone hears it, and somehow that only makes the applause grow louder. Demi beams beside me like she orchestrated the chaos herself. But I know the owner of this place curated this crowd into exactly what they've become.

With both hands, Demi hurls me into the thickening circle of regulars, who swarm me with praise and hilarious comments.

Then I feel it.

That shift in the air.

Everything hushes inside me, even with the room still buzzing. My body registers him before my eyes do.

I turn... and there he is.

Hector Xavier Alvarez.

Walking toward me. Time bends around him. Every line of his body taut and powerful. A black tee hugs his frame as if it knows it's wrapped around something sacred.

His eyes are locked on mine. Focused. Unflinching. No hesitation. No noise. Just him.

He stops right in front of me.

Curling one strong arm around my waist, he lifts and settles me gently on the bar's edge. His hands linger on my thighs, tracing the shape of me with quiet devotion. As if I'm something both fragile and unbreakable.

The room hushes.

The entire bar goes still, a breath caught in every throat at once, including my own.

Then he speaks.

"I've had a lot of versions of this place in my mind," he says, his voice low, gravel-smooth, unshakeable in a way that makes my whole body lean toward him. "And a lot of versions of myself."

He goes still, eyes distant, as if tracing a thread that runs back through everything he's ever been. "I used to stand right here and picture what this bar could be. What *I* could be. Different setups, different nights, different faces coming and going. Sometimes I imagined success. Sometimes I imagined walking away from it all. But none of those versions ever felt right."

He looks up at me again, eyes locked, sure as anything.

"Because *you* were in none of them."

My breath catches.

I can't blink. Can't move. Afraid that even the slightest movement will shatter this moment.

"You crashed into my life like a storm—well, that was mostly Demi," he says with a small, crooked grin that pulls a soft laugh from the crowd and a *"You're fucking right"* from Demi, "but you... you made everything make sense."

He takes a breath, and I feel it echo in my own chest.

"I love you so damn much, it rewired me. You and Bash. You didn't just give me something to look forward to. You *became* home. You're the peace I never thought I deserved, and the angel that pulled me out of the dark."

The air around us stills. My heartbeat is so loud in my ears, I can barely hear the world anymore. I mouth *I love you too*, not wanting to interrupt him but wanting him to also know I feel the same.

"I've lived a life where I've had to fight for everything. Every inch of ground, every breath, every fragment of peace. But loving you... loving you doesn't feel like a fight."

His voice drops, roughened by restraint, every syllable striving not to splinter.

"It feels like coming up for air."

My throat burns. My vision blurs with tears, but I don't move to wipe them away. I want to feel every second of this.

He steps one pace back, releasing my hand, but his eyes never leave mine.

Right there on the bar floor, between the peanut shells and boot scuffs and spilled whiskey I'm sure Will is pissed about—Hex drops to one knee.

From his pocket, Hex pulls out a ring. It's worn around the edges with an antique setting whispering of other hands, other promises, none quite like this one. The band is delicate but strong, etched with the faintest vine work that catches the light if you tilt it just right.

It's subtle, elegant, but nothing flashy. At the center sits a bold onyx diamond, deep, dark, and perfectly cut as if carved from midnight itself. It doesn't need to sparkle to be seen; it holds attention just by existing. A stone that says I've seen the fire, and I'm still here.

It's not traditional. It's not what anyone else would've chosen.

But it's *perfect* for me.

And somehow... Hex knew that. Knew exactly what I would want, even though I'd stopped letting myself picture a ring a long time ago.

My hands grip the edge of the bar. White-knuckled.

I look down at him, chest tight, heartbeat crashing against my ribs, ready to surrender itself to him completely. I never thought I'd get this moment. Not at thirty-nine. Not with everything that came before. Not after the wreckage of a decade-long relationship that blessed me with my child. The heartbreak. The fight it took to get here.

But here he is.

Hex.

He looks at me the way believers look at light breaking through stained glass. I'm his proof that hope wasn't wasted.

"Legs," he says, voice rough but clear. "You are mine. You are my Angel."

Then softer, I hear the question I thought would never grace my ears: "Will you marry me?"

My throat tightens.

Tears push at the back of my eyes, but I hold them there. Not because I'm trying to be strong. Because I want to see him clearly. Every line of his face. The reverence in his expression. The way his hands hold still—not shaking, not reaching—just waiting.

I slide off the bar. My knees brush the edge of his thigh as I lower myself in front of him.

I reach down and lift his chin with two fingers, feel the rough stubble graze my skin, and suddenly all I can think is—

He looks even better on one knee than he did on two.

My heart swells until it presses against everything inside me, stretching wide enough to crowd out breath... thought... everything.

I lean in close, just enough so no one else can hear but him. "Let's fucking do this."

He surges up as if gravity lost its hold. His hands lock around my waist, lifting me clean off the floor into a kiss that feels like coming home. Starting over. And setting fire to every plan we ever made just to build something entirely new together.

The bar erupts.

Cheering. Glasses pounding. Someone screams "HELL YES!" from the back. ZZ Top Beard howls like a banshee. Trucker Hat throws a coaster, imitating a wedding bouquet. Biker Glitter Queen pulls a flask from her bra and toasts the ceiling.

"Hey, no outside liquor, Maryann!" Will shouts, then turns to Hex and me, "About damn time!"

I smile into Hex's mouth and can't help but giggle with happiness.

Demi's full-on sobbing and fanning herself with something laminated.

I don't even know what I'm laughing at anymore. Maybe it's the cheering, maybe it's the coaster in the air, maybe it's the way Hex hasn't let go of me, arms locked like I'm still something he's afraid to lose. But I can't stop smiling. My cheeks hurt. My heart cracks wide open, and love floods in, filling every hollow I didn't know sat empty.

For the first time, in a long time, I'm not waiting for the other shoe to drop. I'm not thinking about the past, or the mess, or what comes next. I'm just *here*. In this wild, rowdy bar, with this wild, *steady* man, surrounded by people who love us in their own, chaotic way.

I look to my best friend Demi, who is still blotting her eyes with what I now recognize is a drink specials insert. It's a proud moment for her as well, as she points her menu in the air victorious and announces:

"This will be the best fucking wedding I ever plan!"

CHAPTER FORTY-ONE

Hex

"I t's starting to hurt," she mutters, voice strained.

I slide closer, my thumb brushing the inside of her wrist as I catch her hand. "Tapping out already?" I murmur against her ear. "Didn't think you'd fold before the outline was even done."

"I'm not folding. I'm adjusting." Her eyes flash up at me, watery but fierce. "He's only done the outline?"

I can hear the panic, and it makes me laugh. "No, I'm kidding. He's shading now."

Sable grips my hand harder, nails digging in just enough to make me feel it. God, she's gorgeous when she's wild and stubborn and trying so damn hard not to give in.

"Don't make me punch you with my non-tattoo arm."

I lean in, close enough she can feel the heat off my mouth. "You try it, Legs, and I'll make him give you a second tattoo that says crybaby across your ass cheek."

The artist snickers behind his machine. I keep holding her hand like I'm not the biggest sucker for her in the room.

She's doing so fucking good.

I glance over. The skin is flushed and raw but beautiful beneath the slow reveal of black and gray lines. The outline of the angel wing is already mapped out, stretching from the top of her shoulder down to just above her elbow. Completely her.

Remembering the night she said how strange it felt to never have any-thing permanent enough in her life to ink into her skin. It did something to me. To never feel that...

Then to have her look at me a week after proposing and say she wanted one: "*The angel wing. Just one. Just the one you drew.*"

So I sketched it again. Poured everything I had into it. The softness. The strength. Designed to move with her, curving so fluidly it will seem one breath away from lifting her off the ground.

Bash watched me draw it. The kid is so enamored with creative arts, just like his mama. Every time he pointed out a line gone too thick or a curve off mark, the design grew more meaningful.

Her first tattoo. She walked into the shop nervous as hell and doing her best to fake calm. But I could feel the tremble in her hand. See the way her breath shortened when the stencil hit her skin. The nervous chatter she couldn't control.

Still, she didn't flinch.

Not once.

"You're doing incredible," I whisper, rubbing my thumb across her knuckles.

She turns her head, eyes meeting mine through lashes that are heavy with heat and a little bit of pain. "Yeah?"

"Yeah," I say, kissing her hand. "Tough as hell, angel."

"Have I officially graduated into my grown-up pet name?" she asks.

The artist looks up from her arm and gives me a nod. "Almost there. Last bit of shading."

Sable exhales, steady now. Focused.

I glance at her hand in mine, at the ring I picked that fits her like it always belonged there, then back to the ink stretched across her skin.

"Not quite," I breathe, kissing the back of her hand, then trailing my mouth lower. "But I'm gonna lose my shit the first time I get to call you *wife*."

She laughs. Soft. Real. Like it lands somewhere deeper than she expected.

The woman I love wears my art on her skin like it's a badge of honor, inked in trust and permanence.

And I've never been more fucking sure of forever.

The artist smooths ointment over the tattoo with careful fingers and wraps it in a thin band of medical film, securing it tight against Sable's skin. The wing curves perfectly, the way Bash suggested I draw it. Every feather inked in with the kind of detail that makes my chest ache. She looks down at it, eyes wide, as if her mind is just now registering what her body now carries.

Mine has.

It was always meant for her skin, her story, her soul.

We thank the artist and head out, hand in hand. It's still early afternoon, warm and slow, the kind of day that wants you to go home and do nothing.

Back at the loft, we kick the door shut behind us and drop our stuff near the couch.

Bash is still at school for another forty-five minutes.

Sable stretches her arm out carefully, already wincing at the soreness. "No way I'm going back to the shop today. This thing hurts."

"That's your dominant arm too," I say, moving to the kitchen to grab her a glass of water.

"I know," she groans, holding it up and mimicking a sanding motion that accidentally—and very clearly—looks like a hand job. She pauses mid-move, eyes narrowing in mock offense.

"Nope," she says, shaking her head. "That's no good. Can't even pretend to be productive."

I smirk as I step back toward her, glass in hand.

"Oh, I can think of something else we can do for forty-five minutes." I hand her the water, brushing her hip with mine. "Your arms are not required, but your legs are mandatory."

She barely has time to laugh before I scoop her up, one arm under her knees, the other at her back. She yelps and clings to me, grinning through a wince.

"Hex!"

"Shhh," I murmur, pressing a kiss to her shoulder with care as I carry her to the bed. "Doctor's orders."

I lay her down slow, careful not to jostle her arm too much. She hisses when her elbow brushes the sheet, and I freeze.

"You okay?"

"Yeah," she says, breathy. "Just... don't touch the wing."

I give her a grin that feels downright predatory. "Your elbow is nowhere near where I want to be."

Sable bites her lip as I slide my hands down her hips, easing her pants past her thighs, then off entirely. I drag my palms up her inner thighs, moving with the kind of patience that says I've got time. Because I do. For her, I always do.

"I'll keep away from your wing," I murmur, dragging my mouth along the soft skin of her hip. "But everything else is fair game."

Her breath catches as I nudge her thighs open. She's already warm. Already wet.

"I love you," I say against her skin. "The way you taste. The way you lose yourself for me."

She lets out a soft, trembling sound as I kiss her inner thigh. The hand on her good arm fists the sheets.

Long, deep strokes of my tongue make her hips twitch. Soft moans turn into broken gasps. I don't stop. I don't rush. I keep one hand on her stomach to keep her still, the other gripping her thigh while I worship her with my mouth.

Her breathing goes ragged. She tries to muffle her sounds, biting her lip, eyes squeezing shut, but I don't let up. I want her to feel everything. To let go.

"Come on, angel," I whisper, voice low and rough against her skin. "Let me have it."

And when she breaks—head thrown back, free hand clutching my wrist, desperate for something to keep her grounded—it's fucking beautiful.

She shudders through it, panting, her body flushed and glistening, her eyes barely open as I rise back up and press a soft kiss to her mouth.

She hums, dazed and content. "That definitely beat going back to the shop."

I settle beside her, and she curls up into me, cheeks still pink, arm draped carefully over her stomach. I brush a strand of hair from her face and press a kiss to her temple.

She's quiet for a second, then smiles.

"I can't wait to see Bash's reaction," she murmurs. "He was so excited this morning. Totally bummed I wouldn't let him stay home from school and come with us."

I grin, imagining his wide eyes when he sees the ink. "He's gonna lose it."

"Yeah," she says, eyes soft, voice fading into something sweeter. "He'll love it."

She dozes off, her hand on my chest, body tucked close.

I watch her sleep.

She's tucked into my side like she belongs there. Like I'm not dangerous. Like I didn't once drag a man into the woods and bury what was left of him so no one would find the teeth marks I left.

I've killed for people I cared about. Hurt others without blinking. Moved bodies. Burned evidence. Sat across from the devil and offered my soul just to make sure someone I loved didn't have to suffer.

But this is harder.

Not the proposal. Not the ring. I knew the second she looked at me like I was worth keeping, I'd ask her to be mine. That part was easy. She already was mine.

What's hard is this silence. The stillness. The part where no one's bleeding and no one's screaming and nothing's on fire... and I'm supposed to exist.

I know how to be a weapon. The one who kicks the door down. Who handles it. Who never flinches.

I don't know how to be hers.

Not like this. Not without looking over my shoulder.

The ring on her finger should feel like peace. It does. And doesn't. Because peace is foreign. Peace is something I give to other people, not something I wear like a second skin.

She thinks I can be this man.

A partner. A future.

But the truth is, I've spent so long surviving in the dark, I'm not sure I'll know how to breathe if no one's trying to kill me.

The street, the fights, the bar, I know how to move in those places. I don't know how to sit still and be loved.

But for her, I'll learn.

When she leaves to pick up Bash, I wait until I hear the door close, then head downstairs.

The bar's mostly quiet. The buzz of the cooler whirrs in my ears, the scent of wood polish at my nose, and the vibration of plotting in the air.

Will and JT are at the far end of the counter, both hunched over a notepad, a bottle of bourbon between them.

They look up when I walk in.

JT lifts a brow. "Sable asleep?"

"No," I say, sliding onto a stool. "Went to grab Bash from school."

Will spins the bottle in his hand, then nods toward the paper. "Good. We've been talking."

"Not talking," JT says. "Laying out options."

"Scouting possibilities," Will adds. "Carefully."

They don't say his name. They don't have to. I know we are talking about Stauder and the lingering debt Will promised to pay.

Just the idea that fucker thinks he still has a grip on everything that matters to me, boils my blood. And I know the second Will looks at me with that steady, unflinching calm, we're past the planning stage.

This isn't a conversation.

It's time.

"We've got a way in. Infrastructure softens. He's gotten comfortable." He taps the coaster, numbers marked in pen. "Security rotates on this twelve-day cycle. And like clockwork, Ned makes a drop himself that same day."

He traces the loop once. Then again. Then again.

"I want to watch it repeat. Make sure it's consistent. But if it is—" His finger stops. "That's our window."

I glance toward the loft stairs.

Picturing Sable in my bed, her bare shoulder, the ink still fresh. I think of Bash's grin when he sees it. Think of what it took to get us here.

And most importantly, I think of what I'll do to make sure no one takes it away.

I'll erase his name from the goddamn earth.

I look back at them—*my brothers*. Weapons.

"Track it." I nod. "We wait. And when the time is right, we make him disappear."

Will

Hex and Sable's engagement party is not the worst thing I've ever been forced to attend. That honor still goes to JT's "I'm totally fine" twenty-fourth birthday, when we had to talk him out of fulfilling his dream of leaping from the Fortnite Battle Bus—by way of skydiving drunk in a banana costume.

But this?

This is definitely top five.

Tonight's just for family. The chosen kind.

Sable's mom, Marilyn, is behind the bar—*God help us*—trying to convince Hex that her newest cocktails deserve a permanent place on the menu. She's all charm and volume and "mixology flair," whatever the fuck that means, sliding garnished glasses across the counter to Sable and whoever the hell is willing to taste one.

Hex is actually humoring her, nodding along, taste-testing things with that little brow-lift that says he's got no intention of arguing. Not tonight.

Bash is here too, tucked to the side in one of the booths, playing a game on his tablet and pretending not to listen to the grown-ups. I've caught him glancing up more than once with that knowing look kids get when they realize their mom is happy and safe and settled. There's a stillness in the kid that seems new.

So yeah. This is not our usual kind of night.

It could've been sweet—almost touching—if the human glitter bomb wasn't standing on a barstool, radiating the kind of confidence usually reserved for cult leaders and drag queens.

Demi.

Sable's unhinged, redheaded best friend. She's loud, half-drunk, and draped in a dress that's ninety percent sequins, ten percent sin, and absolutely no apologies. Fuck, she probably made it herself and that might make it even worse. She's singing—or trying to—with Sable, both of them swaying off-key through some country pop song Hex clearly endures solely because he's stupid in love with her. It's awful. Painful, even. If there were dogs within a two-mile radius, I'm pretty sure they're howling.

I can't even begin to describe the audacity that is Demi's behavior.

She's already barefoot. That alone makes me twitch. An hour ago, she chucked her heels into a planter out back with the fury of someone betrayed by their footwear. She's spilled at least six drinks—nope, *seven,* correction: *eight.* And I've watched her lick not one, but *two* surfaces she should absolutely not have been licking. Her tongue claimed the jukebox second. She said it *"tasted like memories."* I had to physically look away before my soul left my body.

Every time she laughs too loud or throws an arm around someone, I feel this weird heat climb up the back of my neck. The kind of heat that makes you clench your jaw and grind your teeth, looking around the room for confirmation someone else sees this mess too.

But no. Everyone's used to her.

Everyone except me.

I don't know what pisses me off more: the way she keeps violating my unspoken rules about cleanliness and public decency, or the way one look from her has my body forgetting I ever knew what self-control meant. Several times, I considered taking *myself* to the back and punching myself in the semi-hard dick.

I don't want to think she's hot. I don't want to notice the way her dress clings to thick hips. Or how her smile lights up the room. Or how her laugh, even when it's entirely too loud, somehow sticks to the inside of my ribs.

But I do. And I hate every inch of myself for it.

I've been keeping an eye on her all night. Not because I care, but because someone has to stop her from setting something on fire or offering JT a lap dance for the third time. Hex won't say anything. JT thinks it's hilarious. So it's me, standing here in the back, arms crossed, stomach sour, watching her swirl another one of Sable's mom's mystery-colored cocktails she absolutely does not need.

Hex walks up beside me without warning. Doesn't say anything right away, just leans on the wall and watches the madness unfold.

"Man," he says eventually, "I need a favor."

My head snaps toward him. "Absolutely not."

"You don't even know what it is."

"I don't need to. If it involves her"—I jerk my chin toward Demi, who's currently trying to climb back onto her barstool with all the grace of someone mounting a horse after three margaritas—"it's a no."

Hex lifts a brow, the kind of slow, knowing arch that says he's already won. "She needs a ride home."

"Call her a fucking Uber."

"She's banned from the app."

"Then call her a Lyft. Or a helicopter. Or a garbage truck. I'm not letting that woman into my car, Hex. She'll leave fingerprints on the dash and glitter on the seats and probably touch things just to fucking piss me off."

Hex doesn't even bother arguing. He just gives me that slow, infuriating smirk that says *you're my best friend, and you're gonna do this whether you like it or not.*

"Take her home," he says it so casually, as if he's asking me to pick up milk instead of gamble my upholstery and mental stability in one go.

I stare at him. Hard. Then sigh with the solemn resolve of a man heading into something he knows won't end well. "Fine."

I round the bar, push through the crowd, and grab Demi by the waist, pulling her off the stool, before she can attempt another drunk gymnastics routine.

"Ooooh," she purrs, swinging an arm around my neck like we're lovers. "You finally giving in to your dark, twisted feelings for me?"

"I'm giving in to nothing except social obligation and mild peer pressure."

"Mmm," she says, pressing her body against mine far too eagerly. "Say it slower."

"I will drop you." I threaten.

"You'd better not. I'm not wearing underwear."

I lift her up and toss her over my shoulder, making sure her skirt is covering her ass just in case she wasn't lying. She squeals, laughing, legs kicking while I head for the back door.

"You're officially kicked out again," I grunt, gripping her tighter as she squirms.

Halfway across the room, she goes quiet. Too quiet.

Then she mutters, "I think I might puke."

My entire body stiffens and through gritted teeth, I growl:

"You better fucking not."

Acknowledgements

To anyone who's ever used art to survive themselves: *I see you.*

No words have ever flowed through me so freely and I couldn't ignore that they demanded to be shared with the world.

I wove pieces of so many important people in my life into its pages—my mother, my brother, my best friend (though she is not nearly as wild as Demi), even Andrew is based in reality. He was never intended to be any sort of villain in this story; just part of making it relatable and something worth reading. But in doing this, the need for privacy grew and grew.

Life throws some pretty wicked curve balls. You can let them strike you out or if you're brave enough, you can knock that shit right out of the park.

My mom and my best friend keep me swinging and I couldn't go without thanking them. They are constants, confidants, my fiercest support. My gratitude to the two of them is endless.

To my editor—who received my "I'm not publishing" message the same day she returned my edits—thank you for helping me figure out how to pivot, and for not shying away from confessing your obsession with my characters.

To my alpha readers, beta readers, ARC readers, and book besties—thank you for cheering me on as I stepped into this darker side of storytelling. You've made this ride infinitely more fun!

I have a beautiful, complicated life—one that is wholly my own. I wouldn't change a single thing.

About the Author

While Calla Tate is a pen name, I'm overjoyed to still be able to connect with readers. Follow me on IG **@callatatebooks.** *You can also reach me at* **callatatebooks@gmail.com.**

For more information on future projects, visit:

www.callatatebooks.com